ALEXANDRA CONNOR

The Turn of the Tide

HarperCollins*Publishers*

HarperCollins*Publishers*
77–85 Fulham Palace Road,
Hammersmith, London W6 8JB

www.harpercollins.co.uk

A catalogue record for this book
is available from the British Library

ISBN 0 00 775520 1

Typeset in Sabon by
Palimpsest Book Production Limited, Polmont, Stirlingshire

Printed and bound in Great Britain by
Clays Ltd, St Ives plc

THE TURN OF THE TIDE

Alexandra Connor was born in Oldham and still has strong connections to Lancashire. As well as being a writer she is also a presenter on television and BBC radio.

She is a Fellow of the Royal Society of Arts.

Acknowledgments must go to Blackpool Tourist Office and Library. Thanks, Tony Sharkey. Gratitude also goes to WH Smith, Blackpool, who managed to track down the reference books I needed, and to Sussex Eye Hospital, Brighton, who gave me some valuable insight. Also I must thank Nicola Plant for setting me straight legally, and Harry Bott, Esq. whose military knowledge was invaluable.

Gull Road, Blackpool

No. 139 – LEN BRADSHAW and ROSE

No. 140 – THE WILLIAMS FAMILY –
and No. 142   RUBY and ALFRED, TRUDIE,
LESTER and JOE, and
GILBERT BEARDSLEY

No. 117 – CLOVIS DYER

No. 111 – NAN WILMSLOW

PROLOGUE

Of course, rain. Rain at three thirty on a winter afternoon, making early shadows, the windows freckled with water. Outside a newspaper boy shouts the headlines, a bus braking sharply as it turns into the main street. And beyond, a man passes on the street, whistling, cheerful on his way home.

Inside, another man rises to his feet and addresses the jury. He is not whistling, not cheerful.

'Will the foreman of the jury please rise?'

One more man assumes his part, getting up and looking determinedly ahead.

'Ladies and gentlemen of the jury, have you reached a decision upon which you are all agreed?'

The man begins to answer, his voice breaking. A cough and then he resumes.

'We have.'

'Do you find the defendant guilty or not guilty?'

PART ONE

Love and scandal are the best
sweeteners of tea.

Love in Several Masques
Henry Fielding 1707–1754

ONE

'I'll call you once more to move your bleeding arse and then I'm coming up!' Ruby snarled up the narrow stairwell at the back of the house on Gull Road.

Propelled out of bed at the thought, Joe Williams glared at his brother, who was already up and dressed.

'Why didn't you give me a shove?'

Lester shrugged into the mirror. 'I nudged you a couple of times, you just turned over. I called you too.'

'I didn't hear you.'

'You heard Mam.'

'Everyone heard Mam,' Joe said, padding over to the bedroom door. 'You off down the pier?'

'Sure am.'

'It's Saturday!'

'Rich pickings on a Saturday,' Lester replied, looking at himself critically.

He was a good height now he was eighteen. All that worrying about being a runt had been a waste of time. Turning his head, Lester studied his face. If he was honest, Joe was the better-looking twin. He had the finer features, those melting brown eyes the girls liked. Lester's eyes were a kind of sucked-out hazel, with green flecks like pondweed. Over his shoulder, Lester watched Joe pad round, looking for his socks. Ten minutes separated them. It could have been a lifetime. Lester was the older brother, older by six hundred minutes. If you were counting.

'JOE!' Ruby's voice scorched up the stairs again.

'I'm up, Mam! I'm up!'

'Up to no bloody good!' she snapped, making the landing, flinging open the door and staring at her sons.

Ruby Williams was the tallest woman in Blackpool – good enough for the freak show, she liked to joke. She also had arms like a panel beater and a voice that could peel an onion from the end of the pier. Her husband, Alfred, proposed when he was drunk. Idle, with a bad back, a port-wine mark on his left cheek and a wild taste for lies, he hadn't worked since anyone could remember. Ruby did all the working. And Ruby kept all the money.

'I've new guests coming this afternoon. I don't want you lads hanging around with stubble and bad breath, putting people off.'

Despite himself, Lester loved his mother. It was impossible most of the time to understand why, but he admired her bloody-mindedness. The twins' father lied about everything. He had been a spy in the Great War, he insisted; his father had been a doctor, and he only had one liver. It was no good telling Alfred that everyone had only one liver. No good saying he meant *kidney*; the lie remained.

Useless, but amusing, Alfred lived his life exactly as Ruby told him to. She was the brains of the family, she said repeatedly, and no one doubted it. Somehow she had scraped together enough to buy one of the small houses in Gull Road – number 140. Then a year later she bought number 142, which had been occupied by an old man for years and stank.

After the old man died, it had been empty for a while. No one wanted a house that was rank. But Ruby didn't mind: Ruby could clean anything. And she did. And when she had cleaned it she knocked the two houses into one – and her private hotel, Sea View, was born.

Lester thought back. It was doubtful if Ruby had been trained in plumbing, electricals or joinery, but – during his childhood – Ruby had somehow fixed the boiler, window-frames, mangle and backdoor lock. She even managed to put in a second bathroom, her gigantic frame squeezing pipes into implausible shapes, her booming curses making the top floor shudder. Oh yes, Lester thought fondly, she was a hell of a mother.

'What you looking at?' Ruby barked.

Lester shook his head. 'I was thinking –'

'No time for that!' Ruby replied, studying her son. 'What are you all dressed up for anyway?'

'I'm going to work –'

'It's Saturday,' Ruby retorted. 'Since when did you work on a Saturday?'

'I've got a bit of a deal . . .'

His mother's heavy features darkened, her cheeks turning as red as her lipsticked mouth. 'A bloody deal! Hah! That's the way they all start. What kind of deal, I'd like to know.'

'It's kosher –'

'You been talking to Eddie Cohen again? You want to watch out, he'll have you sucked into his business like a rat up a drainpipe.'

'I'm going to have my *own* business.'

Ruby slowly looked Lester up and down. Oh, he was a cute one all right. There were no flies on him. Good thing too, because although Joe was funny, he was also a bit of a dope and needed someone to look out for him.

'You're *eighteen*, Lester!' she barked. 'How the hell can you have your own *business*?'

'I'm saving up. You know, filling up the slot machines on the end of the pier –'

'Harry Sayer does that. I remember when his youngest got his tongue stuck in the pull-out drawer. Daft little bugger.'

'Harry's off sick now. Asked me to fill in.' Lester paused, thinking ahead. 'I reckon if I do a good job, he'll ask me to take over. It's not bad money –'

His flow was interrupted by the appearance of his younger sister at the door. Trudie was thirteen, full-busted already, and a gossip. Anything that went on in Gull Road, Trudie knew. And Trudie shared everything with her mother. Ruby might rail at her daughter for her slovenliness, but Trudie could always wheedle her way back into Ruby's good books. *You know what I heard about the new priest at the Sacred Heart? . . . And what about the greengrocer's cousin?*

No one even knew that the greengrocer *had* a cousin – except Trudie. She looked and acted old for her years and had already mapped out her future. 'Helping' her mother at the hotel, she would pick out a husband just as soon as she was ready. Get herself set up in some nice little flat nearby, where she could have a baby and twitch the curtains all day.

'You fall out with your tailor?' she asked Lester snidely. 'Or are you wearing that jacket for a bet?'

He passed her in the doorway and then turned at the head of the stairs.

'I'll be back around four, Mam –'

'Bring us some onions off the corner shop, will you?' Ruby replied.

Joe hurried after his brother down the stairs.

'Oi!' Ruby roared. 'Where are *you* going?'

Joe turned his liquid eyes on his mother imploringly. 'I'm helping Lester today. Didn't he tell you?'

'But –'

'I have to go, Mam. See you later.'

The sun was blinding as they left the cool darkness of the house. In the front window the 'Vacancies' notice was up on the window sill, next to a potted aspidistra and a cheap statue of an Alsatian.

'Who said you could come with me?' Lester asked his

brother, Joe still buttoning up his shirt as he fell into step.

'Aw, come on, I can't hang around there all day. You know what she's like when there's guests coming.' Joe paused to rebutton his shirt. 'Did you smell that bacon?'

Lester nodded.

'I never got any,' Joe said ruefully.

'No one did. Mam had half a piece left and cooked it so that the new arrivals would be impressed.' He lit up a Black Cat cigarette. 'I didn't see Dad this morning.'

'He's in bed.'

'He's always in bed. He should have sores the size of dinner plates on his arse.'

Lester regarded his brother thoughtfully. 'Why *are* you following me?'

'I thought I could help you out –'

Lester cut him off. 'I don't need help.'

'You might,' Joe said, the unmistakable pleading in his voice. 'Aw, come on, Lester, let me tag along.'

A familiar voice broke into their conversation at that moment, a rangy man in a loud suit waving to them from across the street. Waving back, Lester waited for Len Bradshaw to approach.

He was sweating, his high forehead shiny under his trilby, a bookie's ticket jutting out of his top pocket – and the squint in his left eye more pronounced than usual under the sunlight. Not one to let anything hold him back, Len had cunningly managed to make a trademark out of his defect, his nickname round the racetrack being 'The Lazy Eye'. It was useful for a ticktack man to stand out from the rest, and Len certainly stood out.

Head and shoulders above the punters he would perch on his box, waving his white-gloved hands animatedly to his bookie employer, George Ogden, across the track. No one was quicker than Len at signing the odds, something George knew only too well – just as he knew that Len desperately wanted a pitch of his own.

'When I'm dead,' George said repeatedly, his stoat face cunning, 'you can have my licence and pitch.'

'You'll live to be a bloody hundred to spite me,' Len always replied, weary of the eternal carrot being dangled in front of him.

But how else could he get a pitch, unless he inherited one? All the other bookies left theirs to sons or relatives; George Ogden was the only bachelor around with no family, thank God. And no friends. Except Len.

'We've not seen you around lately, Mr Bradshaw,' Lester said, as Len fell into step with the brothers.

'Been busy, lads,' he replied, fanning his face with his hat. 'It's hot today. Too hot for April.'

To hear their father tell it Len Bradshaw was a hell of a womanizer. 'Don't be fooled by his wall eye,' Alfred confided. 'He's had more women than the Aga Khan. It's the squint,' he went on. 'The ladies feel sorry for him . . .' Not that Len was in love with any of them. His only love had been for his late wife, Vera. It was doubtful if there was ever going to be another Mrs Bradshaw. Besides, Len had his daughter to think about. And raising a girl on your own wasn't easy. Oh no, Len would say, it's a bugger of a job and no mistake.

'Too hot,' Len repeated, blowing out his cheeks. 'Never had it this hot in early April.'

'How's business?' Lester asked, knowing the answer already, and winking at Joe.

'Not good,' Len replied, as he always did, 'not good at all.'

'But I heard you cleaned up on Lady Dancer the other day.'

Len smiled wryly. 'You heard that? You heard wrong. Lost a fortune that afternoon on a bloody horse that ran like a slug. I tell you, if it had gone any slower it would have lapsed into a sodding coma.'

Joe couldn't resist provoking him. 'How's Mr Ogden?'

12

Len bridled. 'He's well enough.'

'That's a bugger,' Joe whispered under his breath, Len shooting him a warning look.

'You want to watch that mouth of yours, Joe Williams! No one likes a smart arse,' Len snapped, his attention suddenly taken by a buxom woman waving to him from the Promenade.

Smiling, Len hurried off just as a tram passed, a girl laughing with her companion on the back seat. Lester felt a tweak of envy. It was Saturday, he would have liked to be out on the town with a girl, not working. He would have liked to buy a couple of ice creams and sit on the pier, nuzzling someone's neck like the dozens of courting couples glistening under the welcome sunlight.

'What are you thinking about?' Joe asked, his head on one side.

'About the future,' his brother lied, reverting to his usual train of thought. 'About making money, Joe. About a big house, with a big car –'

'And a big woman?'

Smiling, Lester punched his brother playfully on the shoulder. 'Nah, I'm going to marry the best-looking girl in the county. You see if I don't.'

'Who's that?'

'I dunno,' Lester replied honestly, swapping his bag of tools from one hand to another. 'I haven't met her yet. But she'll be the woman every man wants – and she'll be mine.'

Joe pulled a face. 'What if she won't have you?'

Oh, but she would, Lester thought. When the time was right. But not now. Not yet. When he had money in his pocket and people called him *Mister Williams*, then he would think about romance.

But not a moment before.

TWO

The galling thing about living so closely to other people was that everyone knew everything about you. Disgruntled, Rose Bradshaw slid off the windowledge and looked across to the Williamses' private hotel. Rose couldn't remember the prospect of Sea View ever being different. Just the sign changed: 'Vacancies' or 'No Vacancies'. Otherwise it was the same colour of paint on the door, the same plaster figure on the windowledge and probably even the same potted plant.

It had been that way for as long as she could remember. In contrast, her father liked change. In fact Len liked change so much that their furniture never remained in the same place for more than a month. And sometimes even the pieces changed. If he had had a good day at the track Len would buy something. Unfortunately the house was small and usually another piece of furniture had to go to make room. Like the pummelled leather armchair, which put in one short glorious appearance and then vanished. 'I don't like leather,' Len had proclaimed. 'When you sit on it it sounds like you've farted.'

Rose didn't ask where the chair came from, or where it went, but when a piano materialised in place of her dressing table, she had had enough.

'You can't do that!' she had exploded.

'Now then, Rosie,' Len had remonstrated, 'you could learn how to play –'

'Who has a piano in their bedroom?'

'Just my point,' Len had said hopefully. 'Any girl can have a dressing table.'

Smiling to herself, Rose remembered the incident. Her father had given way, of course, and the piano had gone within twenty-four hours . . .

The sun came through the window at that moment, Rose blinking and moving away. Just as she did so, a small woman with a dowager's hump passed by on the other side of the street, waving: Clovis Dyer, Len's older sister by nearly ten years. 'Clutter Clovis', as she was known around Blackpool.

She had earned her sobriquet because nothing escaped Clovis's hoarding mania. Having lost her husband in the Great War, and having no children, her whole attention had focused on collecting. The problem was that Clovis collected *everything*. She had – as Len said repeatedly – no bloody idea. He might like to swap around his possessions, but at least he made room for them by getting rid of other pieces. Clovis didn't like to get rid of anything.

Gradually her house – at number 117 Gull Road – had filled up. It had begun in the front room, spread into the kitchen and then the unstopping tide of tat had eventually snaked its way upstairs. And there was always room for more. Indeed, Clovis had become the scourge of every jumble sale, carrying, pushing or dragging her spoils home.

Boxes full of bobble hats, tea cosies and jigsaws jostled for space with tea trays, stacks of *Picture Post*s and carpet rolls. For some reason Clovis had developed an ardour for floor coverings. Any colour, any pattern, any size of roll found its way into number 117, along with numerous offcuts. Propped up against the walls like so many rigid drunks, Clovis's inanimate family increased steadily until she couldn't open the boxroom door. Undeterred, she then began to fill her own bedroom.

It wasn't large, and by the time Clovis had cramped a

15

pair of grocer's scales, a rusty pram, twenty glass bottles, an old parrot's cage and four rolls of her beloved lino into it there was just enough room left for her bed. And the way to the bed was hazardous. Only someone with the skill of a mountain goat could navigate the route. But although Clovis was sixty, and had a dowager's hump, she was nifty on her feet.

So the tat kept coming . . . Before long the clutter had moved into the hall, and entry to number 117 was only for the hardy – like Len, who had long since accepted his sister's foibles and would sit and have a cup of tea with Clovis, surrounded by cliff faces of clutter.

Watching her aunt pass by, Rose relaxed. Clovis wasn't going to drop in. Instead she seemed bound for the house of her friend, Nan Wilmslow, number 111.

The sun felt kind on Rose's face, her skin warming. It was too good a day to lose, she decided, getting to her feet. She would call at Sea View and see if Trudie wanted to go down to the Promenade with her. Not that *she* would get the attention – Rose never did. It was Trudie who got the boys panting.

Reluctantly, Rose moved to the fly-blown mirror over the sink and looked at her reflection. She had her mother's thick dark hair, wide mouth, fine nose and high cheek-bones. But she had her father's squint. The lazy eye had found another victim.

Rose turned away. It was no good being depressed. It was life, and you had to get on with it. When she had been younger, it hadn't been too bad. But now she was thirteen and growing up, and suddenly she wanted the boys to like her. Not make fun of her. Not overlook her.

She might be young but Rose Bradshaw had learned fast that the boys weren't going to clamour to court her. They wanted the perfect girls, to show off with. To impress their peers with. Not some kid with a glide in her eye. Knowing he blamed himself, Rose's father had always been kind:

'You look so bonny in profile,' he'd said often. But who could live in profile, Rose thought. You had to turn round and look people in the eye eventually, didn't you?

Trudie could give the boys the eye. But Rose couldn't. She always looked down, staring at her feet . . . One day, she told herself, one day she would have enough money to get her eye fixed. One day.

But she knew it would never happen. It was just a fantasy, like all Alfred Williams' fantasies. A daft daydream, with no chance of coming true.

THREE

Catching sight of Len Bradshaw, the Widow Miller turned away hurriedly as her chauffeur continued driving down the Blackpool Promenade. Counting to five before she looked up again, she then watched Len's lithe frame merge into the distance. He was an appalling man, she thought, still mortified that she had once been related to 'The Lazy Eye'. By marriage, not choice.

After all, Edward Bradshaw hadn't been a bit like his brother. And she had been young, very young. Besides, she had been in love with Edward, and love distorts everything. A shudder ran through her, her ex-brother-in-law was a ticktack man! Dear God . . .

Winding down the car window to let in some of the comforting sunshine, the Widow Miller glanced at the royal-blue sea. It looked warm, but appearances were very deceptive. Anyone attempting a swim in April would have the air punched out of their lungs instantly. Still, it was of little importance. The days of her swimming in the sea were long gone. She wouldn't be seen dead on the beach now, never mind getting herself messy in the water.

The Widow Miller smiled to herself. It was so pleasing to be rich. Not that her present comfort was due to Edward Bradshaw. He had tried hard, and distanced himself from his appalling relatives, but poor Edward had died young and poor. It had been lucky for her to meet Hubert Miller so soon after. Everyone had said they were suited. After all, she had come from money, and although her family had managed to lose a small fortune, she still remembered, and *longed*, to spend. Hubert might have been dull and unprepossessing, but he had had a lot of money. And, luckily, no imagination.

It was ridiculous, the Widow Miller thought. Why have money if you don't know how to indulge yourself? Hubert had been busy with his architect's practice and had had neither time nor inclination to rid himself of the riches he had accumulated. His wife had been a big help there. Hubert had grand designs at work, but all his passion had been in bricks and mortar, not in living. Nor in bed.

Luckily his wife's main desire had been spending money. She had not required a tremendous lover, and had had no interest in deep conversations or romantic trips. Her satisfaction had come from a well-upholstered sofa, or weighted silk curtains. The Widow Miller had experienced passion with Edward Bradshaw – *had* been in love once – but that was long over. After Edward, any orgasmic delight came from choosing brocade or discovering the perfect tone of Sèvres blue.

Naturally, when Hubert died she arranged a gracious funeral, with her late husband in an immaculate suit, lying in the best, most expensive, carved mahogany coffin available in the North-West. As Len had said at the time: 'It's a pity she couldn't have tipped him out and kept the bloody thing as a coffee table.'

And so the elegant widow had inherited Hubert Miller's fortune. She then sold up the marital home and bought a glorious house in Lytham St Annes. Next door to Blackpool, but on the classy part of the coast. The well-to-do relative barely tolerating her slightly seedy seaside sister.

There was only one reason that the Widow Miller had any remaining interest in Blackpool. Rose Bradshaw. Having no children herself, she had fond memories of Len's daughter when Rose was a baby. In the distant days when she was married to Edward Bradshaw and wondering if they might have their *own* family . . . The Widow Miller shook her head in disbelief. It would never have worked. She wasn't maternal in the least and if she had ended up with a batch of kids, living in some Blackpool backstreet, it would have killed her.

No, she was too selfish for children. But she *had* taken to the baby Rose; remembered the summer she had been born, and Len's pleasure, even though his wife had died soon after. He had pushed Rose – or Rosie as he called her – out in her pram and even taken her to the races, all the women piling round to look at the baby . . . The Widow Miller snorted softly. Opportunist, she thought. Len Bradshaw had only done it because he knew women couldn't resist a baby.

But then neither could she . . . Fiddling with the collar of her coat, the Widow Miller stared hard at the back of her chauffeur's head, lost in thought. She had seen quite a lot of Rose when the child was little, but after she had married Hubert all connection was severed. It was incredible, but then Len Bradshaw had *cut her off*! Never even gave her a chance to reject him first. Suddenly her birthday and Christmas cards were returned to her and all connection with Rose severed.

Not that she would have admitted it to anyone, but it had hurt. Hubert's money managed to lessen the rebuttal, but the Widow Miller missed Rose. And over the years that followed she had avidly gathered all the titbits of information she could find about Miss Bradshaw. She was bright. She was healthy. *She had a squint.*

The Widow Miller winced. Dear God, why hadn't that fool Len done something about it? Why hadn't he taken his daughter to see someone? It would ruin the girl's chances in life . . . Irritated, she kept staring at the back of her chauffeur's head. *She* had the money to take Rose to see a specialist, to pay for an operation. She would like to do that, like to see Rose blossom. *Despite* her idiot father. But she knew that Len wouldn't hear of it. Oh no, he'd rather have his daughter squint than let his ex-sister-in-law help them out.

It was so silly of him. But then Len Bradshaw had always been silly where the Widow Miller was concerned.

Len had seen the chauffeured car pass, and noticed his old sparring partner duck down in her seat out of sight. Idiotic woman, he thought, pausing to roll a cigarette. The sun shimmered on the sea in front of him, trickling down the steel carcass of the Tower, the long lazy stretch of Central Pier and the Pavilion. His mind went back to when the Widow Miller had been married to his brother. She'd been plain Hettie Lyon then, and madly in love with Eddie. For a while . . .

God, Len thought, inhaling on his cigarette, that ageing bag in the big hat had once been the doting Hettie. Fussing around her husband, making pies for Eddie, living in Holland Road, the next street to Gull Road and the Bradshaw home. Hettie, who had been born into a fortune and thought that money didn't matter then. Hettie, who got freckles across her nose in summer and sat on the back step playing pontoon with her brother-in-law. Hettie, who went red around her ears when she laughed and told the dirtiest stories in Blackpool. Adorable Hettie.

Once. Then a few years passed and Eddie didn't manage to get them out of Holland Road and the shabby house. He didn't get on at the council offices because he wasn't bright; he was just loving and worshipped his wife. But what good was that? Hettie began to wonder. Who needed to be idolised in Holland Road? So as Eddie *failed* to make his fortune, Hettie remembered how her family had *lost* theirs – and suddenly she wanted out.

By that time Len and his late wife, Vera, had had Rose.

Fascinated with the baby, Hettie used to call to see Rose and sit on the back step in the sunshine. She moaned to Vera about Eddie, and Vera, being Vera, had defended her brother-in-law. Which wasn't what Hettie had wanted to hear. And all the time, she fussed over the baby, brought her presents, and begged to be allowed to take Rose out in the pram. It was as if she had wanted to encroach on the family by stealth, to *buy* her way in.

Len had resented it, although Vera was more tolerant of her sister-in-law – even when Hettie had begun to regale both Vera and Len with tales of her family's former wealth; even when she had taken to chivvying Eddie in front of them and talking about how she could have married a rich man.

Then one evening – in midsummer – Vera had gone out and Hettie called by to see the baby. On the back step she had sat in a violet dress, her blonde hair coming unfastened at the back, the top of her breasts exposed as she rocked the child. The evening had been a drowsy one, the far-off sounds of the pier and the holidaymakers coming lazily on the soft air as Len offered her a lemonade.

'Nothing stronger?' she had asked, her expression pert.

Surprised, he had poured her half a pint of beer and stood beside her, looking up into the darkening sky. A few birds had passed, the sound of a couple laughing coming loud from Shepherd Street, only a block away. In Hettie's arms, Rose had fallen asleep, her breathing sonorous. Moments had swung past, taking their languorous time. Then Hettie had taken a long draught of her beer and smiled, froth lingering on her top lip for an instant before she had wiped it away with her fingers.

'It's late,' Len had said at last. 'You should be getting back. Eddie will be worried about you.'

She had looked down at the baby and then, to Len's astonishment, begun to cry.

At once he'd sat down beside her. 'What is it, Hettie?'

22

'I can't . . . I can't . . .' she had trailed off, then turned, her face caught in the kitchen light coming from behind them.

He thought at that moment that she was blindingly appealing; had found himself – with the sounds of far-off laughter and the scent of lilac coming like a ghost in the backyard – moved by her. Which was what Hettie had planned. Turning, she had bent her head backwards and closed her eyes, inviting him to kiss her. And for one second – one infinitesimal second – Len had wanted to.

But the moment had passed and then he'd seen her for what she was – an opportunist on the make.

'You should go home,' Len had said again, getting to his feet.

Surprised and embarrassed, Hettie had risen awkwardly, passing Rose over to him. Her face had been flushed, her voice thin with spite.

'You're just like your brother, a *weakling*.'

Holding on to Rose tightly, Len had faced his sister-in-law. 'Hettie, I know you're unhappy, but you don't really want me –'

'You're right there!' she'd hissed, walking out into the backyard. 'Who *could* want you, Leonard Bradshaw? Eddie might not be much, but at least your brother doesn't have a walleye.'

Grinding out his cigarette, Len winced at the memory. From that day onward, Hettie had hated him; despised him for rejecting her. He didn't doubt for an instant that Hettie would have rewritten history over the years. By now *he* would be the one who had made a pass at *her*. How much more palatable that version would be to a vain woman.

Their relationship had been all but severed from that night. Hettie might still visit Vera and the baby, but Len's card had been marked. Scorned and bitter, she declared her own personal 12 August on him. Every pot shot she could take, she had taken. Every time she could aim a verbal swipe at him, she had done. She carped at Eddie about Len being a wide boy, and even hinted darkly to Vera about her husband's roving eye.

She was a bitch, Len had realised as he fought to undo the damage. The sexy woman in the violet dress had gone, leaving a vicious harpy in her place. Steadily and relentlessly Hettie had continued to track down Len's good name – but before she could blast it into oblivion, tragedy struck.

In this poor Eddie was as considerate as ever. That year a flu epidemic killed Vera, and her brother-in-law had followed only months later. Len suddenly became a widower; his sister-in-law, a widow. Shattered by the loss of his wife, Len had watched Hettie dry-eyed at Vera's funeral, and had rejected her offer to look after Rose for a while. You want my child, he had thought, aghast, not bloody likely! He would look after Rose, Len told everyone. He was her father. He could manage. Alone. And he did.

He had known all along that his sister would be no help. Clovis had no interest in children. Clovis had no real interest in anything animate; taking to the pram more readily than the baby. But after a while Clovis got curious. Besides, she was living only a few doors away and had got tired of hearing about her niece from neighbours. Even Nan Wilmslow. And everyone knew that Nan was a woman of few words.

So by the time Rose was eighteen months old Clovis had grown used to the idea of being an aunt and visited the baby regularly, always bringing weird jumble-sale presents, like iron doorstops and copies of *The Family Doctor*. But if Rose had needed feeding or changing, Clovis wasn't capable. She couldn't give care, only presents.

Hettie had sent presents too for Rose's birthdays and Christmases, but Len had returned every one. He knew there was no generosity in Hettie's actions; she just wanted access to the child. Or was it access to *him*, Len had wondered over the first few years.

Then thankfully a saviour had arrived in the portly form of Hubert Miller, Hettie undergoing her own personal assumption into the celestial realms of the richest Blackpool drawing rooms. No longer Hettie Bradshaw, she had become *Mrs Henrietta Miller*. And Mrs Miller had no time for the past.

A car horn sounding loudly snapped Len out of his reverie, a motorist waving his fist at him.

'Watch where you're bloody walking!' the man shouted as Len jumped back onto the pavement. 'I could have killed you!'

Oh no you couldn't, Len thought. He had survived Hettie's assassination attempt. After her, everyone else was an amateur.

FOUR

The *private hotel* on Gull Road – as Ruby grandly called it – consisted of two houses knocked together, which spanned three floors, and Ruby Williams owned them all. Not bad, she thought often, not bad at all for a tinker's kid. Not that people knew Ruby's origins; she had covered her tracks well.

From her earliest recollections she had known that a traveller's life wasn't for her. Hadn't fancied living off her wits and being moved on from site to site. Besides, she was too tall to live in a sodding caravan. So she'd upped and offed on her own at sixteen. No one had messed with Ruby; no one had dared. She was too big and too fierce. On the markets she had learned a bit about buying and selling; had even managed to put aside some money. But she had stayed away from the betting shops her family had loved, and instead took a second job as a cleaner. She was strong, was Ruby, could scrub out a house in no time. And offices. The demeaning work hadn't mattered to her, it had only mattered that they paid her. Then slowly Ruby had got more ambitious and taught herself how to cook a little – nothing fancy, but good solid food for the labourers who called by the van she had parked on some waste ground off the main road into Blackpool.

Some men – usually the bigger ones – had tried to chat her up, but Ruby had none of it. They got their food and mugs of tea and they got moved on. By the time Ruby was eighteen she had a bank account, a new van, a thriving little business and a half-share in 'Madame Jasmina – Sees all that the future has in store'.

Pitched in a tiny hut on the centre of North Pier, Madame Jasmina had intermittent asthma attacks and a desperate need for a partner. So why not Ruby? Are you a seer? Madame Jasmina had asked when Ruby approached her. I'm gypsy stock, she'd replied honestly. That had been enough. Besides – Ruby had thought – who needed second sight to tell someone's fortune? And anyway, if what she said was rubbish, who would argue with a six-foot woman?

Opening the guest register, Ruby allowed herself to reminisce a little longer. It had been a hot summer, she remembered, when a young man had come by, tipsy with his friend, to have a reading. Or rather, to have a good laugh. Steaming in the cramped wooden hut, Ruby had regarded the men wryly, then flinched. Before her sat her elder brother, Gilbert. The only person who had ever bullied her. The brother who had peed in the water butt where she used to wash her hair; and put a ferret in her knickers. That bloody Gilbert.

Making sure the veil was covering most of her face, Ruby decided – there and then – to get her revenge.

'My Lord! . . . I see many things for you . . .'

Gilbert sniggered.

Little prick, she thought, hadn't changed a bit.

'. . . I see fame and fortune . . .'

Gilbert stopped laughing then. He'd always fancied himself and wanted to go on the stage.

'. . . I see your name in lights . . .'

'Aw, come on!' Gilbert's companion moaned. 'This is crap.'

'Leave off!' Gilbert replied, watching his friend slouch back in his seat, sulking. Mesmerised, he looked back to the veiled figure. 'Go on.'

Oh, I intend to, Ruby thought darkly.

27

'. . . you'll be known all over the world. Admired, envied . . .'

'Get away!'

Idiot.

'. . . As far as Egypt . . .'

'Bloody hell!'

Cretin.

'. . . even further. *America.*' Her voice trembling with the enormity of what she was foretelling, Ruby watched her brother glisten with hope.

'. . . and you'll have seventeen children.'

'Jesus!' Gilbert's companion said, sitting upright. 'No wonder you'll be known all around the world!'

Staring into the crystal ball, which told her precisely nothing, Ruby pressed on.

'. . . Oh yes, seventeen children . . . and three wives . . .'

Gilbert was glassy-eyed at that. Women hadn't been on his agenda at all.

'Hang on!' his companion said suddenly. 'You *can't* have more than one wife –'

Ruby silenced him with a glance, then turned back to her brother.

'. . . Oh. Oh no! Wait a moment . . . what's this?' She stopped, frowning.

Gilbert's companion smirked. 'Only *one* wife, right?'

'No, I see . . .' Ruby paused, allowing her voice to tremble further. '. . . God, I see terror, loss, fire . . .' She stared into her brother's glazed eyes. '. . . I see the envious out to get you. Oh no, no! I see all your money gone. Your fame over. I see poison –'

'Yeah, well, I've been smelling a rat ever since we came in here –'

Ruby stilled Gilbert's companion with another blistering look. Then, suddenly and terrifyingly, her voice turned into a wail, Gilbert jumping in his seat as Ruby leaned towards him for the final flourish.

'. . . I see *Death*!'
And then Gilbert had passed out.

Sighing with satisfaction at the memory, Ruby glanced back to the desk in the hallway. On top she had placed a brass bell and a register for her guests to sign. She had learned long ago that you couldn't ask too many questions, but her appearance deterred the working girls. Ruby would turn a blind eye to the occasional 'Mr and Mrs Smith' who came for a weekend in the season, but there was no way Sea View was being used as a knocking shop.

Looking round, she inspected the hallway, the scrubbed walls and the brushed rug. Clean and tidy, good. She had half an hour left before the first guests would arrive for the Easter break. Mentally she ran through her checklist. Beds made, food in, tablecloths on, and the note on each table – 'Sixpence for use of the Cruet.' She had other rules too: one bath per person daily, or there was a charge for the hot water. And as for food – Ruby would cook whatever the guests brought in for their evening meal – unless it was foreign muck. There wasn't an extra charge for cooking that, because anything foreign that arrived in Ruby's kitchen was immediately propelled out of the back door by a throw the England cricket team would have admired.

You couldn't beat having your own kingdom, Ruby thought, especially if it didn't have bloody wheels and stayed put . . . The sun crept into Gull Road, slithering into the hallway of Sea View. On the ground floor was a dining room with six tables, next to it the lounge with the aspidistra. At the back was the living kitchen and yard. On the first floor were six bedrooms and a bathroom. The cramped family bedrooms – all four of them – were at the top of the house, crushed together, with one rickety bathroom in between.

Four bedrooms. For Ruby and Alfred; Trudie; Lester and Joe; and . . .

'Ruby,' an affected voice said suddenly. 'Ruby, my dear . . .'

She could hear feet padding down the stairs behind her and turned, her eyebrows raised. Funny how things worked out, wasn't it? Ruby thought. Here was her brother, all these years later, living with the sister he had spent his childhood tormenting.

'I've a terrible headache,' Gilbert whined, his soft-fleshed face pink, his hair spiralling out of control without the usual layer of Vaseline to keep it under control. 'Oh, Ruby, I could do with a cup of tea.'

'So could I. Make me one now you're up,' she replied smartly, moving into the kitchen, Gilbert trailing behind her.

He was dressed in a pair of striped trousers, a loose white shirt flapping around his fleshy form. On his feet he wore Turkish slippers, curled up at the toes like scorpions aiming to strike. 'From a fan,' Gilbert had explained the previous Christmas, 'someone who admired my Widow Twankey at the Grand . . .'

He liked to dress eccentrically, did Gilbert, copying a picture he had once seen of Aubrey Beardsley, the artist. The fact that Beardsley had been tall, thin, with a long aquiline nose, did not faze Gilbert. In his mind's eye he looked like the artist. And *once*, he had. So much so that he had even adopted the painter's surname as his stage name, calling himself Gilbert Beardsley. But that had been many years ago, before fat, rainy matinées and pantomimes at the end of the pier had swallowed him whole.

Relenting, Ruby pushed a cup of tea over to her brother and sipped her own, watching him. To hear Alfred tell it, Gilbert was *one of those* . . . The theatrical circles in which Gilbert moved might find it acceptable, but off the pier and out of make-up, her brother was a moving target for bigots. And the police.

Yet instinct told Ruby that Gilbert wasn't sexually active

any more. He had been once . . . He thought she didn't know about Larry Ford, but she did. Often wondered if that was why Gilbert had been so ignominiously turfed out of the travellers' coterie. Their father was a wide boy, all right, but he wouldn't have tolerated any *sexual* shenanigans. But had there been anyone since Larry? Nah, not likely, Ruby thought. Her brother was too aware of the police. He might play the pantomime dame and dress like God knew what, but Gilbert was too scared to share a bed with any of the Blackpool *demi-monde*. No matter how much he might want to.

'I hear they were looking for a clown for the Tower Circus,' Gilbert said, pushing his untidy black hair away from his pale, sad eyes.

His voice had undergone a strange metamorphosis over the decades. He might have been born a gypsy, but now he sounded like a Shakespearean actor: grand and poignant at the same time.

'You're not a clown, Gilbert,' Ruby replied smartly, 'not professionally, anyway.'

He looked miffed. 'I could do it.'

'I thought you said you were only going to be a serious actor from now on.'

'All the greats play comedy as well as tragedy.'

'Really?' Ruby countered. 'I've never seen King Lear with a red nose and braces.'

Footsteps overhead caught Gilbert's attention. 'Alfred up and about?'

Ruby glanced at the clock over the kitchen range and shrugged. 'Past eleven. Must be.'

'I heard him tell one of your guests that he was a banker.'

'The only money Alfred gets close to is the stuff he sleeps on.' Ruby could see her brother's eyes flicker. 'You think I'd really be that dumb, to put my money under the mattress?'

'I just wondered –'

'Well, you can *stop* wondering! The money I earn is in

31

the bank. Where it should be. Incidentally,' Ruby added, her tone razor sharp, 'you owe me rent.'

'Oh, come on, Ruby! I paid you only the other day.'

'That was for last week.'

'I'm a bit short,' Gilbert replied plaintively. 'I'll pay you when I'm working again.'

The front doorbell interrupted their conversation, Ruby about to leave, then turning back to her brother.

'You want to stop wasting your money, Gilbert. Pay me my rent first – *then* spend what's left.'

He was all righteous indignation. 'I spend my money wisely!'

'Like buying that stuffed fox, you mean? What did the bloody fox ever do to you? And I know you bought that set of encyclopaedias –'

'They were a good buy!'

'They're all the same volume!' Ruby hurled back. 'You have ten copies of the *Encyclopaedia Britannica* from G to I.'

Piqued, Gilbert looked away. 'The man I got them from said he'd make it right with me –'

'Hah!'

'I'll have you know that he's a well-respected member of the profession, Ruby –'

'What profession? Thieving?'

Another ring on the bell stopped Ruby's flow, Gilbert staring gloomily into his tea as she left the kitchen, slamming the door behind her. Her brother would never learn. He would believe what he wanted to believe and buy ten volumes of the same book because the bindings looked impressive. Not that he would ever read them. Because Gilbert couldn't read.

Ruby paused, momentarily sympathetic. Her brother had also hidden his origins well. No one would have thought that Gilbert Beardsley was gypsy stock. No one would have known that he learned his lines in the back kitchen of the house, Ruby reading them to him over and over again until he knew them by rote. No one at rehearsal would imagine – as Gilbert stared at the script in front of him – that the words meant absolutely nothing.

It was all top show with Gilbert. Funny clothes, funny voice, funny stories, funny Turkish slippers. All so funny. All so sad.

FIVE

Swinging her handbag, Trudie was whistling and eyeing up the boys on the pier. Well aware that she was being watched, she sat down on a bench and crossed her legs, Rose beside her. The sun was surprisingly hot, her forearms beginning to turn pink after a few minutes. Blast it! Rose thought, pulling down the sleeves of her cardigan hurriedly, she was going to burn. Please God, just don't let me start itching . . .

Trudie had no problem with the sun. In fact, she hadn't even noticed it, her attention elsewhere. Only yards away a youth stood with a group of his friends, showing off, his shiny bicycle leaning against the iron railings of the pier.

'I bet you he's a good kisser.'

'Aw, Trudie!' Rose replied, exasperated. 'How would you know?'

'Because I've kissed dozens of boys.'

'I don't believe you!' Rose replied, wriggling uncomfortably on the bench.

Damn it, her skin *was* beginning to itch. She shouldn't have come out. Besides, it was no fun any more: now that Trudie had discovered boys. Before, they had gone on the amusement rides: one of them distracting the owner so that the other could sneak on and get a free ride. They had other ploys too. Rose was a dab hand at looking pathetic; it was the only time her squint came in useful. She would stand, sobbing quietly, until the ride's owner came over to her. Then she'd tell him that she'd dropped her money and couldn't afford a turn. It usually worked. And both of them were adept at 'the orphan trick': latching on to the back of a big family, in the hope that they wouldn't notice and pay for another kid.

But now, Rose thought miserably, there was no throwing up on the big dipper or swiping the tops of kids' candy floss as they passed. Now Trudie was only interested in one thing. The one thing that terrified Rose.

'I bet he uses his tongue . . .'

Rose's mouth fell open. 'What!'

'That's what they do, you know. When a real man kisses, he uses his tongue.'

'What for?'

'To clean the bloody windows!' Trudie snapped. 'What d'you think?'

Her skin itching frantically, Rose gave in to the temptation and scratched it, her nails raking long red weals under the sleeves of her cardigan.

'I don't believe you, Trudie! I think it's disgusting anyway.'

'It's not. It's sexy.'

Blowing out her cheeks, Rose squirmed on the bench. She was patently aware that she looked a lot younger than Trudie. No breasts for her yet, no mysteries of the monthly curse, no sudden turning from a kid into a siren. Whilst her friend could pass for sixteen easily, Rose had remained in plaits and short socks. And she felt like an idiot.

A sudden shadow fell across them: the boy with the bike approaching.

''Lo there, good-looking.'

Trudie smiled up at the youth, his hair falling over one eye, one hand holding the handlebars of his bike.

'Oh, 'lo there,' Trudie replied nonchalantly, recrossing her legs.

'I've been watching you,' the boy went on.

'Have you?' Trudie answered, nudging Rose as she began to scratch her arms again. 'Well, there's lots to watch round here.'

'I dare say,' he went on, smiling, 'but I've only got eyes for you.'

Dimpling up, Trudie simpered on the bench.

'You want to have a ride on my bike?'

She looked at it thoughtfully. 'It's only got one seat.'

'We could share it,' the lad went on. 'You'd have to hang on tight, though. You know, put your arms around my waist –'

'Cheeky,' Trudie replied, delighted by the thought.

Beside her, Rose was staring at the floor, trying not to scratch. Why did the boy have to come over, she thought, looking through the slits in the wooden planks at the water lapping below. She could smell the ozone, the familiar odour of her childhood, and hear the gulls calling over her head.

'Aw, come on, have a ride with me,' the youth went on. 'Dump your kid sister –'

'Oi!' Rose said, her head snapping up. 'I'm not her kid sister.'

Totally unmoved, the lad kept talking to Trudie. 'What d'you say? Fancy a spin?'

'We should go home –'

'Rose, don't nag!' Trudie chided her, then turned back to the boy. 'I suppose I *could* go for a little ride with you.'

'And leave me here?' Rose asked, folding her arms belligerently.

Trudie glanced back to the lad, her voice hopeful. 'Have you got a friend?'

To Rose's mortification the boy looked over to her, studied her carefully, and then shook his head. 'She's a kid –'

Flushing, Rose got to her feet. It was always the same. Would anyone *ever* want her?

'I'm going home!' she said, half expecting Trudie to follow. As she walked down the pier, Rose could hear the water

36

lapping below her feet. A gull swooped down from the raking blue sky. Trudie would run after her, she told herself, any minute now she'd follow. She always did . . .

But not this time. In fact Rose was halfway down the pier before she finally dared to turn to look back. Balanced on the bike with the floppy-haired lad sat Trudie, whooping with delight, her legs at all angles.

Wobbling dangerously, they skidded round and about the tourists, one woman nearly losing her footing as they hurtled past her. The sun high overhead, Trudie, the boy and the bike cast an alien shadow on the pier's weather-bleached boards as Rose watched them longingly.

And as she watched, the bicycle's bell rang out; high and shrill over the calling of the gulls.

'Isn't that our Trudie?' Joe asked, shielding his eyes from the sun. Beside him, Lester was filling one of the pier's slot machines, a large canvas bag lying by his feet.

'Pass me that screwdriver, will you?'

When Joe didn't respond, Lester sighed and then followed his gaze down the pier. 'Hey, that's Trudie!'

'I know, I just said that,' Joe replied, still watching his sister. 'Who's the lad?'

'How would I know?'

'Some out-of-towner,' Joe replied darkly, while Lester bent to rummage in his bag again. 'Mam would kill her for fooling around . . . bloody hell, her skirt's up round her arse now!'

At once Lester dropped his screwdriver and stared at the giddy couple on the bike. 'Go and have a word with her, will you, Joe?'

'Why me?'

'Because I'm working,' Lester replied.

But his attention was shifting, his gaze now fixed on his sister. The boy was standing up on the pedals now, Trudie clinging on to his waist, passers-by watching.

'What the hell does she think she's playing at?'

'She's going to fall,' Joe said grimly, suddenly catching sight of Rose approaching. At once, he waved her over, Rose's feet dragging as she saw the brothers. ''Lo there, Rosie, are you with our Trudie?'

She shrugged, looking down. Joe was nice, but Lester was heavenly. Rose had adored him for years, could hardly speak in his presence. Not that he would notice her. *No one* noticed her.

'She *was* with me,' Rose said churlishly, scratching her left forearm.

Lester was still staring at his sister; didn't even know Rose was there. In fact, Rose thought peevishly, if her head was on fire he wouldn't have noticed.

'Who's the lad?' Joe asked.

'I dunno.'

'You were with her.'

'Well, I'm not with her now!' Rose replied, her tone piqued.

Slyly, she snatched a glance at Lester. he was so good-looking, she thought – that blond hair and hazel eyes. And he was smart, everyone said so. He'll go far, her father had told her, you mark my words, Lester Williams will go far . . .

'Why did you leave her?'

Rose blinked. *Lester was talking to her!*

'What?' she croaked.

'Why did you walk off and leave her!'

His tone was curt, as though his sister riding that bicycle with a yob was *her* fault! The one person Rose wanted to think well of her was chastising her. God, life was a pig.

'I didn't walk off!'

'You're not with her now,' Lester replied, without noticing Rose's discomfort. 'You should have stayed with her –'

'I'm not her keeper!' Rose hissed suddenly, Lester taken aback. Her temper was up. Here she was, having been

38

dumped by Trudie, dismissed by some lad, and now told off by Lester Williams. They could all go to hell. Every one of them. 'I don't have to look after your blasted sister!'

'It's just that you're a good influence,' Lester began, somewhat surprised by the red-faced kid in front of him. 'You're a nice girl; you keep Trudie steady –'

'I don't want to keep Trudie steady!' Rose hurled back, her arms itching, the sun knifing her in the back. 'And as for that boy – she's kissed him. *With tongues.*'

For years afterwards Joe would say that he had never seen his brother move so fast. Within seconds it seemed that Lester had the lad off the bike and pinned against the iron railings of the pier. It was only Joe's intervention that prevented a fight. Trudie was marched home in disgrace.

Leaning against the side of the Rock Emporium, Rosie watched them go. Her triumph had been short-lived. Slowly, she turned to the group of lads, now a way off. The boy with the bike was rubbing his arm where Lester had grabbed him, his friends ragging him. He didn't look so sure of himself any more. In fact, he looked like a kid who had been cut down to size.

It was strange, Rose realised, how quickly you could change from hating someone to pitying them.

SIX

Strategically placed across the course, Len signalled to George Ogden as the bets began to be laid for the next race, at two thirty. Going hard. You could say that again, Len thought wryly. Standing high on his box, Len moved his white-gloved hands deftly, tapping his wrist to indicate that one horse was 5-4 and then tugging his ear to show that another was at 11-10 odds. Having been a ticktack man for nearly fifteen years, Len could work on automatic pilot at many of the smaller meets, but this was Haydock Park and he would do well to keep his eyes and ears open.

For Len had a potential rival. Out of nowhere a whey-faced man of around twenty-five had slid into George Ogden's life. *Roy Howell*. Roy bloody Howell, Len thought. Rhymes with owl. And he looked like a flaming owl too: big bulging eyes of pale green, over a small hooked nose and a mouth that never moved unless absolutely necessary. Roy Howell, George's new clerk.

It was a well-known fact that the bookies' clerks were the geniuses of racing.

'You get a good clerk,' George had said often enough, 'and you're quids in.'

He was right. After every race a punter would come over to his bookie and ask for his winnings. A good clerk could tot up the money to be paid out on the spot. With no mistakes. No overpayment. No pissing off his bookie boss.

Will had been George's clerk for as long as anyone could remember. Now suddenly he'd disappeared – and the first Len had known about it had been half an hour ago.

'Morning, Len,' George had said, his shifty face turning to the owl behind him. 'Heard about Will?'

'Your Will?'

George had nodded his feral head, his grey hair flopping under his trilby. 'Disappeared.'

'Disappeared? *Will?*'

Pulling a face, George dropped his voice. 'Had to. Know what I mean?'

'He *never* cheated you!'

'Will? Do me a favour.'

'What then?'

And it was at that moment that nemesis appeared.

'Oh, there's someone I want you to meet, Len. Roy Howell. My new clerk.'

And that had been it. Before Len had had any time to ask questions, they had parted to get the odds before the first race.

Across the course he was now watching them: the weasel George with the owl Howell, the latter sitting behind his master's stand, hunched over the betting records.

'Hey! Len!' a punter shouted over to him suddenly. 'You asleep, or what?'

'*Me*, asleep? I don't even close my eyes at night, I'm so scared of missing something.'

'Give us the odds on Happy Lady then, will you?'

The odds were looking good for Happy Lady, but Miserable Man standing on the podium was beginning to look like a bit of a loser.

The new guests at the Sea View private hotel were standing to attention before Ruby, Mr Liddle – a twenty-one-year-old railway clerk – overawed. The hotel had been recommended to them by friends. Don't be put off by the

41

landlady, they had said, she's a bit of a tartar, but she runs a nice house. And she can cook.

No one had mentioned that she was a bloody giant.

'If you buy your food, bring it to me before noon, I'll make your dinner. *But no foreign muck*,' Ruby said, toning down her booming voice for the newcomers. It paid to make the right impression from the off. 'You've got hot water. And clean towels in your room.'

Mr Liddle nodded. He didn't quite know why, only that it seemed the right thing to do. Beside him, Mrs Liddle was silent, her tiny round form dwarfed by their landlady. Mesmerised by the apparition, Mr Liddle suddenly found his attention focused on Ruby's mouth. She was wearing lipstick, he realised – nothing remarkable on most women, but on her it looked like someone had painted the surround of a bakehouse oven.

'I don't like food kept in the rooms, or any drink. But you can have a key. If you're out after ten you let yourself in. Oh, and don't bang the door, it makes the dog go mad.' With that, Ruby smiled, Mrs Liddle flinching. 'There's a radio in your room. There's not many hotels around here who have radios for their guests. Not in their rooms anyway.'

'What about –'

'No playing music after eleven,' Ruby interjected.

'We thought –'

'And if I were you I'd steer clear of the pier after dark. Can get a bit rough, if you know what I mean. For out-of-towners, like yourselves.'

After taking her new guests to their room, Ruby climbed the second flight of stairs and entered the bedroom she shared with Alfred. He was trying to put on his socks, his beer belly making it difficult to reach his feet.

'New guests,' Ruby said, bending down and pulling on her husband's socks for him. 'Good thing too. Funds were getting a bit thin, Easter being so late this year.'

'When I were young –'

'You were *never* young, Alfred,' Ruby replied, passing him a shirt to put on.

She never knew what to make of her husband, never had. He hadn't been good-looking, or likely to do well. And his bad back put paid to any exertion – at work or at play. So what *had* been the attraction?

'I were dreaming of you,' Alfred told her, scratching his balding head. 'Remember how we got locked in that van when we'd stolen in for a cuddle?'

'It wasn't a van, Alfred, it was a broom cupboard.'

He frowned. 'Are you sure?'

'I was born on the move,' Ruby replied patiently. 'I know when something's got wheels on it. And that broom cupboard had no wheels.'

'It still moved around a bit,' he said, winking. 'I had wonderful hair then.'

'You're a liar! Your hair started to fall out on your twenty-third birthday. You got drunk to get over it,' Ruby replied, sitting down on the edge of the bed. At once, the springs protested. Alfred looked over to her quizzically.

His wife might be six feet tall and hefty, but there was something about Ruby that still turned his heart after nearly twenty years of marriage. Not that he could tell her that; Ruby wasn't one for sentiment.

'Lester's got something up his sleeve,' Ruby said suddenly. 'Talking about setting up his own business.'

'I had my own business once.'

'Alfred, you never did! You never had a *job* for more than a month.'

'My infirmity held me back,' Alfred replied, rubbing his lower spine. 'Things were never the same since I injured myself working for the royals.'

Ruby loved this story. In fact, she suddenly realised just what it *was* that she loved about Alfred. His lies. Those fabulous swoops into surreality, so at odds with her own pragmatism.

'*Working for the royals!*' she laughed loudly. 'You fell off the bloody kitchen roof when you were in gaol, Alfred.'

'Ah, but I were in gaol for spying –'

'And I was Mata Hari,' Ruby answered him, lying back on the bed, her hands locked under her head.

Below her she could hear her guests moving round. Four rooms booked already, good. Soon she would have to be busy again, getting dinner ready. But not for a little while. The kids were out and Alfred was rested enough to have dreamed up a good new story.

'I never told you about my spying, did I?'

'No, Alfred, you never did.'

'I worked . . .' he struggled for the right words, '. . . in disguise.'

Smiling, Ruby rolled onto her side and cupped her chin in her hand. How in God's name could her husband have been disguised with a port-wine stain as big as a hand print on the left-hand side of his face? It was ridiculous – like all Alfred's stories. But she wouldn't have stopped him for the world.

The first time she had met Alfred he'd bought a pie off her van. A labourer then, he had been working on a nearby building site and was freezing cold. But cheeky.

'By hell,' he said when he saw her, 'you're a big 'un, aren't you?'

'You should see my father,' Ruby had replied, watching Alfred bluster.

'I meant nothing by it!' he said, accidentally dropping his pie onto the muddy ground.

Leaning further out of the van's serving hatch, Ruby had looked at the pie, then back to Alfred.

'That was clumsy.'

'I don't suppose –'

'No.'

Alfred had stared at the pie mournfully. On his cheek

Ruby could see the port-wine stain and for a moment it looked like the ace of spades.

'That's lucky,' she had said suddenly.

'Dropping my bloody pie?'

'Nah, that thing on your face. The ace of spades. It's lucky.'

He had touched it, embarrassed. 'The ace of spades is black.'

Ruby had shrugged. 'Same shape, though . . . Now, you want another pie, or not?'

Nine months later she had married Alfred Williams, a fool in life, a genius in lies. And it was only Alfred who knew Ruby's origins. Only Alfred who had any idea that a six-foot woman could weep like a baby. Only Alfred – lazy, daydreaming, overweight Alfred – who would never, *ever* betray her.

A sudden commotion below broke into Alfred's story, Ruby off the bed and down the stairs before her husband made it to the door. In the hall stood Lester, gripping his sister's arm. Joe shrugged as he looked at his mother.

'Trudie was –'

'Not here!' Ruby snapped, jerking her head to the kitchen.

In silence they followed her, Joe closing the door behind them. In his basket by the fire slept the dog, a mongrel called Chase, who was impervious to everything and everyone most of time. Unless someone banged the front door. And then he would leap to his feet and bark hysterically.

'We've got guests,' Ruby said sternly. 'It's the season, in case you'd all forgotten. So from now on, keep it quiet, and keep it to the back of the house.'

Ruby looked at her children in turn, then realised that Gilbert was still sitting at the kitchen table, still mooning over his stale tea.

'I've a terrible headache –'

'Shut up, Gilbert!' Ruby snapped, looking back to Lester. 'So what's all the fuss about?'

'Trudie was larking about with a boy –'

'I wasn't! I wasn't!' she said, breaking free of Lester's grip and staring at her brother fiercely. 'I was just talking.'

'On a bike?'

'You can talk on a bike, you know,' Trudie sneered. 'Being mobile doesn't paralyse your vocal cords.'

For a moment Ruby was impressed by her daughter's eloquence. But it didn't last.

'*You were larking about on a bike with a boy?*'

'I was talking –'

'Who was he?'

'Some lad.'

'What's his name?'

'I dunno.'

'Where does he live?'

'I dunno.'

'You don't know! But you were larking about on his bike!' Ruby roared, then dropped her voice as she remembered the guests. 'You're my daughter and you'll behave decently –'

'I was just –'

'Don't interrupt me!' Ruby retorted. 'I won't have you growing up a slut.'

'I was just talking . . .' Trudie wailed.

'It's no crime to talk –'

'Shut up, Gilbert!' Ruby and Lester said in unison.

'*Were* you on the bike with this boy?'

'Aw, Mum . . .'

'Trudie! Were you on the bike with this hooligan?'

'I used to ride a bike –'

'Shut up, Gilbert!' Ruby snapped again.

'You *were* riding the bike together, weren't you? Holding on to him, I suppose? Showing me up?'

Before he could stop himself, the words came out of Joe's mouth: 'And showing her legs –'

With one quick movement, Trudie turned and jabbed Joe sharply in the ribs.

'– when she fell off! Only when she fell off!' Joe added hurriedly.

'You fell off the bike?' Ruby was suddenly anxious.

The mood had shifted. Lester gave his brother an exasperated look as Trudie winced and began to rub an imaginary bruise on her shoulder. In that instant the brothers knew she was off the hook.

'I'm all right, Mum, no damage done.'

'Only because she fell on her head,' Lester said under his breath.

'Do you need a doctor?'

'I'm fine, Mum,' Trudie replied, giving Lester a triumphant look. 'Don't worry, there's no harm done.'

SEVEN

At four thirty-five that same afternoon Len Bradshaw found himself in the racecourse bar with George. Same as usual after a race. Only this time Will wasn't there, the Owl was. And the Owl didn't drink, which made Len very nervous. Whoever heard of a bookie's clerk who didn't drink? It was weird. Bloody weird . . . Fixing Len with his round, seaweed-green eyes, Roy Howell said precisely *nothing*.

But George did.

'Shame about Will –'

'You didn't tell me what happened to him,' Len replied, turning to his employer, aware all the time that the Owl had him fixed in his sights like a fieldmouse.

'He's gone.'

'Yeah, you said that. Gone where?'

'Ran off with a woman.'

'He's seventy if he's a day!' Len replied disbelievingly. 'I doubt if he'd got it up for the last two decades.'

'People can surprise you,' George replied, the Owl's eyes burning holes in the back of Len's head.

'What about . . . ?'

'What?' George asked, inhaling on a cigarette and holding the smoke in his mouth for a second before exhaling. 'What about *what*?'

'About . . .' Len jerked his head slightly to indicate the

man behind them, '. . . bloody hell! You know, George.'

'Ah, you mean Roy.'

'Yeah, *Roy*.'

'Nice boy. Roy.'

Holding on to his patience, Len took a long gulp of beer. He knew that George was playing him like a fish and resented it.

'Roy Howell.'

'Yeah, George, you've told me his name. Several times.'

'Quick brain.'

The bar had filled up, the noise level rising. Around them hung a fug of smoke, a scattering of torn betting slips on the floor, the winners buying drinks at the bar. Len had lost count of the times he had stood in the same bar at Haydock Park with George, nodding to acquaintances and envying the bookies with their pitches. It was so difficult to get a pitch – usually only through recommendation, a word in the right ear, or by someone conveniently dying. One day, Len had told himself consolingly, one day I'll have a pitch and a label on *my* jacket and *my* name by the track: 'Leonard Bradshaw – The Lazy Eye'.

'It just seems odd . . .'

'What does?' George asked, taking another sip of his whisky.

'That Will went off so sudden, and Roy's . . .' the name wedged in his throat, '. . . filling in so quick.'

'He's not.'

Len frowned. 'He's not what?'

'He's not filling in.'

Dizzy with relief and the pungent cigarette smoke, Len smiled warmly. 'Oh, I get it! Roy's just temporary.'

'Nah,' George replied, his red-rimmed eyes mischievous. 'He's not filling in, he's here to stay. He's my nephew.'

There was to be no protest, Rose realised at once, not tonight. Standing in the narrow hall she stepped back onto the stairs as her father pulled and tugged a dilapidated chair through the front door.

'Bloody thing!' Len hissed. 'Get in, get in, you bugger!'

There had been a problem. A big problem, Rose knew. Because that was the only time Len was angry with her. Like the time he had been cheated in a game of cards after the late show at the Winter Gardens Pavilion. Or the time he had loaned an old friend five quid – *five quid* – and the man had run off with it. It didn't count that Len got the money back three years later. The money *and* two of his ex-friend's teeth. The point was that he had been betrayed. And that was something Len Bradshaw couldn't stomach.

'Get out of the way!' he barked at Rose, giving the chair one final push through the door and ripping off the lock at the same time. 'Oh Jesus! Jesus Christ!' Len exploded, kicking the back of the chair, then the door. 'Bloody chair! Bloody life! Bloody bastard!'

Exhausted, he then sat down heavily on the step. After waiting for a moment, Rose joined him.

'It'll be cold on your arse. Get something to sit on.'

Obediently she did so, coming back with the evening paper and offering her father half.

'Nah, you have it. It's important for a girl.'

Rose wasn't quite sure how sitting on newspaper was vital to her gender, but duly tucked the *Evening Gazette* under her and then laid her head on her father's shoulder.

'What happened today? Did you lose?'

'Bloody everything,' Len replied, taking out his tobacco and rolling himself a cigarette.

Rose loved to watch him; waiting for the moment when he put a match to the spindly smoke and the end lighted up. She would count to three, then inhale, letting the smoke nuzzle against her nostrils. She thought that she would know her father anywhere by the smell of his baccy.

'What happened, Dad?'

50

'George Ogden – bloody wizened old ferret – has got a nephew.'

'Is that bad?'

'I won't get his pitch or his licence if he's got family!' Len retorted heatedly. 'All these years he's told me he didn't have anyone. I stayed with him because of that.' He looked at his daughter incredulously. 'You know how long I've been with that toerag, Rosie? Too bloody long.'

'Too bloody long,' she echoed.

'You shouldn't swear,' Len said quickly, but his heart wasn't in it. 'That man's played me for a fool. Bloody sod.'

'Bloody sod,' Rose intoned solemnly.

'You should have seen his face when he told me. He was laughing at me! And that nephew of his –'

'Bloody pig.'

Len stopped and stared at his daughter. Then nodded in agreement. 'Yeah, bloody pig. Face like something you'd see on a slab in the wet fish shop. Eyes big as doorknobs. Spooky bugger . . . I needed that pitch, Rosie, needed George Ogden's licence. I've waited for it for years!' Len paused, inhaling again to stop unfamiliar tears of frustration coming. 'Last time I worked it out George had to be over eighty. *Bloody eighty!* I mean, I've never wished him ill – although he's been a bugger to work for – but I was sure I'd get his licence when he died.'

Rose sighed. It seemed the only thing to do.

'If I didn't have you, life wouldn't be worth living,' Len said quietly, looking out over the street to the hotel opposite. 'Lights in the first-floor window. Sea View must have guests, God help them.'

'Another couple arrived today,' Rose offered, glad that she could tell her father something to take his mind off his troubles. 'Mrs Williams said they were staying for Easter – and that she has others coming.'

What Ruby had also said was that if she caught Rose sitting on the doorstep ogling her hotel she would give her something to stare *at*. But Rose thought it wasn't the time to burden her father with that piece of information; especially as he happened to be sitting on the step at that moment, ogling the hotel opposite.

'We could move.'

Rose raised her head. 'What!'

'We could move away, Rosie. Go somewhere else.'

'But I like it here. I've got school here and friends.'

'You could make new friends, get a new school,' Len replied. 'We could make a new start.'

At that moment Clovis came round the corner, pulling a kid's cart behind her. Slowly she made her way over to Len and Rose, then stopped and perched on the side of the cart, her dowager's hump pushing her head forward like a turtle's.

''Lo there, Clovis,' Len replied, looking resignedly at the cart. 'What's that?'

'I got it for a good price,' Clovis answered, by way of reply.

'What's it for?' Rose chimed in.

'A *very* good price . . .' Clovis went on, her face pink from exertion, her heavy tweed coat falling open as she fanned herself with one darkly veined hand. '. . . I never thought I'd get it so cheap.'

Len sighed. 'You've nowhere to put it.'

'I've loads of space!' Clovis replied, her tone abrupt.

'But what's it *for*?' Rose repeated.

'For storing things!' Clovis answered impatiently, as though any fool would have known. 'You two can't see quality when it's staring you in the face.'

Having got her breath back, Clovis got to her feet again, picked up the cart handle and walked off – Len and Rose watching her go.

'She's bonkers.'

'Bloody bonkers,' Rose agreed.

A few moments passed before Len spoke again. 'Why *don't* we move somewhere else? Think about it, Rosie. We could, you know. There's nothing much here for either of us.'

Rose had hoped that Clovis's appearance would have taken her father's mind off moving. Disappointed, she stared at the worn paving stones. A new start wasn't what she wanted at all. She liked living in Gull Road, liked having a best friend living opposite. Had grown up surrounded by people and stories that were familiar – the Williamses, Clovis, Nan Wilmslow. And besides, there was her hero, Lester, living only yards away . . .

'We're happy here, Dad.'

'We could be happy somewhere else.'

'But how d'you know that you won't get George Ogden's pitch?'

'I've told you, he's suddenly got a nephew. The pitch will go to Roy Howell now.'

'He might die too,' Rose said hopefully.

'He's in his *twenties*!' Len replied, exasperated. 'Not many people die in their twenties. And never when you want them to.'

'He might be murdered.'

'Oh, Rosie!' Len replied, laughing grimly. 'What made you say that?'

'Mr Williams told me that three men had been murdered only the other day –'

'Alfred Williams is a liar, everyone knows that.'

'But he *might* be right. George Ogden's nephew might get killed.'

'I wouldn't put a bet on it,' Len replied, getting to his feet then sighing when he caught sight of the chair jammed in the hallway. It was unwieldy, old-fashioned and long past its best. 'What d'you think of that, Rosie?'

She stared at the battered armchair for a long moment before replying.

'It's awful. *Bloody awful.*'

'Yeah,' Len agreed. 'Just like life.'

EIGHT

Up at the Raikes Road School Miss Cork found herself staring at Rose Bradshaw's empty desk. Glancing at the one next to it she was surprised to see Trudie Williams picking at her split ends. Usually they played truant together. But this time Rose had gone it alone. Now why was that, Miss Cork wondered, glancing back to the scrappy piece of paper the school secretary had just handed her.

Dear Miss Cork,
     Our Rosie can't come to school today. She's bad with a cold and should be home in the warm.
     Yours sincerely,
     Len Bradshaw

Miss Cork liked the 'yours sincerely' touch, but the handwriting was a dead giveaway. And she was certain that Len Bradshaw didn't write with a green crayon . . . Sighing, Miss Cork set the other pupils to work and then glanced out of the window. The warm weather had passed; now there was a chill in the air, the trees shivering in a cold wind.

Rosie Bradshaw had a good brain. She had potential. Not like Trudie Williams, who was only interested in getting married – if she didn't get pregnant first. No, Rosie could go on to get some further education, possibly even a profession, if only she would apply herself. But recently Rosie had no interest in anything any more. The change in her had been sudden. From being an attentive student she had changed into a sullen, stroppy kid with a chip on her shoulder.

Miss Cork couldn't put the change down to puberty. Trudie might have developed impressively, but Rosie still looked like a child. Maybe that was the trouble; maybe seeing the rest of her class shoot up around her made her insecure. Girls, Miss Cork knew only too well, worried about things like that. Puberty was a difficult time. Suddenly you were propelled from being a child into being a woman, and that meant having to compete.

And Rose wouldn't fare too well in competition . . . Miss Cork glanced down at her hands, thinking. A squint wasn't life threatening, and she knew that Len Bradshaw wasn't a rich man, but she was also sure that if Rose's mother had still been alive she would have sorted it out. Life was hard – who needed anything to make it harder? And it wasn't as though Rose was the insensitive kind.

Only the previous day Miss Cork had seen an episode that had haunted her. Rose had been playing jacks in the playground, an older girl coming over to her and watching.

'Give me them.'

Rose had looked up, surprised. 'They're mine.'

'Not for long,' the older girl had replied, knocking Rose over and taking the jacks. To her credit, Rose had run after her tormentor and tugged at her arm, her anger obvious to the onlookers who had gathered round to watch.

'Those are mine! Give them back!' she'd shouted, the older girl grinning and lifting her hand aloft.

'They *were* yours, but now they're mine.'

Furious, Rose had jumped up to try to catch hold of the girl's raised hand.

'Give them back!'

The watching pupils had been spellbound; some laughing,

some younger ones nervous as they watched Rose stand up to the older, bigger girl.

'Give them back!'

Then suddenly the girl had paused, looking Rose up and down. 'Sod off,' she had said scornfully, 'you cross-eyed runt.'

So was *that* why Rose wasn't in school today? Miss Cork closed the book in front of her. Her gaze raked along the rows of pupils and came to rest on the third row.

'Trudie Williams, come outside a moment, will you?'

'I haven't done anything!'

'I didn't say you had,' Miss Cork replied, beckoning for Trudie to follow her into the corridor.

'Where's Rose?'

Trudie had never been known to answer a question directly. Besides, this was a teacher.

'Who?'

'Your best friend. Rose Bradshaw.'

'I dunno,' Trudie replied honestly. 'Sick?'

'Good guess,' Miss Cork said drily. 'Sick with what?'

This was a minefield.

'A headache.'

'Not a cold then?'

Trudie squirmed. Honestly, if Rose was going to play truant why hadn't she warned her so she could get the story straight? And why hadn't she taken her along?

'A cold *and* a headache,' Trudie said confidently. 'You know what I mean. You get a bad head and then a sick stomach – it's a flu kind of thing. Very serious. Very bad for you. That kind of thing.' Trudie blathered on, unable to resist embellishing the tale. 'I heard someone died in Lytham.'

Miss Cork's sandy eyebrows rose: 'Who?'

'The priest,' Trudie replied confidently. 'He was giving Mass and he keeled over on the spot. Died in church.'

Miss Cork had to admit that it was good entertainment, if nothing else.

'You're lying –'

'Not me, miss!' Trudie replied hotly.

'You're always lying, Trudie, and you shouldn't. People won't trust you if you lie.'

'But I never lie,' Trudie lied.

God, what *was* the point talking to the girl, Miss Cork thought. It was common knowledge that her father wouldn't have recognised the truth if it ran over him. Hadn't she had the misfortune to run into Alfred Williams at the last sports day? Only to be told that he had once sprinted for England.

'I were the fastest man in the county,' Alfred had said, winking, his porkpie hat ludicrously small on his fat head. 'I dare say I could outrun Jack London – with a bit of training, mind.'

'You *run*, Mr Williams?'

At that very moment Alfred had been yanked away by his monumental wife, Miss Cork left with the indelible image of Alfred Williams waddling down the Olympic track in a porkpie hat.

And now here was his daughter telling even more extravagant lies.

'Trudie, listen to me, I'm worried about Rose. She's changed lately.' Miss Cork chose her words with care. 'Are things all right at home for her?'

'Yeah, sure.'

'Is she worried about anything?'

Trudie's expression assumed a far-off look as she knitted up the next lie.

'Rose is fine,' Trudie replied at last. 'She did say she was going to run away from home, though.'

'Run away? Are you sure, Trudie?'

'Well, not *run* away,' Trudie replied, shifting her feet. '"Get away", I think she said.'

'Where would she be getting away *to*? And why?'

'I dunno,' Trudie went on gamely. 'But you're right, she's

not like she was. We used to share everything, but not lately. She's got secrets, has Rose.'

'What kind of secrets?'

'How would I know? They're secrets.'

Miss Cork took in a slow breath.

'Just let me know if she's in any trouble, will you? I don't want to tell Rose off, I want to help. She's a bright girl, she could do well in life. Even go on to further education.'

As Miss Cork said to her mother later, the words 'further education' had an astounding effect on Trudie Williams. Never, in all her years as a teacher, had she seen anyone go so pale, so fast.

Whilst Miss Cork had been talking to Trudie, Rose was sitting in the railway station, at the far end of Gull Road. She liked it there, watching people come and go, wondering if some of the passengers might be heading for Sea View. Usually she came with Trudie. But she was fed up with her friend, ever since she had dumped her at the pier. Sod Trudie! she thought. I can get by just fine on my own.

A man passed the bench where she was sitting, Rose automatically looking away. *Cross-eyed runt*... The words had punctured what remained of Rose's small confidence. If she'd had some money she'd have taken a train there and then and got away from Blackpool.

To go where? Rose wondered, sinking further into the bench. The station master made an announcement over the loud speaker. The words crackled, inaudible where Rose was sitting. If things had been different she might have been going somewhere with her mother. Rose tried to imagine her mother, but she had no memories to draw on.

It was a shame that there were no maternal figures around, Rose thought suddenly. Ruby Williams was hardly the type you'd run to, Miss Cork was too strict, Nan Wilmslow was creepy, and as for her aunt – well, Clutter

Clovis was just plain crazy. Rose touched her stomach furtively. She would die alone, she realised. She *could* have told Trudie. But then she would certainly have told Ruby, and that was unthinkable. As for Dad . . .

Rose looked down. She couldn't tell her father. It would break his heart. Alone and afraid, Rose kept staring at the grubby station floor. Loneliness – sharp as a cat's claw – scratched at her heart.

NINE

'So where is she?' Len snapped, standing on the doorstep of Sea View.

'I dunno,' Trudie whined, as a train drew into the station beyond and blew its whistle. 'Miss Cork was looking for her.'

Distracted, Len's glance darted around him. The street was busy with people coming home from work, Alfred strolling down from the pub on Sheppard Street, his porkpie hat perched on the top of his head.

'How do, Len?'

'Have you seen Rosie?'

Alfred shook his head. 'She's not missing, is she? I heard about a girl once –'

'Not now!' Len barked, hurrying down Gull Road, crossing Coronation Street and moving on into Charnley Road.

He knew that Rosie had played truant a couple of times, but since he had found out she'd promised never to do it again. And he had believed her – because his daughter had never lied to him. Until now.

Behind him the pier rose over the house tops and he could hear the screams of pleasure from people on the big dipper, having fun. Well, why not? Len had had enough fun of his own. Until recently. He had plenty of feminine company and a daughter he adored. And hope – until that toerag Ogden had squelched his dreams into the dirt.

Perhaps he had unsettled Rosie by all the talk of Roy Howell. Or maybe she had been alarmed by the thought of moving to another town. But it had all been just that – talk! Len wasn't really going to uproot them. He'd been born in Blackpool and married to Vera when he first came to Gull Road. So many things at number 139 still reminded him of her. To leave Gull Road would be to leave behind Vera. And he couldn't do that. Not now, not ever.

But did Rosie realise that? Did she realise that her father had just been running off at the mouth, pissed off as he was with Ogden's games? Len stared around him. Every road was familiar; he knew most of the people who lived in most of the houses, just as they knew him. He knew which men came to the track without their wives knowing, and which were hopeless gamblers who would risk the rent on a bet. He even knew why one lad had been murdered. But Len wasn't about to tell anyone. Some secrets were best left secret.

But didn't Rosie know that they would never leave Gull Road? Didn't she know that it was their security to look across the street to Sea View and gossip about the guests? It had always been one of the highlights of their summers, wondering about the new arrivals: where they had come from, who they were, what they did. Rose had a good memory for faces; could recall who had been before, and when. Which Len never could. He could remember everything about a horse – but a person, no way.

And now where was his little girl? Len suddenly panicked. He had always known where she was when she was little, and if he'd had no one around to mind her, he'd take her to the track with him. Even as a toddler Rosie would stand on his box between races, and pull on her father's white gloves. As they flapped on her little hands she would copy Len's actions, tapping her head or her arm, the other tick-tack men laughing as they watched her. She was quick too; picked up the movements rapidly and never forgot them. In fact, father and daughter had developed their own ticktack: across a room they could communicate by signing, and no one else ever knew what they were saying.

And she loved the racing, the horses; Len knew that well enough. Hadn't Rose begged him to teach her all the moves? Begged for her own pair of white gloves? Played hell with him if he didn't let her go round to see the jockeys later and pet the horses? And hadn't she talked – for years – about how she was going to be a ticktack woman? No good Len telling her it wasn't a proper job for a woman – that had only made her keener.

And now his fabulous, funny kid was missing . . . Len stopped walking, aware that he was out of breath. She was, he realised at that moment, his life. Without her there was nothing. Trying not to panic, Len wondered where to go next. It was the season and that meant newcomers to the town. Strangers. All types. And he'd heard all kinds of things. It was no secret that many came to Blackpool for a dirty weekend. And then there were the young men on their own, coming on their bikes, on the tramway or train. Coming whistling down the Promenade, eyeing up the girls. Looking for a kiss and a cuddle, and more if they could get it.

Stop panicking! Len told himself. Rosie's only a kid. She's only thirteen, not interested in boys. *Or maybe she was.* What the hell did he know what went on in her mind? She might have a boyfriend *now*, someone he didn't know about. Someone she met secretly. Shaking his head, Len turned round on the street, looking down towards the station and, beyond that, the sea, dark and deep.

A man called out to him suddenly. 'Oi, Len! You looking for your Rose?'

He nodded, crossing over. 'You seen her?'

'Down the station. I've just got in myself and there she was, sitting on a bench, looking lost.'

Panic flooded through Len as he thanked the man and

began to run towards the station. After a couple of minutes a stitch started in his side but he kept on. His daughter, his Rosie, might be waiting for a train. If he took too long he might miss her. Might arrive and find the bench empty. His daughter spirited away. His world gone.

Ruby looked the new arrivals up and down. Mr and Mrs Noble. Not so noble in appearance, she thought snidely.

'We thought there was a sea view,' Mrs Noble said, her tone assertive.

There is, Ruby thought, if you go upstairs and stand on a chair to look out of the window.

'You said there was a sea view.'

'I never did,' Ruby said flatly.

'But your hotel is called Sea View,' Mr Noble chimed in.

'I could have called it Snowdonia View, but you wouldn't have expected to see a bloody mountain.'

Behind her, Trudie suddenly emerged, walking to the front door and then pausing. Quickly, she eyed up the young Mr Noble. He returned the compliment, suddenly losing interest in whether or not there was a sea view. There was a good enough view indoors.

'Teddy . . .' Mrs Noble said quietly, tugging his sleeve to get his attention, '. . . what d'you think? I mean, there's no view.'

'We can walk to the sea, luv. It's not far.'

Throwing Mr Noble a last look, Trudie went out. Now *that* would be interesting, she thought, to have a good-looking guest for once.

Back inside, Mrs Noble was in full whine.

'But we booked expecting a sea view.' Throwing all caution to the wind, she looked at Ruby and launched in: 'Perhaps we could have a discount? I mean, for not having a view.'

Ruby glowered, like a bear wakened too early from hibernation.

'A *discount*?' she repeated, her booming voice ominously low. 'I'll have you know that there's nowhere as good as here – not for the money you're paying. And you'd have had a radio in your room.'

The same one that the Liddles were having use of, Ruby thought. The radio that did more mileage than the trams.

'But –'

'I don't need to be insulted!' Ruby went on, folding her arms and towering over the flushed Mrs Noble. 'I've had to turn people away because you'd booked in advance. Now if I'd been an unscrupulous woman I'd not have given a damn! But no, I kept my word, and now you – *you* – come here and tell me that my hotel's not good enough for you.'

'I just said there wasn't a sea view –'

'How many other hotels have radios?' Ruby went on, her voice now developing its impressive timbre. 'Anyone can have a sea view – but not a radio in their room.'

'Let it drop,' Teddy Noble urged his wife, before turning back to Ruby. 'We'll take the room.'

'I might not want to let you have it now!'

Both Nobles blanched.

'But –'

'I've plenty of people wanting on a cancellation,' Ruby went on. 'I don't need your money. Although where you'll find another hotel – *decent hotel* – with vacancies on such short notice is a mystery to me.'

'We'll take it,' Mr Noble repeated, picking up his suitcase and walking towards the stairs.

At once, Ruby blocked his way. 'Just hang on a minute.'

Teddy Noble had had enough. He was tired and well aware that they wouldn't find another hotel so late at night. Sea View looked clean, and there was a good smell coming from the kitchen. Besides, he was getting fed up with his whining wife and wanted to get his feet up.

'How much?' he asked Ruby wearily.

'Half a crown. *A day.*'

He winced, then nodded. 'You win.'

'I usually do,' Ruby replied, watching Mrs Noble gather up what was left of her dignity. As she passed her on the stairs, Ruby said slyly, 'And if you still want a sea view – buy a postcard.'

'What you doing here?' Trudie said, sliding onto the bench next to Rose. 'You look awful.'

Rose said nothing, just kept staring ahead.

'Your dad's running about like a scalded cat,' Trudie went on. 'Last sight I had of him was him off down South King Street.'

Silence from Rose. She just sat deathly pale and still.

'What is it? Come on, we're best pals, you can tell me anything.'

'Hah!'

'You're not still sulking about that boy on the pier, are you?' Trudie asked her. 'I mean I could be cheesed off with you – telling Lester about using tongues. What the hell were you doing?'

'Getting even.'

'It nearly worked. Lester was right het up . . . God, Mum would have killed me if he'd told her!'

'You'd have lied your way out of it,' Rose said blithely.

Trudie winced. 'Hey! What's got into you?'

'Nothing.'

'You sick?' she asked, then brightened up. 'Or have you met a boy?'

'No! Boys aren't interested in me . . . Anyway, none of that matters now.'

'Boys *always* matter,' Trudie replied, chewing her thumb-nail and looking round. Another announcement crackled from the station speaker, a woman running after a toddler only a couple of feet away from them. 'What did you mean just then – "nothing matters now"?'

'Oh, go home, Trudie!' Rose snapped, folding her arms and turning away.

'I'm not going home! I came to find you and find out what's wrong with you.' Miffed, Trudie suddenly remembered an earlier conversation. 'Miss Cork was asking about you. Said you were clever.'

'So what? It's not important now.'

Exasperated, Trudie turned her friend round to face her. 'What *are* you talking about?'

'I'm dying.'

Shaken to the core, Trudie let her mouth fall open. A long moment passed before she spoke again. 'You're dying?'

Rose nodded, a tear rolling down her left cheek.

'How d'you know?'

'I'm bleeding.'

'Where?'

'You know . . . down below.'

It took Trudie only a millisecond to understand.

'You're not dying, you cretin!' she said, laughing and then dropping her voice. 'You've got your period.'

Shaken, Rose stared at her. '*My period?*'

'Yeah, didn't anyone explain?' Trudie asked, then rolled her eyes. 'No, course not! I mean, your dad could hardly tell you what was going to happen, could he? God, Rosie, *dying*! You're growing up, that's what you're doing. You'll get breasts now, like me. And *hair* . . .'

Rose didn't hear what Trudie said next, she was too lost in thought. She was finally going to grow up. No more runty kid. Soon she would be tall, like all the other girls. And she'd have breasts. Maybe breasts that were big enough for the boys to forget her lazy eye. The thought melted against her.

Slowly she turned back to Trudie. 'What do I do now?'

'You get interested in boys,' Trudie replied, grinning. 'That's what you do.'

Overhead the loudspeaker crackled into life again, just

as Len ran into the station and onto the platform. He was dishevelled, out of breath, almost panicked. Seeing the two girls, he hurried over and hugged Rose to him frantically.

'What is it, Dad?' she asked, amazed.

'I thought you were leaving me.'

'Why would I leave you?'

'I dunno,' he said lamely. 'You never go off on your own usually. Are you all right?'

I'm changing, Dad, she wanted to say. I'm growing up and I won't be your little girl for much longer. I'm going to be a woman . . . But she knew she had to keep the knowledge to herself. This was something she *couldn't* share with him. So instead Rose Bradshaw linked arms with her father and together they walked out of the station into the changeling night.

Len had been right all along. His child *was* leaving him. But a woman would come to take her place.

TEN

1934

It didn't quite work out the way Trudie had planned.
Certainly Rosie changed physically – growing steadily in the
years that followed until she was slightly taller than her friend
– but mentally she remained the same. Developing breasts
and a natural swaying walk might invite some interest, but
Rose never encouraged or pursued it. Inside she was still the
runty, boss-eyed kid that the boys would always overlook.

'Aw, come on! You'll never get a lad unless you cheer
up,' Trudie said, exasperated.

It was a hot day at the rock factory. And yet, although
she had seen it a hundred times before, Rosie watched the
four assistants rolling a length of pink rock on the steel
worktop. Over their heads, a supervisor hovered, making
sure that the immortal word 'Blackpool' would run evenly
through. Trudie didn't like the work; didn't like *any* work.
But as she said, who could spend every day at Sea View
with the all-seeing Ruby? So Trudie had taken the job, her
wage partially mollifying her mother.

It was one of the many seaside attractions available, day-
trippers coming to watch Blackpool rock or humbugs being
made and then, inevitably, buying some. Business had
always been good, but lately a busker on the sands had
taken to throwing sticks of rock into the crowds, kids
chivvying to catch the souvenirs.

'I just don't feel like going out tonight,' Rose said quietly, sneaking closer to Trudie as the supervisor walked off.

Using the back of her forearm, Trudie wiped her forehead. 'It'll be a laugh –'

'I don't know the lads.'

'You'll never know *any* lads if you don't look sharp about it,' Trudie replied.

A kid called out from the onlookers. 'Oi, has anyone ever eaten a stick of rock that big?'

Trudie looked at the kid. 'Yeah, we had a bloke from the circus come. He swallowed it whole.'

A gasp went up from the audience.

'*Swallowed it whole?*'

'Yeah, then he ate three bags of humbugs in one go – and a donkey off the beach.'

Having come back on duty, the supervisor hurriedly relieved Trudie from her post at the table.

'You go and get your break, Trudie,' he said, dropping his voice to a barely audible whisper. 'And stop making up wild bloody tales.'

Wiping her hands on her white coat, Trudie walked out of the factory, Rose beside her. Then she paused to light up a cigarette, blowing smoke into the hot air.

'You're getting to be a right bore, Rose.'

'Hey!'

'But you are. You never want to go anywhere.' Trudie inhaled again. 'You and me go back a long way, but we're not kids any more. And I want some fun. All the girls in the factory like having a laugh.'

'So what are you saying – that you want to go out with them?' Rose asked quietly.

'I just said that I wanted some fun. Oh, come on, Rose, you're my best pal. We could have some right laughs with all the lads around now. It's the season, the pier's full of blokes.'

'It's because I'm still at school, isn't it?'

Trudie rolled her eyes. 'No! Although I have to say I don't know why you're still there.' She shot Rose a questioning look. 'You want to be a teacher or something? God, if you do, you must be mad. I mean, fancy ending up an old maid like Miss Cork.'

Smarting, Rose looked away. She had pleaded with Len to let her leave school, but he had insisted that she stay on until she had taken her school certificate. Then he had pleaded with her to stay on longer to take more exams.

'But I want to work at the track with you,' Rosie had objected.

Len was mortally tempted. 'No,' he'd replied at last. 'Miss Cork says you've got a good brain, so you have to use it, Rosie.'

'I want to work with you –'

'Working the track's not right for a girl!' Len snapped. 'I'd have you with me like a shot, you know I would, luv. But that would be selfish. You get what education you can.' His expression darkened with anger. 'I might have to kowtow to that bastard Ogden, but you could be your own boss in life.'

'Oi! don't you stand there daydreaming!' Trudie said, finishing her cigarette and grinding it out with the heel of her shoe. 'You're not a kid any more, Rose, so don't act like one.' She waited for a response. But when one didn't come, Trudie's tone hardened: 'So, are you coming out tonight, or not?'

ELEVEN

Afterwards everyone remembered how hot it had been that night.

After a sultry day the evening darkened, a huge September moon slung low and lazy over the coast. All around, midges cluttered the air, the lights of the pier like glow-worms skimming the dark, flat field of sea. There had been little rain for days. The trippers were tanned or reddened by the heat, couples dozing on benches as the sun went down, others snogging under the pier; more dressed up for the evening, aiming for the Winter Gardens.

On the still air every noise travelled clearly. From the Orchestra Hall of the Pavilion, seeming almost eerily close, came the melting sounds of jazz, imported from America. Walking in step, Trudie and Rose made their way down Church Street to the fairground on the South Shore.

'What's his name?'

Trudie paused to take a lipstick out of her bag. 'Johnny Grover.'

Rose nodded, watching Trudie apply the lipstick skilfully. It was Ruby's, but it looked better on her daughter.

'What's he like?'

'Nice enough, I guess,' Trudie replied, dropping the lipstick back into her bag and linking arms with Rose.

This was more like it, she thought to herself, now Rose was trying to enjoy herself. After all, no one could have blamed her for dropping her friend if she'd *insisted* on being a bore.

'It's a strange night,' Rose said suddenly, turning to glance up at the moon. 'God, that looks weird, like it's stuck on the sky. Not like it's real at all.'

'Oh, you do go on!' Trudie said impatiently. 'Don't talk like that with the boys, will you? They'll think you're strange. Lads like girls who can laugh at their jokes, flirt with them, make them feel good about themselves.'

'Dad wants me back by ten, no later.'

Trudie didn't doubt that. 'Jesus, Rose, we haven't even met them and you're talking about going home! I don't know why I bother with you –'

'Oh dry up!' Rose replied shortly. 'I'm here, aren't I? That's what you wanted. Now get off my back.'

Suitably chastened, Trudie walked beside Rose, wondering if she was going to speak again. But Rose's thoughts were elsewhere. The moon *did* look odd, hanging directly over the end of the fairground, tipping the top of the big dipper with silver, and raking the sea beyond. There was no breeze.

A voice called out suddenly: 'Hey, Trudie!'

Both girls turned to see a couple of lads hurrying through the crowd towards them.

'Hello there, Mike,' Trudie said, her head on one side as she smiled at his companion. 'And hello, Johnny.'

He smiled easily, already up for a good time.

'So you must be Rose?' he said, looking at her with interest.

And then she glanced up and read – as she did so often – the disappointment in his face.

'See you later!' Trudie said quickly, moving off, Mike's arm already round her shoulder.

A long silent moment passed between the abandoned, awkward couple. Johnny said nothing, Rose mortified and longing to go home.

'You don't have to take me out,' she said at last. 'I don't mind. There are loads of girls around: you'll find someone else in a minute.'

To her complete humiliation, he wavered, looking round. Then he turned back to her.

'Nah, we might have a good time,' he said, hurrying off, Rose following in his wake.

It was obvious to her that Johnny was trying to keep in sight of Mike and Trudie, dreading the thought that he might be left alone with his not-so-prepossessing date. Almost running after him towards the fairground, Rose pushed her way through the cluster of people, the sounds of the barkers loud in her ears.

'Roll up, roll up! Come on, you likely lads, come and have a go at this. Try your luck, hit three ducks in a row and you get a prize. Roll up! Roll up!'

Mike stopped, and Johnny hurried to his side.

'Let's have a go, hey?' he asked his friend eagerly. 'Best shot buys the drinks.'

Mike immediately paid his money and took up one of the air guns, the barker starting off a tin row of ducks, which glided jerkily across the back of the tent. Closing his left eye, Mike took aim, hit two and then missed the third.

'Bad luck,' Johnny said cheerfully. 'Now my turn.'

Just nipping the first duck he caught the second full on the head and the third full on its side, the duck shuddering with the force of the shot.

Beaming, Johnny turned – and smiled at Trudie.

The following hour went on in the same fashion, Rose trailing behind the other three, Trudie flanked by the two lads. For Rose, the humiliation was complete. Not only did her date not want to be seen with her, he was even pretending she didn't exist. And as for Trudie . . . Oh, thought Rose bitterly, you're having your day in the sun, aren't you? And at *my* expense.

Never again, Rose swore to herself, never again. Her old

73

friend could make allies with the girls at the rock factory, but not with her. She'd had it with Trudie Williams. And besides, Rose realised, Trudie was getting just a little too much satisfaction from her triumph.

Finally, around nine, they stopped at the big wheel. Rose stared up at the wheel stretching skyward, almost scraping the bottom of the ominous moon. God, it was a strange night, Rose thought, shivering despite the heat.

'Come on, slow coach!' Trudie called out to her. 'We're going on the big wheel.'

Well, why not, Rose thought, glancing at her watch and momentarily grateful for her father's curfew. Paying the charge, all four of them clambered on, Mike and Trudie taking one bench seat, Johnny then realising that he would have to share the bench behind them with Rose. Reluctantly he climbed in beside her.

'You like heights?' he asked, leaning forward towards Trudie and ignoring Rose.

'I like excitement!' she replied, full of herself, full of the evening, the triumph of having two admirers hanging on her every word.

'Pull the bars across your waists!' the fairground attendant shouted. 'Across your waists and keep them there. And keep your arms down at all times. At all times.'

He then set off the machine. The wheel rose with its passengers, through the bath-warm air, into the night, the movement making a welcome breeze. Beguiled, Rose stared up at the moon, her hands clutching the iron bar across her stomach, Johnny shouting something to Mike and laughing.

I'd like to stay here on my own, Rose thought longingly, up in the warm air, under the moon. Beneath them the fairground lights illuminated the underside of the wheel and the skin beneath their chins, whilst the moon stroked long fingers of white on the tops of their heads. Slowly, gradually, the wheel climbed, then reached the top. I could get out here and climb onto the moon, Rose thought, walk on its white face and lie on the clouds beside it . . .

Then suddenly the wheel began to descend, the air starting to rush past them and chill their faces, women screaming with excitement, Johnny clinging to the iron bar across his waist. Mike was laughing, Trudie grinning, her mouth open as she alternately laughed and hollered. The wheel was coming to a point halfway in its descent – the fairground a long dizzy way below their feet – when Trudie suddenly began larking about. She was overexcited, her face flushed as she yelled with excitement, her arms above her head, her hair blowing out behind her.

Alerted, Rose shouted to her, 'Put your arms down, Trudie, and hold the bar!'

But the words were lost on the whooshing air, the noises of yells deafening. And *still* Trudie hollered. She was giddy, overanimated, revelling in the lads' attention and the thrill of the ride. Then – in one insane moment – she began to rise up on her seat, trying to stand.

Shocked, Mike tried to drag her back, Rose watching the scene in front of her disbelievingly. Jesus, she thought, what *is* she doing? Giddily, Trudie flailed her arms around . . . The idiot was showing off! Rose thought, watching horror-stricken. Trudie was acting crazy, daft under the moon, letting all the lads have a look at her, riding the wheel.

'Trudie, sit down!' Rose shouted. 'TRUDIE, SIT DOWN. IT'S DANGEROUS!'

Trudie's arms were high above her head, her mouth open as she shouted something and laughed.

And then she slipped.

In staccato images Rose watched Trudie slide over to one side, her left arm momentarily hanging over the edge of the seat, her hand relaxed. Then she saw the arm caught, and heard the sickening crack as Trudie's limb struck one of the metal surrounds of the wheel.

The impact made the carriage shudder for an instant, Trudie letting out a terrified scream, her face incredulous as though she didn't understand what was happening. Below, the fairground attendant looked up, running to stop the wheel. But he already knew that he would be too late to prevent the downward motion pulling Trudie out of the seat and throwing her thirty feet onto the ground below. As Trudie struggled to keep her balance, her eerie screaming reverberated around the fairground, filling the night air, people looking up from the ground and staring, horrified at the deadly tableau above. Blood pouring from a slash to her wrist, Trudie screamed louder and louder, the sound hoarse and animalistic, Mike frozen in terror as Rose suddenly leaned forward.

The wheel was still trying to move on, Rose's stomach pressed tightly against the metal bar of her own seat as she grabbed Trudie under the shoulders and, with all her strength, pulled. Blood was spurting everywhere from the severed artery in Trudie's wrist, the wheel shuddering, both cars now leaning forwards.

Around them was panic, children screaming on the ground and on the wheel as they watched, adults staring at the grisly scene, one woman fainting three seats behind.

Again, Rose pulled, Trudie now a dead weight as she fainted, the bar against Rose's stomach cutting into her waist and squeezing the breath out of her. His face splattered with blood, Johnny sat motionless in his seat, watching as Rose secured her grip under Trudie's armpits. Then, with one last gargantuan effort, Rose hauled her back into her seat.

Unconscious, Trudie flopped against the bench, her blood still spraying over the wheel and the crowd below. And then the wheel began to move again, beginning its downward descent at a terrifying rate.

'Give me your belt.'

'What?'

'Give me the belt off your trousers!' Rose snapped at Johnny. She tied it around Trudie's upper arm and pulled it as tight as she could.

The blood stopped pumping just as the wheel reached the ground, the shaken owner hurrying over to them.

'Jesus Christ!' he said, looking at Trudie and at the bloodied carriage. Breathing heavily with shock, he then glanced at Rose. 'You saved her life, girl! That's what you did, you saved her bloody life.'

Luminous with pride, Len showed the *Blackpool Gazette* to everyone on the racecourse. That was his girl, his Rosie, the local heroine who had saved her friend. What about that then? he said to Roy Howell; that's my girl. My daughter.

'She was very brave,' the Owl conceded, his sea-serpent's eyes devoid of emotion.

'Brave! I'll say she was brave!' Len replied, glad to have one over on his tormentor. 'She could have fallen out of her own car, but she didn't think of that, did she? No, not for a minute. And there were lads there too. But they were no bloody good. Sat there like lemons, too cowardly to have a go themselves.' He beamed with joy. 'Heart as big as a lion, Rosie has. And more courage than ten men.'

God Lord, the Widow Miller thought as she read the *Blackpool Gazette*, they were writing about *Rose Bradshaw*. She scanned the article avidly. Rose had saved a girl's life! Well, that was something. Not that she hadn't always expected Rose Bradshaw to be exceptional.

But to save someone's life . . . To endanger your own in the process, that showed uncommon courage . . . The Widow Miller looked at the newspaper again. The photograph of Rose was indistinct, her squint not apparent. She looked a handsome girl, but badly dressed, her hair appallingly styled. The widow took out her reading glasses and had a closer look. Oh dear, she thought, the girl's appearance *was* dull, and yet she had potential. And her character was obvious.

Life had become tiresome over the years, the widow thought. Charity, bridge, tennis and travel had become stale. Even shopping was becoming a bore. She was ready for a new challenge, otherwise she would grow old well before her time. She sighed to herself. She had little desire to marry again. What she wanted, she could have – without having to mollify a man to get it. Now she wanted a *project* of her own. Something she could nurture, watch grow.

Or if not something, *someone*.

'Hey, you!' Ruby called over the street as she spotted Rose. 'I want a word with you.'

Crossing over, Rose followed Ruby into Sea View. Through the dining-room door, Rose could see that four of the tables were occupied with guests. The smell of cooked eggs was strong as she followed Ruby into the kitchen.

'Close the door,' Ruby said, looking Rose up and down.

In the chair by the kitchen range, Alfred was sitting with the paper resting on his paunch. He smiled warmly when he saw Rose. 'Rosie Bradshaw!' he beamed. 'The whole town is talking about you.'

She flushed. 'How's Trudie?'

'Out of hospital at the end of the week,' Alfred replied. 'Said you'd been in to see her. Thinking about what happened made me remember the time I saved a man from drowning –'

'Not now,' Ruby said, cutting him off in mid-flow.

'He were a big man, fought like –'

'Not now,' Ruby repeated, walking over to Ruby. 'I'm not one for sentiment, but I wanted to thank you for what you did. You know, saving our Trudie like that.' She paused, unusually hesitant. Then – to Rose's complete amazement – she grabbed hold of her and gave her a squeeze. 'You're a good girl, you are, Rosie Bradshaw, and I'll not forget

78

what you did. No, you can rest assured, as long as I live I'll never forget the debt I owe you.'

'Trudie would have done the same for me –'

'Nah!' Ruby said pragmatically, releasing her grip on Rose and standing back. 'She'd have panicked. Not one for thinking clearly, isn't our Trudie. But you! You didn't panic. I'll tell you straight, you've gone up in my estimation, Rose Bradshaw, and that's a fact.'

Basking in the unexpected compliment, Rose smiled.

'Oh yes, you've proved yourself,' Ruby went on blithely. 'And to think that I always thought you were an oddity before.'

Life wasn't what you expected, Rose realised. The days of being constantly overlooked were over. She was someone now, had snatched respect from people who had dismissed her previously. It was nice to be recognised, to have people come over to talk to you in the street. Even nicer to be courted by the ones who had had no time for you before.

Like Johnny Grover. He had even asked Rose out again, but she'd refused. Then the bug-eyed Roy Howell smiled at her and mumbled something about her being a proper heroine . . . For the first time in her entire life Rose Bradshaw was the focus of attention, and to her complete surprise, she adored it. Her confidence – so shaky – grew with every passing minute. She was someone; she was a force to be reckoned with.

But how long would it all last? How long would the attention continue? How long before she slid back into dreaded obscurity again?

Deep in thought, Rose walked home from the hospital after seeing Trudie. She was recovering fast, the doctors certain that she would regain the full use of her arm in time. And it was all due to her: to Rose Bradshaw.

Running footsteps behind her made Rose turn, surprised

to see Lester approach. He was out of breath, smiling as he looked at her.

'You can't half walk fast!' he said, laughing.

Rose was suddenly flustered. This was Lester – *Lester Williams*, whom she had idolised since childhood. And he had sought her out.

'Hello there, Lester,' she replied, her voice pitched a little too high for comfort. 'I was miles away.'

'I could see that. You going home?'

She nodded.

'Mind if I walk with you?'

Mind if I walk with you?

'No, no I don't mind at all,' Rose replied, her heart hammering.

'I haven't had chance to say thank you for what you did for my sister.'

'It was nothing.'

'Yes, it was. It was a hell of a lot.' He paused, taking a box of chocolates out of his pocket and handing them to her. 'It's not much, for what you did. But I'd like you to accept – as a thank you.'

Lester Williams was giving her chocolates . . . Rose's hand shook as she took them. Then suddenly Lester leaned down and brushed her cheek with a kiss.

'Sorry I have to rush off,' he then said, 'but I have to get back to work.'

Rose blustered. 'Now? I mean . . .' she gazed at the chocolates, blushing, 'thanks . . . I mean . . . thanks, Lester.'

Smiling, he moved off, but stopped at the end of the street. Watching him, her mouth dry, Rose waited. Look back, she willed him. *Please, look back* . . . And then he did. Lester Williams turned and waved at her once more.

In that instant Rose felt as she supposed Gilbert felt going on stage: stepping out of the shadows into the full glare of admiration. Until then hers had been an apologetic existence. But now she had escaped from that. She was free.

And going to *stay* free. And God help anyone who stood in her way.

At last, Rose Bradshaw had found some power. All she had to do was to work out a way to keep it.

PART TWO

The dragon-green, the luminous, the dark,
the serpent-haunted sea.

The Gates of Damascus
James Elroy Flecker 1884–1915

It's still raining.

I'm watching the jury, trying to read the verdict in their faces. So many blank looks, so many eyes, which avoid mine. You can't imagine how well I've got to know these twelve faces after looking at them day in and day out. I suppose they all have families. Parents, wives, husbands, children. I suppose that they eat and drink and put their heads down to sleep like everyone else. I suppose they talk, walk, see and listen.

I know they listen. They've been listening for days; hanging on every word. Hanging – now that's a word that terrorises me.

There's a juror on the front row who caught my eye yesterday before turning away. I know I read some sympathy in the look. But then maybe I want to believe that – amongst the dozen arbiters of my fate – there's one who feels for me.

The rain's coming down hard outside, the foreman of the jury mumbling something inaudible to the clerk of the court.

'Speak up,' says the judge. 'Speak up . . .'

TWELVE

Dear Rose,

This is rather awkward to write, my dear, but I knew you when you were a baby. I'm Hettie – ring any bells? No doubt you realise that your father and I do not get on, but I'm hoping that the past can be overcome somehow.

I would so love to see you, Rosie. Please be in touch.

With very best wishes,
Mrs Henrietta Miller

Frowning, Rose pushed the well-thumbed letter back into her pocket. Should she reply or not? She'd had the letter for a while now – maybe she'd left it too long for a response. From where she stood in the wings her gaze moved to a sideways view of the dancers on stage. If she was honest Rose was glad to have left school – even though Len was racked with guilt about it. Dear God, didn't he know that she *wanted* to help him? To bring in her own wage to supplement her father's meagre earnings that year? She had never wanted to be a bloody teacher – that had been Len's ambition, not hers.

Only one thing rankled: why hadn't Len let her work with him on the track? Even when she begged him, her father remained firm.

'The track's not the place for a girl. It's not respectable.'

'I don't care about being respectable!'

'People would talk, Rosie. You'd get a bad name.'

She had stood up to him, certain he would give way. 'Dad, I've been on the racetrack since I was a baby –'

'Well, a baby's one thing, a young woman's another,' he had sighed. 'Look, luv, I'd have you round me all the time, you know I would, but there are some roughnecks on the track, and I don't want you depending on the likes of George Ogden.'

'But if it's all right for you –'

'It's not all right with me!' Len had replied, uncharacteristically irritated. 'I *have* to work with Ogden, you don't. Look, luv, if I was a bookie, with my own business, it might be different. You and I could work together, have our own pitch – but you being a ticktacker? Over my dead body!'

'Wish me luck, sweetheart,' Gilbert said suddenly, breaking into Rose's thoughts as he came to stand beside her. He was dressed in a tail coat, his make-up heavy, a long white evening scarf draped extravagantly over his copious shoulders. Preoccupied, his eyes fixed on the female singer on stage as he waited for his cue. From a distance he would look glamorous, Rose thought; from the stalls no one would see the sweat patches under his arms, and around his neck. God knew how many other actors had worn that jacket and Rose knew only too well that the silk scarf wasn't just for effect, but to cover several cigarette burns and a couple of decades of stains.

'I knew her when she was playing Ophelia at Oldham Rep,' Gilbert said, sighing. 'She married the director, you know, then left him for a bassoon player. A month later, he'd dumped her. You can never trust a wind player, I say.'

Smiling, Rose leaned against the wings. 'You know, I used to imagine that I could act.'

Gilbert raised his blackened eyebrows. 'You should have a try. With that squint you could corner the market in character parts.'

Flushing, Rose looked down.

Gilbert was immediately contrite. 'Oh, my dear, I didn't mean . . . Oh God, I can't believe I said that.' Gently he reached over and turned Rose's face into profile, the illumination from the stage striking her like a spotlight. 'You're a good-looking girl, you know. You've fine bones and a strong jaw line – but you should do something with your hair.'

Embarrassed, Rose stepped back. 'I like it the way it is.'

'You like it falling all over your face because then people can't see your eye.'

'Well, why not?' Rose snapped, shushed immediately by the stagehand. Her voice dropped into an impatient whisper. 'I don't want character parts! If I did go on the bloody stage I'd want to be the heroine. A *beautiful* heroine.' Ashamed of her brusqueness, she nudged Gilbert with her elbow. 'I was only kidding about wanting to act. I like my job here. I see all the comings and goings from the ticket booth – and I get to see you a lot.'

Rose watched the singer finish her song and take a bow.

'Wish me luck, sweetie,' Gilbert said, hurrying out onto the stage.

He was playing a dramatic part someone had codged up about a wealthy man who had lost his ladylove. It was sentimental and badly written, but Gilbert wrung out its pathos as adeptly as a farmer could wring a chicken's neck. Alone on the stage of the Pavilion Theatre – his act sandwiched between the tenor and a family of Hungarian jugglers – Gilbert roared and emoted through his lines. It should, Rose thought, have been embarrassing, but Gilbert Beardsley wasn't going to have anyone laugh at him. He was too much of an old hand: been treading the boards for decades. He might not have made it to the Old Vic or Broadway, but he could hold a Blackpool matinée audience in a wrestler's grip.

'. . . my darling . . .' he intoned, speaking to the audience.

A woman in the front row was sucking a boiled sweet as she listened. '. . . *what is life without you? What is money without you? I can no longer speak . . .*' He paused.

Only a handful of people knew that Gilbert Beardsley couldn't read. But Rose had seen Ruby sit with her brother, time after time, in the back kitchen of Sea View, reading him his lines. He would listen, repeat verbatim, and then act out the words, Ruby hurling abuse every time he faltered. His efforts had seemed heroic to Rose. Ruby's dire warning always sounded in her ears as she left.

'Not a word of this to anyone, you hear? If this gets out about our Gilbert, I'll know who couldn't keep her big mouth shut.'

Needless to say, no one ever told on Gilbert. And no one ever dared to ask how Ruby knew how to read. After all, as Trudie confided once, her mother and uncle had come from the same tinker stock. Not that this had been a secret to Rose. Her father had told her long enough since that Ruby and Gilbert had been travellers. Just as he told her that they were Catholics – his inference making it the first and only bigoted remark he had ever made.

Sometimes he recalled other things about the past. About his wife, Vera, and once, only once, about Hettie, his late brother's consort. Hettie, a.k.a. Mrs Henrietta Miller – the woman whose letter now resided deep in Rose's pocket.

'It's over! My love has gone . . . It's all over . . .' Gilbert intoned brokenly from the stage.

The woman in the front row had stopped sucking her sweet and was watching Gilbert with glistening eyes. Gilbert was a triumph, Rose thought. People loved to come to the seaside for fresh air, a bit of slap and tickle and to have their emotions chewed like gristle.

With one last longing look, Gilbert left the stage, the audience clapping enthusiastically.

'So,' he asked Rose as he entered the wings, 'did I serve Madame Tragedy well?'

'No one better,' she replied, following him into the dressing room he shared with the Hungarian jugglers.

Pushing some clothes off a chair, Gilbert sat down. Rose leaned against his dressing table as he began to take off the thick pancake make-up he was wearing.

'So what's the matter, my dear?'

'Why should anything be the matter?'

Gilbert gave her a long dramatic look. 'Because you look a bit peaky.'

She could feel the letter in her pocket and slowly drew it out. 'I got a letter.'

'No point asking me to read it, sweetheart,' Gilbert replied, smiling. Carefully he wiped off his darkened eyebrows to expose his own thinning, grey strands of hair.

'It's from Henrietta Miller.'

'*The Widow Miller!*' Gilbert replied, all ears. 'What on earth does she want, writing to you?'

'She wants to see me.'

'You should go,' Gilbert said, slapping some cream onto his rounded cheeks and rubbing them hard. 'She's got oodles of money, you know. And no children to leave it to. Besides, she always had a soft spot for you.'

'I can't remember her,' Rose admitted, 'from when I was little, and Dad won't talk about her.'

'They had a falling-out,' Gilbert confided, dropping his voice. 'You know your father and the ladies.'

Rose vaguely remembered hearing about Len's women in the past, but his dalliances had always been secret and never serious. And for the last decade or so he had been happy with Doris, a woman who lived out beyond Preston, and who was so discreet that Rose rarely saw her even now.

But her father and Hettie? That *was* a thought . . .

'Was he in love with Hettie?'

Gilbert paused, a glob of cream in his right palm, the left side of his face smeared with goo.

'No one's sure . . . She was friendly with your mother,

91

always visiting, especially after you were born. But after Vera died, she didn't seem to come round as much. Then suddenly she didn't come round at all. It was quite a mystery at the time.' He smeared the cream over his mouth, his melodious voice muffled for an instant. 'Then she married a man with money and had no time for Gull Road any more.'

'So why d'you think she's written to me?'

'Well, there's two reasons. One, she read about you in the paper and was impressed. Or two, she might want to gloat about your father's little hiccup,' Gilbert replied, wiping off the remainder of the cream and then throwing the smeared towel onto the table in front of him. Outside they could hear the audience gasp as the Hungarian jugglers went through their act. 'After all, Hettie must have heard about your father's misfortune.'

'I suppose everyone has.'

Gilbert nodded. 'I'm not being much help, am I?'

'Not really,' Rosie replied frankly. 'I wanted to know about Hettie and Dad – what the story *really* is about those two.'

'Can't tell you any more than I know,' Gilbert said, leaning towards her. 'But that doesn't answer your *real* question, does it? About whether you're going to reply to Mrs Henrietta Miller or not?'

'Should I?'

Gilbert raised his eyebrows. 'There's no *should* about it. You do what you think's right.'

'That's no help!'

'I'm doing my best,' Gilbert replied honestly. 'No one usually comes to me for advice.'

'Well, I have, so concentrate,' Rose said, taking the letter out of her pocket and staring at it. 'Do I tear this up and forget it? Or answer it and see where it leads me? What should I do?'

'Dear God,' Gilbert intoned, 'I'm not sure I can handle the responsibility.'

A moment shuddered between them before Gilbert spoke again, his voice sonorous.

'"There is a tide in the affairs of men, Which, taken at the flood, leads on to fortune".'

Baffled, Rose stared at him. 'What?'

'It's Shakespeare. *Julius Caesar.*'

Rose shrugged. 'What does it mean?'

'It means you have to take a chance. That you have to grasp the nettle, go with the tide, screw your courage to the sticking place . . .' Gilbert looked into Rose's blank face and sighed melodramatically. 'It means *answer the bloody letter*!'

THIRTEEN

The misfortune Gilbert had mentioned had taken place the previous Saturday when Len's temper with Roy Howell had snapped at Catterick racecourse. Apparently the Owl had pushed him too far and Len had belted him, sending the Owl *and* George Ogden's stand into six inches of mud. It had been a wet autumn, and the Owl's suit was spattered with dirt when he got up again, a couple of torn betting slips sticking to the seat of his pants.

All very funny – for everyone but George Ogden, who lost out on the bets on the three thirty and blamed Len for buggering up his profits. The fact that his nephew had a bruise the size of a poached egg on his face came secondary. Later, George had left the racecourse without so much as a word to Len.

Within hours the news had been over town: Len Bradshaw had finally lost his patience. But he'd lost more than his rag, he'd lost all hopes of old Ogden's licence too . . .

Back home, Len's temper had cooled. He knew full well that he shouldn't have hit Roy Howell – but the Owl had had it coming for long enough.

Anyway, Len had had disagreements with George Ogden before; it would blow over. Soon things would be back to normal. But would they *this* time, Len asked himself, clammy with unease. Before it had been just George and

Len. The Owl hadn't been around then. But *now* he was here in all his glory – Roy Howell, old Ogden's nephew, flesh and blood, heir apparent. Oh Jesus, Len thought, why the bloody hell did I hit the bugger?

For the next few days Len had waited to hear from George about the coming meet at Haydock. But word never came. His boss would call by, Len reassured himself. After all, he only lived in the next street. He'd call in, or Len would bump into him . . . But he didn't. Another day passed and *still* Len hadn't seen or heard from his employer.

And then – out of nowhere – Len got an infection in his throat, his temperature raging. No, he didn't want the flaming doctor, he told Rosie. He'd be better in an hour or so. Only he wasn't, and when George finally called round to Gull Road, Len could hardly be bothered to mollify him.

'I think you owe me an apology,' George began, his weasel eyes sly. 'You hit my nephew.'

'Roy Howell and I don't get on! We never have,' Len snapped. His throat was burning, acid eating into his vocal cords, and before he knew it the question he had wanted to ask for years finally slid out. 'Anyway, George, why didn't you let on you had a nephew? You always said you had no one; let me think you were on your own. Then Roy Howell popped up out of nowhere and I'm sidelined.'

'You're not sidelined, Len. You and me go back a long way,' George replied, sitting down at the kitchen table and glancing at the headline of the *Blackpool Gazette* – 'Italy – Teachers to Wear Fascist Uniform'. 'Goes to show,' he said, tapping the paper, 'even the high and mighty don't know what's round the corner.'

His head on fire, Len regarded his boss impatiently. 'Oh, for God's sake, George, if you've something to say, bloody say it!'

Surprised, George kept his own voice calm. If he had expected an apology, he was fast realising that he wasn't going to get it.

'I have to put my nephew first. After all, he's my own flesh and blood.'

'Yeah,' Len replied sarcastically. 'Part of that *phantom* family of yours. Incidentally, did he have parents, or was his an Immaculate Conception?'

His expression needle sharp, George stared at Len. He had been annoyed to see his clerk nephew struck by his ticktick man. It was bad for business and, besides, George was starting to have doubts about Roy. At first he had been delighted to have his nephew work for him. The Owl was quick and seldom made a mistake, those huge, seaweed-coloured eyes missing nothing – even at the Grand National. But lately Roy had begun to drop hints about his uncle retiring. *Retiring!*

Greedy little shit, George thought peevishly. How unreasonable could a man be? No one had any real patience any more.

'Roy's parents are dead.'

His voice getting more hoarse by the minute, Len replied: 'Maybe you've got some love children around? Or wives in Wigan? Or maybe your father's still alive, George? After all, your lot live for ever.'

So, George thought, Len was pissed off, was he? Mind you, not many men would have been as tolerant for as long. Roy certainly wasn't. And all over such a little thing, George thought: a little badge in its little leather holder – but which meant enough to have two men at each other's throats. Oh, the power of it all, George thought, relishing the moment.

'I need you tomorrow at Cartmel.'

'I can't do it,' Len said, ill and reckless. 'I'm not up to it this time.'

'But you never get ill!'

'Well, I'm ill now!' Len snapped back. 'That's another thing, George – how many times have I let you down in all the years we've been working together, hey? Not once,

96

not bloody once.' He paused, to clear his rasping throat. 'And what thanks do I get? Sod all.'

At that moment Rose walked in on them, her coat over her arm. She had grown up, George thought; but then she must be nearly seventeen by now. His ferret eyes took in every detail. Rose, the boss-eyed runty kid he remembered had developed into a statuesque brunette. In fact, she would have been quite a stunner – if she'd had her eye fixed. Amazing that, father and daughter both with a squint . . .

'What's up? Rose asked, looking from one man to the other.

'Nothing to do with you, missy,' George replied. 'I'm here to talk to your father.'

'He's not well.'

'Leave it, luv,' Len replied. 'This is men's talk.'

'Hah!' she replied curtly.

George ignored her. 'Are you coming to work tomorrow, or not, Len?'

'Are you crazy?' Rose shouted.

'Hey!' George replied. 'Keep a civil tongue in your head –'

'He's bloody ill!' she snapped. 'Dad can't work. Just look at him!'

Len winced inwardly. Only the other night he had had his ear bent about Rosie's language, his sister banging on and on . . .

'She swears too much,' Clovis had said, looking over to Nan Wilmslow. 'Doesn't she? Doesn't our Rosie swear too much?'

The cadaver nodded.

'Hang on!' Len had replied in exasperation. 'Rosie's just been taught to stand up for herself –'

'*And* taught how to swear. It's all your fault, Len. Anyone would have thought you'd raised a boy. Well, it'll do Rose no good,' Clovis had gone on. 'Men don't like a woman with a foul mouth.'

'Just drop it, will you? Rosie will do fine just the way

she is.' He was nettled. 'You don't know what you're talking about, Clovis, criticising my girl. I *won't* have her criticised – by you or anyone else. Rosie will do herself proud one day. She'll find herself a husband. That's what I want – a good man who'll look after her. Someone who'll know what a gem they've got.'

Len had said the same to George, but both Clovis and George Ogden had doubts about Rose Bradshaw's future. None of the local men thought of her as marriage material. They admired her – after all, she had turned out to be quite a heroine – but she was too much one of the lads, too feisty, too blunt to lust after. Besides, she wasn't conventionally pretty. And in Blackpool, where there were hundreds of pretty girls, Rose Bradshaw didn't stand much of a chance.

Still smouldering from Rosie's words, George looked back at Len, his tone threatening. 'I need you. The meeting's at Cartmel tomorrow –'

Rose interrupted again. 'Dad, you can't go! That's miles away and you're not fit enough.'

'I need him –'

'You didn't need him on Wednesday at Carlisle,' she replied, turning back to George. 'You managed then – or did you find someone else to fill in whilst you left my father to stew?'

George hated clever women. Almost as much as he hated ambitious nephews.

'Now look here, Len,' he said darkly. 'You can't afford to pass up on this. You're always telling me you need the money –'

'I *do* need the money,' Len replied, 'but I'm not up to it this time.'

The expression on George Ogden's face altered in that instant. He *always* got what he wanted from Len Bradshaw – but not this time. Now his ticktack man was letting him down – at the very time he should be trying to get back into George's good books.

'I'll go.'

Both men stared at Rose.

'You what?' George asked, his wrinkled face irritated.

'I said I'll go and stand in for Dad –'

'You're a girl!'

'I know that! But I can do it,' she insisted, secretly excited by the prospect. 'I've been going to the races since I was in my pram. I've watched Dad work and I know what to do.'

'Rosie –'

She turned to her father. 'Dad, I *can* do it. Let me.'

'The hell with that!' George replied, getting to his feet. 'I'm not having some half-witted kid wrecking my business.'

Slowly, Rose walked over to George Ogden. She was taller than he and had the satisfaction of knowing that it made the old man uncomfortable. She had never liked George Ogden. It hadn't sat well with her that her father had had to kowtow to him for years. And besides, Fate had finally presented her with an opportunity to get into racing. Her father was ill; he couldn't object. She could almost smell the horses and hear the thud of the hoofs on the track . . .

'Mr Ogden,' Rose said quietly, 'I can do it –'

'Rosie, no!' Len snapped suddenly, his face flushed with fever as he heaved himself to his feet. 'I've had to lick this bugger's boots for years, but you don't have to –'

'Dad!'

But he was beyond caution.

'You're an old sod, George Ogden. You'll not keep me hanging about any longer, though. I've had it with you, your flaming nephew, your crap pitch *and* your bloody licence. Frankly you can take it all and shove it where the monkey shoved the nuts.'

FOURTEEN

Snow had fallen the previous night, making the roads icy, the sky heavy, ominous as Rose walked up the narrow, gravelled drive. Now this was some house, Rose thought as she reached the door of Heathcote Place. Checking her reflection in the glass, Rose then took a calming breath before ringing the bell. A moment passed. She rang again. This time it opened at once.

'Good morning,' an old woman said briskly, letting Rose into the hall. 'Are you Miss Bradshaw?'

Rose nodded.

'Mrs Miller will be with you shortly,' the old woman explained, gesturing for Rose to take a seat.

Sitting down, Rose looked about her. The floor was marble, like the floor in the Marble Hall of the Alhambra Palace, the walls over hung with dour, oversized paintings. Rose stared at the nearest one and wondered why someone living in Lytham St Annes would want to have a painting of Scottish cattle.

Her thoughts wandered. It had been difficult to lie to her father, but Len wouldn't have approved . . .

Rose's attention was suddenly caught by a dog standing at the head of the stairs – a pedigree dog obviously, not at all like the Williamses' mongrel, Chase. The dog looked at her; she looked at the dog, and then the animal walked off.

Another minute passed, Rose shifting awkwardly in her

seat. She shouldn't have come. But then again, she had to know why she had been summoned. Her gaze wandered, settling on a macabre painting of a parrot pecking at a monkey's paw.

'Rose?'

Jumping to her feet, Rose smiled uncertainly at the woman facing her: Mrs Henrietta Miller.

'How d'you do?'

'I do very well,' she replied, laughing lightly.

Showing Rose into the drawing room, Hettie closed the double doors behind them. More paintings cluttered the walls, and a long low table was crowded with artefacts. The room was bitterly cold.

'Sit down,' Hettie said, looking at Rose critically. 'You can't imagine how pleased I am to see you after so long. I was worried that you wouldn't reply to my letter.'

All the time she was talking she was studying Rose. Good height, good figure and fine facial bones. Hair messy, hands too big, and that dreadful squint . . . But there was plenty of raw material to work with.

'Are you hungry?'

Rose nodded. 'A bit.'

The truth was that she was freezing and thought that some food might warm her up. God, Rose thought, looking at Hettie in her lightweight suit, doesn't she feel the cold?

'We'll have high tea,' Hettie went on, ringing a bell and then giving the old woman orders before sitting down again.

'Are you warm enough, dear?'

Rose was finding it difficult to speak. 'It *is* a bit cold in here.'

'Really? I don't ever seem to feel the cold. It's strange that. I've been to many specialists, but no one can find out why. I just must be cold-blooded – like a snake,' she laughed, bending down and setting a taper to the laid fire, then resuming her seat. 'Now, my dear, tell me about yourself.'

101

'Not much to tell.'

'I think there is. I read about you in the paper.'

'Oh, that was nothing –'

'It was a good deal. You saved your friend's life. Most impressive, I would have thought.' Hettie paused, pouring the tea, which had been brought in for them, and passing Rose a cup. 'I wanted to approach you then, but the timing didn't seem right. I didn't want you to think your act of bravery had prompted me into action. That would have been too gauche.'

Rose had no idea what 'gauche' was, only that it was something Hettie would never be. Cautiously she stole a glance at the Widow Miller. She was obviously in her late forties, dressed with comfortable elegance, her hair streaked at the front with two wings of white. Striking was the word that came to Rose's mind. Hettie was striking and very sure of herself. Maybe money did that.

'What is it?'

Rose blushed, ashamed that her scrutiny had been so obvious. 'Sorry, I was just thinking how smart you look.'

Hettie waved the compliment away with a flick of her hand. 'No small talk! We have to get down to business, Rose.'

'*Business?*'

'Yes, the business of you,' Hettie replied, leaning towards her. 'Your father doesn't like me –'

'But –'

'Oh, come on, if we're to be friends we have to be open with one another. Your father doesn't approve of me – I imagine that's why you didn't tell him you were coming to see me? You *didn't*, did you?'

Rose put down her teacup. 'No . . . But I didn't like lying about it.'

'Well said,' Hettie countered, surprised by the feisty tone in Rose's voice. This girl was no walkover. 'Your father did a remarkable thing in raising you without a woman's influence – I mean, a woman's *constant* influence.'

Rose noted the jab, but fielded it. 'My father's girlfriends are *his* concern, not mine.'

'I dare say,' Hettie replied drily, liking Rose more and more by the minute, 'but you must admit that you would have liked a mother figure around when you were growing up?'

'It wasn't important. Dad did what he could.'

'Don't be angry with me, Rose!' Hettie retorted lightly. 'I'm not criticising your father, it's just that I would have liked to have been involved in your upbringing more. I tried to be – I sent you letters and presents – but your father always returned them.'

Rose felt under threat suddenly. Should she apologise? But if her father had cut Hettie off, he would have had a good reason. She remembered what Gilbert had told her and proceeded cautiously.

'That's the past.'

'Indeed it is,' Hettie answered, her tone unreadable. 'And now we have to think of the future. I'll be honest with you, Rose, you impress me. You're good-looking, obviously intelligent and courageous. I could help you, Rose. With me beside you, you could do well in life.'

'I get by –'

'You get by!' Hettie snorted. 'What kind of life is that?'

Rose bristled. 'My kind.'

'Hah! Don't look a gift horse in the mouth, my dear.'

'I'm used to horses – and they *never* do what you expect.'

Stunned, Hettie regarded Rose for a long moment and then laughed softly. Putting down her own cup, she then walked over to the window, looking out on to the impressive garden.

'You're old for your years, Rose, and you've a quick tongue. A clever woman with wit can do well – but a clever, *beautiful* woman with charm can rise to the top.' She turned back to her visitor, looking her up and down. 'Have you a boyfriend?'

'No . . .' Rose said, suddenly uncertain.

'Ah, but I think there's someone you like.'

Flushing, Rose cursed her awkwardness. 'Maybe there is.'

'So why isn't he your boyfriend?'

Rose looked up, her expression confrontational. 'Why do *you* think?'

'I really don't know.'

'Boys don't like me.'

'Why?'

'Isn't that obvious?'

'Is it your manner? Or your appearance?'

'Look at me!' Rose said sharply. 'I've got a squint. And don't say you didn't notice –'

'Of course I noticed! Something you got from your father,' Hettie replied impatiently. 'Len should have had it seen to long enough since.'

'My father isn't rich!'

'No, but I am,' Hettie went on. 'I can get that eye of yours fixed, Rose. I have money, plenty of money. It would mean very little to me to pay for the operation. In fact, I already have the name of a specialist on Rodney Street, in Liverpool.' She paused, seeing Rose's expression was changing from hostility to vulnerability. Touched, Hettie hurried on. This was not a girl who would appreciate pity. 'I want to do this for you, my dear.'

'Why?'

She certainly was blunt, Hettie thought.

'Because it would give you a better chance in life.'

'But why should that matter to you?'

'Because I have no children of my own,' Hettie replied, sitting down again. 'Look, I'm a selfish, spoiled woman with a lot of money and no one to spend it on. I was very fond of your mother and of you, when you were a baby. I wanted to stay close to you – but that wasn't to be.'

She wondered why it was proving so unsatisfying to be

charitable. Surely Rose Bradshaw should have been on her knees, thanking her by now? But then again, Hettie thought, if she had reacted that way she would have admired her less. Rose's sheer truculence was a challenge.

'I can't let you do this,' Rose replied finally. 'I can't. You're not family. I hardly know you –'

'So what?' Hettie said, raising her arched eyebrows. 'Oh, come on, do it for me, if not for yourself. Let me feel good about myself. Let me imagine I'm a nice person with a kind, big heart.'

Amused, Rose studied Hettie. 'You're very blunt, aren't you?'

'Takes one to know one.'

'I suppose it does,' Rose agreed, her thoughts running on. 'But my father wouldn't approve. He wouldn't like you to pay for the operation.'

Again, Hettie flicked away the objection, then rose to her feet. Taking Rose's hand, she guided her guest over to the mirror hanging above the fireplace.

'Now forget your father for one moment and think about this.' She turned Rose's face to the mirror. Immediately, Rose looked down. 'Think about looking into a mirror and seeing yourself perfect. Think about brushing your hair away from your face and seeing two beautiful eyes staring back at you.' Hesitantly, Rose glanced into her reflection, Hettie smoothing her guest's hair away from her forehead. 'Look at that perfect oval face of yours, Rose. Look at your skin, your jaw line, your eyes.'

'I don't want to –'

'Yes, you do!' Hettie replied impatiently. 'Now look into the mirror again – and instead of seeing some kid who hides behind a stroppy manner and a thick fringe, see a stunning woman. That's what I'm offering you, Rose Bradshaw, a chance to get what you want in life. Not make do. Not get by – but triumph!'

Staring into the mirror, Rose found herself enticed by

Hettie's words. Her assessment took in her face as though she was seeing it properly for the first time. Hettie was right – she had good bones, a strong jaw line and green eyes that could be compelling. That *could* be . . .

Annoyed, Rose shrugged her shoulders and moved away, letting her fringe fall back over her face.

'Dad wouldn't allow it –'

'Of course he would!'

'It would make him feel so small if I accepted your offer,' Rose responded, fighting two emotions: wanting the help, and not wanting to hurt her beloved father. 'I know him: he would be crucified to think that he couldn't provide for me.'

'But, as you said, he's not a rich man,' Hettie replied evenly. 'The operation costs a lot of money. No one would expect Len to have those kind of funds.'

'So how could I let *you* pay for it?'

'Don't be a fool, Rose.'

'What!'

'I said – don't be a fool,' Hettie replied, her tone steely. 'I understand that you don't want to hurt your father, and that's very commendable. But just tell me something – and tell me honestly – does he know how much you hate the way you look?'

Rose flinched, the blow hitting her full on.

'Well, *does he*?'

'No . . .'

Hettie's eyebrows rose again. 'How noble of you to forfeit your own chance in life to avoid hurting your father. I can imagine how pleased Len would be to know about your martyrdom.'

Furious, Rose turned on her would-be benefactor. 'You bitch!'

'Yes, I'm a bitch,' Hettie replied, her tone razor sharp. 'I'm bitch enough to have you thrown out of here now. But I won't.'

'And why is that?' Rose countered, her own voice brittle. 'Or maybe I already know. This act of generosity isn't really for me. It's a way of getting back at my father, isn't it?'

What an evil young woman this one could be, Hettie thought, seeing Rose's spirit and wincing at the deadliness of her aim. Obviously the upbringing in Gull Road had sharpened her claws early. But then again, Hettie wouldn't like to have seen her money and interest wasted on a simpering nobody. Rose Bradshaw had her mother's looks and her father's passion – an intimidating combination. And when she was made beautiful . . . God knows what she could become.

'I don't want revenge on your father,' Hettie said at last. Her tone was injured. 'My offer was simply designed to help you. My motive was to play at being a mother figure and benefactress – from a distance. Maybe I'm trying to reclaim something of the past, a time when I was happy. Maybe I just want to do something to help a child I once loved.' She shrugged, Rose watching her, shame filling her mouth like battery acid. 'I'm not anyone's daughter, anyone's wife, or anyone's mother. I am a man's widow. Nothing more. That's why I can only offer friendship and money. And I *still* offer them to you.'

'I'm sorry,' Rose said, mortified. 'I'm so sorry.'

'So you'll accept my offer?'

A moment strung its juddering length between them.

'I want to –'

'Then say yes.'

'But, Dad –'

'Talk to him, let him know how much you want this chance. He loves you, Rose, and he's a big enough man to let someone help you. Just ask. Please, just ask.'

Pausing, Rose considered the offer. If she had the operation, she would be beautiful, able to look the world in the face. The power she had temporarily tasted would finally become her regular nourishment. The idea was intoxicating.

'I'll ask him.'

Hettie smiled to herself. She knew a fighter when she saw one.

FIFTEEN

It can't be! Lester thought, craning forward to get a better look and then nudging Joe with his elbow. 'Hey, look over there – is that who I think it is?'

Both brothers peered across the track to where an erect young woman was standing on top of a box, head and shoulders above the betting crowd. Wearing her own new white gloves, Rose was ticktacking, sending the odds for the three o'clock race over to George Ogden. Her hands moved fast, almost in a ballet of their own in the cold December mist, as she tapped her wrist to signal that Turkish Harem was in at 5–4.

Len was all but recovered, but Rose insisted that he take some more time off – partly to let George's anger subside, and partly to give her more time on the track. And God, how she loved it. Loved the sights, the scents of horse and earth and even the muck. How she loved to look over the heads of the bookies and punters, high up on her box, knowing that she was different and that she stood out. Knowing that people talked about her. *So what* if it wasn't a suitable job for a lady? Hell, she was no lady, she was Len Bradshaw's girl, and this was her piece of Heaven.

'Hell's bells! It's Rose Bradshaw!' Joe said, jumping up to get a better look over the heads of the crowd. 'I heard she was filling in for Len, but I didn't believe it.'

Mesmerised, Lester watched her.

'She's good. Bloody hell, she's good!' he said, laughing. 'Put five bob on Turkish Harem for me, will you?'

'Which bookie?'

'Rose's bookie!' Lester said impatiently. 'Who the hell else?'

For a while life had been running smoothly for Lester. He had – as he promised – set up his own business. For the previous two years he had been selling tourist goods in one of the booths at the end of North Pier. Then he had bought a camera and put Joe into business taking snapshots of the day-trippers. He was a lousy photographer, but he was good-looking and the women liked him. So despite what their partners said, Joe flogged his snaps.

And Lester expanded, buying up another booth and another – and then only the previous week he had got his first car. Now all he needed was a girlfriend, Joe had teased him, totally without ambition himself. But not without a girlfriend. Whilst his twin brother had been pursuing his ambitions, Joe had been pursuing Maisie Hollinbrook from Stork Street.

Pushing through the crowd, Joe laid Lester's bet on with George Ogden.

'Hello there, Joe,' the old man said warily. 'I didn't think I'd be seeing you around here for a while.'

'Keep your voice down, Mr Ogden!' Joe replied, looking round. 'I told you, I don't want anyone knowing about our little arrangement.'

The old man nodded. 'No one will, son. Unless you renege on your payments.'

Snatching the ticket from George's hand, Joe could see Roy Howell smirking behind the stand, and leaned towards him menacingly.

'Oi, snake eyes! What the hell are you grinning at?'

The Owl's expression sobered up at once. Joe turned away and hurried back to Lester.

'Here,' he said, passing him the ticket. 'Jesus, I hate that Howell bloke.'

'Everyone hates him,' Lester said, looking out to the course and waiting for the race to start. 'I can't believe it's really Rose out there. God, what a girl.'

Surprised, Joe searched his brother's face. As twins they each knew instinctively what the other was thinking and feeling. Was that tone in Lester's voice what he thought it was? Joe sighed to himself. No, he had only been mistaken for a moment. Lester *wasn't* in love with Rose, it was just admiration.

His attention wandered, then settled on his own problems. What a bloody idiot he had been to keep betting after he'd lost. What a chump! Hadn't he always known that was what morons did? But he had done it anyway – and now he was in hock for ten pounds to George Ogden. With no means to pay it back fast. Joe had heard plenty about how George got his debtors to pay; how they got a call in the early hours of the morning from a couple of heavy-weights . . .

Joe shivered. He could ask Lester to help him out, but not for the whole sum. As for Ruby . . . Joe winced at the thought of asking his mother for assistance with a betting debt.

'We're off!' Lester said suddenly, holding some binoculars up to his eyes.

Bloody binoculars! Joe thought. Now where the hell did he get those? Admiringly he looked at his brother. Lester was a cute one, all right; could make money out of sand. Joe's thoughts drifted again. He *had* to find some money himself and get old Ogden off his back. But how? It couldn't be too hard, could it? He was Lester's brother, after all, and everyone agreed that Lester had the Midas touch.

Perhaps he should be a bit more reckless, Joe thought, watching as Turkish Harem came in first for his brother.

Naturally . . . Yes, Joe thought to himself, maybe he would have to take another risk.

Lester couldn't be the only lucky one.

Having read the evening paper twice, Nan Wilmslow looked up at Clovis. She was used to her friend's house. Other people might give number 117 Gull Road a wide berth, but Nan liked it. It made her feel smug about her own tiny, tidy flat at number 111. Nothing out of place there, not even a fly daring to clutter the windows in summer.

'Dangerous.'

Clovis ducked her head out from behind her paper. 'What is, Nan?'

'Hitler. Says his empire'll last a thousand years.'

This was the longest sentence Nan had uttered in months and had Clovis's full attention.

'Never! That silly little bugger couldn't run a railway for a week.'

'Dangerous,' Nan murmured again darkly.

'Here, hold this,' Clovis said, passing a ball of string to Nan, whilst she began to wind it from her end.

She had known Nan Wilmslow for over forty years, long enough to see a misfit girl change into a quiet wife and a virtually silent widow. But although she didn't talk much, Nan was well known in Blackpool and around the North-West for her remedies. Anyone with a fever, a cough, an ulcer on the leg – anything in fact – came to see Nan.

Rumour had it that her parents had been farmers up in the Lake District, virtually cut off from civilisation, and that her grandmother had been a witch. God knew how much was fancy, but the real truth was that somehow, some-where and from someone Nan Wilmslow had learned about herbal remedies.

And other things – like laying out the dead. Nan might only be just over five feet in height, but she had the nerves of a pugilist. Many years earlier, Clovis had gone with her

112

on a call – something she would never do again. Nan had been summoned to a slum house where a woman had just given birth. The baby had been deformed. Nan arrived and picked up the screaming child. It had been born with its internal organs outside the body and was screaming, the mother desperate to hold on to her child, the father almost catatonic. For years afterwards Clovis would think back and wonder *how* Nan had managed it, but before everyone's eyes that poor baby had died peacefully, slipping away from a life that would have been short and agonising.

Clovis knew that Nan had somehow put an end to the baby's sufferings. But how she did it was – and *remained* – a mystery. It took guts to do that, Clovis had thought, watching with admiration as Nan wrapped the dead baby in a sheet. Guts, and a sound understanding with God. Once, a concerned Len had asked Nan if she could do anything about Rose's squint, but her response had been odd. Help will come to her without looking, Nan had replied mysteriously. But it hadn't so far.

'Not too tight!' Clovis admonished her now, as she tugged on the string. 'I heard yesterday our Rose is doing a right good job at the track. Her father'll be pleased, I suppose. Not that it's a respectable job for a woman.' She looked over to Nan. 'I've said to Len often enough – that girl of yours is turning into a firebrand. You want to watch her, now she's grown up. But will he listen? Not likely! Men don't, do they?'

'No.'

'I mean, who ever heard of a ticktack *woman*? And yet there she is, up on the box, everyone looking at her whilst she signs the odds. Laughing with the bookies, giving the lads cheek. Full of confidence, Lester Williams told me. Full of *herself*, more like . . . Makes you think. I mean, Rose isn't usually one to like people looking at her. What with that eye and all.' Clovis paused, winding up the last bit of

113

the string and tucking it into her pocket. 'Makes you wonder what Rose Bradshaw would have been like if she *hadn't* had a bad eye – you know, if she'd been a regular girl. With her looks and nerve, she could have been a real handful . . . It makes you think, doesn't it, Nan?'

The corpse in the chair nodded. 'Yes.'

'Makes *me* think,' Clovis went on, nodding also. 'Makes me think that perhaps God knew what he was doing when he gave her that funny eye.'

The only advantage of having your arm damn near ripped out of its socket was the fact that you could dodge work. Trudie sighed to herself, watching her mother sew a button on one of Lester's shirts. It was the time of year the Williams family dreaded: when Sea View had no visitors, money was tight, and Ruby was underoccupied.

'Bloody smell!' Ruby snorted, looking over to Trudie. 'Did you go into room four?'

'Yeah, Ma.'

'Could *you* smell anything?'

'Yeah.'

'Like what?'

'Like fish.'

Down went the shirt with a slam on the kitchen table.

'I knew it! I said so this morning to your father. Although talking to that slab of meat is like trying to plait sand. There *is* a smell in that room. I've cleaned it from top to bottom, but there's *still* a smell and I can't get rid of it whatever I do.'

Listening half-heartedly, Trudie watched her mother riddle the ashes in the grate and then turn and point the poker at her.

'You remember Robert Upton?'

Oh God, Trudie thought, the Robert Upton story.

'Yeah, Ma. He topped himself here.'

Ruby nodded. 'Cut his throat in room two. You can't

114

imagine what it was like going in there and finding him. Mind you, I should have known. No one in their right mind books a room in November.' Ruby let her thoughts wander. 'It was a shame, though; he was a nice-looking man.'

'I bet he didn't look so good with his throat cut.'

With a deft flick of the shirt, Ruby clipped her daughter behind the ear.

'Don't speak ill of the dead!'

'I didn't even know him!' Trudie wailed, lapsing back into her chair.

'I had enough trouble cleaning out number two, I don't need another bothersome room.' Ruby thought back. 'That Noble couple were in room four this summer. The little ratty Mrs Noble who comes every year – and asks for a discount every year.'

'And you never give her one,' Trudie replied, raising her eyebrows. '*And* you took the radio away when they came this summer. She was mad about that. Asked for a discount again.'

'I don't give discounts,' Ruby replied firmly. 'Maybe they did something to the room?'

'They haven't been here for months!'

'Yeah, but the smell's got stronger gradually . . .' Ruby frowned, '. . . and Mrs bloody Noble looked mighty peeved when I had that run-in with her.'

'No wonder. When she said she was a teacher you said you weren't surprised – because having her as a guest had taught you a lesson.'

'It was a joke!'

Trudie rolled her eyes.

'Maybe the smell will pass.'

'Nah, it's getting stronger every day,' Ruby replied, walking to the door. 'I'm going upstairs and I'm going to pull every piece of furniture out and find that bloody fish stink. You can give me a hand.'

Trudie pulled a mock sympathetic face and pointed to

her arm. The wound had healed, although there was a livid scar running from her elbow to her wrist.

'I can't, Ma.'

'You don't need your arm to smell, Trudie.'

Luckily Ruby's attention was diverted by the arrival of an uncharacteristically morose Joe. Walking into the kitchen, he avoided his mother and sister's eyes and made for the bread tin. In silence, he cut himself a slice and smeared it liberally with jam.

Trudie looked around the room dramatically. 'You feel that, Ma?'

'What?'

'I think a ghost just walked in.' Trudie's tone was uneasy. 'I can sense a presence in here. Hello?' she called out, looking past Joe and into the corners of the room. 'Is there anyone there? Talk to me, I can help you. I mean you no harm. Trust me –'

Joe sighed. 'Dry up.'

'Ma, it's talking to me! Gentle ghost, tell me your troubles.'

She expected her brother to have a laugh and kid along with her, but for once Joe wasn't interested. Instead he slouched off with his bread and jam, slamming the door closed behind him.

Wearily he climbed the two flights to the top floor of number 142, walking into the bedroom he shared with Lester and flopping onto the bed.

He had been wrong. George Ogden hadn't waited to send round a couple of heavies at night: they had buttonholed Joe on the pier. Just as he was about to take a photograph of an out-of-season tripper. The woman had looked astonished to see her would-be snapper hauled off, Joe's feet trailing along the wooden planks of the pier as he was dragged away.

It would have been funny – if it had happened to someone else. But it had shaken Joe. He had always been the protected one, Lester always looking out for him. But

Ogden's heavies had chosen their moment well; Lester wasn't anywhere to be seen. They had dragged Joe into one of the elaborate shelters on the Promenade, the winter rain lashing against the structure, the strings of Christmas lights doing a demented jig in the wind.

And then they had told Joe that George Ogden wanted his money paid within a week. Joe had said nothing. There was nothing he *could* say because he knew that it would make no difference. He wouldn't be able to pay back the money. Not in a week, or a month. Maybe not even two months. After all, everyone knew there weren't that many tourists around in the winter.

So now here he was holed up in Sea View, wondering why he had placed another bet on at the end of the day's races. With another bookie, of course. But it still lost. Of course. Why had he been such an idiot? Why had he risked the little money he had? And lost it.

Closing his eyes, Joe pulled the counterpane over his head. Lester was the clever one. Lester was the reckless one. Lester could duck and dive and still come out on top. Joe should never have kidded himself that he was like his brother. He didn't have the confidence, the nerve, or the brains. Apart from appearance, Joe wasn't like his twin at all.

And he was scared, *really* scared, for the first time in his life.

SIXTEEN

Hettie had expected to have heard from Rose by now, but no word had come. Every day she checked the post and asked the housekeeper repeatedly if there had been a telephone call. But the answer was always the same: no contact. It puzzled Hettie. After all, if she had been presented with such a generous offer she would have snatched her benefactress's hand off.

But that was her. And Rose obviously wasn't like her. Sighing, Hettie rose to her feet and paced up and down the morning room. Then she paused and walked to the phone. She would call Rose; she knew that the Bradshaws had a phone; it was imperative for a bookie's runner to be contactable. Yet as she lifted the handset something happened that surprised Hettie. She felt nervous.

Of what? she asked herself. She was only going to telephone Rose. But what if Len answered?

Hettie put down the phone and lit a cigarette. Hubert had always hated the habit, but Hubert was dead and this was her house now. Her thoughts turned back to Rose. If she had had a daughter she imagined that she would have been like Rose.

Suddenly Hettie longed for what she had missed, her maternal urge resurrecting itself unexpectedly. Why had she allowed herself to miss the pleasure of grooming a child? Of teaching it manners? Of making her offspring acceptable

118

to society? A daughter would have extended Hettie's influence, made her important for considerably longer. A widow was something, but a mother was quite another.

She would have had kudos if she had been a parent, Hettie thought. Doors would have opened to her, and she would have had the pleasure of living vicariously through her daughter. But she had left motherhood too late, and now her belated dreams of being a surrogate parent looked set to be scuppered.

Hettie didn't like that idea a bit. She had always got what she wanted in life and did not see why the pattern should change. Inhaling deeply, Hettie considered her options. Of course, she could simply wander into the Pavilion and buy a ticket for a show. Rose worked in the ticket office, after all. But the thought of being seen in Blackpool, buying a ticket for a pantomime, was too much for Hettie.

Once upon a time she had loved pantomimes. In the old days, when she had been married to Eddie Bradshaw, they had gone out with Vera and Len to watch Gilbert Beardsley perform. He had been good, Hettie remembered – for a seaside actor, anyway. He'd been young then, like all of them, and afterwards they'd chatted to Gilbert backstage as he cleaned off his make-up, his feet encased in a brand-new pair of Turkish slippers.

It was amazing what the theatre and special effects could do, Hettie thought. Gilbert had seemed so glamorous that night: dark-haired, slim before he had run to fat, that heavenly voice brushing against the gilded angels on the Pavilion ceiling and putting its arm around every woman in the audience. She had – Hettie admitted slyly to herself – even carried a torch for Gilbert Beardsley, briefly. Until someone repeated a lurid rumour and suddenly Gilbert wasn't glamorous to Hettie any more. Just a freak in make-up.

No, Hettie thought, her attention drawn back to the present. She wasn't going to buy a ticket at the Pavilion just to make contact with Rose Bradshaw. The girl was ungrateful, callous even. Surely manners should have insisted that she gave Hettie an answer – even if it was in the negative.

But Rose wasn't like that, Hettie realised. Rose wasn't the type to feel beholden. And besides, she was too fond of her father to see clearly. Was it *really* possible that a young woman would throw away such an opportunity, simply to spare her father's feelings? Apparently it was, Hettie concluded with amazement.

There was no choice. She would have to wait a little while longer and hope for Rose to come to her senses. But she wouldn't wait for ever . . . Smouldering, Hettie finished her cigarette and stared at her expensive court shoes. Dear God, didn't the stupid girl realise she had a mentor? Had she been blind, as well as rude, when she had visited Heathcote Place? Couldn't she see the money and power Hettie had? And more amazingly, didn't she want some of it for herself?

That was the part that Hettie had found most difficult to accept. Rose might be the sensitive type, and loyal to her father, but Hettie had recognised something in Rose Bradshaw that Rose might not have recognised in herself. *Ambition.* For what, Hettie wasn't quite sure, but Rose had a longing to get on. But to achieve *what*? Money? A certain man? Or power?

Instinctively Hettie believed it was the last option. Rose Bradshaw wanted power. And power was something most people – except the lucky few – weren't born with. Power was created. You made yourself powerful by talent, or guile. Or by marriage – as Hettie had done. But to get power, whether you made it or bedded it, it helped if a woman was beautiful.

Hettie sighed to herself and then wondered just how long it would take Rose Bradshaw to realise that.

It was too cold for George to be out, Len thought. Jesus, he was bloody freezing himself, and he was a relatively young man by comparison to his employer.

Their argument had gradually faded into a memory. At first Len had thought he'd gone too far, but although George smouldered from the insult, he was too wily to dump the reliable Len. Especially as his nephew was acting shiftily.

Having given the odds for the last race, Len stood on his box and looked over the course to where George Ogden was standing, rubbing his hands to warm them. As ever he was wearing his trilby and a heavy overcoat, the collar turned up around his stoat's neck.

And behind him, in the gloomy air, sat the serpent-eyed Howell. Len winced as the Owl turned in his direction, his bulbous eyes holding Len's glare for a moment before looking away. Spooky bugger – Len thought to himself, climbing off his box and making for the bar – more like a bleeding frog than a man.

Recklessly buying himself an expensive whisky, Len downed it in one, relieved to feel the liquor warm his stomach and send a welcome glow through his limbs.

'Hello there, Len.'

He looked up, nodding to another bookie as the man took a seat next to him.

'Flaming cold out there.'

'Too cold for me, Des,' Len replied, stretching his hands out to the fire to warm them. 'Had a good day?'

'Seen better,' the man answered. 'I were watching that Howell bloke. Looks a bit shaken to me. Mind you, from what I hear, he has reason.' He leaned towards Len and dropped his voice. 'Is it true?'

Baffled, Len looked at him. 'What?'

'You know.'

'No, I've no bloody idea what you're talking about.'

The man looked suddenly shifty, as though he had said too much. 'Oh, it's nothing –'

Len caught hold of his hand. 'I think it is, Des. And I think I should know about it.'

'It's just my fancy . . .'

'Share it with me.'

'I heard . . .' he looked round to see that no one was listening, '. . . that Howell was fishing about – you know, getting some more work on the side, working other courses, with other bookies.'

Len shook his head. 'Never! He's got enough on with George.'

'I heard different.'

'He wouldn't risk George finding out he was working for others.'

'He would if he thought his uncle was a bit slow.'

Len laughed. 'George Ogden slow? Yeah, like a wolf's slow.'

Des shrugged his shoulders. 'I heard it from two different sources.'

Len looked at Des's empty glass. 'You want a refill?'

A moment later Len was back from the bar with a drink for Des and another whisky for himself. He was praying that what he was hearing was the truth. If it was, he could finally oust his rival. George Ogden didn't like disloyalty, and he would take it badly being made to look a bloody senile old fool.

'Tell me, Des, are you on the level with this?'

'So help me God.'

'I don't want to go to George and end up with egg on my face.'

'I won't steer you wrong, Len. I mean, you've been badly treated by that old sod. We all think that. What with Howell turning up out of nowhere and being Ogden's *nephew* – with all that means . . .'

Len nodded. 'I have to be sure, Des. If I go to George with this, he'll get rid of Howell. I know that much. But if I'm wrong, he'll get rid of me.'

Des shook his head. 'You've nothing to worry about.'

'I'm pushing fifty,' Len said evenly. 'I've waited years to inherit George's pitch. But if I go to him with a lie about his nephew, I'll lose my job, never mind any chance of his licence.'

'Trust me,' Des replied, 'the word's out. Everyone's talking about Howell.'

Staring into his glass, Len frowned. Was it true? He didn't doubt that Des believed it and had passed it on in good faith. *But was it true?* Or was it – and was he clever enough – a lie planted by the Owl himself? If it was – and Len exposed him and was proved wrong – *Len* would be the one to be banished and Roy Howell would inherit everything.

Len flinched at the clammy thought. No more ticktack work for a while. He'd have to find a new bookie employer and that might not be so easy. Times weren't quite as buoyant as they had been, the Depression was taking effect and Len had his future and his daughter to think about. The world wasn't looking quite as predictable as once it had. And the younger men were coming up; and they were all in a hurry. Like Howell.

Len had never liked the Owl, and was liking him less and less with every word he heard. And not just because he wanted George's pitch. Len didn't like the idea of the old man being ripped off, and certainly not by the likes of Howell. Left to his own devices, alone with his uncle, what would happen? If Len was cut out of the picture, who would stop Howell's progress then? George was very old, frail – just how far would the Owl go?

'What is it?' Des asked, seeing Len wince.

'I was thinking about Howell.'

'Well, if you want my advice, stop thinking and get moving. Or that fish-eyed bugger will screw you up good and proper.'

SEVENTEEN

Christmas Day came in cold in Gull Road, ice at the windows, the doorsteps glacial with frost. In the distance, steam rose from the occasional train, which dragged itself into the station as sea mist snaked along the Promenade and curled about the streetlamps. Down in the basement at number 111, Nan had invited Clovis to Christmas dinner, whilst at number 139, Rose was just about to serve the pudding to an unusually silent Len.

For the third time in only a minute, Len sighed and glanced across the road towards Sea View.

'Looks like Ruby's set the chimney on fire again.'

Hurrying over, Rose looked out of the window – at the precise moment Ruby exited number 140. Glancing up at the chimney she then turned – and before they could duck – caught sight of the Bradshaws.

'I've told you often enough – stop ogling my hotel!' she yelled, before rushing back in, Trudie laughing at the front-room window.

'Can they put it out?'

'They do every year,' Len replied, pushing away his half-eaten pudding and lighting his pipe.

'What's the matter?'

'Huh?'

'You love Christmas pudding and you've hardly touched that – what's up?'

'I've been thinking, luv,' Len replied, glancing back to Sea View. Ruby was outside again, fat Alfred waddling down the steps and staring up at the chimney, Gilbert standing beside both of them in his Turkish slippers.

'What are you thinking *about*?' Rose pushed her father.

'Roy Howell.'

'Ah.'

He smiled wryly at her. '*Ah?*'

'Yeah, ah.'

'I've been hearing a few rumours about the Owl . . .' Len went on. He had promised himself that he wouldn't talk about it over Christmas, but it was proving too hard to stay silent. Besides, he always valued Rose's opinion. '. . . rumours like he might be working for some other bookies.'

Rose raised her eyebrows. 'Really?'

'George would take it badly if he was. I mean, the Owl being his nephew and all.'

'D'you think it's true?'

Len looked at her thoughtfully. 'I wondered about that. But it was Des who told me, and we go back a long way. He wouldn't steer me wrong.'

'So what are you going to do about it?'

'I should tell George.' Len paused. 'But I'm not the sneaky type.'

'You're just the loyal type,' she replied deftly. 'You worried that George might think you were just trying to get rid of Howell?'

'He's bound to, isn't he?'

'But if it's true, he'd want to know. And if he found out that you knew and had said nothing, he'd take that badly – and wonder if he could still trust you.' Rose got to her feet and began to clear the dishes. 'I think you should tell him.'

Len nodded. 'You're smart, Rosie, like your mother. Vera would have said the same.' Gently he reached out, took

Rose's hand and squeezed it. 'Thanks, luv. We can talk about everything, can't we?'

Not quite, Rose thought ruefully, thinking of the Widow Miller. Not quite.

At three in the morning on New Year's Day 1935 Lester sneaked back into Sea View – to find his mother waiting for him in the kitchen.

'So what kind of a time d'you call this then?'

'Aw, Mam, it's New Year –'

'And you've been celebrating, I see,' she replied, looking her adored son up and down. He was a fine man, she thought, not as handsome as Joe, but he had a ready look and a confident manner that could turn a girl's head easily. 'Why didn't your brother go with you?'

Slumping into a chair by the kitchen fire, Lester pushed the dying coals with the toe of his boot.

'He didn't want to; wandered off this afternoon in a right state. I don't know what's the matter with him lately. Joe's usually the one who's always telling me to get out and enjoy myself.'

Having made them each a mug of tea, and slopping in liberal amounts of whisky, Ruby sat down beside her son. She was wearing her old blue candlewick dressing gown, her hair in rags, her great hands dwarfing the mug.

'Joe's not himself. Hasn't been for a while. I thought I'd have a word with you about that. See if you knew what was the matter.'

Lester shrugged. 'He won't talk to me.'

'That's a first.'

'Yeah.'

'Maybe he's in love. I know he's been seeing a lot of Maisie Hollinbrook. Daft little cow.'

'She's all right. A bit silly –'

'Like Joe.'

'– but all right.'

'Don't you think that your brother might be better with a more settled girl?' Ruby asked, glancing up as heavy feet lumbered overhead.

'Is Dad up?'

'Don't be daft! It's Gilbert. He was late in too, drunk as a lord, singing "Barnacle Bill" at the top of his voice.' She frowned. 'He told me that this was going to be a good year for the whole family.'

'Maybe he's right.'

'It's not started out so good for Joe.'

Sobering up, Lester said, 'You worried about him?'

'I never used to worry about your brother, but that was because he was always with you. I thought that Joe could be daft if you were around because you'd get him out of any trouble. But he's changed, keeping to himself, and that's not like Joe. He's not talking to you either. So yes, I'm worried.'

'I've tried talking to him.'

'Will you try again?' Ruby asked, finishing her tea and putting down the mug. 'I don't like to think Joe's in trouble. But most of all, I don't like to think he can't come to us for help.'

Turning off the light a few minutes later, Lester followed his mother upstairs. It had been a good night. He had danced with some of the best-looking girls in Blackpool and kissed Beth Hodges on the pier as the old year was counted out. His mind was full of new ideas: he was going to expand, buy a place on the North Pier, save up some real money and see if he couldn't plan to open a dance hall in a few years. Why not? He could do it. If he kept his head and his nose clean. If he kept the right company and didn't get side-tracked by the likes of Beth.

But although it had been a good night, Lester's satisfied mood had deserted him when he caught some of Ruby's anxiety. His mother wasn't the worrying type; if she was uneasy, there was a good reason for it. In the bedroom he shared with Joe, Lester splashed his face with some cold water and glanced over to his brother's bed. Instinct told him that Joe wasn't sleeping.

'Hey, Joe, you awake?'

Silence.

'Joe, you awake? Want to talk?'

The body in the bed never moved. Lester walked over to the window and peered out. In the distance a few fireworks still spluttered into the New Year sky, the moon coming out fitfully as the sea mist thinned. He was just about to talk to Joe again when Lester's attention was caught by someone staggering into Gull Road.

At first he thought it was a drunk, but as the moonlight hit the figure Lester saw that it was George Ogden. Weaving around, the old man lurched about in his trousers and vest, waving his arms desperately.

Startled, Lester ran out, and down the street towards him. George turned to Lester, blank-eyed.

'He's robbed me! He's bloody robbed me!' George was screaming, lights now going on in the surrounding houses.

Lester threw his jacket over George's shoulders. 'Come in, George, it's bloody freezing out here.'

Wildly, the old man shook off Lester's jacket and his grip. 'I'll have him! I'll bloody have him! No one robs me and gets away with it!'

A light in number 99 Gull Road came on, a woman leaning out of the first-floor window.

'Get home and sleep it off!'

'It's OK,' Lester called back to her. 'I'm looking after him –'

'Not well enough!' another man called from a bedroom window further down the street. 'Some of us want to sleep!'

'George,' Lester said, grabbing hold of the old man's arm, 'come with me.'

But George Ogden shook him off again, weaving around in his vest, his head bald without its trilby, his wizened arms pearl-white in the moonlight.

'Get off me! Don't touch me! I want him found, you hear me? I want that bugger found!' His voice was piercing, becoming incoherent as the door of the Bradshaws' house opened and Len walked out, yawning.

Seeing his employer in his vest he stopped short.

'What the hell are you doing, George?'

'He robbed me!'

'*Who* robbed you?'

'That bloody toerag nephew of mine! That's who!' George shot back, suddenly beginning to cough, his frail form doubling over.

'Bring him in here, Lester,' Len ordered, moving back to let them enter.

Rose had also woken at the noise and was standing in her dressing gown at the bottom of the stairs. Confused at seeing Lester, she hurried past into the kitchen and set the kettle on, her head turned away. It seemed that as soon as George got inside, his fighting spirit left him. Suddenly deflated, he crumpled into a chair, Len throwing a rug around the old man's shoulders. He had never seen George Ogden vulnerable, but now his employer was pathetic in a grubby vest, his bony, bare feet turning blue with cold.

'You're going to catch your death,' Len said kindly, passing some tea to George. 'Drink that.'

Lester and Len exchanged frowns over the old man's head. Rose folded her arms and watched silently.

'He's gone . . .' George said finally, his voice now weak and distant.

'You mean Roy?'

He nodded, his head large on the overthin neck. 'He was my own flesh and blood – I never thought he'd do me a bad turn.' George drank the tea sloppily, his hands shaking. 'He fooled me, Len . . . I should never have trusted him. Never have let him into the business.'

Banking up the fire, Rose was aware of Lester's attention suddenly. He smiled, Rose flushing and glancing away.

'George, tell me what happened, will you?' Len asked, drawing up another chair and sitting next to his employer.

'Roy Howell took all my money. I went out for a drink to celebrate the New Year . . .' George paused, as though he could hardly believe it, '. . . when I came home the shit had cleaned me out.'

Len winced. 'Did you have money at home?'

'Enough,' George replied, giving him a shifty look. 'I know what you're thinking! I could have trusted you. Would have been better to tell you, and not confide in that bleeding bastard . . .' he gripped Len's arm, '. . . but he were family. He were my nephew. I thought that mattered. I thought that counted for something.'

'Did he take anything else but money, George?'

'My medals, some furniture . . .' he trailed off, defeated, old. 'He'd planned it for a while, must have. Must have waited until tonight when he knew I'd be out. Must have got a van or a cart and taken the stuff when there were few about who'd stop him. Anyway, he were my nephew – who *would* have stopped him?'

Len turned to Rose. 'Get some warm clothes of mine, Rose, will you? George can't sit in this blanket. It's not comfortable –'

'I don't care!' the old man snapped. 'It were my own bloody fault, Len. I treated you badly and now I'm going to pay for it.'

'Yeah, well, pay for it when you're warm, George,' Len replied.

Lester followed Rose to the stairs. He waited at the bottom of the stairwell for a few moments until she returned carrying a shirt, jumper and trousers of her father's. Walking down the stairs towards him, Rose felt Lester's scrutiny and was suddenly awkward, losing her footing and slipping on the last step.

At once, Lester caught hold of her. 'Hey, steady on.'

'I missed the step,' she said, looking away from him.

'Poor George,' Lester said sympathetically. 'Some New Year, hey?'

She nodded, willing him to let her go. The embrace would mean nothing to Lester, but everything to her. He had probably held and kissed a dozen girls that night, but she had spent her time with her father – thinking of Lester. As she had done ever since childhood.

And now here he was, holding her.

'I should give these to George,' Rose said abruptly, turning. 'He'll be cold.'

Then, without thinking, she turned back. And kissed Lester Williams full on the mouth.

EIGHTEEN

The following morning the snow started in earnest, all races off. Taking some food over to Holland Road, where George lived close to the house that had once belonged to Hettie and Eddie Bradshaw, Len let himself into his employer's house and called up the stairs.

'Hey, George, you up?'

There was no answer. Frowning, Len walked into the kitchen. In all his years working for George Ogden he had never been invited into his house – and now he knew why. Len knew that the place had been rented by George for years, but he hadn't expected how beggared it would look. Surely to God George had earned enough to make himself comfortable? Len looked round at the chipped sink, the bare table, the cheap, water-spotted blinds and the empty grate.

In the backyard, Len found some nutty slack coal and brought it into the kitchen, setting it in the grate and lighting it with the help of the previous day's *Racing Times*. It spluttered into light, casting a dull, smoky glow into the room. There were no mementos of family, no personal items of any sort – and if there had been Len doubted that Roy Howell would have bothered to steal them. Taking down a chipped teapot, Len rinsed it and began to make some tea, listening for the sound of George moving about above.

The place felt damp to Len, and the few pieces of cheap

furniture were long past their best. Obviously Howell had taken anything of value, along with the money and George's old medals. Walking upstairs quietly, Len opened the bedroom door and looked in. The old man was sleeping, snoring softly, thin curtains drawn but letting in the melancholic light.

No wonder George had spent so much time at the races, Len thought. This was a cheerless bloody place to live. Setting down the tea by the bedside, Len saw George stir awkwardly, trying to rise. The old man's expression was relief when he saw his visitor, followed immediately by panic.

'George, what's the matter?'

Opening his mouth, the old man tried to speak, but the words came out muffled, incoherent. Panicking, George tried to get up, but couldn't, falling back against the thin blankets and beginning to shake uncontrollably. Anxious, Len moved closer to the old man and touched him. He was icy cold. His eyes never left Len's face as spittle came from the left corner of his mouth.

And then Len realised what had happened. George Ogden had had a stroke.

'Not now,' Trudie whined as she watched her mother drag the furniture out of room 4. 'It's a holiday today.'

'It's no holiday for whatever's making that smell,' Ruby replied shortly.

Heaving back the bed, she kneeled down and looked under it, then, disgruntled, pushed it back into place. A moment later she had the washstand out, followed by the dressing table.

'You've already done all this,' Trudie went on, her tone bored as she sat on the bed. 'Maybe a rat died somewhere.'

'I don't have rats in my hotel!' Ruby stormed. 'And anyway, rats don't smell of fish.'

'Maybe they're *seaside* rats,' Trudie offered, rolling onto her back and gazing up at the ceiling. 'Anyway, why don't you ask Dad to help you with the lifting?'

Ruby gave her daughter an exasperated look. Then she grabbed one end of the sideboard, and with one almighty effort, pulled it away from the wall. There was nothing behind it.

Out of breath, Ruby flopped onto the bed beside her daughter.

'I can't find it.'

'No kidding,' Trudie replied, staring up at the ceiling. 'It's New Year, Mam. We could go out – you know, have a walk round town. There's a sale on at the Co-op –'

'I'm not setting foot outside this house until I've found the source of that smell,' Ruby replied, closing her eyes for a moment. 'Your Dad brought me some flowers last night.'

Trudie stared at her mother. 'Dad? *Flowers?*'

'Don't act so bloody surprised! He was quite a romantic in his youth.' Ruby sniffed at the air. 'I can still smell it.'

'What kind of flowers?'

'I dunno. Just flowers. Probably got them off some grave, but it was a nice thought.'

'That was a hell of a racket last night. I heard Lester go out late.'

'George Ogden was robbed. His nephew nicked everything.'

Sitting upright, Trudie stared at her mother. '*He never!*'

'He did. Cleaned out George's place and did a runner. I doubt they'll ever find him,' Ruby replied, sniffing again. 'Maybe it's gas?'

'He always looked shifty,' Trudie stated, still thinking about Howell. 'He wasn't normal.'

'Because he never made up to you, you mean?' Ruby replied, teasing her. 'If it's gas, we should report it.'

But Trudie's thoughts were still with the previous night. 'Why was Lester involved?'

'He heard the commotion and went out to help George. Then Len took him into his place.' Ruby paused, thinking of her son. 'Lester was quite pissed when he first came in – before all this trouble with Ogden.'

'He'd been seeing in the New Year,' Trudie said gloomily. 'Lucky sod. I was stuck here.'

'You were stuck here because I didn't want some girl of mine hanging about drunks.'

'But Lester went.'

'Lester isn't a girl.'

'I think Rose knows that,' Trudie replied artfully.

Her mother turned to look at her. 'What d'you mean?'

'You know, Mam.'

'No, I don't. Tell me.'

'Rose is in love with Lester. Always has been.'

This was news to Ruby. '*Rose Bradshaw!* Well, I'll be damned. I mean, I knew she liked him – what girl doesn't? – but in love with our Lester? Wonders will never cease. Has she told you?'

'Nah, Rose has never let on, but I've seen her over the years looking at Lester. Watching him. And she's never really gone for anyone else.'

'I didn't think she was interested in lads.'

'She isn't. Except Lester.'

'I thought she was just shy. You know, because of her eye . . .' Ruby went on, having mercifully forgotten the smell for a while. 'She's a nice kid, but Lester will never have her. She's not pretty enough, not special. He'll not go for Rose Bradshaw. Poor Rose isn't ever going to be in the running. He just thinks of her as a little girl, your best mate, the kid he's seen running around Gull Road all his life. She doesn't have a chance of nabbing our Lester.'

Musing, Trudie ran her finger along the scar on her arm.

'I wouldn't be too sure of that, Ma,' she said evenly. 'There's more to Rose Bradshaw than people think. God knows, she's a lot tougher than she looks.'

But Ruby's attention had wandered. Heaving herself off the bed, she walked over to the wardrobe and was just about to push it back against the wall when she noticed something. Frowning, she disappeared behind the wardrobe and emerged waving a dried-up kipper.

'The bitch!' she hollered. 'It was that sneaky little Mrs Noble. She – or that toerag husband of hers – nailed it at the back of the bloody wardrobe thinking I'd never find it! Leaving it to rot there and stink the place out. Make a fool out of me, will she? We'll see about that. And to think that I once let them have the use of that radio for free!'

Wincing, Trudie followed her mother downstairs where she grabbed some paper from the reception desk. Hurriedly, Ruby wrote a brief note:

Mr and Mrs Noble,

INVOICE

One kipper   bed and board for four months –
Total £28. 19s.

Finally she slid the kipper into an envelope, addressed it, then pulled on her coat and made for the postbox.

George had been admitted to hospital but found it hard to make any sort of recovery. For several days Len visited him, reading to him and talking about the past. But Len knew that the old man was finished. The shock of what Howell had done had hobbled George Ogden and he had no reason to fight back to health. He was an old man, tired of living.

Outside the hospital window George saw only winter-bare trees and the gloomy mist blowing in from the Irish sea. Somewhere – a long way off – his beloved horses were still out there, still running, still blowing steam from their nostrils into the cold air. But he knew he would never see them again . . . Every one of George's years came back to him, each punctuated by his passion. He could remember the races at Haydock, Catterick, Cartmel and the Grand National. Ascot too, where he'd watched the toffs lose, and yet every time George Ogden had gone home, his pockets had been full.

Names danced before George's eyes as he lay in that grim hospital bed. Not the names of women, or children, but horses – Benny's Girl, Lady Dancer, Golden Fleece and so many others, all running down tracks on the flat, or at the steeplechases. Gorgeous, God-struck creatures, manes flying, driving themselves upwards and over the fences towards the winning post.

George stirred, whistling under his breath. At least trying to.

'What's he doing?' Rose asked Len as they sat by George's bedside one afternoon.

'He's whistling for the horses,' Len answered her. 'George always whistled for them by the track after a race. Gave them titbits. Probably gave them more than he fed himself.'

Soon after, Rose left to go back to work, but Len stayed on. It grew dark and still he stayed with George Ogden, because although he had had his differences he knew that George was dying. And Len couldn't leave him to go alone.

'You remember The Pearl Fisher?' Len asked, George's eyes fixing on his as he tried to nod. 'We won some money on that lucky bugger. And the Grand National in 1926 – those were the days, George. I can remember the first time I went with you, Will was working as your clerk then and he gave me a tip. I lost a whole week's bloody wages listening to him!' Len laughed, staring into George's immobile face. Pity shifted inside him. You were an old bugger, he thought, played me along, all right, but I'll not leave you now. 'I was thinking about that time we all went up to Cartmel races – God, it was a hot day – and afterwards we went back by Lake Windermere. You had your first car, a right bone-shaker, but we thought we were everybody.

Vera took off her shoes and stockings and paddled in the water . . .' Sadness overwhelming him at the memory, Len hurriedly changed the subject. 'We've had some good times, George, you and me. Some real good times.'

Suddenly he was aware of the slightest pressure on his hand. Leaning further towards George, Len tried to hear what he was saying. But he couldn't understand him. Again, George tried to form his words, and again he failed. Finally after a long moment, he tried again.

'Sorry,' he said at last, 'sorry . . .'

Those were the last words George Ogden ever spoke.

NINETEEN

Probably because of the freezing weather, Gilbert got a cold, which turned into laryngitis and he couldn't perform. A young man of twenty-three took over. It was, Gilbert professed, a blasted liberty.

'How can they think he has the experience to play Wilde's *Earnest*?' Gilbert rasped. 'Why did they choose him anyway, instead of Reginald? Reginald's been my understudy for years –'

'And never had a chance to get on the stage, since you were never ill before,' Ruby interrupted. 'I dare say the management thought that a younger man would put more bums on seats.'

'Youth is one thing, but class is another.' Gilbert started coughing, then sank back into his pillows. 'I think a little beef tea would help, Ruby.'

'I'm sure you're right, Gilbert,' she replied, walking to the door. 'Give me a call when you've made some.'

Not to be outdone by his brother-in-law, Alfred decided that he had pleurisy and took to *his* bed. Which wasn't much of a change. And Ruby – although she moaned bitterly about looking after them both – was delighted. It was quiet in January, the rooms empty of guests. No one to order around, no regular meals to make, no sand walked into her hallway. Oh yes, Ruby thought to herself, two sickly men would keep her occupied. And stop her worrying so much about Joe.

Trudie, on the other hand, wasn't about to spend the beginning of the New Year drowning in a fog of inhalants and friar's balsam. Work was bad, but being at Sea View was worse. Getting off the 48 Marton tram, Trudie made her way down Central Drive, arriving at Myers bargain stores at thirteen minutes past nine.

'You're late.'

'Why? What's happened?' Trudie shot back to the flustered young manager.

It was a lousy shop, everyone knew that, but off season it was quiet and that suited Trudie. Besides, she was enjoying herself flirting. There weren't so many boys around off season and she was looking for company.

'You want to calm down, Mr Philpot,' she cooed, 'or you'll end up having a stroke like poor Mr Ogden. He died last night, you know.'

'Be that as it may. You should still get here on time,' Mr Philpot blustered, hopelessly out of his depth. 'There are plenty of girls looking for work.'

'Not at this time of year, there aren't.'

Pouting, Trudie pulled on her overall and then took her place behind the counter. Above her head she could hear footsteps coming from the grim lodgings of Overseas House. No competition for Sea View there, Trudie thought to herself, leaning forward when she caught sight of Joe on the opposite side of the street.

Knowing full well it would irritate Mr Philpot, she still knocked on the window and eagerly beckoned for her brother to come over.

'We can't allow boyfriends in here –'

'He's my brother, Mr Philpot,' Trudie said archly. 'I didn't think you were the jealous type.'

It took a while for Joe to find a break in the traffic, then he crossed over, looking around warily. Finally, grim-faced, he walked into Myers, then leaned on Trudie's counter with his head down.

'Well, hello there, sunshine,' she quipped. 'Where have you been? Ma's been going crackers.'

'You shouldn't have called out for me,' Joe mumbled, 'drawing attention, like that.'

Trudie's eyebrows shot up. 'Who are you afraid of?' she asked, half laughing, then sobered up. 'Jesus, Joe, are you in trouble?'

'I can handle it –'

'You can't! You can never handle anything,' she whispered. 'Not on your own anyway. Why don't you come home with me and talk to Mam?'

Joe winced.

'OK, skip Mam. But you could talk to Lester,' Trudie said, beginning to get anxious. 'Hey, you're scaring me, Joe. What's up?'

'I'll sort it out on my own –'

'But you're not sorting anything out, are you? Running off like that, for two days! Christ, we're all so worried about you.' She stared into her brother's unshaved face. 'I said you were with Maisie –'

'Aw, Trudie!'

'Look, it's better they all think that than worry about you and what you've been up to.' She dropped her voice. 'What have you been up to?'

'I can handle it.'

'You know you can't –'

He bristled. 'Thanks, Trudie!'

'It's the truth. You're good-looking, Joe, but not that bright.' She smiled at Mr Philpot, hoping that would send him running. It did. Anxiously Trudie then looked back at Joe. 'Tell me.'

'Then you'll tell Ma.'

'Why does everyone think I can't keep a secret?'

'Because you can't, Trudie,' Joe replied curtly, 'and this time it would be dangerous for you to know.'

Her eyes fixed on his. 'That does it!' she snapped. 'If

you don't tell me what's going on, NOW, I'll call a copper.'

'You wouldn't!'

'I bloody would,' she replied, scowling at a customer who was repeatedly trying to get her attention. 'Now, Joe, tell me. What trouble are you in? And don't lie.'

'Money.'

'Aw, everyone's short –'

'I'm in debt, big debt,' Joe went on, looking round, his voice hardly audible. 'Two heavies came to see me, Trudie. They said I had to pay up, or else.'

'No!' She was incredulous. 'It's like the movies.'

'Christ!' Joe snapped. 'This isn't a game, you know. I've been moving around for two days. Thought I'd get out of Blackpool, but then I thought I'd be better to stay nearby home.'

'I'll get Lester –'

'I can look after myself!'

'I can see that,' Trudie replied drily.

'I just have to get hold of some money,' Joe went on, his face pinched, shadows under his eyes from lack of sleep.

The easy-going brother she had always known had disappeared, trodden underfoot by worry. She was going to have to get help for him, Trudie thought, ever protective. There *had* to be a way to get him some money. Surely.

She looked around, her voice sly. 'How much money d'you need?'

'*What?*'

'How much?' she repeated. 'I could borrow it from here, Joe –'

'You mean steal!'

'No, just *borrow* it.' Her voice dropped lower, a whisper as she leaned towards him. 'The manager's crazy about me, I dare say I could get out of any trouble I got into –'

'Stop it!' Joe snapped. 'You're mad. I can't steal – and wouldn't let you steal for me.'

'So what are you going to do?' she countered. 'Lester's

told me about these kinds of men before. They're too much for you to handle. Talk to Lester – he's got money, he'll see you right.'

'I can handle it!' Joe repeated angrily. 'I'm sick of hearing about "Lester this, Lester that", as though I'm the bloody idiot brother and he's come sodding genius. OK, he's smart and I haven't been, but I'm not going to give him – and everyone else – the satisfaction of letting him get me out of a hole.'

Trudie shrugged. 'Get beaten up instead then. Or worse.'

Wincing, Joe paled. 'It's just a debt.'

'Beg for more time then. Ask for longer to find the money.'

'I tried that, but they laughed in my face.'

Trudie was getting more uneasy by the moment. 'Maybe they'll listen if you explain. They must have a boss, talk to him.'

'He's not the type to listen.'

'How d'you know?'

'Everyone knows George Ogden's ruthless.'

To Joe's complete amazement Trudie started to laugh. She laughed so loudly that the few customers in Myers turned and frowned at her. Mr Philpot came hurrying over.

'What on earth is so funny?'

'What did I tell you when I came in, Mr Philpot?' She turned and winked at Joe. 'About Mr Ogden?'

'You said he died yesterday.'

'Yes,' Trudie said, laughing giddily and unable to stop. 'That's right. George Ogden died yesterday.'

Back in Holland Road, Len was clearing out his employer's old home. He found exactly five pennies and a farthing, a cheap clock with 'Souvenir from Aintree' written on it, and George's old trilby. If that was the substance of a life, Len thought, it was a pretty poor lot.

He then walked into town, stopping at the corner of

Regent Road and Church Street to make arrangements for the funeral. Because George had been robbed there was no money to pay for a grand event, but Len wasn't going to see him buried in a pauper's grave. Instead he stumped up for the funeral himself; kept it cheap, but decent. Then before going home, Len took a detour and dropped George's few coins into the church collection box on Read's Avenue. He wasn't too sure if George had been religious, but thought – as the service was being held there – it was the best place for the donation. As for George Ogden's remains – Len had plans for them.

Quickening his pace, Len then headed back home and put George Ogden's trilby on the top of the sideboard in the kitchen, near to the radio.

'There you go, George, you can hear the racing now.'

Finally Len sat down. He felt drained. By what, he wasn't sure. But maybe he had been more attached to the old man than he had thought. Or maybe it was reaction to the news that George's licence and pitch were now, finally, his. Somehow the old man had made arrangements at the hospital, telling the doctor his wishes. Not Len, the doctor. All the time Len had sat selflessly with him, George had kept his secret, provoking him to the edge of the grave.

Len pulled the evening paper towards him, but for once he wasn't interested in the racing. Instead he picked up his pen and printed his name on the top of the paper – 'Leonard Bradshaw – The Lazy Eye'. Jesus, it would look good on the track, Len thought, his name in amongst all the other bookies. At last.

He laughed softly to himself and then looked round guiltily. It was wrong to celebrate when a man had died. But Len was human, after all, and suddenly he was intoxicated by the fact that his hopes were finally realised. *He was a bookie*, with his own licence and pitch. He had arrived. He had waited and waited, but he had won out in the end.

And maybe *now* he could have Rosie working alongside him. The thought glowed like a ruby . . . Len Bradshaw and Rosie Bradshaw – 'Bradshaw & Daughter, Bookmakers' – oh, that would be something, wouldn't it? That would be bliss. And he'd see to it that Rosie was treated all right; with respect. After all, he was a bookie now. No more tick-tack for Len, no more being a bookie's runner. No more underdog. He was top man. He had made it.

'Jesus, Vera,' he said out loud, 'if you could see me now.'

Sliding on the snow, Joe hurried towards Rigby Street. He paused by the model windmill, which disguised the toilets, and got his breath back. George Ogden was dead! And Joe's debt had died with him! Greedily Joe sucked in the air and then coughed as the cold hit his lungs. He had never been a malicious man, certainly not one to gloat over the tragedies of others, but he had to hand it to God – Ogden's death had done him a real favour.

There would be no more clowning about for him now, Joe thought, gazing up at the starry sky. He was going to stay on the level. Stay safe . . . The sea mist had given way to cold and snow, the sea black to its depths behind him. A tram suddenly chugged past and Joe waved, stupid, giddy with relief. Trudie was right: he wasn't like Lester, hadn't got the brains *or* the balls. He was second-rate. But some-how, suddenly, second-rate seemed bloody good.

Having got his breath back, Joe continued up Stork Street, past the boarding houses with their 'Vacancies' signs – none in the same class as Sea View, just a grim, unsmiling terrace.

Then at number 50, he stopped. There was a light on in the front room, another dim bulb shining over the front door. Joe rang the bell.

A small young woman with thick auburn hair answered. 'Joe!'

He ssshed her immediately, drawing Maisie out onto the step and wrapping her in his coat.

'I was worried about you, Joe. Where have you been?'

He kissed her forehead avidly, searching her pretty, if rather vacant, face. 'Maisie, everything's OK again –'

'I didn't know there was anything wrong.'

'There isn't any more.' Joe looked to the lighted window. 'Is your dad in?'

'Listening to the concert on the radio,' she replied. 'I wouldn't interrupt him now, it's Gracie Fields on.'

Silly Maisie, Joe thought with delight. Silly, glorious, affectionate, simple Maisie.

'Do you love me?'

She looked into his face, flushing with excitement. 'You know I do!'

'I love you too,' Joe told her, kissing her on the cheek and then longingly on the mouth. She smelled and tasted of new bread. And safety. 'I want to marry you, Maisie Hollinbrook.'

She took in a breath before replying. 'But, Joe, think for a minute. Mum'll say we're too young, you know she will. You've no home and no real job . . .' She snuggled against him, snow falling on her pale red hair. 'Where would we live?'

'We'd rent a place. Somewhere cheap. There's rooms in Gull Road. It would do for a start.' Joe pulled back, scrutinising her. 'I'll never make much of myself, Maisie, but I'll work hard, get us our own home before too long. Lester's always got jobs going; he'll always look out for me.' Joe paused, suddenly uncertain. 'I know my brother's the fancy one. I mean, he's got a car now, people look up to him, call him "Mister Williams". Everyone knows he'll go far. They don't think that way about me, Maisie. I'll always be just Joe. A bit thick, a bit slow on the uptake, but I'll love you, take care of you better than anyone. I'd never look at another woman or let you down.'

She was listening carefully, without speaking. God, had he made a mess of it, Joe wondered. Had he not made a good enough case for himself? But he *couldn't* lie – could only tell her the truth and then she'd know what she was getting. Know what kind of a man, and a life, she could expect.

'I'm being honest,' Joe went on. 'Lester's the clever twin. I'm not special.'

'I'm not special either,' she replied, her face buried against his neck. 'We're two not very special people, you and me. But it's *you* I want, not Lester.'

And, for Joe, that was more than enough.

Totally preoccupied, Lester sat in the driving seat of his car and turned off the engine. It was still snowing, the Promenade virtually empty, the illuminations jerking and darting in the wind. At the age of twenty-two he had done well, Lester thought, letting his fingers run over the leather car seat. Business was good: no more filling slot machines for him. He had employees now.

And good clothes. The kind he would have to keep away from his mother, or Ruby would be sure to ruin them. Not deliberately – she was proud of her son – but Ruby's reputation with washing was well deserved . . . It was satisfying to look good, Lester thought, like a businessman. But then, he *was* a businessman now. Come summer, he would get himself a booth outside the open-air baths on the South Shore. If the weather was good, he would make a killing. Everyone wanted ice cream and drinks when it was hot. Not that he would stand behind the counter himself. He would get someone else for that, leave himself free to follow other commitments.

Lester tried to continue with these thoughts, but found his mind wandering and that irritated him. God, it was just a kiss, he told himself. He'd been kissed before. But not by Rose Bradshaw. What on earth had got into her? She was a kid, Trudie's school friend. Lester shook his head, trying to work out what had happened. *She was just a kid!* Hadn't she been around all his life? Hadn't she wandered in and out of Sea View, almost like family? *That* was the point, Lester thought uncomfortably: kissing Rose Bradshaw was almost like kissing his kid sister. Almost incestuous.

Shaking his head again, Lester stared out of the window at the surfing snow. The sea looked bloody freezing to him, and yet there were a few lunatics who had had to take their New Year swim, whatever the weather. Imagine that, Lester thought. Why the hell would someone go and do something as daft as that? It was cold enough to stop your heart.

Why had she kissed him? Lester sighed to himself, trying to dismiss the image. Rose was the kid he'd ragged, kidded about with . . . But she hadn't looked like a kid the other night, he thought. And that squint hadn't shown when she'd closed her eyes, her head tilted upwards for an instant.

She was Rosie Bradshaw, Lester thought, hurriedly dismissing the image and turning on the car's engine. She was Trudie's pal. And she certainly wasn't the kind of girl he was looking for. He wanted glamour. Not a girl who had grown up under his nose, a kid with a glide in her eye. *A kid who had saved his sister's life* . . . Lester flushed, shamed by his own callousness. Rose was an incredible girl. No, a woman. She was quick-witted, strong, funny and brave. She was caring too, a female a man could rely on. A woman a man could stand shoulder to shoulder with.

But not a woman with glamour, and, despite himself, Lester wanted a golden girl, not a surrogate sister. Rose had just acted on impulse, he told himself, that was all. Her kiss had meant nothing. It had been just a reckless gesture. One of those things. A crazy moment. God knows, he had had plenty of those.

But not with someone like Rose . . . Sighing, Lester restarted the car and pulled out onto the Promenade. She was a hell of a girl. But not the one for him.

TWENTY

Dear Rose,

By now you have had time to consider my proposal. If you decide against accepting my help, that is your choice, but I would like you to tell me your decision face to face.

Please do me the courtesy of calling to see me.

Fondest wishes,

Henrietta Miller

'She sounds miffed.'

'And you sound *awful*,' Rose said, studying Gilbert as he sat up in bed. 'How long before your voice comes back to normal?'

Waving aside the question, Gilbert rocked his head on the pillow fretfully. His thinning hair was fluffed out, his eyebrows grey without the penciling. Behind him were a selection of photographs of him in various roles, one signed with a flourish – 'Regards, George Formby'.

'You'll have to go and see her,' Gilbert croaked. 'It's only manners.'

'I thought if I ignored it she might just fade into the background.'

'The Widow Miller could no more fade into the background than an elephant at a flea circus.' Gilbert blew his nose loudly into a massive white handkerchief and then fixed Rose with a stare. 'Did you see the matinée?'

She nodded. 'I sneaked in after the curtain went up.'

Affecting a nonchalant air, Gilbert asked, 'Was he good? My *new* understudy, was he good? Not that I care, but I'd just like to know what he's doing to Oscar Wilde.'

'I don't think he's doing much to Oscar Wilde,' Rose said artfully, 'but he's bloody murdering the part of Jack.'

Flushing with relief, Gilbert leaned back into his pillows. 'Well, it's an experienced actor's role. Not something a mere juvenile could handle. Perhaps the management will remember that when my new contract comes up.' Gilbert paused, then looked Rose up and down, frowning. 'What's up?'

'I've told you – Hettie's letter.'

'There's more! I can tell.'

Embarrassed, Rose looked down at the coverlet whilst the ranks of encyclopaedias stared down at both of them from the top of the wardrobe.

'I kissed Lester.'

Gilbert leaned forward. 'I didn't hear that –'

'You know you did!'

He smirked. 'Well, maybe I did. Maybe I just wanted to hear it again . . . What was it like?'

'I can't tell you that!'

'You told me my nephew kissed you!'

'No, I didn't, I said that I kissed *him*!' Rose corrected Gilbert, irritated.

'What happened next?'

'Why should anything have happened next?'

'There's always another scene.'

'This is real life, Gilbert, not theatre.'

'Sounds a lot like pantomime to me, sweetheart,' he replied deftly.

'He wasn't expecting it and he was embarrassed. I could tell.'

'Never!'

'He *was*, Gilbert. He ran off like there was a devil after

him.' She burned with humiliation. A moment passed before she spoke again, and her voice had hardened. 'I want that bloody operation, Gilbert. I want to have my eye fixed.'

'Ah,' he said thoughtfully. 'I see. *Lester* . . .'

'It's not just because of Lester!'

'But my nephew brought it to a head?' Gilbert queried, sneezing twice before continuing. 'To be honest, I would have snatched Hettie Miller's hand off long before now.'

'So would I – if it hadn't been for Dad,' Rose replied, thoughtful. 'I don't know how to go about it, Gilbert. If I tell Dad I've been in touch with Hettie he's bound to be annoyed.'

'We don't know that for sure.' Gilbert blew his nose again loudly. 'He might not be annoyed at all. And the longer you keep it a secret, the more he'll think there's something to hide.'

'There is.'

'Look,' Gilbert said, leaning towards Rose, his fleshy jowls ruddy with his cold. 'Your father has finally got what he's wanted in life. He's a happy man, in a mind to be magnanimous. Think about it, Rose, why shouldn't *you* have what *you've* wanted for years?'

She shrugged, getting to her feet and reaching for her coat. 'Maybe Dad doesn't know how much I want it.'

'Maybe *you* didn't – until now.' Gilbert watched Rose walk to the door. 'Oh, and as for Lester, naturally I'd kill anyone who said a word against him, but think about it, sweetheart: if he can't see past your squint he's not the one for you.'

The meeting had been called off after the first race. Len took down his pitch 'Leonard Bradshaw – The Lazy Eye', loading it into the back of his old Austin. Who cared if the meeting hadn't been profitable? There were going to be hundreds of races; he was in no hurry. He'd got what he wanted and now nothing else much mattered. In this happy frame of mind, Len walked into the bar and ordered a pint, surprised to see Rose materialise beside him only moments later.

''Lo, there, luv. What brings you here?'

'My half-day,' she replied evenly. 'I thought I'd just check up on you, see how the new bookie was doing.'

He smiled, pecked her on the cheek. There was a glow about her, Len thought, watching as Rose ordered herself a tomato juice. She seemed skittish, on edge.

'So, how did it go?'

'Race called off for bad weather. We all suspected it.'

'Is being a bookie how you thought it would be?' Rose asked him, putting her head on one side.

'Better,' Len replied honestly, dropping his voice. 'I need a clerk, though. There's no good men around that haven't been snapped up. And we all know how important it is to get the right one. Someone I can trust.'

'You'll find him,' Rose replied firmly, then changed the subject. 'I went to see Gilbert. He's sounding awful, you should see him. And Alfred's lying on a couch in the kitchen, moaning like a woman in labour.'

Len laughed, watching her curiously. Had she guessed what he was going to ask? Maybe she had at that. They were so close, and there had never been any secrets between them.

'I told him that his understudy was lousy. But I lied,' Rose admitted, pulling a face. 'He's good and good-looking. I reckon he'll pull in the women –'

'What do you want to tell me, Rosie?'

She stopped, stared at him. God, had her father found out about her visiting Hettie? Did he know what she was about to ask him? Maybe he did. It really wasn't so surprising. After all, they'd been inseparable for years.

'Dad . . .' she started tentatively, '. . . well, it's something I've been thinking about for a while . . .'

He was right, Len thought, she *was* going to ask to join him in the business! What better solution could there

152

possibly be – having Rosie as his clerk? And in time Rosie would inherit his licence and pitch. God, it was almost too good to be true.

'Go on, luv.'

'It might seem strange . . .'

For a woman to want to be a ticktack man, Len thought. No, not strange for his Rosie.

'. . . but I've really given it some thought. And now seems the right time . . .'

Rose paused. Her father was watching her, smiling. He *did* know! Thank God, she thought. Her beloved father knew what she was going to ask him and approved. Must do, or he wouldn't be smiling.

'Go on, luv,' Len urged her again, putting down his drink and trying not to laugh out loud.

'. . . I mean, I grew up with it . . .'

You certainly did, Len thought. No one grew up more surrounded by the racing game.

'. . . but it matters more to me now . . .'

He wanted to hug her, his heart almost bursting. But Len wasn't about to spoil his daughter's surprise. She had to tell him, ask him, in her own way. In her own time. After all, didn't he – above everyone – know that good things come to those who wait?

'. . . it would make such a difference to my life, Dad . . .'

'It would that, luv.'

'. . . and being a girl, it matters.'

'You're better than any ten men,' Len replied, willing her finally to ask him the question he was longing to hear.

'. . . so I want to have my eye fixed.'

Len blinked, unsure that he had heard right. Rose's face came in and out of focus, such was his surprise, and it took him a moment to recover. *His daughter wanted to have her squint repaired.* She didn't want to join the family business, she wanted to have an operation on her eye.

'Are you OK, Dad? You look sick,' Rose asked anxiously,

leading Len to a pub bench and then sitting down beside him.

'I'm fine, luv,' he said at last. 'I was just a bit dizzy there. Smoking too much.' He winked at her, his heart in a clamp. 'So, you want your eye done?'

'I do, yes,' Rose agreed, hurrying on. 'Now hear me out, Dad, without interrupting. Henrietta Miller was in touch with me a while back. I didn't mention that I'd been to see her – I didn't want to upset you – but she's offered to pay for the operation.'

Len could hear buzzing in his ears. *Hettie!* Bloody Hettie. What the shit was she doing back in his life? His daughter's life? And coming back to offer all kinds of goodies. Like an operation for Rose. An operation he didn't have enough money to cover.

'I wondered how much your eye bothered you. You should have said, should have told me . . .' Len began, all the steam evaporating out of him. 'I should have realised a long time ago; should have helped you more. *Hettie . . . Hettie Miller.* Jesus . . .'

'I didn't want to tell you –'

'I should pay for it.'

'You haven't the money, Dad.'

'I'll get the money!' Len said, suddenly irritated. 'I'll borrow it. You'll have your operation, Rose, but your father will pay for it. We don't need the likes of Hettie Miller.'

'You can't afford it and you're not borrowing it,' Rose said unshakeably. 'Hettie wants to help.'

He turned to look at his daughter, his voice sharp. 'Why?'

'She's got no one,' Rose answered him. 'She wants to feel good, that's what she said. She had all that money and no one to spend it on. She said that she and Mum were friends in the past –'

'Hah!'

'Weren't they?'

Len sighed. 'For a while, they were. For a while Hettie

154

was in love with my brother. But poor Eddie wasn't man enough for her. And Hettie got lonely . . .'

He drained his glass. How much was enough to tell Rose? How much should he confess? Or leave out?

'Was there . . . was there something between you two?' Rose asked timidly.

'She would have liked that,' Len replied, 'but I wasn't having it. I loved your mother and when I rejected Hettie she was cut up about it. She bad-mouthed me round town for a long time. Then Vera died – and Eddie followed,' he paused, the memory still smarting, 'and Hettie was suddenly alone. She wanted another family. *Mine.*'

'Oh . . .'

'She did care about you, Rose,' he said generously, 'but Hettie's caring is like being absorbed alive. She has to control in order to care. It's a kind of loving, I guess. But not my kind.' Slowly he began to roll a cigarette, but his fingers were shaking slightly and slivers of the baccy fell onto the pub floor. 'You should have told me, Rose –'

'I wanted to! But I was so afraid I'd hurt you, bring up the past –'

'Not about bloody Hettie!' Len snapped. 'About your eye. I never realised how much it upset you. I should have done; I should have thought about it. Your mother would have done. She would have sorted it out . . .'

Confused, Len trailed off. It was all getting a bit much for him. By now he had expected to be celebrating Rosie's entry into the business, but instead he was watching a despised rival making a better offer. One he couldn't match. His helplessness tore into him. That it should be Hettie who was being magnanimous! Her, of all people.

'Look, Dad, forget Hettie,' Rose assured him, worried by her father's response. 'You're right, we'll save up for the operation. It won't take too long –'

'Oh, come on!' Len said, unexpectedly angry with her. 'You and I both know that's bloody rubbish! You've an opportunity here, Rosie, take it. Take the bloody woman's money and get your eye fixed. You're a good-looking girl; you could be a real stunner.' He smiled awkwardly. 'I'll not stand in your way. Besides, it'll do that woman good to help someone. God knows, normally she only helps herself.'

'Are you sure you don't mind?'

'Oh, I mind,' Len replied truthfully, 'I mind that I don't have the cash to pay for it myself. I mind that it's her money. But I don't mind if it makes you happy.'

'Dad –'

'You have to promise me one thing, though, Rosie.'

'Anything.'

'Hettie might say she's doing it for kindness because she cared about you once. It might even be true, she might have changed. But from what I remember that woman always wanted her pound of flesh. I'm not going to prevent you getting a head start in life – God knows, everyone needs one sometime – but watch out for Hettie. Watch her, Rosie; be wary of her. Whatever she says ask yourself what she *really* means. Whatever she suggests, wonder *why* she's suggesting it. If I know her, she wants a toy – a pretend daughter. Fine. Let her fix your eye and buy you things. You might get a welcome lift up the ladder. Might meet some rich man that way. Might make a good marriage.'

Len's heart felt as though someone was dragging a needle across it. But he wasn't going to ruin his daughter's chances, wasn't going to say: I was so sure you'd want to be with me, work with me. I was certain you'd want the pitch I'd longed for so much. And the licence.

That tatty little piece of paper in its cheap holder. God, Len thought suddenly, why would she? Why *would* she?

'Dad?' Rose asked him, reaching for his hand and squeezing it. 'I won't do it if it causes any ill feeling between us.'

'There'll be no ill feeling,' he reassured her. 'Just don't let her take you away from me, will you? Don't let her turn your head and make you despise Gull Road – and me.'

Her eyes filling, Rose laid her head on her father's shoulder, her voice a whisper.

'I love you, Dad.'

'I love you too,' he said, staring ahead blankly. 'But I warn you, Rosie, if that woman ever hurts you – if she injures a hair on your head – I'll kill her. So help me God, I'll kill her.'

TWENTY-ONE

At five thirty the following day Rose left the ticket office at the Pavilion and caught a tram to Lytham St Annes. The last few minutes she walked. The snow had stopped falling and was lying crisp and pristine on the pavements. Fascinated, Rose walked a short way and then turned to see the single set of her footsteps behind her. There was little moon. Far off, the lights from the Tower glowed and a lonely car beeped its horn into the night.

Excitement was making her light-headed. *She was going to get her eye fixed.* After so long keeping her head down. It would be a miracle. Rose stared at her boots in the snow. Would the world look different afterwards? If she could face people, look them full in the eye, would she change? Would her future change?

She had been worried by her father's reaction, but relieved none the less. If the truth were known, Rose would have been crushed to lose her opportunity. Slowly she walked on. Then an unwelcome thought hit her. What if Hettie had changed her mind? After all, Rose had hardly been polite on her last visit, almost throwing Hettie's kindness in her face. But then again, if she was about to go back on the offer, would she have been in touch?

Reaching the drive of Heathcote Place, Rose found herself hurrying. Suddenly she was in a rush to get everything arranged. To see people's reactions when they saw her afterwards. To see Lester's response . . . Rose banished the thought. This was for her, not for Lester Williams.

A moment later Rose was shown into the drawing room. Hettie was talking to a gaunt man seated on the settee beside her.

'Oh, I'm sorry,' Rose began. 'I should have phoned first to see if it was all right to come –'

Smiling, Hettie rose to her feet. 'Not at all, dear. Mr Fallow is just leaving.'

Mr Fallow looked as though this was the first he had heard of it, but rose nevertheless. After they left the room, Rose could hear them talking in the hallway.

'May I call and see you later in the week?' he asked, his voice nasal.

'Of course, Cedric. You're welcome any time, you should know that by now.'

When Hettie finally walked back into the room she looked pleased with herself. Humming, she adjusted the cuffs of her silk dress and then smoothed her hair. It seemed – for an instant – that she had forgotten that Rose was there.

Then she rallied. 'So good to see you, Rose. I imagine you got my letter?'

'I'm sorry I dropped in unannounced –'

'Mr Fallow is an old friend of mine,' Hettie said, her tone light. 'Actually he's an admirer.'

Rose was startled by the confession, but said nothing.

'He's a widower, you know. And rich. We've known each other for years and I fancy Cedric's taken quite a shine to me.'

Uncertain of what to say, Rose remained silent. Had Hettie lost interest in her, now that the widower Fallow had such a part in her life? God, Rose thought uneasily, not now, don't back out now.

'A woman should always have admirers,' Hettie went on blithely. 'It keeps her young.'

Then she studied her visitor for a long moment. Was she

toying with her, Rose wondered anxiously, remembering what her father had said about Hettie's mean streak.

'I shall have the fire banked up,' Hettie went on, ringing for the housekeeper. 'I know you like to be warm.'

For another ten minutes Hettie talked about herself and the widower Fallow. In an agony of suspense Rose listened, but did not dare to turn the conversation around to herself. Then finally, as the fire crackled into life, Hettie broached the subject.

'So, have you made your decision?'

'I want the operation,' Rose blurted out, adding hurriedly, 'I mean, yes, please. If you still mean it . . . I'd love to have my eye fixed.'

Hettie nodded. 'Fine.'

The atmosphere was odd, strained.

'I've told Dad.'

'Oh,' Hettie said simply. 'How did he take it?'

'He wants me to have it done.'

'But sent no thanks to me?' Hettie queried, answering herself. 'Of course not, he's a proud man. A poor one, but proud.'

Stung, Rose began to dislike Hettie for the first time.

'He can't help being poor. It's not because he hasn't worked hard all his life.'

'Oh, listen to you!' Hettie replied, laughing. 'How you defend him! I wasn't criticising your father, dear. I was just making a comment, stating a fact.'

'Anyway, I've been thinking,' Rose went on, 'I could pay you back for the operation. In time.'

'I suppose your father suggested that?'

Len had, that morning, after he had spent a sleepless night thinking about Hettie's unwelcome interest in his daughter's life.

'We *both* think it's a good idea,' Rose answered firmly. 'I can't just accept your help without offering to repay you. It wouldn't be fair.'

This was not what Hettie wanted. How could she have control when she wasn't *in control*? No, she needed to make sure that Rose (and indirectly Len) were in debt to her. This wasn't to be a loan, but a magnificent gesture. Something that would tie Rose to her for ever. Not a business transaction, but an emotional one.

Hettie regarded her surrogate daughter carefully, then she sat down beside Rose on the settee. Her perfume was subtle, but sensual, stirring some far-distant memory.

'Don't let's talk about this being a loan. It's absurd! I've told you, I've plenty of money and I don't want you to insult me by offering to pay me back.'

'I didn't mean to insult you,' Rose said, mortified.

'Sometimes in life we have to learn to accept things graciously,' Hettie went on, her tone lightening. Really, Rose had a lot to learn. 'Anyway, no more talk about money. We'll have to organise your operation now. That's the important thing. I'll take you to see Mr Walker –'

'Mr Walker?'

'The surgeon,' Hettie explained, getting into her stride. 'The one I mentioned on Rodney Street. They do say he's the best in the North. It will take a while, you know – a week in hospital –'

'*A week!*' Rose was shaken.

'Of course. Didn't you realise that it was an important operation, dear? You'll have to lie very still and quiet for a while, hardly moving your head after you've had your surgery.'

Rose swallowed. In her eagerness to have it done, she had never thought about the minutiae of the procedure.

'But I thought it would just be simple.'

'Not at all!' Hettie replied, delighted to show off her superior knowledge. 'You'll have to have a general anaesthetic to knock you out, then they'll correct the squint, and then you have to recover, whilst your eyes are bandaged.' She assumed a soothing tone. 'Mr Walker says that there will be *some* pain, but he'll do his best to keep it to a minimum.'

Hospital, pain . . .

'You looked shocked, Rose. Didn't you realise what it entailed?'

'I never really thought about it.'

'Well, you have to think about it now. You have to prepare yourself.'

'Can I recover at home?'

'Not for the first week. You have to stay in hospital. But after that you can finish your convalescence at home.' Hettie was relieved to have clarified that point. She didn't want to act as nurse, only as benefactor. Besides, if Len was such a good father he could look after his daughter perfectly well on his own. 'It will be worth it, Rose. If there *is* some pain, so what? Think of the outcome, of the change it will make to your life.'

Rose was thinking about *just* that.

'I'll have to take time off work –'

'So take time off!' Hettie said imperiously. 'It's not much of a job anyway.'

Rose bristled. 'I like it at the Pavilion. I get to see people and to watch Gilbert perform. Anyway, I probably won't be there much longer. I want to work more at the races, now that Dad's got his pitch.'

Raising her eyebrows, Hettie's expression became glacial. 'Rose, my dear, you must be joking. I mean, you don't really want a career – what woman with any sense does? And certainly not on the race course.'

'But –'

'What we have to do is to find you something respectable until you get married.'

A clammy sensation overwhelmed Rose. Hadn't her father warned her that Hettie liked to take over people? Hadn't he also said that she never did anything for nothing? So how much was the operation *really* going to cost? And was it worth it?

'That young man you've got your eye on will be running after you soon,' Hettie said, picking her way into Rose's thoughts and manipulating her to perfection. The fact that Hettie had grander matches in mind for her protégée was something she would talk about later. For the present the lure of Lester Williams would serve her well. 'Imagine how surprised he'll be when he sees you . . .'

Rose had imagined it – many, many times.

'. . . We'll have to get you some new clothes and a new hairstyle too. You won't want all that fringe covering your eyes any more. Oh, think about it,' Hettie urged, her voice animated, kind. 'You'll have the world at your feet. A little judicious tweaking and we'll make a countess out of you.'

One part of Rose wanted to get up there and then and leave Hettie and Heathcote Place, turn her back on the manipulation, the subtle tightening of the ropes around her. But she didn't move. She didn't *want* to be controlled – but she didn't want to live in the shadows any longer. She didn't *want* to turn her back on the racing – but how much was she prepared to fight for it? And she didn't want to lose her freedom – but she wanted Lester more.

TWENTY-TWO

Standing at the back door, Len rolled a cigarette and smoked it greedily as Trudie sidled in at the back gate.

''Lo there, Mr Bradshaw. How's Rose?'

'All right – she's doing well in fact,' he said, his tone relieved.

'We've been talking about her all day,' Trudie went on.

Ruby's vast frame suddenly emerged at the gate.

''Lo there, Len. How's your girl?'

'Bearing up,' he replied, surprised at her interest. Then he remembered Trudie's accident and beckoned for the two women to come into the kitchen.

Still wearing her apron, Ruby pounded in, her impressive frame towering over the range. Beside her, Trudie looked round, then flopped into the rocking chair.

'I wanted to stop by and say hello to her,' Ruby went on, 'but I thought better of it. What with it being her operation today, it's a bit soon, I guess –'

'She'll be able to see people in a day or so,' Len replied, setting the kettle on to boil.

'Oh, don't bother with that,' Ruby said, drawing a couple of bottles of stout from out of her voluminous pockets. 'You need a drink when you've had a shock.'

Trudie's mouth fell open. '*You* haven't had a shock, Ma.'

'No, but you will have, when I knock you off that bloody

rocker!' Ruby snapped back, offering one of the bottles to Len. 'Here's to your girl –'

'What about me?' Trudie wailed. 'Don't I get a drink?'

'I could only sneak two out, or your father would have seen,' Ruby replied, easing herself onto the battered kitchen sofa. 'All the street's talking about the operation, Len. And fancy it being Hettie coming up trumps?' After wiping the top of the bottle with her apron, she sipped her beer lustily. 'Ah, that's good. Alfred won't miss a couple of bottles.'

'How is he?'

'In bed.'

'Ill?'

'Idle.'

Thoughtfully, Len downed more of the beer, Trudie watching both of them.

'I could ring the hospital again.'

'It's late, Len: better leave it until morning,' Ruby replied evenly. 'I've a meat pie back home, still warm. You're welcome to it, Len.' She turned to her daughter. 'Oi, Trudie, go and get that pie – and be quick about it.'

Moaning, Trudie left for Sea View, leaving Ruby watching Len carefully.

'Your kid will be all right. She's a fighter, is Rose.'

'I know, Ruby,' Len replied, touched by her concern. 'Thanks.'

'I've a soft spot for Rose.'

'Me too.'

'And the operation went well?'

'Couldn't have gone better, Mr Walker said.'

'So why the long face?'

Len smiled to himself. Ruby was no fool. 'I'm pleased for Rosie, don't get me wrong –'

'But miffed that it was Hettie who forked out the cash?'

He nodded, ashamed of himself. 'It went hard with me.'

'But you had the guts not to let it stand in Rose's way,' Ruby said, 'and that's the important thing.'

Still looking out of the kitchen window towards Sea View, Len spotted Trudie returning, holding the pie. His voice wavered.

'You're a good friend, Ruby Williams.'

'I am that,' she replied, 'but you can come away from that window now, and stop ogling my bloody hotel!'

Len wasn't the only member of the Bradshaw family to like a smoke. Carefully rolling her own cigarette, Clovis relished the first puff.

'That's good.'

Nan Wilmslow said nothing, just waved the pungent smoke away with her hand.

'I've been wondering what our Rose will look like, now her eye's fixed,' Clovis went on. 'She's coming home tomorrow, and the bandages come off next week.'

'Right.'

'I'm glad we went to visit her, Nan, but I shouldn't have taken those magazines of mine. Bit stupid that, when she can't see,' Clovis went on, thinking of the body on the hospital bed.

She had never seen Rose so still, both her eyes covered with bandages, for some reason, her voice quiet. Fragile, delicate, her head never moving as though she was frightened to do anything to spoil the operation. Nan had gone with Clovis, saying nothing, but rubbing Rose's hands with some pungent, transparent lotion. It had smelled soothing in amongst the hospital disinfectant.

'She looked scared.'

'Nah,' Nan replied.

'She did! She looked worried, like she was afraid of it not working.'

'It'll work,' Nan replied simply.

'That doctor was a tartar,' Clovis went on, 'and that

sister on the ward! Must be difficult, lying there, and not know what's going on around you. Just being able to hear, and do nothing.'

Nan didn't answer, just kept looking straight ahead.

'And fancy Alfred Williams turning up, going on about how he'd been in hospital seven times,' she snorted. '*Seven times for brain surgery!* Hah! They'd have to find it first.'

Inhaling on her cigarette again, Clovis turned her gaze towards a roll of lino standing in the corner.

'Nice bit of stuff, that. I might give it to Rose, for a homecoming present. There's nothing like a bit of lino to lift the spirits.'

It had been hard for her to be so dependent on other people, Rose thought, grateful to be back in her own bed at Gull Road. God, how the days had dragged and there had been so much pain. No one had prepared her for the pain. They had mentioned it, but when she came round after the anaesthetic her eye had felt as though it had been burned with acid.

Mr Walker had told her all about how they had adjusted the muscles in her eye and stitched them in place, the squint repaired. Repaired, Rose had thought, was it really? Was it really? So many times she had wanted to take a look, but hadn't dared; hadn't even risked moving, except when she had to. And the indignity of being helped onto a bedpan! And of being blind, both eyes bandaged at first. What was that all about?

But she hadn't complained. How could she? She had got her wish, all she had to do now was wait. Things had improved when they had taken the bandages off her good eye. Suddenly she wasn't so isolated, and greedy to take in anything she could see. Like visitors. Hettie came, always alone. Then there was Alfred and his balmy stories, Trudie and her mother with cakes, Gilbert doing a monologue of Noël Coward's. And Joe, making her laugh when she was trying to keep her head still. But no Lester. He sent a card instead, which Trudie read out.

It had been difficult, but Rose had tried not to brood on his absence. Instead she stuck to her surgeon's instructions meticulously. Never grumbling at the endless rounds of drops, the quick blurred flash of light before her eye was bandaged again. They told her not to touch her eye; she didn't. They told her not to get up quickly; she didn't. In fact, if they had told Rose to lie with her head in a bucket of ice, she would have. There wasn't going to be *any* reason for this operation to fail. When the bandages came off Rose Bradshaw would be another person, someone to be reckoned with. Someone beautiful.

And then Lester would come calling. He would, wouldn't he . . . ? Rose sighed to herself, then checked her emotions. Stay still, she willed herself, only two days left and then the bandages come off. Hettie had made arrangements for that too. Rose would be collected and taken back to the hospital with Len, and then Mr Walker would review his handiwork. What Hettie *hadn't* said was whether or not she would be there at the critical moment.

Len hadn't mentioned it, and neither had Rose. Whether her father and Hettie met or not, it didn't matter to her. This wasn't going to be their day. It was going to be *hers*. The day Rose Bradshaw had longed for, dreamed of, waited for. The day that would determine the rest of her life.

And there were only forty-eight hours to go.

PART THREE

From birth to eighteen a girl needs good parents.
From eighteen to thirty-five, she needs good looks.

Sophie Tucker 1884–1966

O that 'twere possible
After long grief and pain
To find the arms of my true love
Round me once again!

Maud
Alfred, Lord Tennyson 1809–1892

There's a problem. The judge is leaning forward, talking to the clerk of the court. I can hear the murmur of his voice, but not what he says.

Get on with it, I want to shout, but don't. There's no point hurrying now. There was, once. But no longer. If I look to my right there's a painting hanging just beside the window. An indifferent portrait of someone dead and gone. Someone who had family once, and a story. But not like mine. If it was, he wouldn't be on display here. Tucked away instead, where they put our kind.

And still it rains. I want the verdict, but there's a problem. I think I already told you that. Maybe the judge is deaf; maybe there's a mistake somewhere. And now I'm thinking the trial will be stopped. No verdict, no sentence, no punishment.

A woman coughs, my head turning towards her. She looks at me, and although she's embarrassed, she holds my gaze. Will she tell her children, and their children, that once she looked a murderer in the face?

I never wanted to be famous.

TWENTY-THREE

Before Ruby had walked far a quick shower forced her to take shelter in the doorway of Charles Harding & Sons, Estate Agents. Sighing impatiently, she glanced at the photographs in the window. So they were selling freehold houses for £495, were they? Robbing bastards.

The shower passed as suddenly as it had begun, Ruby humming to herself as she continued her walk. The weather had been sultry, April arriving in a froth of blossom, the Promenade cluttered with trippers. And all her rooms taken. It felt good, Ruby decided, to have a successful business.

Not that she was the only one. Len had come on in leaps and bounds in the short time he had had his licence. Even his walk had altered, a confident, quick step replacing his previous measured gait. That was what confidence did for you, Ruby decided, her thoughts skipping at once to Gilbert.

Her brother was worrying her. Oh, he was doing well enough at the Pavilion, and was booked for the summer season, but there was something about Gilbert's manner that made her uneasy. Maybe he was tired. Hadn't she told him often enough to take a break? But Gilbert wouldn't hear about it.

Finally turning into Gull Road, Ruby walked into Sea View and continued, uninterrupted, into the kitchen. Her guests were all out for the day, no dinners to make until later. Hotel policy. And God help anyone who came back early.

'Hello there,' she said, spotting Gilbert. 'I didn't think we'd see you until tonight.'

He turned to look at her, his face puffy, his eyes wiped of emotion.

'Bloody hell! You look a sketch,' Ruby said shortly. 'You taking on too much?'

'I have to take the parts when they're there. Otherwise God knows when they'll come again,' he said, dropping down onto the sofa, next to Alfred.

'When I was an actor –'

'You never acted, Alfred,' Gilbert replied, sighing.

'I bloody did! I were courted by Hollywood. Cecil B. de Ville –'

Gilbert winced. '*Mille*. It's Cecil B. *de Mille*.'

'Not in them days, it weren't,' Alfred replied, warming up. 'When I were younger I was quite handsome. You ask your sister, she'll tell you.'

Ruby pulled a face. 'You always looked like a model for coffin handles, Alfred –'

'Hey, now!' he replied, folding his hands over his paunch. 'My good looks faded when I got fat. Before that, I was a masher.'

Gilbert had heard it all before, and wasn't in the mood to listen to it again. Thoughtful, he pulled off his jacket, eased off his shoes and then loosened the collar of his shirt. A flicker of light caught Ruby's attention.

'What's that round your neck?'

Flushing, Gilbert tried to hide the gold chain. 'Nothing . . .'

'It is!' she persisted, pulling back his collar to look. 'You're wearing jewellery, Gilbert!'

Discomforted, he got to his feet, snatching up his jacket and shoes and making for the door.

'You don't miss anything, do you? Not a thing! You want to mind your own business, Ruby. People like to live their own lives without being spied on.'

With that he left, banging the door closed behind him.

'Hell fire,' Alfred said simply.

Ruby glanced over to her husband. 'Have you noticed anything different about Gilbert lately?'

'Like what?'

'I dunno. Anything.'

Alfred considered the matter carefully. Ruby never usually asked his opinion on anything.

'Is he taller?'

'Taller!' Ruby roared. 'What the hell are you talking about? Gilbert's pushing fifty; people don't keep growing after childhood –'

'I heard about a man who grew a foot a year.'

'Yeah, probably the same bloke who puts the lights on the top of the bloody Tower without a ladder!' Ruby replied, walking out and making for Gilbert's room.

She was about to knock when she heard a sound inside. Carefully, Ruby opened the door a couple of inches and looked in. Gilbert had his back turned to her, his arms wrapped around himself as he rocked, rhythmically, back and forwards.

And cried.

Having wondered about it for some time, Hettie took the bull by the horns. She had no reason to be afraid of calling at Gull Road to see Rose. After all, she was just visiting her protégée. Coming to call on the young woman she had taken under her wing. It was a reasonable thing to do. Anyone could see that.

The trouble was that Hettie decided to arrive in style, her chauffeur-driven car pulling up outside number 139, a bevy of onlookers suddenly drawn to watch. At number 111, Nan Wilmslow was looking out of her window, immobile; Clovis staring avidly from number 117. As for Sea View – from there, Trudie could hardly believe her eyes.

'Hey, Ma, look at this!'

'You've got work to do, Trudie,' Ruby replied. 'Get on with it.'

'But –'

'Trudie!'

'Ma,' she persisted, 'it's the Widow Miller.'

Ruby was by the window in an instant. 'God, look at that bloody car,' she said longingly.

'Look at the driver –'

'*Chauffeur*,' Ruby corrected her. 'He's called a chauffeur.'

'I don't care what he's called, he's handsome,' Trudie replied, staring hungrily.

But Ruby wasn't interested in the hired help. Instead her gaze fixed on the woman who was just getting out of the car.

'Hettie Miller!' she said flatly. 'I remember her when she bought her dresses from the Co-op, and glad she was to have them. Now look at her! Those shoes must have cost some poor sod a week's wage.'

'She's loaded, she doesn't care,' Trudie replied, agog. 'I thought the Widow Miller would be older, but she's still quite good-looking.'

'Not having to work keeps you young,' Ruby countered. 'And that woman's never worked for decades. Not since she lived in Gull Road.'

Aware of the attention she was causing, Hettie smiled and then waved at the onlookers.

'Hellfire, she thinks she's the bloody Queen!' Ruby snapped, opening the window and calling out: 'Oi, Hettie! Still fancy some pig's trotters?'

Flushing, Hettie turned away. Then she hurried up to the Bradshaws' door and knocked. A long, agonising moment passed before it was opened.

'Hettie,' Len said, his tone guarded.

She smiled awkwardly: embarrassed at seeing him again and mortified by the laughter coming from behind her.

'Oh, hello, Len. I came to visit Rose, see how the patient's doing. Soon be time for the unveiling.'

Silently, Len stepped back to let her enter.

God, what a hole, Hettie thought as she moved into the Bradshaws' kitchen. But then she had lived in a similar place. Once. When she was married to Eddie. The thought shuddered inside her as she looked round, spotting the paper opened at the racing pages and Len's chipped, white enamel mug.

'How's Rose?'

'A bit impatient,' Len replied cautiously, studying Hettie. She had some nerve, calling in out of the blue, he thought. But then again, how like her to catch him off guard. 'Tomorrow's the big day.'

Hettie smiled her professional smile. 'It certainly is. Tomorrow Mr Walker will finally take off the bandages. It's so thrilling.' She rapped on the window and motioned to her chauffeur. A few moments later he came to the door carrying a batch of parcels.

'What are those?' Len asked, his tone suspicious.

'A few things for Rose. I thought she'd like something pretty to wear tomorrow, so everyone can see her look her best for her re-emergence,' Hettie smiled. Excited, spiteful. 'I mean, having this surgery has been so important to Rose. Something she's waited all her life for.'

He wanted at that moment to grab Hettie by the throat and choke her. Wanted to see her eyes bulge and her clever composure destroyed. It wasn't enough that she had paid for Rose's surgery, now she had come laden with gifts too. Just to underline – publicly – her generosity. And his inadequacy.

'You've done enough for Rose –'

'Nonsense!' Hettie replied dismissively. 'Is she upstairs?'

Len wanted to throw her out into the street. But he couldn't. So instead he nodded, jerking his head to the stairwell.

'She's in bed.'

'Well then, time for a little visit,' Hettie replied, turning and holding Len's look for an instant.

Malicious triumph registered in her blue eyes. Victory. A look that said: see what it's like to feel uncomfortable, Len? So Hettie *hadn't* forgotten the past, he realised. She had remembered his rejection only too well. And had never forgiven him for it.

Without replying, he watched her mount the narrow stairs, the chauffeur following awkwardly with the packages. Embittered, Len walked into the kitchen and took in a deep breath to steady his rage. It was worth it for Rose, he told himself. Worth it for her that he was being made to feel small. And only because his daughter was benefiting would he allow Hettie to rub his nose in it . . . But if the time ever came when business was just between the two of them it would be different.

Enjoy your triumph while it lasts, he thought dourly. Because one day it'll be my turn.

TWENTY-FOUR

What Hettie hadn't counted on was that the following afternoon Rose wanted her father to be with her. She was very grateful for Hettie to take her to Mr Walker's consulting rooms on Rodney Street: but when it came to the moment when the bandages were due to be removed, Rose rejected Hettie and chose Len instead.

'You don't mind if Dad goes in with me, do you?' she asked.

Hettie shot Len a savage look before replying, 'Of course not, dear. Whatever makes you comfortable.'

'It's just that –'

'It's fine,' Hettie interrupted, her voice borderline shrill. 'Honestly, Rose, it's fine.'

Biting her lip, Hettie then watched as Len walked with his daughter into Mr Walker's consulting rooms. Really, she thought to herself, what a nerve! After all she'd done, Rose should have asked *her*. Never mind, Hettie consoled herself, Len could have his moment of victory. God knows, it would be short-lived. Everyone knew who had paid for the operation.

Still smarting, Hettie stared at Mr Walker's closed door. It was infuriating to be shut out, she thought self-pityingly. Didn't anyone realise how hurtful it was? If Len had had any breeding at all he would have stood back – but what could you expect from a peasant?

She had to admit that Rose looked wonderful in the pale blue suit she had bought her. And who knew the girl had such good legs until they were shown off in silk stockings? Obviously Len had never shown any interest in his daughter's appearance. And as for Rose's skin . . . Hettie felt a quick flicker of envy. It was fine skin, the kind that would burn in the sun, but fine nevertheless.

But then Rose's transformation had been only partially completed. The rest would have to wait until the bandages were removed. Hettie glanced at her watch: three fifteen . . . She would organise Rose and then make sure she, Hettie, was back in Lytham for six o'clock. After all, Cedric Fallow was calling by tonight.

Mollified, Hettie smiled to herself. Cedric was unattractive, with his nasal whine and long, bony body, but he was well off and obviously lonely. And – as everyone knew – Hettie was like catnip to widowers. Oh yes, Cedric needed moulding into husband material. It was for his own good, in fact. Hettie rested her eyes for a moment: soon her whole life would change, she thought contentedly. She had been crazy, thinking she didn't want to marry again! A husband and a daughter would be a delight. What a lot to think about again. Two people to look after, cultivate, improve, control.

She was only being generous, after all. Because whether he realised it or not, Cedric needed her – and Rose, well, the poor girl would have been a dead loss if Hettie hadn't taken her in hand. Opening her eyes, Hettie stared at the consulting-room door impatiently. What *was* keeping them? Good God, suppose something had gone wrong? What if the surgery hadn't worked? What if Rose's eye was now worse? The thought made Hettie clammy with unease. It would be ghastly, unthinkable.

It would be such a waste of effort. And money.

Inside Mr Walker's consulting rooms Rose sat very still in the overstuffed leather chair. Her heart was slamming against her ribcage, her mouth ash dry. Slowly the nurse unwound the first bandages, Mr Walker then taking off the eye pad.

'Miss Bradshaw, open your eyes now.'

Rose couldn't. Wouldn't.

'Miss Bradshaw, open your eyes.'

She was sure that she would faint, her breathing was so short. Then suddenly Rose felt her father take her hand and squeeze it.

'Come on, luv, open your eyes.'

Slowly, nervously, Rose opened her eyes a fraction. She had already seen her new clothes with her good eye – but now light poured into her repaired eye and made her wince. She couldn't see through it! The operation hadn't worked!

'Slowly, take it easy,' Mr Walker said. 'Now, look at me.'

Gradually Rose opened her eyes again and gingerly looked ahead. The light was overwhelming – but then suddenly the world was in focus, Mr Walker's navy suit looming in front of her as she stared ahead. Carefully, he then inserted some drops into her corrected eye and examined it with an ophthalmoscope.

'Fine . . . Oh, hold on a minute.'

Rose could hardly breathe. 'Is it all right?'

'Miss Bradshaw –'

Her legs hardly able to hold her upright, Rose struggled to her feet, Len holding on to her arm to steady her. Slowly, Rose walked towards the mirror and then paused, looking down.

'I can't, Dad.'

Frowning, Len tipped up her chin and studied her face. 'Oh, luv . . .'

'What is it?' she asked, panic-stricken when she saw her father's eyes fill with tears. 'Oh God, what is it?'

'Look,' Len said simply, turning her face to the mirror. 'Just look.'

And she did. For the first time in her life Rose Bradshaw

looked herself full in the face. Her eyes were perfect, no sign of a squint, her whole face and expression changed. Greedily, Rose studied her forehead, her eyebrows, her mouth, then her gaze moved back to her eyes. She had never noticed the slight uptilt at the corners before, or her dark lashes. For a lifetime she had avoided mirrors, ducked away from scrutiny, hidden behind hair, behind people.

But no more . . . Mesmerised, Rose examined herself. Was this her? Was this Rose Bradshaw? Behind her, she could see her father's reflection in the mirror and winked at him. Look at me, Dad, she wanted to shout, this is me. This is *really* me.

'Are you happy?' Mr Walker asked.

'*Happy?*' Rose repeated, beginning to laugh. 'Yes, I'm happy. And I'm pretty! Bloody hell, I'm *pretty*!'

TWENTY-FIVE

As Ruby said, they were both as daft as each other, so it was bound to work. Ruby watched as, sitting beside Joe in the kitchen, Maisie fed him the last of her scone. Like two babes in the wood, Ruby thought. Let's hope the world doesn't eat them up alive. Especially now, when times were getting a bit hard. 'The Depression', the papers were calling it, talking about the leagues of men round the North-West all looking helplessly for work. Which wasn't there. Not now that so many industries had folded. Men who thought they had jobs for life in the mills and factories were suddenly aimless, unhired, unwanted. Desperate.

In Blackpool it wasn't so bad. People always tried to get a holiday, or even a day away to escape the harsh reality of the northern towns. But for how long would the holiday trade be exempt? Ruby sighed: no point crying before you're hurt.

'So, you two,' she said, looking from her son to Maisie, 'what did you think of number ninety-nine?'

Reluctantly, Joe glanced away from Maisie. 'We went this morning –'

'And?'

'It's small and cold. A bit damp too.'

'Nothing that can't be fixed,' Ruby replied matter-of-factly. 'You should have seen this place when your father and I first came here. Water running down the walls in the back.'

'I thought yellow,' Maisie said suddenly.

'Yellow what?'

'Yellow walls in the front room, Mrs Williams.'

Joe beamed. Yellow walls were an inspiration. 'And yellow curtains?'

'It'd be like living inside an egg,' Ruby replied, secretly laughing to herself. 'Mind you, I think I've got some yellow odds and sods put away. You'd be welcome to have them. But aren't you both jumping the gun a bit? I mean, you're not even married yet.'

'We soon will be,' Joe reminded her. 'Only a month to go and Maisie will be Mrs Williams.'

'You better call me Ruby then, or they'll be no end of confusion. Or you could call me Ma.'

Maisie's pale blue eyes widened. She had a ma, and she wasn't a bit like Ruby.

'I could call you Mother, if that would be all right,' she suggested timidly.

'Mother's fine,' Ruby replied, pulling down two vast pans from the top of the range and setting some water on to boil. 'You told Lester?'

Joe nodded. 'Told him last night; he was made up. Said that I'd made a good choice. I told him he should be thinking about getting married himself.'

'Oh, Lester won't marry for a long while,' Ruby replied, beginning to cut up some vegetables. 'Can you cook, Maisie?'

The girl seemed baffled by the idea. 'Well . . .'

'I can cook,' Joe interrupted. 'Maisie can keep house.'

'You'll be working, Joe. Maisie will have to learn how to put a meal on the table for when you get home of a night.' She turned to her future daughter-in-law. 'And you'll need to get your wedding dress.'

'I can make do with something I've already got,' Maisie

replied, unusually practical. 'Ma and Dad haven't got that much money and I don't mind.'

'I could have a word with Clovis,' Ruby suggested tentatively. 'At the last count she had three wedding dresses in her hoard.'

'They'd be second-hand,' Joe answered his mother, aghast.

'Yeah, they would, but they'd save you both a lot of money. Money you could put to better use – like buying yellow paint.' Ruby's attention was suddenly caught by the sight of Len entering the house opposite. 'Now that's something I *can't* wait to see!'

With an effort, Joe dragged his attention away from his fiancée again. 'What?'

'Rose – now she's had her eye done. Today was the big day. Hettie Miller drove them back from Liverpool. I couldn't get a look at Rose, though. Len was hurrying her into the house as though he was hiding the Crown Jewels.'

Kneeling on the sofa and looking out of the window, Maisie sighed. 'I wonder what she'll look like now?'

'Whatever she looks like,' Joe replied lovingly, 'she'll never match my girl.'

The following morning was warm, the sky faultlessly blue. Having got herself dressed in her new clothes, applied a little make-up and brushed her hair away from her face, Rose walked to the top of the stairs. And froze.

'Dad!'

Hurrying out of the sitting room, Len looked up anxiously. 'What is it?'

'I can't.'

'Can't what?' he asked frowning.

'I can't face anyone.'

'Oh, for God's sake!' he laughed. 'Get yourself down here, girl. It's a perfect day and I'm taking my daughter out.'

185

It should have been the easiest thing in the world, but for once Rose was nervous at leaving the house. Having been hidden away for a while, her courage was failing her. What would people think? She knew she looked amazing, but what if that was just in her imagination? What if there was no real change? If she was still Rose Bradshaw, the runt with the squint?

Slowly she came down the stairs towards her father.

Len shook his head in disbelief. 'I never knew I had a beauty for a daughter,' he said, quiet with pride as he offered her his arm. He could feel her shaking, and squeezed her hand quickly. 'Come on, luv, time to let the world see you.'

As Len and Rose Bradshaw left their house, Maisie called to Ruby and Joe so that they could watch. In complete disbelief Ruby took in the silk stockings, the expensive suit, the thick, styled hair, and then her eyes fixed on Rose's face. The girl who had stared out from her window opposite for so many years had gone. A striking, groomed woman stood in her place, looking out at the world with a beauty's grace.

'Oh, bloody hell!' Ruby exclaimed, snatching open her front door and running across the street. 'My God, Rose Bradshaw, you're a wonder.'

Flushing, Rose smiled. Joe and Maisie were following behind Ruby, who was now standing staring at the vision.

'God, Rose, you're a cracker!' Joe turned back to Maisie quickly. 'And you, luv, of course.'

Maisie giggled happily, looking at Rose's clothes. 'You look like something off the films.' She moved closer, studying Rose's face with guileless curiosity. 'Oh, you're so pretty now!'

'I bet Lester will think so,' Joe said mischievously.

Ruby threw him a warning look.

'What did I say?' he pleaded, as his mother turned away from him and looked Rose up and down.

'I would never have believed it, but you're a wonder now. You've lovely eyes. No bugger noticed before, though, did they?' She turned to Len. 'You must be made up to see her like this.'

He was glowing. Even getting George Ogden's licence wasn't this good. The fact that Len hadn't been able to afford the operation was a niggling thought he suppressed fiercely. Who cared whose money it had been? It had made his girl.

'You two going out?'

Len nodded eagerly. 'We sure are, Ruby. Off for a walk down the Promenade,' he smiled, mock-grand. 'I feel that Blackpool should have the benefit of seeing a *real* beauty around these parts –'

'Oh, Dad!'

'He's right,' Ruby replied. 'You've hidden away too long, Rose. It's your day in the sun. Make the most of it.'

Surrounded by her gaggle of admirers, Rose was still smiling when she noticed a car pull up opposite, in front of Sea View. Her heart beating thunderously, she watched the driver's door open and Lester get out. He was preoccupied – looking for his keys for several moments – before he finally glanced over.

For an instant he didn't recognise Rose. He merely felt a jolt of attraction for the woman in the pale blue suit, who was regarding him levelly. Then, incredulously, Lester recognised *Rose Bradshaw*. His sister's best pal, the girl across the street, the runty, little funny face he'd thought of as a kid. This was the girl he had seen every day, every month, every year, for a lifetime. The girl he had sometimes been offhand with, the girl he had never taken seriously. The same girl who – only recently – had kissed him and embarrassed him: made him squirm at the memory.

The girl who had been a beauty in disguise.

And as Lester looked at her then he saw Rose Bradshaw

for the first time. Not as a child, or a surrogate sister. But as a full-blown glamorous woman.

And in that instant realised the opportunity he had missed.

TWENTY-SIX

Four days later Gilbert was outside the Golden Bear pub, drunk, his clothes dishevelled. Luckily, it was Nan Wilmslow – of all people – who found him and helped him home. Quite what Nan was doing out and about past eleven at night no one asked: Nan was a law unto herself. But as for Gilbert – Gilbert hadn't been drunk in years – or certainly not drunk enough to be lying in his vomit outside a pub.

Having knocked loudly on the back door of Sea View, Nan could hear a window being thrown open on the top floor. Ruby's head poked out, her hair in rags.

'If that's a guest, let yourself in with a key! And don't bang the door, it makes the dog go mad.'

As she said it Chase leaped to his feet in the kitchen and began to bark, throwing himself rhythmically against the back door.

'It's me – Nan!' the old lady hissed up at the window.

Ruby hurried downstairs just as a guest came out of the first-floor bathroom.

'Oh, hello, Mrs Williams,' a flustered Mrs Brown squeaked, surprised by the giant in curling rags. 'Is everything all right?'

'Nothing to worry about. But you could turn that radio down a bit, if you don't mind,' Ruby replied haughtily, descending the next flight two steps at a time. Finally she snatched open the back door to find the town's most unlikely couple weaving in an inebriated embrace.

The dog moved even faster than Ruby. Seeing his opportunity, Chase leaped up and grabbed hold of Gilbert's arm.

'Oh, leave off!' Ruby snapped, sending the dog flying and then heaving her brother into the kitchen.

'What a stink!' she snorted, regarding Gilbert with horror. 'You've sicked up all over yourself.'

Hardly visible under Gilbert's other arm, Nan murmured simply: 'The Golden Bear.'

The three words explained everything. Hauling her brother onto the kitchen sofa, Ruby looked down at Gilbert's diminutive rescuer.

'You must be stronger than you look, Nan. Thanks for bringing him home.'

She nodded in reply. Enough words had been said for a week.

'He's drunk,' Ruby said, stating the obvious. 'Pig!' Her head moved closer towards Gilbert, her eyes widening. 'Is he wearing make-up?'

'Actor.'

'I know he's a bloody actor, Nan! But he never goes out in make-up – he usually washes it off after a show.' Ruby paused, smacking the dog round the head when it snarled again, then shaking her brother: 'Gilbert, wake up. Gilbert, wake up!'

But he was dead to the world, snoring peacefully. Sighing, Ruby crossed to the range and put on the kettle.

'Have a cuppa with me, Nan?'

She nodded.

'I don't suppose a lot gets past you, does it?' Ruby went on as she set out the cups. Above their heads they could hear a cistern emptying, one of the guests making a late call to the lavatory. 'About Gilbert – I don't have to spell it out for you, do I?'

By way of reply, Nan shook her head.

'Good. Well, between you and me, lately I've been worried about my brother. You know what I mean – there was that man in Abingdon Street who got three years in Strangeways for . . . messing about. I don't want the same for Gilbert.' She sipped at her tea, watching Nan over the rim of the cup. 'People don't have much truck with anyone different, do they?'

Nan met Ruby's gaze steadily, but she said nothing.

'Folk are scared of anyone out of the ordinary. My family were, and Alfred's too stupid to understand or he'd have acted different with Gilbert long enough since. As for me, well, maybe I should be disgusted, but I've lived too long for that. All I know is that Gilbert's been lonely all his life. If that's the price you have to pay for being queer, it seems a lot to ask of anyone.' She paused, wondering. 'I don't suppose – what with you knowing all about herbs and things – I don't suppose there's anything we could give Gilbert?'

Nan shook her head.

'No, I thought not,' Ruby replied, sadly. 'It was silly to ask. I just wondered . . . Loneliness is a wicked thing, Nan. And incurable.'

Apart from Cedric's nasal whine, his bony hands and irritatingly pompous manner, he would do. Oh yes, Hettie thought, he would do. Still enjoying her recent triumph with Rose, she was now hellbent on the next leg of her own personal marathon.

'Do tell me, how is your son these days?'

Cedric pulled a pained expression. 'Stuart's a worry to me, Hettie. He never seemed so bad before, but then maybe it's more difficult for him now, with my being on my own.'

'Oh, I do so understand. If his mother had still been alive . . .' Hettie let the inference hang. The influence of a woman was not to be sniffed at and it would be in her favour if Cedric realised that. Fast. 'Still, Stuart's taken over your practice; inherited your empire. You must be very pleased to have him follow in your footsteps.'

'Stuart's a good dentist,' Cedric admitted, 'but a little high-spirited.'

He could afford to be – on a big wage, with a Jaguar in the garage and no money worries. No wife either . . . A plan began to form in Hettie's mind. Why hadn't she thought about it earlier! Really, it was so obvious. *Stuart and Rose*. In time Rose would become the younger Mrs Fallow, Hettie would have her new husband in Cedric – and her stand-in daughter even closer.

Passing Cedric some elaborate marzipan cake, Hettie smiled her most winningly. 'Perhaps Stuart has a girlfriend?'

'No one suitable.'

Pleased, she studied Cedric's good suit, polished shoes and expensive watch. His house on Lytham's sea front was old-fashioned, but grand. Big enough to house two couples. She could sell up her own property and put the money away – it never did for a woman to be without funds – then set up home with Cedric. The thought tingled deliciously against her ribcage.

'No nice, steady girl he's interested in?'

'No,' Cedric said dismally. 'Stuart is seeing some actress . . .' the word struck Hettie with all the force of a dinner gong, '. . . but she would not be the right wife for a dentist.' Cedric leaned towards Hettie, his tone confidential. 'He's nearly thirty, more than ready to settle down. I said so this morning, but Stuart just laughed.'

'Ah, the young,' Hettie said indulgently. 'What do they know about life?'

'Quite.'

'But I would have thought your son would value your judgement.'

Cedric's eyes found a spot on the ceiling and he sighed expansively. 'You understand – but he doesn't. I said to him, think of the name, the Fallow name. There have been

Fallows in Lytham for five generations. His mother was from Shropshire, but we don't talk about that . . .'

Hettie assumed a sympathetic expression.

'We Fallows have a reputation to uphold, I said.' Cedric's gaze left the ceiling and rested on Hettie. 'Do you know that the Fallow dental practice is the longest-established in the North-West? We've filled the teeth of the landed gentry, and even a film star – I name no names – but a gentleman of worldly status. Now, I ask you, that counts for something, doesn't it?'

God Lord, Hettie thought, what a windbag.

'It certainly does, Cedric.' She poured him another cup of tea and leaned towards him. 'Who was the actor?'

'My lips,' he said, his tone even more nasal, 'are sealed.'

'Not to me, *surely*?' Hettie gave him an imploring look. An admiring, imploring look. It had been a while, she thought, but she was in a class of her own when it came to men.

'I can't tell you. Honestly I can't,' Cedric insisted.

'Maybe . . .' Hettie paused, '. . . when we know each other a little better?'

He flushed with confused pleasure.

Honestly, Hettie thought, it was almost *too* easy. 'A little more cake, Cedric?'

'That would be lovely,' he replied, trying vainly to balance his cup, saucer and full plate.

Hettie had done it deliberately, of course. Smiling, she leaned forward to relieve him of his plate, her fingers brushing the back of his hand as she did so.

'Here, let me help you, Cedric.' She allowed her eyes to express her emotions. 'I would *always* help you. You know that, I hope.'

Cedric swallowed, the marzipan hop-scotching drily down his throat. 'My dear . . . oh, forgive me, Henrietta.'

She flushed on cue. 'Please, Cedric, it would be a honour to think that you thought of me as "your dear".'

A moment passed between them. Hettie was wondering how much longer had to pass before she could turf Cedric out and sit back to listen to the radio. There was going to be a jazz concert transmitted live from the Winter Gardens at seven, and she didn't want to miss it.

Meanwhile Cedric was working his way through his marzipan cake and wondering if Henrietta would like to go out for dinner. He could see that she was smitten by him; her every action made it obvious. It was in her manner, her eyes, her voice. Oh yes, Cedric thought, he might not be a young man but he could still turn a woman's head.

And then they both looked up, caught each other's eye, and smiled.

TWENTY-SEVEN

Gilbert woke with a hangover, rolling over in bed and thinking for an instant that he might throw up. The nausea lifted slowly – then someone banged the front door below, Chase barking insanely. Opening one puffy eye, Gilbert looked at the clock. How in the name of God was he going to get on stage tonight, he wondered, relieved that there was no afternoon matinée that day. He should never have got drunk; he couldn't hold his booze, never could.

A knock on his bedroom door made him wince, Trudie walking in and passing him a concoction in a tall glass.

'What is it?' he whispered.

'From Nan Wilmslow,' she replied, looking at it suspiciously. 'She says it'll either cure you, or blow your arse off.'

Gilbert moaned, then drank the emulsion in one gulp. It slid down his throat like a greased eel.

'So, what happened?'

'When?'

'Aw, come on,' Trudie admonished him. 'Last night.'

'I don't want to talk about it.'

'You've still got your stage make-up on,' Trudie told her uncle, walking to the window. 'And you're not the only one who's suddenly all tarted up.'

Gilbert struggled to sit up in bed. He was relieved that Trudie was talking about something else. And curious too.

'What are you going on about?'

'Rose,' Trudie replied, biting the corner of her index finger and staring across the street. 'You should see her, all done up –'

Gilbert was suddenly galvanised. 'How does she look?'

'Different.'

He caught the spite in Trudie's voice and winced. So the operation had been a success, had it? Perhaps *too* much of a success. Trudie had always been the looker before, not poor Rose. But now, suddenly, the tables appeared to have been turned.

'Is she pretty?'

'Dressed up like a dog's dinner, covered in make-up, her hair all done –'

'Trudie, is she *pretty* now?'

'In a flashy way.'

'Oh, come on!' Gilbert admonished her. 'Rose deserves some luck.'

'Well, she's got plenty now! That old bag the Widow Miller taking her under her wing and throwing money at her. You should see her clothes! Jesus! Why didn't she take a shine to me?' Trudie wailed. 'You should see everyone stare at her now – "Look at Rose, she's a beauty, who'd have thought it?"' Her voice was thick with malice. 'Amazing what having a bloody squint fixed can do for you.'

Shocked, Gilbert rounded on her. 'Rose Bradshaw saved your life!'

'So what?' Trudie hurled back. 'I don't have to go around licking her boots for ever, do I? I mean, anyone would have done the same –'

'Like the two boys you were with, you mean?'

'I wouldn't talk about *boys* if I were you, Gilbert,' Trudie countered spitefully, 'not after what people are saying about you.'

Flushing, Gilbert pulled the sheet around him. His stage make-up was smeared around his cheeks, his black eyebrows half rubbed off. He looked comical and pathetic at the same time.

'You should see yourself!' Trudie mocked him. 'What a mess.'

Shaken, Gilbert looked away. 'Don't take your spite out on me, Trudie. I'm not going to be your whipping boy.'

'Nah. I reckon you might have your own *personal* whipping boy. Hey, Uncle Gilbert?' Trudie replied, walking out and banging the door.

'If my Gordon had still been alive, we'd have been married for over twenty-five years now,' Clovis muttered under her breath as she surveyed the huge table laid out in the middle of Gull Road.

They were making preparations for the King's Silver Jubilee, everyone chipping in to set up a street party, banners suspended across the street, from one upper window to the other, Sea View bearing a Union Jack over the doorway. It had been an overcast day, but around two thirty the sun had come out. Ruby was now ordering everyone around with plates of pies, muffins and cakes. Sullen, Trudie slammed down the offerings on the table, whilst the white tablecloths fluttered in the muted breeze.

'Honestly, I don't see why we have to go to all this trouble,' she moaned, Clovis pushing past her with a tray of scones.

'It's for the Royals.'

'What did the Royals ever do for us?' Trudie chimed back.

Nan gave her a baleful look.

'I want the tongue and ham in the *middle* of the table,' Ruby barked, 'otherwise those greedy bastards at number twelve will scoff the lot.'

'Why can't someone else organise all this?' Trudie wailed, pushed quickly aside by Joe as he brought a pile of plates to the table.

'Why can't you stop moaning?'

She pulled a face at him. 'Listen to you! All sunny now you're a married man.'

Joe glowed – two days married and *still* laughing about it.

'Why don't *you* get yourself someone steady, Trudie?'

'I want to play the field.'

He nudged her with his elbow. 'There's many a lonely old nag said that.'

Stung, she slapped an apple pie down on the table and rounded on her brother. 'There's more to life than marriage!'

'You mean, like a career? Like working at Myers?' he responded mischievously, winking and trying to lighten the atmosphere.

But Trudie wasn't having any of it. She was fed up with her job, with Sea View and with her new boyfriend. About to be *ex*-boyfriend. And most of all she was irritated by Rose. The whole town had been talking about her transformation, the manager at the Pavilion insisting that she had brought in more trade by just *sitting* in the ticket office. Smouldering at the thought, Trudie remembered the old days. But they were just that: *the old days*. Gone. Over. There was to be no more lording it over her friend, no more being magnanimous. Trudie was feeling the unexpected discomfort of coming second – and it chilled her to the bone.

'Help me here!' Joe called out to his new wife, Maisie turning, her simple face flushed with exertion. 'I need a hand. There's loads more places to set and we've not got enough cups set out . . .'

The street was alive with people, families moving in and out of their houses, men watching the women, Nan Wilmslow ducking and diving like a wren in a family of jackdaws.

As the sun crawled higher in the May sky, the warmth

increased, Maisie flicking her hand to scare off some wasps as they circled the jam tarts.

Hustling past her son, Ruby caught sight of Trudie – the only person standing idle.

'Oh, come on! Give us a hand –'

'Aw, Ma, what's all the fuss for?'

'You know what it's for!' Ruby replied angrily, overheated and out of patience. 'Why are you being such a flaming pain in the arse today?'

At that precise moment Rose walked out of number 139, carrying a bowl of flowers.

It was too much for Trudie. She took one look at her glamorous, unexpected rival and threw down the cutlery she was holding.

'Oh, sod it!' she snapped, everyone looking up in amazement. 'Sod the food, the bloody weather, the bloody Silver Jubilee!' Then she turned to Rose: 'And above all – sod *you*!'

Waiting at the end of North Pier, Lester watched Beth Hodges walking towards him. She hadn't seen him yet, that much was obvious. Deep in thought, her head was bowed, her eyes fixed on the pavement. She had been right to assume that no one would miss her from the street party – no one had. Not even her mother, who would be occupied for hours, the Silver Jubilee the perfect excuse for a gossip. Indeed, Beth reckoned that she had at least a couple of hours before the party drew to a close and someone noticed her absence.

'Hey there,' Lester said simply, walking towards her. 'Who'd have believed it would be this quiet down the pier?'

'It's all the Jubilee parties,' Beth replied, sliding her hand through his arm. 'I'm glad you came.'

'I wanted to see you,' Lester said, but his tone was cautious.

'I wanted to see you too,' Beth answered, walking over

to the railings and staring down into the balmy sea.

Around them they could smell the peculiar Blackpool aroma of ozone, and fish and chips, a gull circling, calling overhead. A little way off, a pleasure boat tooted its hooter, its gauzy flag fluttering in the half-hearted breeze.

'We had a good time the other night,' Lester said.

Beth turned to look at him. She was striking: hair black as a magpie's wing, her face heart-shaped, her eyes vividly blue. In time she would either become grand or darkly savage in her looks – Lester wasn't sure which.

'I like you a lot,' she said simply, smiling and touching his cheek. 'Don't look so worried!'

'I'm not,' he replied.

But in truth, he was. There was an intensity in Beth Hodges that he hadn't as yet seen, but suspected. Some darkness of spirit which shadowed her. She was good fun, but he wasn't in love with her. Unexpectedly Lester's thoughts turned to Rose. She had shaken him to the bone; as she had shaken many other people. Suddenly she was a force of nature, a woman men admired, thought about, wanted. A woman *Lester* now thought about. But in the weeks since her transformation Rose had kept her distance.

Oh, she had been polite and chatted easily enough to him, but always when there were others around. In fact, it seemed that she avoided intimacy with him. And that made it difficult for him to talk to her, to explain. Because he needed to say – I was wrong, forgive me for dismissing you so easily. Give me another chance. I won't reject you again.

But he wasn't going to get that chance, was he? Rose was on the up, going higher and further than anyone would have imagined. She had the Widow Miller behind her now; that meant power and money. Lester thought of Trudie's jealousy. Rose and his sister had been friends since they were babies in prams, but suddenly Trudie hated her. Rose hadn't changed – she was exactly the same person – but all her attempts at a reconciliation with Trudie had been rebutted.

Why? Because she had beauty and power. And because she was out of their league.

'What is it?'

Jolted out of his reverie, Lester turned to Beth. 'I was miles away.'

'With someone? Or on your own?' she asked, her voice flirtatious, but her expression suspicious.

'What a thing to ask!' Lester replied, jollying her along. 'Do I ask you what you were thinking about?'

'I would tell you – I was thinking about you,' Beth answered, her hand sliding along the rail and resting against his. 'I was thinking about how you kissed me, how good it felt. I was thinking that I would like you to kiss me again.' Her hand slid over his and squeezed it. 'I would like you to hold me and touch me.'

He turned and studied her intriguing face. Their relationship had started as a flirtation, little more, but over the months it had slowly, insidiously, developed into an intense romance. Repeatedly Beth had assured Lester that she wasn't looking for anything serious. They were both too young, she said. And she wasn't like Maisie, the settling-down type.

Lester had been relieved to hear it; he wasn't ready to settle for a long time. And never with Beth Hodges. He had made that clear from the start. We can go out and enjoy ourselves, he had said, but it won't lead anywhere. I'll not lie to you, Beth: I'm in my early twenties and not looking for a wife. Only a fortune.

'There you go again,' Beth said suddenly, teasing him, 'off in a dream world. Without me.'

He turned to her again. Beth's head was tipped back, reminding him of the time Rose had stood in the same position. The one and only time they had kissed. Anxious to blot out her image, Lester put his arms around Beth and kissed her eagerly, desperately.

In time he would forget Rose. He would *make* himself.

TWENTY-EIGHT

Around five o'clock on the following Saturday, Maisie set fire to the chimney of number 99 Gull Road. Panicking, she ran out into the street, someone else calling the fire brigade. She didn't know it was packed up with newspaper, she told them, flushing. Look next time, luv, the fireman replied patiently.

Not blessed with much intelligence, Maisie was, however, willing. She set about decorating the walls of their flat at number 99, but used the wrong paint and it peeled off within a week. Then she decided she would learn how to cook, turning on the gas and forgetting to light it. Only the timely arrival of Joe prevented another accident. If there was anything on the floor, however tiny, Maisie tripped over it. If she could bump into it, drop it, set fire to it, drown it or crush it, she did. For a dainty woman she was – as her adoring husband told everyone – ridiculously accident-prone.

Of course Joe could see nothing wrong with that. He struggled down meals that would have felled a boxer, and tea that was weak and barely hot. Having thought his mother had mastered the art of laundry butchery, Joe discovered that Maisie could outdo even Ruby. So after a while, Joe washed his own jumpers, Maisie mixing the soap powder in the sink for him and watching her husband lovingly. Then she let down the drying rack from the ceiling and sighed as Joe arranged his clothes in it.

'You're so clever.'

Leaning over, he kissed her cheek. 'It's nothing.'

'I should do it.'

'You do other things.'

Maisie frowned. 'Not really, Joe. You do most things now.'

This was true, but he didn't mind. Even coming home from work and repairing the meal his wife had attempted to make for him wasn't a chore. Nothing he did with Maisie was a chore.

'We'll go to the baths on Saturday if it's hot.'

Maisie flushed. 'I don't like going there and putting on a swimming costume.'

'You've a figure any woman would be proud of!' Joe told her. 'All the lads look at you.'

'They don't!'

'They do!' he replied, sitting down and pulling her onto his knee. 'I'm so happy here, Maisie. I know it's not much – a rented flat that's not too grand – but what with Lester giving me work, we've enough money to get by nicely. In time we could move. Maybe buy a place one day . . .'

She laughed happily. 'You worry too much about tomorrow, Joe! We're doing fine, you and me. I like working at Collinsons part time.'

'Soon you won't have to work!' Joe replied, his pride tweaked.

'It's not hard, waiting on tables –'

'If Lester was married, you can bet *his* wife wouldn't be working.'

'Oh, stop going on about your brother! It doesn't matter what Lester would do. This is *our* life,' Maisie replied, her tone mock-stern. 'We're not ambitious, like Lester. We're ordinary, Joe. But we're happy. Let's just enjoy what we have and not worry about what we haven't got.'

Nodding, he squeezed her. 'I love you.'

She rested her head against his shoulder. 'I love you too,

Joe. You know, I sometimes wonder what I would have done if you hadn't married me. I would have stayed at home, or married someone horrible.' Her eyes widened at the thought. 'I couldn't live without you, Joe. Not even for a day.'

'You won't ever have to,' he replied, suddenly serious and holding on to his wife tightly. 'I'll never leave you, Maisie. *Never*. Whatever happens, they'll never part you and me.'

So much for the winning bet! Len thought, throwing down his slip and looking over to his clerk, Bunny Lambert. He had hired Bunny when he realised that his daughter wasn't going to come into the business. She didn't say anything directly, but she looked so glamorous now and was obviously so much under Hettie's influence that a career on the track was never going to materialise. And in a way Len understood. The old Rosie would have thrived in the business, but the new one had choices now. Choices a beautiful woman would be mad to ignore.

Not that Bunny Lambert wasn't a damn good clerk. With a pale, bland face and thin, blond hair, Len's clerk looked like a glass of milk – all one colour. He had earned the nickname Bunny from the coat collar he wore. He might swear blind it was ermine, but some wag had insisted – years ago – that it was rabbit. And the sobriquet had stuck.

'Lean day,' Len said.

Bunny nodded dolefully as he passed the takings. 'Cold too. I thought summer had come, but it's freezing again.' He glanced around. 'Some bloke was looking for you earlier, Len.'

'Who?'

'Dave . . . Dave Lincoln.'

Len's eyebrows rose. 'He's a copper, is Dave. What did he want?'

Shrugging, Bunny rose to his feet. 'I dunno, just said

he'd like a word at the bar after the races.' Stretching his long arms above his head, Bunny winced. 'When I'm rich, I'm going to live abroad. The cold gets into your bones here.'

'Whisky help?'

'Might, at that.'

'You buying?'

Bunny gave him a long look.

'Yeah, right,' Len said, both of them walking away from the track towards the enclosed bar.

It was packed with race-goers, the toffs in the upper bar, the snug smoky with cigarette fumes and the open fire. A satisfying smell of meat pie and beer curled around the wooden panelling and nicotine-stained ceiling as Len walked up to the bar.

He had a lot to think about. The much-publicised Depression was hitting racing and now some meetings were badly attended, men holding on to any wages they had earned. Even the odd flutters were falling off. In Blackpool, where the main industry was tourism, the Depression hadn't taken grip completely, but gradually it was seeping in. People who had usually saved long and hard for their summer holiday or weekend break now found that they needed the money to pay the rent. Only the other day Ruby had mentioned that two of her regular couples had already cancelled. Who the hell could afford a holiday, she said, when they hadn't got a job?

Dave Lincoln was at the bar and Len saw him immediately, and greeted him with enthusiasm.

'Long time no see, Dave.'

'Len, good to see you. Must be two years.'

'*Two years*,' Len repeated, amazed. 'God, time passes so bloody fast.'

'It does that,' Dave agreed, motioning for Len to follow him to a cramped table, crowded into a corner. 'We can have a talk here.'

Curious, Len studied the man he had known since primary school. A big man even in his teens, Dave Lincoln had been a good amateur boxer in his prime, joining the police force in his late twenties. Once they'd been close friends, but circumstances had gradually forced them apart. Occasionally, they had had a drink together, but otherwise the two men had seldom mixed. Which was why Len was interested to hear from Dave Lincoln out of the blue.

'Is it about Roy Howell?'

Dave shook his head. 'Nah, that sod's disappeared off the face of the earth. He's covered his tracks well. No, it's something more personal, Len.' He looked around, dropping his voice further to avoid being overheard. 'You know the Williams family that live across from you in Gull Road? You know them well, don't you?'

'Known them for years. We're friends, Dave.'

He nodded. 'I thought as much. You friendly with Gilbert Beardsley?'

'Not really. Rose is close to him, especially since she began to work at the Pavilion, but Gilbert's a theatrical, not a racing man.' Len paused, looking Dave up and down. 'Why?'

'It's difficult . . .'

'I can't hear you,' Len said, straining to catch Dave's words.

'I said, it's *difficult*,' Dave repeated, pulling his chair closer. 'There's word around that Gilbert's been . . . he's mixing with some funny types, Len. Oh, you know what I mean. Queers.'

Len winced at the word *and* the implication. 'Nah, he might have fooled around once, but not now. Ruby's mentioned it to me now and again, but I'd put money on it that Gilbert's passed all that.'

Nodding his head thoughtfully, Dave looked around again. 'I don't care myself how people live, as long as it doesn't affect me. But there's others that *do* care. And they make trouble. Moral do-gooders. The type that likes to be *seen* making trouble. You know, people who pick someone out for a scapegoat –'

'Not Gilbert?' Len asked, shaken. 'He's harmless. Come on, Dave, it would have been all around Gull Road if he'd been up to something. You know what it's like: people talk, and I'd have heard.'

'It's very recent, Len. Only a few weeks since Gilbert's been seen with someone with a bad reputation. Louis Wilkes.'

Len shrugged. 'I've never heard of him.'

'I didn't think *you* would have done,' Dave replied drily. 'Look, I'm just tipping you off. I can't tip off Gilbert directly, and I knew you were a friend of the family, so I thought I'd tell you and you could pass it on.'

'I will. You can be sure of that.'

'There's some who'd say that people like Gilbert Beardsley deserve what they get.'

'What would *you* say, Dave?'

'I'd say there're worse things in life,' he replied, draining his glass and then looking back to Len. 'I'm not just being noble. There's something in this for me too.'

'Like what?'

'The bastard who's out to get Gilbert got promoted over me last year. A right politician, if you get my drift . . .'

Len nodded.

'. . . so you could say I have a score to settle. And what better way to get my own back than to get someone else off the hook at the same time? Leave my boss high and dry.'

'Point taken.'

'If you don't throw a scare into Gilbert Beardsley to get him back in line, Len, then make sure you remind him of what's at stake – prison. No more acting, no more normal life. He'll be crucified, and so will his family.' Dave stood up, momentarily towering over Len. 'It were good to see you again.'

'And you.'

'Anything I can do for *you*?' Dave asked suddenly. 'Any favour wants sorting out?'

Len thought for a moment, then nodded. 'Yeah, keep an eye out for Roy Howell, will you? I've a score to settle with that bastard.'

TWENTY-NINE

Staring fixedly at the silver celebration plate on the picture rail, Stuart Fallow aimed and then threw the paper dart he had made. It was a direct hit. The plate wobbled, then righted itself, settling back onto the rail. Typical, Stuart thought, nothing in the old man's house ever got derailed.

'Stuart,' a nasal voice intoned outside the door. 'Stuart, are you in there?'

Without waiting for an answer, Cedric walked into the morning room and looked at his son with a pained expression. He always appeared so louche, Cedric thought, not at all like a Fallow.

'Can't you smarten yourself up a bit?'

Half-heartedly, Stuart combed back his thick wavy hair with his fingers and then elaborately sleeked his eyebrows with his forefingers, his father's expression becoming more mournful by the second.

'And look at your surgical coat, Stuart,' he went on. 'It's so tight.'

Only because yours was as big as Billy Smart's Circus tent, Stuart thought patiently. Honestly, his father couldn't weigh more than eleven stone and yet all his clothes swamped him, as if he expected a sudden outbreak of obesity.

'Are you listening to me?'

Stuart hadn't been, but looked interested. 'Go on, Dad –'

'*Father.*'

'Father, please go on.'

'We've a new receptionist beginning today –'

'What happened to Mrs Oakfield?'

'She left.'

'Did she fall, or was she pushed?'

Cedric stared at his son. What *was* the boy talking about?

'Mrs Oakfield has moved on, and the new lady will begin at nine thirty. She's inexperienced in reception work, but very bright.' Cedric paused, looking at his son. 'You're *not* listening, are you?'

'I am! She's very experienced in reception work, but not very bright.'

'Are you doing this to irritate me?' Cedric asked, an outraged master of pomposity.

'Doing *what*?'

'It ill becomes you, Stuart, to act like a fool. The Fallows didn't progress in life by being giddy.'

Stuart didn't doubt that for an instant; his father was as giddy as haemorrhoids.

'I want you to help our new receptionist as much as you can.'

'Where did she come from?'

'She's Mrs Henrietta Miller's protégée,' Cedric replied, making this as grand-sounding as possible. 'Mrs Miller is a very respected lady, as you know. Any young person whom she chooses to take under her wing must be a person of rare qualities.' Cedric moved to the door, then turned. 'I'll expect you in the surgery in ten minutes, on your best behaviour. You have an impression to make.'

And he didn't mean for a set of dentures, Stuart thought wryly.

At that very moment Rose was walking up to the surgery door. She was early. Should she wait outside? Or go in? Frowning, she glanced up at the windows of the first floor. Hettie had told her that the Fallows' surgery was attached to the house, but what Hettie hadn't mentioned was that the house was a rambling red brick heap. Huge arched windows, with intricate stained glass, peered down from the first floor, the glass door of the surgery depicting a scene of a shipwreck. How comforting, Rose thought, biding her time a little longer.

She had thought that when she left the ticket office at the Pavilion it would be to work on the track with Len. But gradually all mention and thought of racing had faded. Her father seldom mentioned it, and Rose no longer badgered him. Guilt made her feel queasy. She had wanted to work with her father for years, longed to be back at the track, but now other possibilities were presenting themselves – opportunities never before available to Rose . . . Anyway, she sought to console herself, her father had Bunny now. And how *could* she refuse to please Hettie when her benefactress had done so much for her?

So when Hettie told her about the receptionist job Rose felt she could hardly refuse. The money was good, and it was some sop to Rose's conscience that she could bring more cash in to number 139. A bigger wage would mean that she could buy some new furniture, and get her father the gramophone he had had his eye on for months. He deserved it, Rose decided. He had put her first for years; it was time he got something back. After all, she was hardly doing without.

Rose thought about Hettie and felt another twinge of unease. Her mentor was charming, but very possessive. She had a right to want to know about Rose's life, but not to take it over. But the questions had been increasing steadily. *How was her admirer? What did he think of her transformation?* Rose had ducked the queries. She didn't want to talk to Hettie about Lester and, besides, she didn't really know what she felt about him herself.

He had been thrown by her new appearance, Rose knew that much. God, his face had been a study. And she'd seen a look in his eyes then. For the first time, he was attracted to her. But as for following it up – that had been awkward. Then finally an opportunity presented itself, Rose literally bumping into Lester as she rounded the bend into Gull Road.

'Rose,' he'd said simply, fascinated by her and confused. Surely he couldn't fall in love with Rose? No one fell in love with their kid sister, but she wasn't his sister, was she?

For her part, Rose was simply staring at Lester, willing him to say something else. .

'You look really well . . .'

Was that romantic, Rose had asked herself. *Really well*? Or was it something one neighbour said to another. Couldn't a woman recovering from a hernia operation look *really well*?

'All grown up . . .' Lester had gone on, embarrassed by how crass he sounded.

'I've been grown up for a while,'

'Oh, I know, I know . . . but to me you're still little Rosie, Trudie's friend.' Lester felt like a man in a falling lift, his head spinning sickly. 'No! That wasn't what I meant either. I mean, you look older.'

Had it been anyone else other than Lester, Rose would have walked off there and then.

'Nothing more than older?'

'And lovely.'

Her face had flushed. Lester had been severely rattled. What was this new feeling? He had always been in control where women were concerned, but Rose had crept up on him by stealth. He felt uncomfortable around her and yet, at the same time, was desperate to ask her out.

It had been Ruby who broke the spell, yelling out of the front door of Sea View: 'If you go by the market, Lester, get me a pound of carrots, will you?'

Lester had nodded impatiently – but when he turned back to Rose, she had already gone.

Her thoughts coming back to the present, Rose looked at the looming house. It was like a bloody mausoleum, she thought, making a mental note not to swear. The Fallows wouldn't like that . . . Her gaze rested on the red brick walls. The place was enormous, and no doubt worth a fortune, but ugly. Still, the job was well-paid, and all thanks to Hettie. Again. She had started on about Rose's work a few weeks previously: Didn't Rose think it was time she got a more respectable job? Surely she would never go back to the track? That wasn't the place for a lady.

Irritated, Rose had retorted that if the track was good enough for her father, then it was plenty good enough for her! In reply, Hettie had looked hurt, murmuring about only trying to help. Rose's guilt perfectly manipulated, the girl had apologised, and – after a few days of cajoling – agreed to take the dental receptionist's job.

'What are you doing?' a voice said suddenly from above her head.

Surprised, Rose looked up to see a youthful, good-looking man grinning down at her.

'I was too early.'

'You the new receptionist?' Stuart asked in amazement.

''Fraid so.'

'I'm not!' he replied happily. 'Good on the old man.'

She flushed at the obvious compliment, waiting patiently to be let in. A few moments later Stuart was showing Rose around the surgery, taking her coat and pulling out a seat for her to sit down. Amused, she thanked him elegantly. She liked Stuart Fallow. Not that he would have given her a second glance in the old days . . . Stop it, Rose told herself briskly, the old days are over.

Grinning, Stuart pointed out the gory bisection posters of teeth on the wall, and then his certificate, all the time mocking himself. Who on earth would imagine he could have become qualified? Everyone knew he was a complete dunce. Amused, Rose listened. Stuart Fallow was good company, she decided, and good fun.

His father, however, was not.

'Good morning, Miss Bradshaw,' he intoned as he walked in. 'Stuart, you should have called me and told me that Miss Bradshaw had arrived. I was waiting in the morning room.'

'Sorry, Father,' he replied, without a trace of sincerity. 'I was just showing her the ropes.'

Cedric winced.

'Mrs Miller told me you were a highly intelligent young lady, so I imagine you will have little difficulty with the position. Basically you just need to make appointments in the appointments book . . .' he pointed to it, just to make sure Rose understood, '. . . answer the phone . . .' he pointed to the phone, '. . . and take messages on the pad.' Finally he pointed to the pad. Stuart smirked behind him. 'If there is anything you do not understand, please ask my son, or myself. I am retired now, Miss Bradshaw, but I have an active interest in the way the practice is run.' Cedric gazed up, his eyes fixing on the plaster ceiling rose as he continued. 'I expect you to be polite and charming to the patients and, of course, immaculately well presented at all times.' Slowly his gaze returned to her. 'You may have one hour for lunch and the use of our own personal, private kitchen.'

Having finished his speech, Cedric then left.

Stuart flopped down on the edge of the desk, grinning.

'Should you have reason to talk to the dentist,' he pointed to himself, 'or indeed to breathe,' he pointed to his chest and breathed in dramatically, 'please fill out a form, in trip-licate, first.'

Rose smiled back at him. 'Your father's very thorough.'

'He's a Fallow. Very thorough fellows, are Fallows.'

Putting her head on one side, Rose raised her eyebrows. 'You're a Fallow too.'

'Only by birth,' he teased her, jumping off the desk when the doorbell rang. 'Please answer the bell, Miss Bradshaw,' he said, pointing to it. 'That's the bell – B-E-L-L.'

She had made the right decision, Rose thought to herself cheerfully. Oh yes, she was going to be happy here.

'A receptionist in Lytham!' Clovis said with smug pride. 'What did I tell you all along – Rose would make us all proud.'

Nan Wilmslow gave her an impenetrable look, but said nothing.

'She's changed out of all recognition,' Clovis went on. 'Really glamorous. I bet Len had a bit of a worry, you know, wondering if she would go the way of Gilbert . . .'

Nan frowned.

'On the boards!' Clovis explained, exasperated. 'I mean, she's got the looks now and all the confidence in the world. And I dare say if Rose had stayed working at the Pavilion she'd have been snapped up. They do that, those producer men.' She dropped her voice in case there were any producers lurking under the sink. 'They lure young innocent girls off and then sell them abroad.'

'White slave trade.'

Clovis nodded. 'That's it! Sell them off to rich foreign men, for *mucky doings* . . .' she paused; it was too horrible to contemplate. 'Good thing the Widow Miller's taken her under her wing, I say. And now our Rose is a dental receptionist. In Lytham.'

'Off the track.'

Clovis frowned. 'Oh, I don't know about that. The trams run up there, and the buses.'

Nan sighed. 'Off the racetrack.'

'Oh, and a good thing too!' Clovis said vehemently. 'I said to Len not once, not twice, but more times than I care to count – that girl of yours shouldn't be at the race track. I mean, what respectable woman would do a job like that? But could I make him see sense? No chance! Like all men, my brother only sees what he wants to see. It was fine for him, he said. But that wasn't the point, was it? He's a man.

Rose is a young woman, and besides, she was getting very used to sparring with the punters. A bit too used to it, if you get my drift. Rose is where she should be now. In a good job, with respectable people. She's safe and if she plays her cards right she might nab herself a nice husband. One of the patients perhaps . . . But if Rose had stayed working the track it would have ended in disaster. You mark my words, Nan, if she'd stayed at the track there would have been a tragedy.'

THIRTY

Fully aware of just how dangerous a situation Gilbert was in, Len agonised. He knew he had to tip his neighbour off, but he could hardly just walk over to Sea View and tell Ruby what Dave Lincoln had said. It had to be done delicately. Len was beginning to wonder if it had to be done at all. It was hardly easy to talk about: even with an open-minded woman like Ruby Williams. But then again, he'd given his word to Dave Lincoln, so he would have to see it through.

Rolling up a cigarette, Len looked back out through the window. Lester was just arriving home in his car, looking very prosperous. As well he might, Len thought. Hadn't Lester just bought a property on the North Pier that he was going to turn into a dance hall? He had the Midas touch, and no mistake. And so young. Not that he looked it, Len thought. All the hours Lester worked had aged him. Anyone meeting Ruby's son for the first time would assume he was in his thirties.

Len leaned further forward, watching Lester. Instinct told Len that he would continue to do well, build up the seaside empire he had set his heart on. It was in the stars – *even the cards*, Ruby had said once, laughing. And when Lester had amassed his power and money, then what? Marriage? A family? It wouldn't be hard for Lester to find a partner, Len thought. He was attractive and basically a decent man. He thought back to the time Lester had helped him with

George Ogden. Yes, Lester was a good man, but would that common decency survive his wheeling and dealing?

Would all the contracts, back-handers, deals, rivalry and the envy gradually chip away Lester's goodness? Len had seen it happen to other men, and wondered just how tough Lester Williams really was. Len also wondered about what kind of woman Lester would choose to marry and decided that whoever she was she would have to be very strong. Lester wouldn't be an easy man to live with. Ambitious men seldom were.

Then, as he continued to watch Sea View, Ruby suddenly walked out, shaking a rug. Finally, he had his moment! Without thinking, Len banged on the window and beckoned for her to come over. Surprised, she did so, walking into the Bradshaw kitchen and waving away the tobacco smoke from her face.

'Whatever are you smoking, Len? Smells like someone's bloody hedge.'

He smiled. 'Cuppa?'

'I can't now. I got some new guests coming in an hour and I haven't got the room finished.'

'Can't Trudie do it?'

'Hah!' Ruby snorted. 'Our Trudie's going off her rocker. The hotel's not good enough for her, she says. Seeing your girl get that receptionist's job has nearly done her in. I can't talk any sense into her. Jealous as a snake. I'm sorry to say it, Len, because those girls had been friends a long while. I never thought Trudie would act like this.'

'She'll come round.'

'She better,' Ruby said warningly, folding the rug over her arm. 'So, what did you want me for?'

'I have to talk to you about something personal, Ruby.'

'I'm already married, I'd have to refuse you, Len,' she said, winking.

He laughed, then his tone was serious again. 'I've had a tip-off from a copper friend of mine. About Gilbert.'

Ruby sat down heavily on the rocker, all the steam gone out of her. 'Oh Jesus, he's not been caught with his trousers down, has he?'

'No,' Len replied carefully. 'It's just that the police have their eye on him.'

'Dear God!' Ruby said, her face chalk-white. 'I didn't think he'd risk anything. You know Gilbert: he's a coward through and through. Stupid sod. But then he *has* been acting out of character lately, and drinking. Jesus, what have you heard?'

'He's been mixing with someone . . .' Len hesitated; how the hell could you say it? '. . . someone . . .'

'Queer?'

'Yes,' he agreed, 'I suppose that word will do as well as any.'

'Local man?'

'Out-of-towner.'

'Name?'

'Louis Wilkes. Mean anything?'

She raised her eyebrows. 'Not to me. Where's he come from?'

'I dunno,' Len said honestly, 'but he sounded a bad lot. Known to the police, anyway.'

Ruby hung her head. 'God, Len, I've been afraid of this for years. But nothing happened and I thought Gilbert had more sense. He had someone else a long time ago – he doesn't know that I know – but he did. After him, no one.' She paused, staring at the rug on her knee. 'He must get lonely. Everyone needs someone. I've got Alfred, the dope, and the kids, but Gilbert's been a loner all his life. If he didn't have the theatre he'd have been a sad man. Like I said, there's been a change in him lately. He's got secretive. It's not doing him any good, though. Whoever this man is, he's not good for Gilbert.'

Len was at a loss for the right words.

'I suppose I could tell Gilbert to act normal – resist

temptation, at least. But that's too much to ask, isn't it?' She looked over to Len. 'You know that. You've got your daughter. And Doris.'

'Oh, now, Ruby –'

'Don't ssh me, Len Bradshaw!' she teased him. 'You've keep it quiet and away from Gull Road, but everyone knows you have your feet warmed often enough.'

'We're not talking about me,' Len said hurriedly, relighting his cigarette. 'We're talking about Gilbert. If he carries on seeing this Wilkes bloke, it'll end badly, Ruby. I mean *really* badly. Court, a sentence. Prison.'

'Christ.'

'You know what people are like. They'll tear him to shreds. They laugh at his clothes now and his bloody Turkish slippers, but it's just that, a joke to them. Some might wonder about Gilbert, but if they stop to think that he might be seeing a man, having an affair with a man –'

'I've got the point!' Ruby snapped.

'I didn't mean to offend you.'

'You didn't, Len,' she replied, her tone steadying. 'I just can't imagine it myself. I know one thing, though, it would kill Gilbert if he had to go to prison.'

'It would hurt you too,' Len said sympathetically. 'And the business –'

'Bugger the business!'

'That was an unfortunate turn of phrase,' Len replied woefully.

A moment passed between them before Ruby spoke.

'Seems like I'm grateful to the Bradshaw family again. Thanks for the tip-off, Len.'

'It's nothing.'

'What do I say to my brother?' Ruby asked, her voice unusually doubtful. 'Whatever do I say to him?'

Len shook his head. 'I don't know. But you have to put the fear of God into him, Ruby – or someone else will.'

* * *

The act had come over from Russia, or so the billboard said, advertising The Remarkable Rashichovs. No one could pronounce the name, but that didn't matter. They were foreign and exotic, and that was what counted. Enthralled, Gilbert watched from the front row of the Tower Circus. He had finished his last show for the day and was sitting, his hands clasped around a block of chocolate, gawking at the sight in front of his eyes.

God, he was so perfect, Gilbert thought, so effortlessly beautiful. His eyes followed every movement Louis Wilkes made. So what if he wasn't Russian? So what if he wasn't the greatest entertainer of all time? He was an image from the past, from the era of the *commedia dell'arte*; he was a Russian Harlequin, in black and white, a massive fur hat pulled down low over his forehead above the deep-set black eyes.

And everyone loved him. Coming on after the obvious clowns, he elegantly rolled the massive white orb around the ring, then balanced a smaller orb on his arm, letting it run to his fingertips and then tossing it over his head and catching it with his other hand. He danced as no one had ever danced in the Tower Circus before. His steps were perfect, light-footed, piercingly balletic. Under the lights, on his own in the middle of the ring, he was caught in an untouchable bubble – dancing in his own way to his own tune. He was beautiful, talented, charismatic.

And vicious.

At the end of the act, everyone applauded wildly, not quite sure what they had seen, but impressed nevertheless. Then as the regular clowns came into the ring, followed by the performing horses, Gilbert left his seat and moved to the dressing-room tent at the back. The pungent smell of elephant dung and sweat caught Gilbert unawares as he picked his way gingerly towards the tent and knocked on the wooden sign.

'Come in,' Louis Wilkes called out, smiling as Gilbert

walked in, flustered, and knocking a costume from its hanger with the end of his umbrella. 'You came to see me!'

'I would hardly miss you, would I?'

'You might,' Wilkes replied, shrugging. 'Was I good?'

'Incredible.'

Smiling, Wilkes sat down at the mirror and stared at Gilbert's reflection. 'Have you put on weight?'

He flushed. 'No, I don't think so.'

'I don't like men who are too fat,' Wilkes replied, turning and smiling over his shoulder. 'You mustn't be a pig, Gilbert.'

'I haven't had dinner –'

'Good boy,' Wilkes replied, leaning his head on his arm and staring at Gilbert limpidly. 'Are you wearing my present?'

Gilbert felt for the chain around his neck and pulled it out from under his collar. 'I never take it off.'

'Don't make too much of it. It wasn't expensive,' Wilkes replied, turning back to the mirror and watching Gilbert flush. 'We could go out tonight. For dinner.'

'I'd like that.'

'But then again . . .' Wilkes paused, as though trying to remember something, '. . . I have another admirer who offered to take me out.'

'Louis, don't tease.'

'Who said I was teasing?'

'Louis, don't . . . don't. You know how it hurts me when you're cruel,' Gilbert said, his tone pleading.

'But the world is cruel,' Wilkes replied, leaning over and running his forefinger down Gilbert's cheek. 'Love is cruel. That's what makes it worth fighting to keep. Don't you agree, Gilbert? Don't you want to fight to keep it? Don't you want to fight to keep me?'

THIRTY-ONE

Summer dragged its heels for a month, during which news was all over town that Lawrence of Arabia had died, the newsstand reading 'LAWRENCE DEAD – HERO LOSES FIGHT FOR LIFE'. Then the weather brightened, and by the time June arrived the town was crawling with people, the shops chock-a-block, the trams and buses hanging with trippers. The season was in full swing.

Having gone to the Derby at Epsom, Len cleaned up on the Aga Khan's horse Bahram. That night, he and Bunny took the long drive back to Blackpool with their pockets jingling, Len's old Austin chugging home contentedly through the balmy summer night.

That same evening Rose had been held up at the dental practice by an emergency. One of Stuart's patients had broken off a piece of her tooth and it was wedged in between her other teeth and her gum. As the dental nurse had already gone, Rose was drafted in to help, holding cotton wadding and following Stuart's instructions to the letter. Adeptly he grasped the piece of broken tooth, pulled – and it was all over before the patient knew what had hit her. It had hurt, she said, but only for an instant. And she was *so* grateful.

'You have your father's skill, Mr Fallow,' she went on, Rose passing her a clean piece of gauze to hold to her mouth. 'I hope he appreciates you.'

'Oh, my father thinks of world of me,' Stuart replied, shooting Rose a wry look. 'Tells me so every day.'

After Rose had made a further appointment and shown the patient out, it was coming up for eight o'clock.

'Sorry to keep you so long,' Stuart said, stretching his arms above his head and yawning. 'Thanks for staying – and for helping out. You did well.'

Rose glowed at the compliment. 'I enjoyed it.'

'Looking down someone's mouth? You're a weird one.'

She laughed. 'You know what I mean! I enjoyed doing something more than reception work.'

'You could train,' Stuart said, taking off his white coat and throwing his jacket over his shoulder.

'As what?'

'A dental nurse.'

'I couldn't!'

'You could,' he persisted. 'Look, if I can be a dentist, you can be a dental nurse. It's easy.'

If you have the money for the training, Rose thought to herself, then dismissed the idea. She was doing all right as she was; the receptionist wage would have to suffice.

'Well, I'll be off now,' she said cheerfully, walking to the door. 'See you in the morning.'

At once, Stuart ran after her. 'I'll give you a lift.'

'You live in Lytham, and I'm going home to Blackpool,' she said, her eyebrows raised.

'I could do with a drive,' he insisted. 'Get some sea air.'

'Then go for a walk.'

'Is it the hump?'

She frowned, wrong-footed. 'What?'

'Is it my hunchback that's putting you off?'

Laughing, Rose picked up her bag. 'You're crazy.'

'You're right,' he agreed, 'but let me drive you home anyway.'

The conversation was easy – as were all conversations between them. Stuart mentioned that he had a birthday coming up, and that he would be holding a party and would she like to come. Rose replied that she doubted if his father would approve of his mixing with the hired help.

'You're not hired help!' Stuart replied, winding down his window and letting the salty sea air fill the car. 'You come via the Widow Miller – and that's close to being recommended by God.'

Rose turned to look at him, curious. 'Do you know her?'

'Only by reputation. I know that she has my father wrapped around her little finger – and that he thinks he has her under his thumb.'

Rose laughed, brushing her hair away from her eyes as they sped along.

'You're wicked!'

'You're right.'

'The Widow Miller paid for my eye to be fixed.'

Stuart snatched a quick glance at his passenger. 'What's wrong with your eye?'

'I had a squint.'

'Oh Lord . . .'

'Yeah, it was very attractive. You've no idea how it drew the boys.' Her voice was sharp, then mellowed. 'Life's changed so much for me since the operation. I'm grateful for everything Hettie's done for me.'

'But?'

'Why should there be a but?' Rose asked, smiling.

'Because there always is. Besides, it's exhausting being grateful all the time. The person who gives is always better off than the person who receives.'

'That's bloody silly.'

He laughed loudly. 'Miss Bradshaw, you have a foul mouth on you!'

She refused to be scolded. 'I don't believe that the giver has power over the receiver.'

'Really?' Stuart replied, pulling up outside number 139

Gull Road. 'So why are you so pissed off with the Widow Miller?'

Across the street, Lester had just come home. From the dining room he could hear the sound of the guests eating dinner, Ruby pushing past him as he walked into the kitchen.

'You're busy tonight.'

'And no Trudie around to help,' Ruby snapped.

'Need a hand?'

She paused, smiling. 'Thanks, Lester, but Maisie's popped over. If you want a bite to eat there's something on the kitchen table – but stay off the egg and bacon pies.'

Walking up to his room with a hurriedly made sandwich, Lester glanced out of the landing window – just in time to see Rose get out of a sports car. Surprised, he leaned forward to get a better look. The man was a stranger to him. So Rose had a boyfriend now, did she? Lester was amazed by the pain such a notion caused him. Or maybe it wasn't a boyfriend at all, just someone from work. Someone driving her home. Someone young and good-looking, with an expensive car.

It was his own fault, Lester realised. He had steered clear of Rose because he was confused. *Lester Williams, confused? Lester Williams for once not knowing what to do?* Irritated, he leaned further forward. He had been blind to Rose for years and unless he was very careful, she was going to disappear permanently – snatched right out from under his nose. The woman he now dreamed about, longed to touch, to kiss . . . If he didn't make a move quick some other man would get her.

Not bloody likely, Lester thought, galvanised. She's *my* girl.

Throwing the half-eaten sandwich out of the window, Lester ran down the stairs, Stuart's sports car just driving away as he hit the street.

227

'Rose!'

She glanced over to him, surprised. 'Oh, hello, Lester.'

'What d'you mean, "oh, hello, Lester"?' he barked, Rose staring at him in surprise. 'And who the hell was that?'

'What business is it of yours?' she snapped back. 'What I do is my own concern.'

'Not any more.'

'*Really?*' she replied sarcastically, folding her arms. 'For someone who's only just noticed I exist, you have some nerve.'

'Well, I've noticed you now.'

'Yeah, since I had my eye fixed.'

'What the hell has your eye got to do with anything?' he replied shortly.

'Oh come on, Lester, we all know what you're like. You wouldn't have wanted to be seen with some squinty-eyed kid off the racetrack.'

Lester's face was a study. 'Where did the *racetrack* come in?'

'You only noticed me when I had my eye fixed and got all dressed up.'

'I don't believe it! Is *that* what you think?' he replied, laughing.

'I don't think it's funny! And I don't like being laughed at!'

'You don't like being wrong, you mean,' he responded, serious again. 'I didn't notice you before because you'd always been around –'

'Great!'

'I mean, you were like one of the family. You were Trudie's mate! A kid, for God's sake!'

'Well,' she said scornfully, 'being such a kid, maybe I shouldn't be out so late talking to strange men. Good night, *Mister* Williams.'

Infuriated, Lester grabbed hold of her and pulled her round to face him. Then he kissed her firmly on the mouth

228

before she had time to react. Shaken, Rose tried to pull back and then responded, clinging onto Lester hungrily, her arms around his neck, her eyes closed.

And her father watching from the window.

It was all going so nicely, Hettie thought as she eyed Cedric helping himself to another sherry. Rose had settled into her job and Stuart was smitten. Not that it would do for Cedric to know she had planned it all.

'Comfortable?'

He smiled. 'Delightful, my dear.'

'And still happy with Rose?'

'She's a fine girl,' he replied pompously. 'Almost good enough to be a child of mine.'

So she hadn't been swearing around Cedric, Hettie thought. Rose was learning fast. Be what people want you to be, that was the way to win in life.

'Stuart told me that she was an invaluable help the other evening when he had an emergency. The dental nurse had finished for the day, so she wasn't around when the patient came in . . .'

Oh, do get on with it, you old windbag, Hettie thought meanly.

'. . . The patient had a portion of tooth broken off. It was wedged in her gum, between her teeth . . .'

When they married, Hettie thought, Cedric would *have* to get a hobby.

'. . . and Rose helped Stuart as though she had been trained to do so. Remarkable, no nerves at all. Almost as though she was a natural . . .' He paused again to gather his thoughts. 'Of course, that does beg a question.'

'Which is?'

'A girl with a natural aptitude could train.'

'For what, Cedric?'

'To be a dental nurse,' he replied, surprised that she hadn't cottoned on already.

Oh no, Hettie thought, we don't want Rose to be a dental nurse, we want her to be a dental *wife*. We want two Mrs Fallows in that ghastly house of yours, not some jumped-up receptionist. Cedric had to be put right, and put right now. No point letting her plan drift awry, when all it needed was a smart shove back in the right direction.

Smiling as though she hadn't a care in the world, Hettie decided on a radical course of action.

'I can speak to you in perfect confidence, can't I, Cedric?'

'Indeed.'

She smiled, her voice lowered. 'You realise that Rose will be very rich one day.'

Cedric paused, his hand – holding a custard tart – halfway to his mouth.

'She will?'

Hettie nodded, knowing she had his full attention. Slowly, she slid along the sofa towards him, her voice low. 'I'm very fond of the dear girl. She's like my own child. And as I have no children of my own –'

'A tragedy.'

'Quite.'

'You would have been a fine mother.'

'Thank you, Cedric,' Hettie replied impatiently. 'As I was saying, Rose is like my own child, and will inherit my fortune one day.'

'She will?'

'Yes, Cedric, Rose will have all this one day.' Hettie waved her hand around, Cedric following it with his eyes. 'So you see, my dear, I have to make very sure that she marries well.'

'But she's not from a good family –'

'That won't matter so much when she's rich,' Hettie said quietly. 'I myself came from a family who had lost their fortune. Then I married for love. Edward Bradshaw . . . ah, he was a wonderful man. No money, but goodness itself. He died, Cedric, and then fortune smiled on me and I met my beloved Hubert.' It was vital that she explain her background at this point, Hettie thought. No point having Cedric come up with any probing questions later in the day. 'I would have stayed happily married to Hubert, had it not been for his untimely death.' She felt Cedric's cold hand move over her own. 'You know what it's like to lose someone you love? How it breaks your heart, tears up your life, ruins your hopes for the future . . .'

Cedric mumbled an agreement.

'. . . But you went on, my dear. And so did I. We have to find comfort where we may.' She smiled at Cedric bravely. 'Love can be a great sadness.'

'Quite.'

'But hopefully not for my dear Rose. When she marries she will marry for love, but having said that she must marry someone who is used to money. I don't want to think – when I am dead and gone –'

'My dear –'

'It must be faced, Cedric: one day I will be dead and gone . . .' but not before you, chum, she thought, '. . . and Rose will inherit my money. Her husband must be a man of unimpeachable reputation. Someone with a good family background. Someone not likely to act like a fool when his wife gets her fortune. In short, Cedric, a man of reputation.'

He coughed, looked down at his feet, and then took the bait.

'I don't want to speak out of turn, my dear –'

'You never could, Cedric. I rely on you to guide me.'

'Indeed. But I would – I hope this is not too presumptuous, Henrietta – like to put forward my son, Stuart, for your consideration.'

'Stuart!' Hettie said, feigning shock. So the old boy's got the message, has he?

'He's not the most steady character, but I dare say the right woman . . .'

With the right fortune, Hettie thought.

'. . . could settle him down.'

'I thought he was involved with some actress?'

Cedric looked pained. 'Oh, that's nothing! Just a young man acting foolishly.'

'But –'

Cedric hurried on anxiously. 'My son has a good family name, as you know, and a fine practice, which I spent long years cultivating. In short, Stuart might be a good match for your girl.'

My girl, Hettie thought. Yes, Rose is very nearly my girl. And when this little business is sorted, she will be closer to me than anyone. There wouldn't be too much time for Len and Gull Road, Hettie thought, not when there was the call of the Lytham social circuit and the lure of an inheritance to keep Rose in check. Oh, and a husband . . . Hettie smiled to herself. Stuart was a good-looking enough fellow – at least from the photographs Cedric had shown her – and young. The girl would have a suitor no one could possibly have imagined for her. She would have position and money.

Hettie was moved by her own generosity; Cedric saw her eyes fill and squeezed her hand.

'Oh, come now, my dear, we can sort this out. I don't want you to worry about a thing. I will talk to Stuart when the time is right, and we'll see to it that these two young people get together.'

With my fortune, Hettie thought meanly. Oh, Cedric, what a greedy man you are. And old . . . *The Widow Fallow*, Hettie mused, yes, it would do when Cedric was no more. When she was living with Rose and Stuart and their children, in Lytham St Annes. She wouldn't ever be alone again; she'd have a family, people to keep her occupied, lives to plan out.

Then for one delicious moment Hettie could imagine Len's face, and smiled triumphantly to herself. Revenge sometimes took a while, but it was all the better for waiting.

THIRTY-TWO

Without making any comment, Len had watched the romance between Rose and Lester begin and then pick up speed, finally deciding to confront his daughter at the end of June. It had been a smouldering day, leading into a sultry night. Earlier, Ruby had put under Len's door a note that read simply 'I warned Gilbert off, but he's besotted. Any ideas?'

Len had read the note and wanted to put one under Ruby's door, reading, 'I warned Rose off, but she's besotted too. Any ideas?'

But sarcasm wasn't Len's style. Besides, he wasn't sure that Ruby knew the full extent of her son's involvement with Rose. At any other time Ruby would have known everything, but she was preoccupied, and for once her oracle – Trudie – was too sullen to share any gossip.

Reaching for his baccy, Len rolled a cigarette and leaned back in his chair to savour it. He had no idea how to deal with the problem of Gilbert Beardsley, other than warn him off. And Ruby had already done that, to no effect. Len inhaled, wondering why the cigarette didn't taste as good as it normally did.

For all his reputation Len had been faithful to Doris for years. In fact, apart from a brief spell of womanising after Vera's death – which had gained him his reputation in the first place – he was a steady man in love. Thoughtful, he considered Doris. A widow, comfortable in every way, not without a bob or two, and certainly not without a sense of humour. They had good times, he and Doris. Neither wanted to marry again, and liked living apart in different houses and different towns. The arrangement was odd, but it suited them. And it suited Rose, who had no interest in her father's other life.

Len sighed. One thing about getting older – the passion subsided. It wasn't like being in your twenties, when you couldn't get enough of each other, when every day apart scorched you, when you daydreamed about your lover and carved her initials in the back of the bandstand. Len smiled, remembering. He had been that crazy about Vera; white-hot for her, just as she had been for him.

Just as Rose was for Lester now . . . Reflecting, Len stared at the tip of his cigarette, glowing dully. He had known that one day it would happen: his baby would fall in love. But he hadn't anticipated the grinding pain it would cause. Or the unease. Was Lester Williams really right for his girl? Len had his doubts, and yet Lester was treating Rose right – taking her out, buying her gifts, never keeping her out past her curfew . . . Len rolled his eyes. Who was he kidding? Vera's parents had set her a curfew, but if kids wanted to fool around they could do it at six o'clock just as easily as at midnight.

If only he could talk to Rose. But for once, Len was tongue-tied. And he had no one to turn to for help. Certainly not Clovis, who would have picked a roll of underfelt over Cary Grant any day. As for Nan Wilmslow – Len frowned – she was a woman of many parts certainly, but he couldn't see himself even broaching the subject with her. So who else was there? Not Ruby – she was preoccupied with Gilbert – and as for Trudie, she had been spitting feathers since Rose's transformation.

'What *are* you doing?' Rose said, walking in and flicking on the light. 'You're sitting in the dark, Dad.'

Surprised, he stubbed out his cigarette and glanced at her. 'Have a good time tonight?'

'Wonderful.'

She had the look, he thought – oh God, she had the look. I know what that means, love, the bubbles in the chest, the feeling that no one would understand, that no one has ever felt like this before. The time when the lover is everything, every thought, every action stored up to share. The time when even a touch on the hand is potent, the real world distant, populated by people who are drab and grey, because only the lovers' world is coloured. The look that says I'm encased in something deliriously, light-headedly special. And it will last for ever.

Or so everyone believes. Once.

'Rose, luv, I wanted to have a word with you.'

Immediately she sat down next to him. 'What is it?'

'It's difficult –'

'You're not ill?'

'Nah,' Len said hurriedly. 'It's nothing bad. It's about you and Lester.'

Her eyes warmed at the sound of his name. 'Don't worry, Dad –'

'But I do, luv. I'm supposed to, it's part of being a father,' he teased her. 'Is it getting serious?'

'Well,' Rose looked down at her hands, flushing, 'he says he cares about me.'

'I dare say, but what are his intentions?'

'Oh, Dad!' she replied, laughing. 'Don't be so old-fashioned!'

Len found himself unexpectedly blushing, but pushed on. 'OK, have a good laugh at me, but I'm only asking what any parent who gave a damn would ask. I don't want you getting in too deep with Lester. You know what lads are like: they're out for what they can get –'

'Dad!'

'Don't "Dad" me!' Len shot back. 'I have to say this.

Lester's a good lad, but you don't want to get yourself a reputation –'

Rose was on her feet in an instant, her expression blazing. 'Well, thanks for trusting me! I've not done anything wrong –'

'Oh, luv,' Len said hurriedly, 'I didn't mean –'

'What *did* you mean then?' she hurled back. 'You're jumping to the wrong conclusion. It's not like that with Lester and me. We care about each other – and he's not like that, anyway. He wouldn't try it on, not with me. He's serious about me.'

'Rose, sit down and let's talk this out.'

'I don't want to bloody talk it out!' she snapped. 'There's nothing to talk out. We're going out, enjoying ourselves, having a good time and now you want to spoil it –'

'Rose, luv –'

'I waited for this all my life. Longed for Lester to even notice me, let alone care about me. And now you're going to ruin everything.' She was suddenly close to tears. 'He *does* care about me! He bloody does!'

Len studied his daughter carefully before he spoke again. 'So what's the matter?'

'Nothing!'

'Rose, what's the matter?'

Slumping back into her seat, Rose stared ahead. 'I don't know, Dad . . . I thought everything was perfect, but he seems so preoccupied sometimes. You know, like his thoughts are somewhere else. He says it's work.'

'I don't doubt it,' Len replied. 'Lester's always running around after some deal or other. He's a lot on his mind.'

'That's what he says. He says that he wants to get on in life, to make a real name for himself. And that takes a lot of effort. He's explained all that – but sometimes I just want him to be more light-hearted, not so serious about everything.'

This was exactly what Len had expected.

'Rose, Lester Williams is a very ambitious young man. He's never going to be easy, and he'll get worse as he gets older. I'm not criticising him, luv, not for a minute, I'm just telling you what it'll be like. Men like Lester are driven; they have to be chasing after something – usually money and position. All fine and good, if they do it right and legal.' He put up his hands to stop Rose interrupting. 'I'm not saying anything Lester does is illegal, just hear me out! People like him, *ambitious* people, want to change the world. Or at least the part closest to them. They might care and love like other men, but not with the same devotion, because most of their energy is always being pumped into the next deal, the next idea.'

Rose was watching her father carefully. 'But I know he cares about me.'

'In his own way . . . and what you have to ask yourself is – would that be enough?' Len paused to roll up another cigarette, noting with astonishment that his hands were trembling. 'Mind you, luv, I don't know why we're talking so seriously about this. Lester Williams is just your first boyfriend. One of many –'

'But I don't want anyone else! I've always loved Lester. Since I was a child.' She stopped short.

His eyebrows raised, Len glanced up from his smoke. 'Oh, I see. I thought as much.'

'Dad, I can't help it,' Rose said eagerly. 'I *do* love him, I always have. I didn't want to tell you because I felt so stupid. But he's what I've always longed for. And now I have him I can't bear to think about losing him.' She kneeled down beside her father's chair and looked up at him. 'You understand, don't you, Dad? Say you understand.'

'Yes, I do,' he said gently. 'But what I *don't* understand is why Lester didn't fall in love with you before?'

'I was just a kid to him then. Just Trudie's friend –'

'But now you're beautiful, he wants you.'

'It's not like that!' Rose hollered.

'All right,' Len replied calmly, 'but just answer me one thing – if you weren't so pretty, would he still want you? I'm not trying to hurt you, Rose, just make you think, so you don't run off and lose your head over all of this. Lester's a fine man in a lot of ways, but he wants a good-looking woman on his arm. Another conquest to show the world he's got the best.'

'Whatever you think, Lester's good to me, Dad,' Rose said quietly, 'and he could have had anyone.'

'Hey! Don't put him on a pedestal,' Len warned her. 'He's no better than you.'

'I know,' she replied unconvincingly, 'but I want him, Dad. I really love him, and he loves me.'

A knife shot through Len's heart, severed the arteries and tore open the veins.

'Are you sure he loves you?' Len managed to ask after a moment had passed.

'Yes,' Rose answered her father emphatically. 'He loves me and I love him. He's the only man I've ever wanted and the only man I could ever love. Don't laugh at me, Dad, please, it's true. I was meant to be with him. However hard it gets, however much it might turn out to be a struggle, Lester is the only man I want.'

'Then all I can say is take your time, luv,' Len replied, trying not to let the emotion show in his voice. 'Just take it one day at a time. If it's real, it'll last and come out stronger. If it's not meant, nothing in this world – or the next – can save it.'

THIRTY-THREE

Rolling out some pastry for the evening meal at Sea View, Ruby glanced over to her husband. Alfred was sitting in his shirtsleeves, his eyes peering closely at the evening paper, his porkpie hat perched on the back of his head. Forgotten to take it off again, Ruby thought. What a dope. Silently she began to roll the pastry again. One of her guests – Miss Vernon – had complained about the custard. Said it had lumps in it! Wizened-up old bat, Ruby thought, mentally making a note to give her the pie with the least meat and the most pastry.

'Alfred,' Ruby said suddenly, rolling pin in one hand and bag of flour in the other, 'have you ever met a man . . . a man like . . . you know . . .'

'A dwarf?'

'Who said anything about a dwarf?' Ruby snorted. 'What made you say dwarf?'

He shrugged. 'I just thought you were going to say something about a dwarf. I knew a dwarf once, legs tiny like a dog's, bonny face. He could juggle like you wouldn't believe. When he died they buried him in an orange crate.'

Blinking, Ruby let this story run, and then pressed on.

'I was meaning –'

'. . . He had a sister, another little dwarf, and she was a pickpocket . . .'

'Who took things out of men's turn-ups, I suppose?'

239

But Alfred was well on his way.

'. . . she fell in love with the Ringmaster, when they had the old-fashioned Ringmaster at the Big Top. But his family were against it.'

'You don't say.'

'Said he owed it to them to marry someone taller . . .'

Incredulous, Ruby said nothing.

'. . . seeing as how he had a bit of a deformity himself.'

'He couldn't stop lying?'

'No, he had a cleft palate. And one leg shorter than the other.'

'You know, Alfred, I'm sure I would have remembered a Ringmaster like that,' Ruby said drily, then hurried on. 'I was going to talk to you about someone else. *Gilbert*.'

'She used to wear doll's clothes –'

'For God's sake, Alfred,' Ruby snapped, 'stop talking about dwarfs!'

Miffed, he stared at her, shook the newspaper and then disappeared behind it.

Sighing, Ruby walked over to him. 'Alfred, do you know about Gilbert?'

Reluctantly Alfred's head appeared over the top of the paper, his eyes boring into his wife's. 'He's your brother.'

'I know that. But do you *know* about him?'

This was getting too much for Alfred.

'*What* about him?'

'What he's like?'

'Bit fat.'

'No, I meant, what's Gilbert like as a person?'

'Odd.'

'How odd?'

'Very odd,' Alfred replied, surprised that he was even being given a hearing by his wife. 'An actor.'

'But apart from being an actor?'

Alfred struggled manfully. 'He's . . . he's . . . he's *weird*.'

Ah, Ruby thought, so Alfred knew more than he had let

240

on all these years. Maybe he could help her, after all.

'Yes, Alfred, he's weird,' she agreed. 'Now, what d'you think we should do about it?'

'His being weird?'

She nodded. God, it was like drawing teeth.

'Well . . .' Alfred thought for a moment, stroked his chin, and thought again. Finally he leaned towards his wife. 'I know what I would do.'

'You do?' she said thankfully. 'What, Alfred?'

'I'd take away those Turkish slippers,' he said, nodding sagely. 'That's what I'd do.'

How could he not have seen her before? Lester wondered. In the few weeks since he had started to go out with Rose he had found himself besotted. Even his work, so precious to him, could not entirely consume his every thought. She would sneak into his meetings, curl herself around every booth he looked at, call out from in amongst the voices of others. She was his darling, his beautiful, perfect, funny, sassy, precious love. And more than that, she was feisty. Oh no, no pushover was Rose. He was certain she adored him, but she stood up to him too. And he admired that.

Of course, Joe had noticed, teasing his brother and asking him how it felt.

'Getting married soon?' he asked, when he arrived at Lester's office beside the station.

It wasn't much of an office so far. But Lester – typically – had furnished it with the best desk and chair. If you wanted to attract quality, he had said, you had to look the part. As for Lester's clothes . . . Oh boy, Joe had said to Maisie, he must spend a fortune on those. In fact, anyone who didn't know Lester Williams from Gull Road would have thought him a prosperous businessman from Manchester, at least. Maybe even London.

'So, *are* you going to marry Rose?'

Lester looked up from the blueprints he was studying.

'Married! We've only been going out for a bit.' Then he smiled. 'She's a one-off, isn't she?'

'Seems like you're suited then,' Joe replied. 'Anyway, you go lovesick every time someone mentions her name. Looks like the real thing to me, brother.'

Feeling flustered again, Lester glanced down. He *was* in love with Rose, utterly and completely. In fact the depth of his feeling had rocked him. Is this real love? he had asked himself. The thought that without that person, life wouldn't be worth bloody anything? The thought that if he didn't see, hear or touch Rose Bradshaw everyday he would die? And now the thought of marriage – that condition once so abhorrent to him – seemed just a delicious necessity.

'You know, Lester, if you want to make an honest woman out of her, you might have to look sharp. All the men are after Rose now.'

'Well, they can keep their distance. She's mine.'

'Not until you marry her she's not. Anyway, moving amongst the nobs now, she might meet someone any day.' Joe couldn't resist it. 'Like that bloke with the sports car.'

'She's not interested in him!' Lester replied testily.

Joe laughed. 'Oh dear, you *have* got it bad. Poor Lester. *Mister Williams is in a fluster.*'

Lester was mortified. 'I never thought I could feel like this about anyone.'

'You never do. Until it's the right one,' Joe replied, picking up some of the drawings and studying them. 'These the plans for your dance hall?'

Lester nodded. 'If they go through.'

'Big.'

'The bigger the better.'

'It'll be nice.'

'Yeah,' Lester agreed. 'I'll make it the best in this town.'

'I meant if you married Rose!' Joe said, laughing. 'I'd like to have my brother settled, like me. I don't suppose you'd end up in Gull Road, though.'

'Who knows?' Lester said cagily.

In fact, he had already decided that Gull Road was not for him and his bride. They would live somewhere up and coming, not a street full of rented rooms and private hotels. But he could hardly say that, could he? Could hardly patronise his family, infer that what they had wasn't good enough for him. But when everything was settled he would sort it out, make sure no one was affronted, least of all Len.

'What does her father think?'

Lester smiled. He and Joe had always had a mental telepathy.

'He's a bit off with me at the moment. Sizing me up, I reckon. I don't blame him. Rose is all he's got and it took me long enough to realise her value.' Lester stared his brother full in the face. 'To be honest I *didn't* think of Rose romantically until she had her eye fixed. But it wasn't the damn squint, Joe, it was her! She was just a kid to me, Trudie's chum. Then I suddenly saw her like everyone else did – and she swept me away.' He paused, embarrassed by his feelings. 'I was a bit slow on the uptake, wasn't I?'

'For once,' Joe replied, winking.

'I guess another reason Len doesn't approve of me is because I'd take Rose away from him. Leave him a lonely man.'

'Not if I hear right,' Joe replied, leaning against his brother's desk. 'I hear there's a lady called Doris in the background. Maybe Len will have a bit more time for her *when* you take Rose off his hands.'

'You are such a bloody gossip!' Lester mocked him, although he was inordinately pleased by the news. Joe was right: it *would* make it easier if Len had someone else in his life. 'Where d'you hear that?'

'Trudie.'

'She's being a right bitch at the moment. I can't say anything to her without her biting my head off.'

'She's doesn't like coming second, doesn't our Trudie,' Joe

said evenly. 'And you falling in love with her rival doesn't help.'

'She and Rose were best friends once.'

'Not any more. She's jealous, and the fact that Rose might nab her brother isn't helping.'

'Maybe she should find someone of her own,' Lester replied, his tone testy.

Joe shrugged. 'To hear her tell it, no one's good enough. But if you ask me, if Trudie doesn't stop scowling and start smiling again she might find herself alone a lot longer than she thinks.'

This being a Thursday, Rose called to see Hettie. To report, she told Lester, to let her mentor know about how she was getting on. Having accepted the requisite cup of tea and exchanged small talk, Hettie eyed Rose carefully. Goodness, the girl learned fast. Those clothes she had bought Rose were looking good, and she had managed to mix and match them perfectly. As Hettie had suspected from the start, the girl had style.

'Still enjoying your job, my dear?'

Rose could smell the scent of honeysuckle and old roses drifting in from the garden and was drowsily content. Life was sweet; even Hettie's interference couldn't bother her now.

'It's pleasant at the surgery, and Stuart's easy to work with.'

'He seems impressed with you,' Hettie replied, playing with her cuffs; something she always did when she was thinking. 'In fact, his father seems to believe that Stuart might be carrying a bit of a torch for you.'

Without thinking, Rose laughed.

'I don't see what's so funny!' Hettie suddenly snapped. 'You should be grateful for the attention, my dear. A good match there would set you up for life.'

Stupefied, Rose looked at her mentor. Hettie was sitting

with her back to the light, her hair a luminous aura around her face, her expression unreadable. Rose had known for a while that she was out to make Cedric Fallow her third husband, but she had never thought that Hettie's ambitions extended to arranging her protégée's love life. Feeling surprisingly cold in the stuffy room, Rose reached for her tea and drank silently. She would have to find a way to make it clear – without hurting Hettie's feelings – that her life was just that. *Her life*. A life in which Stuart Fallow had no part, except as her employer.

'Hettie,' Rose said, struggling to find the right words, 'you know how grateful I am for everything you've done for me?'

Hettie preened herself, but her mind was needle sharp.

'You've been so generous, paying for my operation, buying me clothes and getting me a good job. But . . .'

'Yes, dear?'

'Well, I have to make up my own mind about who I go out with.'

Hettie moved, leaning back against the sofa, her eyes flinty. 'Going to waste yourself on some lowlife, are you? Waste all my efforts and money –'

'Now look here!'

'No, *you* look here!' Hettie snapped, outraged. 'I didn't invest all my time and money in you, just to have you throw it away. I have plans for you, my dear.' Her tone softened; Rose was speechless. 'Great plans. Sometimes in life we have to plot a little to make the good things happen. You're a lovely-looking girl now, and you have class. You could do very well for yourself.'

And indirectly for you, Rose thought. Nothing like living vicariously.

'Hettie,' she began, her tone reasonable again, 'I don't want my life plotting out –'

'That's what you think now. Later you'll thank me.'

Swallowing her temper, Rose pressed on. 'I have to make my own way in the world.'

'Why? When you have someone to help you?' Hettie replied, her tone soothing. 'I don't think you understand, Rose. I am very fond of you, very fond indeed. I have no family and I would like you to inherit my fortune.' Rose stared at her incredulously. 'Don't look at me like that! It's very simple, my dear. You are becoming a remarkable woman. With my tutelage – and the attraction of one day being a rich woman – you could find yourself a good husband. No working for you, Rose. Just a cushy life, with a nice house and children –'

'And a husband *you* pick?'

Hettie blinked. Really, Rose could be so sharp at times. 'But you like Stuart Fallow.'

'As a boss! Not as a would-be husband,' Rose replied, her tone heated. 'Hettie, you can't run my life for me –'

'I seem to have done for a while now. God knows where you would be if it *hadn't* been for me.' She squinted, smiling cruelly. 'Stayed that runty kid with a glide in your eye, living with your father on Gull Road? Not many prospects there, hey?'

'You bloody cow!'

'How dare you!'

'*How dare I!*' Rose snapped back. 'You did all this for me so that you'd have a bloody puppet to play with? Someone you could jerk around, pick up and manipulate when you wanted? Well, not me, Hettie, not me!'

'I would think carefully about what you're saying!' Hettie threw back. 'Don't give up so much money and power so recklessly, my dear. It came easy to you, but it's hard to earn.' She paused, her tone softening. 'You must forgive me, Rose. Come now, sit down again. We're squabbling like fish wives and that's not good.' She patted the sofa beside her. 'Come on, I might have been a little out of turn, but then so were you.'

Reluctantly, Rose sat down again. She had a good deal to thank Hettie for, and was painfully aware of it. Guilt made her continue to visit Heathcote Place – just as Hettie knew it would.

'I spoke too soon about Stuart Fallow,' Hettie went on, choosing her words carefully. She had to be very adept now: Rose was proving to be more difficult than she had imagined. And after she had promised her a fortune! Dear God, working-class people could be so ungrateful. 'I was just excited for you. Pleased that you had made such an important conquest. Of course, you must choose your own partner. But when you *are* choosing, do consider how rich you'll be one day and pick someone your equal.'

'Hettie, I can't inherit from you,' Rose replied, cautiously. 'I'm not related. Not even your own flesh and blood –'

'You're like a daughter to me.'

Rose persisted. 'But I'm *not* your daughter, am I?'

Hettie could feel a sudden pressure in her chest. Her plans were being turned over, belly up, vulnerable.

'You're not my daughter by birth,' Hettie continued, controlling herself, 'but I care about you deeply. As I would my own daughter. Oh, come now, Rose, who else have I got? You're young, you'll marry and have a family of your own. Think what good you could do with the money . . . If you won't consider yourself, then think of your father, how you could help him.'

Confused, Rose looked down at her hands. What was the right answer – to refuse? Or was Hettie being genuinely kind? Did she really want Rose to inherit the money and put it to good use? Another thought hit Rose almost immediately. What if the inheritance was simply a carrot – like George Ogden's licence had been for her father? Something eternally dangled out of reach? But then Len had got the licence in the end, hadn't he?

'Your attitude hurts me very much,' Hettie said, sounding wounded. 'I want only the best for you and yet you always treat me with such suspicion.'

Guilt struck Rose like a hammer blow. 'I didn't mean –'

'I think you should go now. Think about what I've said and then maybe you'll realise that all I want is the best for you. I'm not the selfish, egotistical woman I once was, Rose. I'm older, I've changed. If you have any kindness in you, let me do something worthwhile with my life. Please, it would mean so much to me.'

It was the second time in a month that Hettie saw her bait being swallowed whole.

THIRTY-FOUR

Hurrying down the Promenade in the heat, Ruby was perspiring, her cotton dress sticking to her back, strands of hair clammy against her neck. She hated the summer; hated the heat; hated the flies. Hated everything about it, apart from the fact that summer meant guests. And guests meant money. Blowing out her cheeks, Ruby paused to lean against the cool iron railings, looking out to sea.

On the beach below her a small boy was chasing after his brother, a man asleep in a deck chair, in amongst the hundreds of other deck chairs. Row after row extended for as far as the eye could see, the sunshine shimmering on the sea, gulls calling and dipping overhead. And on the pier itself Ruby could see the clutter of trippers in their summer dresses and shirtsleeves, waving cheap souvenirs and laughing. Their voices mixed with the sound of the band playing at an open-air concert and the fairground barkers calling loudly into the stuffy afternoon.

Waving a fly away from her face, Ruby stared into the sea and then, on a whim, ploughed her way down amongst the crowd on the beach. Purposefully, she strode on, most people stepping back for a six-foot woman with a nasty gleam in her eye. Finally, at the water's edge, Ruby pulled off her shoes and stockings and then waded out, up to her knees.

The relief was immediate, her body cooling down, the

sound of some boys laughing at her having no effect. Mellowing, Ruby glanced around her, her gaze resting on the horizon. When she was a kid, she had dreamed of having a house near the sea. Nothing could have been nicer, to a child brought up in a caravan, than to have solid earth underfoot and a wide open sea to look at.

Wriggling her toes in the water, Ruby sighed to herself. Joe's marriage to Maisie was a success, that much was obvious, and now Maisie had her glasses she wasn't even bumping into things any more. As for Lester, he seemed very preoccupied at the moment, Ruby thought. But then again, who was she to talk?

She wriggled her toes some more. Then, after allowing one last sweet wave to tickle her knees, Ruby walked back to the beach, her stockings and shoes in her hand.

'What yer doing?' a young lad called out to her, his friends giggling behind him. 'People don't go swimming with their clothes on. Don't yer know that?'

'You been swimming today?' Ruby asked them.

'Yeah. What of it?'

'Been over there?' Ruby pointed to the right of the beach.

'Sure.'

'Well, don't go there again. A kid got eaten by a shark last year.'

The kids took in a united breath.

'Yer kidding!'

'No.'

'I don't believe yer,' the first kid said. 'Why would a shark eat him?'

Ruby leaned her impressive bulk towards the child. 'Because he asked stupid bloody questions. That's why.'

A few minutes later Ruby was sitting on one of the wooden benches on the Promenade. She had pulled her shoes onto her wet feet, but tucked her stockings into her pocket, letting the breeze cool her bare calves. The Pavilion Theatre twinkled in front of her. *Gilbert . . .* Ruby sighed, then found herself looking away from a policeman who glanced in her direction.

What the hell was she doing, she wondered, irritated. She had nothing to be afraid of. She wasn't a criminal. In fact, no one in the family was. Since Alfred's little run-in a long while back, there had been no crooks in the Williams camp. There was just a *would-be* criminal. An up-and-coming criminal. A criminal in the making.

Oh God, Gilbert! Ruby thought impatiently, what the hell are you playing at?

The policeman walked past her, then doubled back, the sun fire hot on the top of Ruby's head. Did he know her? More to the point, did he know her brother? Was he about to stop and ask her about Gilbert? Maybe tell her that he had been arrested . . . ? Oh, stop it! Ruby told herself, stop making up stories. You're getting like Alfred.

But even after the policeman disappeared into the distance, her unease didn't lift. So for once Ruby put her chores on hold and sat for a long while looking out to sea. Gradually the sun moved, dipping down into late afternoon, and still she sat. Before long she would have to return to Sea View, Miss Vernon and her other guests, but not yet. The temperature dropped, becoming soft, the evening yielding. Early lights went on at the pier and around the big dipper. Gradually the trippers moved off the beach, the click-clack of the deck chairs being folded echoing into the drowsy air.

The answer had to be somewhere, Ruby told herself. Somewhere under that cool sea, beneath that warm sand, or bobbing in a rock pool. Somewhere there was the answer . . .

Her eyes moved upwards, her attention drawn by the clouds hurrying overhead. Tomorrow would be fine again. And hot. Bloody hell . . . The clouds met, mingled and then separated, their blowsy white and pink edges parting like theatre curtains.

Of course! Ruby thought. That was the answer. *Of course*.

All the boys that summer were dopes, Trudie thought, letting herself into Sea View and sloping off upstairs. It was pointless even going out. As for her job at Myers – who wanted that? Or any of the others she had gone for? Irritated, she flung herself down on her bed and stared up at the ceiling. The wallpaper was mottled and patchy. She wondered what kind of wallpaper the Widow Miller had and then imagined Rose lying in some elegant bedroom, looking up at the pristine wallpaper overhead.

Why did *she* have to get so lucky? Why *her*, of all people? Trudie fumed to herself. No one expected Rose Bradshaw to make anything of herself, and then the Widow Miller came along and damn near adopted her. She didn't *work* for it. Just got lucky . . . Fuming, Trudie turned over and began to pick at her eiderdown fretfully. Below her she could hear the opening and closing of doors: guests going out for the evening. And then, coming in later, they'd be giggling quietly, or tipsy, making the bed-springs creak.

Some chance Trudie had of meeting anyone who would make *her* bedsprings creak. She was shut in with her family – although Joe had got out, and it looked like Lester would follow soon. *With Rose* . . . Furious, Trudie pulled the coverlet over her head and screamed noiselessly. She could tell it was serious. Even if her mother couldn't see it yet, Trudie knew what was going to happen. She was going to lose her brother to that smug bitch. She was going to be left alone with her parents at Sea View whilst Lester and Rose moved on, got their own freedom and their own home.

It wasn't supposed to have been this way, Trudie railed inwardly. *She* was the one who should have landed a fancy fella and got out first. Whilst Rose should have stayed the squinty-eyed one in the background. Not turning heads, not being given good clothes, not having some swanky job. And definitely *not* stealing her last remaining brother.

It was all wrong, Trudie thought self-pityingly, hate growing inside her like a spring mushroom. It was all wrong. But surely it wasn't going to last. It couldn't, could it? Trudie asked herself. Surely *something* would halt Rose's astonishing rise.

Or *someone*.

It had been a good night, Louis Wilkes thought, as he made his way back to the tent behind the Tower Circus ring. He would change, have a little drink, and then wait for Gilbert. Wilkes smiled wolfishly to himself. The danger always made the sex so much more exciting. The masses would be horrified to know what men like them did; but didn't that make it all the more alluring? And he'd never been caught. Besides, he had an escape route, something poor podgy Gilbert didn't have. Louis could move on if things got too dangerous; but Gilbert was beached.

It was amazing how pathetic people in the provinces were. Poor Gilbert, so grateful for the odd kiss and fumble, grateful enough to buy Wilkes anything he wanted. Dinners, clothes, even a watch. And Gilbert had been so pathetically pleased when he had been given that gold chain. Well, it wasn't gold actually, but by the time Gilbert found that out Wilkes would be long gone. Moved on to another town, or back down South.

Carefully, Wilkes began to wipe off his white Harlequin make-up. Not many could resist him, he thought with satisfaction. His looks had served him well. All he had to do was to make sure that he made the most of them before they decayed. He wasn't going to get like the other ageing queens, touting for business at the rough end of the market. No, whilst he was still fresh, Wilkes was going to clean up where and when he could, and then retire gracefully.

A knock on the tent board alerted him. 'Come in, Gilbert, darling. I've been waiting for you.'

To his astonishment a very large woman entered instead.

Ruby looked at him with open disgust. Jesus, she thought to herself, what kind of freak was this? Incredulous, she took in his powdered face, his perfectly made-up mouth with its exaggerated cupid's bow, and shuddered. This man was trouble, Ruby realised instinctively. He might be slight in stature, but he was as deadly as the roughs she had encountered so often in her childhood. An opportunist, like they had been. Only he was an opportunist of the sexual kind.

Towering over the seated Wilkes, Ruby boomed down at him: 'Gilbert *darling* won't be coming.'

Wilkes looked aghast. 'Don't tell me he's married –'

'I'm his sister!' Ruby shot back, staring at his upturned face. 'You're good-looking, I'll grant you that, but I want you to leave my brother alone.'

'You came here to tell me that?' Wilkes laughed. 'How delicious! Isn't that duty supposed to fall to the father of the outraged virgin?'

Immediately Ruby jabbed her toe under the front rung of Wilkes's chair, flipping the chair – and its occupant – backwards onto the floor.

'Now, listen to me, you big girl's blouse,' she said, looming over the prostrate Wilkes. 'You keep away from Gilbert –'

'You can't make me!'

'I think I can,' Ruby replied. 'How much?'

'You what?'

'Oh, come on, don't act soft. You and I know how these things work – how much?'

Wilkes's expression assumed a shifty air. He wasn't about

to fight for the privilege of seeing the portly Gilbert again at the risk of being mauled to death by his sister. A financial compromise seemed ideal, even assuaging the headache he was getting from the lump on his head.

'I want fifty quid –'

'You want a bloody good thrashing!' Ruby replied, taking some money out of her pocket and slamming it down on the dressing table. 'That's all there is and all you're getting, so don't bother asking for more.'

'I could get more from Gilbert.'

'You try it and I'll go to the police.'

Wilkes's eyes widened, his smile sickly. 'You wouldn't dare! You shop me and you'd give your brother away at the same time.'

'No, I wouldn't,' Ruby replied ruthlessly. 'I'd say I'd seen you in the park, with a man.'

Smarting, Wilkes struggled to his feet, turned to the money and picked it up. Slowly he counted it and then sighed.

'Not bad.'

'It's a one-off.'

Wilkes smiled.

'You got any letters from my brother?'

'Nah.'

'Photos?'

'Nah. Your brother's not exactly the photogenic type.'

Ruby winced. 'Any kind of memento?'

'Like what?' Wilkes asked, provoking her. 'Love tokens?'

'If you want another lump on the head, keep it up,' she warned him darkly. 'Now think carefully, Mr Wilkes, have you got *anything* which could come back on Gilbert?'

'Nothing,' he replied, realising with annoyance that he had lost a valuable opportunity.

'In that case,' Ruby said flatly. 'You leave Blackpool tonight.'

'Tonight! I've four more shows –'

'You go *tonight*, Mr Wilkes,' Ruby repeated coldly, 'or the next time you come off stage there'll be another big burly man waiting for you. Only this time he'll be in bloody uniform.'

THIRTY-FIVE

The Bank Holiday of 5 August broke all records. Scuttling to the coasts around Britain, people flocked in their thousands, Blackpool crammed with day-trippers, Sea View full. On the North Pier there was hardly room to walk, the sun bouncing off the sea, children fishing at the end of the pier, lads larking about in pleasure boats. Hardier types took to the sea, the water warm enough not to paralyse the limbs, the elderly sitting in huddles on the Promenade benches.

The worst of the Depression had passed, and a new optimism filled the air as the unemployment figures fell. There was more work again. There was more money again. Not much, but enough to make people want to go out for the day to forget the hot press of city streets and factory hooters calling them to work. As ever, they came to the coast.

In Lytham, Hettie stayed indoors at Heathcote Place. As she said to Cedric, Blackpool was just too common. But over in Gull Road, where the houses steamed in the summer heat and the noises from the railway station clattered on the hot air, Lester was preparing to take the day off.

'When I were a lad,' Alfred told his son, 'every Bank Holiday there were a murder. Regular as you like. Someone got killed.'

Lester was combing his hair and smiled at his father's reflection. 'That right, Dad?'

Alfred nodded sagely. 'Aye, that's right. There's many a body under this pier that's been hidden for years.'

Picking up his jacket, Lester mulled the information over. 'Wouldn't the tide have uncovered it?'

'Not if it were buried deep,' Alfred said, tapping his nose as though he had personal knowledge of the graves' measurements. 'Not if it were buried *deep*.'

All thought of murder left Lester's mind as he set off down Gull Road. The day was going to be blistering, he thought, walking over to Rose's house and then pausing. No, he'd go for some cigarettes first, then call for Rose. After all, she wasn't expecting him. Who had ever heard of Lester Williams taking a day off? It was to be his big surprise: a whole day spent alone with his girl.

Retracing his footsteps, Lester was just turning into Rigby Street when he heard his name called.

Frowning, he turned. Beth Hodges was leaning against the wall of the corner shop, deep in shadow, her sloe eyes striking in her pale face. Somehow she seemed unreal, as though she didn't belong there; as though she had been waiting, unmoving, for a very long time. She was, as ever, compelling.

'Beth,' he said simply, walking over to her. 'How are you doing?'

She pushed away from the wall, her eyes steady as she looked up at him. 'I haven't seen you for a while. Six weeks, in fact.'

'I've been busy,' Lester said, suddenly shame-faced. 'Look, I'll be honest with you, Beth, I've met someone else. It's serious –'

'We were serious,' she said, her tone suspiciously even.

'No, we weren't!' Lester replied heatedly. 'You know that, and so do I. We said from the start it was nothing but a bit of fun. You said yourself that you weren't looking to settle down.' She was watching him oddly, unnerving him. 'I have to go now, Beth –'

'It's that Rose Bradshaw, isn't it?'

Lester winced. Somehow he didn't want Beth even to mention her name.

'So you know?'

'I heard,' Beth replied, moving closer to him, her tone still measured. 'I heard and I saw you both together. Walking along without a care in the world. All wrapped up in each other. Like *we* used to be.'

'It wasn't the same with us, Beth,' Lester said, his tone even, but not unkind. He felt sympathy for her. But she had made it clear that she wasn't interested in a serious relationship with him, so why was she acting so strangely now? 'I liked you a lot –'

'Hah!'

Taken aback, Lester turned to go, Beth catching hold of his arm. Men longed for Beth, she knew that, just as she knew she could have whoever she wanted. But she only wanted Lester now. It was true that at first she hadn't been interested in anything serious; had made the point clear with Lester. *Just fun.* She was good at fun. It filled the empty pit inside her. What the pit was, where it had come from, Beth didn't know. But fun had always kept it away. Until now.

She was wearing a green dress that seemed too hot for the day and eerily out of place. A dark green dress, the colour of reeds and deep water. A drowning dress.

'Don't rush off,' she pleaded. 'Don't let's argue.'

Lester turned back, reluctantly pliable.

'Beth, I'm sorry, I called round the other day to tell you, but you were out. I should have called back, explained.' He paused, but she did not respond. 'Things have moved so quickly. There's no easy way to say this, Beth, but I'm going to marry Rose Bradshaw.'

Her eyes flickered, but she remained still, her hand around his arm. The pit inside her was suddenly sucking her in. '*Marry* her?'

He nodded. 'I know I said that I didn't want to settle down, but she's the right one for me, Beth. You'll find someone and feel the same way I do one day –'

'Don't patronise me!' she hissed, her eyes black fire. 'You're not going to marry Rose Bradshaw. You're going to marry me.'

Irritated, Lester made to go, but Beth's fingers were gripping his arm tightly. 'Listen to me,' she commanded him.

Unnerved, Lester shook her off and hurried away. The sun beat down on him relentlessly as he crossed the road, his shadow thrown huge and dark in front of him. And as he hurried away, he could hear the sound of footsteps following, and then saw a dark shadow catch up with his own. Soon their shadows were in step, side by side. Two dark shapes walking to nowhere.

'Go away!' he snapped, stopping and turning to face Beth. 'Just go away.'

'Never,' she said simply, her hair inky black, without colour under the sunlight, her skin surreally pale. And the dress, moss green, serpent green. 'Lester, you have to marry *me* –'

'You're crazy!'

'No, I'm not crazy, and you'll see it's for the best in the end,' she replied, following him as he moved off again, her dress making rustling noises like a snake travelling quickly through long grass. 'Lester, you and I are meant for each other –'

'Beth, go home!' he barked. 'What we had is over. There's nothing left. You can't make it more than it was.' His tone softened. 'I'm sorry, but these things happen. It's over.'

'I'm pregnant.'

Lester could feel the sun on the back of his neck and along his shoulders, but it was no longer comforting. It scorched him instead; made his head swim, his thoughts muddled. And in front of him stood Beth, cool in her drowning dress, her eyes never leaving his face. Jesus, Lester thought, what had he done?

'I don't believe you!'

'It's true,' she replied calmly. 'Why would I lie?'

'To trap me.'

'I don't have to trap you,' Beth answered him, her eyes unfathomable. 'You *want* to be with me. You know you do, really. Lester, this baby is a sign. A sign that you and I are meant to be together –'

'It's an accident!' he replied, backed into a corner and imagining himself trying to explain the situation to Rose. Oh God, he thought, not Rose. How would he tell her? And what would she think of him when he did? 'Beth,' he said hurriedly, 'I'll help you, I promise you. We'll sort this out.'

She nodded, already ahead of him. 'I know we will. We'll have the first banns read this Sunday and –'

He shook his head impatiently. 'Listen to me! I can find out who's the best person to see about the baby. I have the money, Beth. We can get all this cleared up.' He was panicking, desperate in the heat, on the boiling corner where she had forced him to stand. 'No one will ever know. And when it's over you can get on with your life –'

'No.'

He stared at her, wanting to hit her, to shake her. Desperately, he looked around. The street was empty except for a child playing on a far corner.

'Think about it,' he pleaded. 'You're confused, Beth. You have to think sensibly.'

'I *am* thinking sensibly,' she replied. 'I'm thinking for both of us. The three of us.'

Lester's mouth dried. His future, so promising only minutes before, was now under threat. Instead of having his beloved Rose, he imagined his life with the enigmatic Beth. In some shady house nearby, with some child, crying in a pram in some backyard. *His wife*, Beth, dark-haired, blue-eyed, sensual and disturbing.

'We have to get this sorted,' Lester went on, hardly able to talk, his mouth was so dry. 'Listen to me –'

Panic was making her sharp. 'No, you listen to *me*! You desert me and I'll tell everyone what you did. Your name will be dirt, Lester, and I doubt your mother would approve of your actions. People don't expect a man to shirk his responsibilities in this town. They look badly on it. Look badly on him. It wouldn't be good for you personally, or your business, Lester. And you know how much your business means to you. You've got to stand by me –'

He backed away from her then. 'I don't have to marry you. I *don't* have to.'

Slowly Beth moved, her dress rustling as she circled him. The pit in her stomach was gaping, terror making her thoughts wild. 'If you let me down, I'll kill myself.'

'Jesus!'

'*I will.*'

And in that moment Lester knew that she probably would. Probably walk into the dark green sea in her dark green dress, spite taking her down in the undercurrent. And when she reached the bottom she would stare upwards with her sloe eyes, her black hair ebbing and flowing with the overhead tides.

'Don't talk rubbish!'

'Don't make me do it,' Beth replied, her voice deadly, blundering on with the threat. 'Because I will, Lester. *I will.* I'd do anything to stop you marrying another woman. I have nothing to lose. All I want is you and I'll do anything to get you. Even kill myself . . .'

He tried to bluster. 'You wouldn't have me if you killed yourself.'

She smiled. 'I'd have you body and soul then, Lester. You and I both know that. So you can't *let* me commit suicide, can you? You don't want that on your conscience, do you? The death of your woman and your unborn child?' She circled him again. 'You couldn't live with that, not you, Lester. It would eat into you, drive you to madness.'

His mind was swimming, drowning in the whirlpool she had created.

'You couldn't kill yourself. What about the baby?'

'What about it?' she countered. 'You don't care about it, do you? Then why should I? Poor Beth Hodges, people would say, she killed herself because the man who had got her pregnant left her.' It *couldn't* happen, she thought desperately. Whatever she did, she *had* to keep him. She would make up for it later: she would love him, make him see how mad he had been even to think of leaving her. 'Think about what people would say – Lester Williams, they'd mutter, he's the bastard who all but killed her. Your name would be mud –'

'You *can't* do this,' Lester said helplessly. 'What's the point? We wouldn't be happy together. You can't *make* someone marry you, Beth. We'd end up hating each other. I don't love you.'

'I love *you*,' she replied, her eyes focused on his. 'And that will be enough to begin with. You'll love me in time, Lester – when I'm your wife and the mother of your child.'

He could feel his heart slow down. Strange, Lester thought, he would have imagined the opposite. But hatred made his pulse slow, his mind clearing. The street was empty suddenly; not even the child out playing now. Overhead the sun grinned maniacally down on the trippers, the Tower, and the dark green sea.

Slowly, he reached out for her and then pulled Beth into the nearby alleyway. She went with him willingly, thinking he wanted her.

THIRTY-SIX

That night came in slow, the water lapping the beach, the lights from the pier shining on the sea. Overhead the sky darkened into indigo, the Tower reaching its inky finger upwards to the moon. On the Promenade, drunken revellers sang and swayed to their boarding houses or late trains. And on Rigby Street everything was quiet.

Staggered by what she had just heard, Trudie hurried back across Gull Road and stood immobile, staring at the Bradshaws' house. There were lights on downstairs, so someone was home. Was this the best time, she wondered. Go on, Trudie willed herself, go over and tell Rose what you know. Go and blow her bloody good luck into oblivion . . . But should she? After all, it would hurt her brother too. But then again, Lester hadn't cared too much for his sister lately.

Go on, a voice urged her. Go on, tell her . . . It would do Rose Bradshaw good to have her world upturned. Oh, people would still stare at her, but for another reason completely . . . Go on, go on . . . Trudie bit her lip, spite like a good meal inside her. For the first time in weeks she felt content, in control again.

A noise made her duck down the basement steps of the house next to Sea View. Joe came out of his home and banged the front door shut. He looked worried. As well he might, Trudie thought. I wonder how much he hero-worships Lester now? In the shadows, she watched her brother enter Sea View and then crept back up to street level.

And then she saw her: Rose, walking home. She was wearing white, showing off her tanned skin, a striped bag flung casually over her shoulder.

'Rose.'

She turned, saw Trudie and stopped. 'Hello there, what are you doing?'

'Waiting for you.'

She smiled, genuinely pleased. 'You want to go out somewhere? The flicks or something?' She moved over to Trudie and linked arms with her. 'I've missed you.'

'Yeah, I could tell,' Trudie replied churlishly. 'Where's Lester?'

'Working. As usual.'

'No, he's not.'

Alerted by her tone, Rose dropped Trudie's arm and stood back. Slowly she scrutinised her friend's over-made-up face, her clothes almost blowsy. She had changed, Rose thought with surprise. She was getting cheap, even her voice assuming a hard edge.

'What you looking at?'

Caught off guard, Rose blustered, 'I was . . . I was just wondering what you meant.'

'About Lester?'

'Yes, about Lester's not working.' Rose looked round. 'So where is he? At Sea View?'

'I doubt it.'

'Oh, come on, Trudie, don't muck about!' Rose teased her, although the atmosphere between them was static with tension. 'What are trying to tell me?'

'Lester's been up to no good,' Trudie replied, smirking, delighting in passing on her messy secret. 'Not quite what you think he is, Rose. In fact, he's been playing you for a bit of a chump.'

Rose winced. Trudie's envy had been obvious for a while, but now she was being openly vicious.

'What are you getting at?'

'What's *he* getting at, is more the point!' Trudie replied, laughing raucously. 'Or rather – what's he *getting*? And from whom?'

'If you've got something to say – bloody well say it!' Rose hissed.

'Oh, listen to you! Do they know that you swear, over at Lytham St Annes? What about the Widow Miller or Stuart Fallow – do they know that you're as common as muck?'

Exasperated, Rose turned and began to walk off, Trudie hurrying behind her.

'He's got another woman.'

Rose stopped, facing her front door. 'What?'

'Lester – my brother – has another woman. Apart from you. Another woman.' Trudie was enjoying herself. 'She's called Beth Hodges. And she's pregnant.'

Stunned, Rose continued to stare at her front door. It needed painting again. She would tell her father and he'd see to it. Red was a good colour.

'Oh, Lester's been a very bad boy,' Trudie continued, almost chanting. 'Getting someone in the family way. And he's going to marry her, Rose. After all, he'll have to do the right thing, won't he? Shame about you, though. I mean, weren't you two thinking of getting married?'

Dropping her bag, Rose turned and grabbed Trudie by the hair, her free hand slapping her hard across the face. Numbed, Trudie took a moment to retaliate, then bit Rose on the forearm, the two of them moving out into the centre of the street. Beside herself, Rose kicked out, Trudie ducking out of her reach and pushing her over into the gutter.

Alerted by the sound of a scuffle, Joe ran out into the street, followed by Ruby, Len bringing up the rear.

'Dear God!' he snapped, grabbing Rose's arm. 'What the hell's got into you?'

But she didn't even hear her father and shook him off, turning back to Trudie. Bleeding from a cut over her eye, Trudie suddenly laughed and then ran at Rose, knocking the wind out of her. Clumsily she fell over, her white dress soiled, her striped bag trampled underfoot as a small group of neighbours came out to watch. And all Rose could hear were the words, *she's pregnant . . . he's going to marry her* . . . Lester, her devoted Lester. The man she had waited for, longed for, finally won. And lost again.

All her frustration came out in that second as Rose clambered to her feet and swung out at Trudie. She didn't care that she was acting like the worst drab in Blackpool; or that she was making an exhibition of herself. She was too hurt to care, and rocked by the fact that it was her oldest friend who had inflicted the damage.

And then suddenly Rose stopped fighting. Her lip was cut and bleeding, her dress torn, her face without expression as she watched a figure come slowly round the corner. Lester saw her in that same instant and realised what had happened. He saw her, and he saw his sister – and knew.

On that sweltering night, Rose Bradshaw and Lester Williams stared at each other. They were only yards away but even that distance was too far to breach. Breathless, the onlookers waited to see what the outcome would be, but only Rose moved. She looked from Trudie to Lester, then bent down and picked up her bag. Her head high, she then walked to number 139 and closed the door behind her.

Len would say later that she cried all night.

PART FOUR

He that would govern others, first should be
The master of himself.

The Bondman
Philip Massinger 1583–1640

Now, in these interminable moments whilst I wait for the verdict, I think of what the jury has been told. Someone was killed. There was a murder. Someone was responsible. After all, look at the evidence . . . As it was offered, it was damning. I can see that – so how could others not jump to the obvious conclusion?

But it's not obvious. Nothing is, really. If you had told me a long time ago that I would end up here I would have laughed at you. After all, I was meant for better things. Hadn't I always been told that? Hadn't I always believed that? My future meant money, position – forever climbing upwards to be somewhere you can never ever see. Until you're there. And then the view's not what you expected.

So you jump off. Or someone pushes you. Or worse, they don't hold out the net when you know you're going to fall . . . I'm still falling. It's still raining. And the judge is still talking.

THIRTY-SEVEN

October 1939

'Joe, stay by me!' Lester shouted above the heads of the soldiers.

Anxiously Joe made his way over to his twin, his face pearl-white.

'Are you OK?'

Joe nodded, his teeth chattering. But not with the cold, with fear. Not that he would admit it – especially not in front of Lester – but he was terrified. They were amongst the hundred and fifty thousand men, together with their vehicles, who had been taken across the Channel to bolster the French defence. The fact that they had made it so far was a tribute to careful military planning. All over Britain soldiers had been moved in small convoys, travelling only at night, until the time had come for them to cross over to France.

And now they had arrived, at dawn, on a cold morning with a long march ahead of them. Joe had realised almost from the beginning that he could never have made it without Lester. Looking around he would see soldiers talking together, some laughing, others withdrawn, silent. Just as he would have been.

He longed for home. For Maisie and his daughter. Missed the black fire grate at number 99, the way the back door jammed, the smell of Maisie's hair on the pillow. He missed teasing her about her glasses, and putting his hand against his sleeping daughter's cheek. Homesickness dug its claws into his belly, his hand tightening over his gun. It hadn't been his idea, the bloody war. Who wanted to fight? Send the politicians in, Joe had said, then we'll see how long it lasts.

Breathing evenly, Lester sat beside his brother, his arms folded, now deeply asleep. How he could sleep was a mystery to Joe, but it seemed that his brother had no fear – none he showed anyway. Lester looked so different in uniform too, Joe thought. He himself looked like a bloody kid in fancy dress, but Lester looked the part.

Down the dawn road, the truck trundled along, moving further into France. Joe would fight, because he wouldn't want to show himself up, but the thought of killing went hard with him. And he was desperately afraid that someone might come up behind him and stick a knife into his back, or blow a hole in the back of his head. Afraid that he would be left, staring blindly up at a strange sky, without ever seeing home again.

And the only thing that stopped Joe from panicking was the sleeping figure beside him. Whilst he had Lester, he told himself, he would be OK. If he stayed with his brother, he would be OK.

THIRTY-EIGHT

Bunny was complaining about the cold again. 'Jesus, Len, it's perishing out here. You sure you don't want to come for a drink?'

For once, Len refused, watching as Bunny walked off. Racing was over for the day. A low mist was starting, the far-off trees leaf-stripped, the ribbon of the course ghostly in the winter light. Sighing, Len rolled himself a cigarette and stared thoughtfully ahead.

Before long, Blackpool would be emptied of young men. Len knew that much. He had seen it before. In fact the last time he had volunteered himself, when he'd been relatively young. Inhaling deeply, Len thought about his work. Would The Lazy Eye continue to make a living during the war years? Because he was certain it *would* be years – Hitler would see to that. Len would bet that he wasn't in it for the short haul. War meant death – the death of people you knew, God forbid. Racing was important, but nothing compared to this. Ah well, Len decided, he'd manage one way or another. Always did.

But would Rose? It still hurt Len to remember his daughter's reaction to Lester's betrayal. And his wedding, that meagre little affair attended by only Beth's mother and those from Sea View, no one else invited. Had that been Ruby's idea? Or Lester's? Len was sure it had been Lester's decision; too shame-faced to be seen marrying Beth Hodges when everyone knew he loved Rose.

But Beth was the pregnant one, and she had caught him. Len sighed again. How many men had been pressed into marriage for the same reason? He would have felt sorry for Lester, had it not been his daughter who had suffered. Acutely embarrassed, Len remembered how he had visited Sea View, beside himself with anger, and hauled Lester into the backyard. No street fight for him. Only the intervention of Ruby had stopped a blood bath, Alfred's porkpie hat knocked off in the commotion, Trudie watching guiltily from an upstairs window.

Memories hurt, Len decided. They did no bloody good, just hurt. And yet they still came back, thick and damp, like the December air. It all seemed so far away now, Len thought, what with Joe and Lester away fighting. But still the memories pushed on . . . Trudie had had her revenge on Rose, but what had it cost her? Len breathed out, his breath vapour in the cold. From being a fresh-faced smart-mouth she had gradually coarsened, her spite corroding her. If she had apologised to Rose, made allowances, their friendship might have survived; but Trudie Williams wasn't the kind to admit that she had ever been wrong.

Lazy and envious, she took against the world. For once blinded, Ruby did not suspect her daughter's fall from grace. But everyone else watched Trudie Williams turn – in only a few years – from a flip young woman to a cynical slat-tern. When she was at home, Trudie was mostly like the old Trudie, making her overworked mother laugh with her stories, and grudgingly helping out with the guests. But outside Sea View Trudie had earned herself a sobriquet no woman would have wanted – Dirty Gertie.

At first she had drunk with the lads and had a fumble under the pier, but the rumours had spread – 'about as quickly as she spreads her legs,' someone had said. Len didn't like to think of any woman wasting her life like that, but he knew that it was Trudie's malice that had turned her. It had been obvious to everyone; and still was.

Grinding out his cigarette with the heel of his boot, Len stared into the chilly evening. Ruby had heard from her sons only that morning, a letter coming and saying the same thing it always did. 'We're OK, don't worry. We're hoping to get some leave soon.' But then months had passed without the Williams boys returning.

Then another letter came to say that they had been picked for special training. The Williams boys were going to be Royal Marines. What the hell does that mean? Ruby had asked Len and he'd explained: that they chose the fittest and quickest for special missions: risky manoeuvres, hit-and-run raids.

It all sounded so heroic, Len thought, but he knew better. And he wondered why Joe had been picked. It was obvious why Lester would be chosen, but *Joe*? Lester would like the risks, but Joe, he liked safety. So maybe he hadn't really wanted to join the Marines, but had simply followed in his brother's wake. As he had always done. Didn't Joe go everywhere with Lester – even to hell and back?

Len rubbed his eyes, his thoughts returning to the present. Maybe the Williams boys would get some leave at Christmas. And he would visit Doris. Len wondered for a moment if he should marry her and then realised that neither of them wanted that. They had been long-term lovers – still were, on and off – but their friendship had extended beyond the physical and both were glad of it. Yes, Len decided, he would visit Doris and then spend the rest of Christmas with Rose. It was no good telling her to accept Hettie's invitations to spend the holiday at Heathcote Place. To Len's pretend chagrin, his daughter always refused. She might attend Hettie's soirées and Stuart's parties, but she spent the most important times with her father.

Len shouldn't be pleased, but he was. He should – he knew only too well – push Rose away; *make* her find her own life. After all, what Hettie had done, and continued to do for her, wasn't to be sneezed at, even though Len was fully aware that the Widow Miller had her own reasons. Oh yes, Len mused, his daughter had managed a cute balancing trick: keeping Hettie and Stuart happy, without committing herself.

It *was* a cute trick – but a wasted one. What good was it keeping a decent, eligible catch like Stuart Fallow at arm's length whilst you longed for a man living in Gate Street? A man with a wife and a son. A man who could never be yours. A man that had been taken away by another woman, and might now be taken away by war.

What good . . . ? Len took in a deep breath, looking over the empty racecourse. Alone, he stood waiting for ghost horses on a ghost track. And wondering how many other ghosts would be created in the months and years to come.

'Keep it straight!' Clovis snapped, her hunched back even more bowed over as she struggled to pull a mattress into number 117. 'Oh, Nan, do keep it straight or we'll never get it inside.'

Nan paused, leaned against the mattress and took a breather. She was wearing her dark winter coat, her grey hair kept in check with a net.

'Heavy.'

Only the top of Clovis's head was visible as she answered her.

'I'll say it's heavy! Good quality, this. I said to our Len only the other day, you can never have too many good beds. And besides, with this war, if no one's sleeping on it, it'll do for protection.' Holding down one corner, Clovis's face suddenly became visible. 'You mark my words, this war will go on for a while. You remember the last?'

Nan nodded.

'I do. Too well.' Clovis paused, fighting emotion. 'Lost my man in that scrap . . . You ready for another go with this mattress, Nan?'

But the cadaver wasn't moving.

'Oi, Nan! Oi, you down there!' Clovis repeated more loudly, then glanced in the direction Nan Wilmslow was looking.

Alfred Williams was walking down the steps outside Sea View in full uniform, a row of medals across his chest.

'Well, I'll be damned! He never won those medals in any war. Got them off the market, if I know Alfred Williams.'

An instant later both of them saw Ruby charge down the steps, grab Alfred by the collar of his uniform, and march him – backwards – into the hotel.

'He's going strange,' Clovis said, laughing.

'Soft in the head,' Nan agreed.

'All those stories he's been telling for years have turned his brain. Mind you, Alfred Williams might turn out to be very useful for the war effort. He could fall over and crush half of the German army without even trying.'

'I just wish,' Maisie said, her eyes watery behind the lenses of her glasses, 'that Joe had taken some more underclothes with him. It gets so cold and he hates the cold.'

Digging her hands deep into her pockets, Rose walked beside her. She had become friends with Maisie soon after the latter's daughter, Lesley, was born in 1936. The same year that Lester and Beth's son, Daniel, was born. Not that anyone had ever seen much of the second baby. Lester and his family lived in Gate Street, beyond the North Shore, and well away from Gull Road. Lester had moved them out there to put some distance between himself and Rose. It was to have been temporary, Lester had told Joe, but the family had never left.

'Beth doesn't bother the same about Lester,' Maisie said, then skidded to a halt. How thoughtless was it to talk about Lester in front of Rose?

Feigning indifference, Rose walked on, her face impassive. But the mere mention of Lester's name conjured up a multitude of feelings.

Over the previous four years he had become even busier. He had also done as he had predicted, and by the time he was twenty-five Lester Williams had been a recognised success. So much so that he now owned two booths, one sea-front novelty shop and had begun building the dance hall. People had called him *Mister Williams* respectfully and had always recognised his car, milling around him, asking for work or offering deals.

Then at night he had gone home to Beth. Though they were forced together by marriage, she had remained an enigma to him. She had passed onto their son, Daniel, her dark hair and sloe eyes, although it was obvious by the child's build and expressions that Lester was the father. People might have talked at first about the rushed wedding, but as Lester's influence grew, people had made allowances. After all, they had said, he did the right thing and married Beth Hodges . . . Yes, some others had replied, but it was Rose Bradshaw he wanted.

And never *stopped* wanting. Bitterness had seeped like damp into Lester's soul. Outside he appeared calm and at times cheerful, but he had never been able to pass the end of Gull Road without a judder. And for that reason he had never returned to Sea View. Ruby called in at Gate Street, with Alfred in tow, and Joe had been a frequent visitor to his brother's house. But Lester – even as the years passed by – had never set foot in Gull Road again.

It was Joe who had told Rose all about it. It was bitter-sweet knowledge, but she had begged for every morsel . . .

'So, what about you and Stuart?' Maisie asked, holding Lesley's hand tightly as they walked along.

'*What* about me and Stuart?'

'Are you ever going to settle down?'

Rose took a moment to reply. 'He should have volunteered, signed up, like your Joe.'

'And Lester . . .' Maisie added quietly.

Rose ignored the comment. Only Joe was allowed to talk to her about his brother.

'Life goes on,' Maisie said, her tone wary. 'It's been a long time, Rose. You should move on.'

'It's nothing to do with Lester!' she lied. 'He's dead to me.'

Oh, but he wasn't, she thought, her eyes burning. He was alive in every day, in every street. And seeing a man who looked like him on Gull Road she would hope . . . But it was never Lester. And since Rose had lost him, no one had managed to carve their way through to her heart. She was attractive to men, but she didn't notice their interest. She had wanted to be perfect for Lester. After him, who cared what other men thought? So no one got close. Only Stuart. And only so far.

'Stuart seems fit enough to sign up,' Rose mused, turning up the collar of her coat against the cold, 'but he says he can't fight because he had rheumatic fever as a child.'

'That's sad.'

'That's convenient.'

'Oh, Rose, don't be so hard on the poor man!' Maisie chastised her. 'I'm sure he'd fight if he could. Anyway, you know how much he cares for you and you're merciless with him. You should settle down. Stuart's nice-looking, well off, and you'd have a lovely home.'

Sighing, Rose confided to her friend, 'Hettie tells me the same thing every week. Without fail. She tells that Stuart won't hang around waiting for me for ever and that I should be grateful to have such an opportunity.' Her tone cooled. 'What Hettie really means is that she wants me to marry Stuart so she can finally bag bloody Cedric.'

'Oh, Rose!' Maisie said, stopping outside the Co-op, its windows displaying the first criss-crossings of tape. 'How *can* you say such awful things?'

'Because they're true,' Rose replied phlegmatically. 'I suspect that Hettie's told Cedric that I'll inherit from her – if I marry his son. So he wants the deal done and dusted. Then he'll marry Hettie and the fortunes are secured all round.'

Maisie's eyes were huge behind her glasses. 'Never!'

'You're such an innocent,' Rose teased her, jingling the change in her pocket. Her mood was becoming more skittish by the moment. 'After all, people have been arranging marriages for centuries, tying up families and fortunes, making deals. I should be grateful – an upstart like me from Gull Road. I should be honoured to have influential people wanting to plan my nuptials.' Her eyes flickered, her voice rising. 'Only I'm not. They can plan someone else's marriage. Not bloody *mine*!'

Blushing, Maisie looked away. Really, Rose should remember her language in front of the child.

'I'm *not* marrying for convenience,' Rose continued, her colour heightening, her mood more agitated by the second. 'Not my convenience – or Hettie's. She was good to me, Maisie, I know she was. But do I have to pay her back for the rest of my life? *With* the rest of my life?'

'I'm sure she doesn't mean –'

'That's exactly what she bloody means!' Rose responded heatedly. 'God, I'm choking here. Suffocating. I have been for a while. I'm getting to hate the job, Lytham, Stuart *and* Hettie. I don't want to be forced into something, Maisie. I don't want to marry a man I don't love because I might never get a better offer.' She pulled her collar away from her neck as though she might literally choke. 'I mean, there's a war on. People might die, there's only so much time for anyone and no one knows how long they've got. God, there has to be more to life – there *has* to be.'

Gently, Maisie touched her arm. 'He'll be all right.'

They both knew who she meant.

A bad fall off the side of the Winter Gardens stage had resulted in a broken ankle for Gilbert. Gradually the break mended, but he was left with a limp. So what? he said in his lush tones. Even better for character roles.

He wasn't so sure about the war, though. At first he had

felt a *frisson* of anticipation – all those soldiers – and then he remembered Louis Wilkes and brushed aside the thought hastily.

His sister had never mentioned it, but Gilbert was sure that Ruby had had a hand in Louis's sudden disappearance. It was not that he would have made the connection himself; only that another performer had mentioned seeing a huge woman visit Louis that evening. And there *were* no women bigger than Ruby.

Another man might have left Blackpool and tried to find Louis, but Gilbert wasn't brave enough. He'd had a sexual skirmish and had loved – and hated – the hunger it had uncovered in him. But Gilbert hadn't been that much of a fool not to know that he had been used. Louis Wilkes had played him like an old piano. Kept him hot and sweaty. Panting on promises.

Walking in at the front entrance of Sea View, Gilbert spotted Miss Vernon. He tried to make a dash for it, but his limp hampered him, Miss Vernon smiling winsomely as she approached.

'Oh, Mr Beardsley, I have to say how wonderful you were last night. Quite a performance.'

Ruby had told him that Miss Vernon had been a tax clerk once. Even long retired, she still had a beady look, her old-fashioned high-necked dress topped off with a no-nonsense bun.

'Thank you,' Gilbert replied, moving off, but Miss Vernon followed him towards the back of Sea View.

'Such a lovely voice you have.'

'Thank you.'

'And such presence. They do call it presence, don't they?' Miss Vernon replied, knowing full well.

It was a matter of some amusement to Ruby that the pernickety Miss Vernon had become a regular guest at Sea View. She might moan about the lumpy bed and raucousness of the summer trippers, but she had set her sights on someone and was not about to be thwarted. The fact that Gilbert had caught her fancy was delicious. She obviously had no idea that Gilbert wasn't interested in women, and was set to track him down like a late tax return.

'I imagine you'll be in the pantomime at Christmas? I mean, even with the war the show must go on. Of course one doesn't want to be frivolous at a time like this – with our boys away fighting – but laughter does so help to keep up the spirits, don't you think? I often said to my employer – Mr Franklin – that the world would be a sombre place without a good laugh . . .'

Glassy-eyed, Gilbert waited for a pause to take his leave, but Miss Vernon had just hit her stride.

'. . . I remember the last war. Well, only just! I was a girl then and my father used to warn me about soldiers. Oh, not that I'm speaking against them, they do a wonderful job, but they can be . . . a particular kind of man.' She flushed, then hurried on when Gilbert looked set to move. 'Not the refined sort, not the kind of man you find in the arts. Not a man who can appeal to the soul. Speaking of the Muse, of Madame Tragedy –'

'If you want pudding, you have to get back to your table now,' Ruby interrupted, Gilbert grabbing the opportunity to move.

'Lovely to talk with you, Miss Vernon,' he replied, hurrying off. 'Always a pleasure.'

A few minutes later Ruby walked into the kitchen, putting down a tray full of dirty dishes and flopping into a chair. Smiling wryly, she regarded her brother.

'How could you lead on that poor old lady?'

'She said she was a *girl* in the last war.'

'Yeah, the War of the Roses,' Ruby replied, watching Gilbert pull off his shoes and reach for his Turkish slippers. They were old now, but he would never part with them for sentimental reasons. Had they come from another

Louis Wilkes, Ruby wondered, suddenly catching Gilbert looking at her.

'What?'

'You look tired.'

'Alfred's been acting odd lately,' she replied, yawning expansively. 'And I can't refuse guests, even at Christmas.'

'We never used to have guests out of season.'

'We never used to need the money so much.'

Gilbert flushed. 'I give what I can.'

'I know,' she replied, tapping his knee. 'You give me more than money, Gilbert. You give me support. Alfred used to do that, but he's gone inside himself since war broke out. I thought I'd hear no end of stories about how he was working as a spy – I was even looking forward to it – but since Joe and Lester went off, he's been down.'

'Does that surprise you?'

'Oh, no, Alfred's always been daft one way or another.'

Gilbert rolled his eyes. 'I mean, did it surprise you that both Joe and Lester volunteered?'

Ruby's eyes met her brother's. 'I expect Lester was glad to get away from his wife. As for Joe, Maisie encouraged him –'

'To volunteer?'

Ruby nodded. 'She said that if Joe went now, he'd be put with Lester. And Lester would look after him, like he always has. But if Joe waited to get called up, he could be sent anywhere on his own. And then anything might happen to him.' Ruby plucked imaginary fluff off her apron. 'I call that brave – for Maisie to do that. And she's right. Lester always *does* look out for Joe. It's some comfort for me and Maisie to know that they're together.'

'Not much comfort, though?' Gilbert asked tentatively.

'What d'you think? I've only two sons and both gone off to fight. And now I've two daughters-in-law left behind. One I can barely stand and the other I love like my own. But I'll have to keep an eye on both of them, and the kids.'

'*We'll* keep an eye on them,' Gilbert said evenly. 'You don't have to do this alone. I like kids.'

'That's because you never had your own.'

A moment snapped its jaws between them, Ruby poking at the fire in the grate with the toe of her boot.

'Sorry, Gilbert. That was thoughtless.'

'It's all right.'

'I didn't think –'

'I don't mind.'

In the dining room beyond they could hear the sound of chairs being pushed back, followed by footsteps as Miss Vernon and Mr and Mrs Grimes left the room.

'That Grimes couple will be at it later. On and off all night. Banging away like a barn door.'

Gilbert smiled. 'What about Miss Vernon?'

'Well,' Ruby remarked, winking at her brother, 'I reckon she's as much chance of having children as you have.'

THIRTY-NINE

As though dazed, Beth walked around the small front room on Gate Street. Touching the common ornaments she had bought, her fingers rested longer on the expensive clock Lester had purchased. What did they want to spend so much on a clock for, she had asked, baffled. And he hadn't even replied, just looked at her as though she would never understand, so what was the point even talking? And now he was gone. Volunteered to serve his country . . . Beth looked at the clock and suddenly wanted to smash its enamel face.

Lester had never come to love her – could hardly tolerate her, in fact. He loved Daniel, their son, but otherwise there was no tie between them. No communication either, just total indifference on his part. She could have borne arguments better – even ill treatment – but the sullen loathing was torment. She had promised herself that she would make up for trapping Lester. He would love her – how could he resist? But he did resist, and her swelling insecurity festered into bitterness.

But she would never let go. Lester knew that, even though Beth had never said it. Some part of her – however illogical – believed that one day Lester would undergo a transformation. See her differently. Love her . . . If she had got close to Ruby it would have helped, but Lester's mother was no pushover, either physically or emotionally. She knew only too well that Beth had trapped Lester, and was only prepared to go along with it because of Daniel.

But if there had been no child, there would have been no marriage. Lester would have married Rose Bradshaw instead and the gilded couple would have had the town at their feet . . . Beth walked over to the child's cot and looked down at her sleeping son. It was a lonely life, cut off with just a toddler for company, even though her mother visited daily. A woman who was now widowed, kind, but remote. A woman who had no desire to get involved in her daughter's problems. A woman who had never realised the emptiness inside her own child.

Beth's passion and intensity had come from her father. You're just like him, her mother had told her repeatedly, you've got all his ways . . . And just as he had passed down his looks, he had passed on his passion – and his dark side.

Beth could hardly remember her father – only as a man sitting in an old chair. He was tired, her mother told her, but that wasn't true. And when he had turned to look at his child, Beth had seen something horribly lost about him. The same unutterable sadness that was in her; the same despair that only Lester kept at bay.

She *had* to keep her husband, Beth told herself again. Without him, what chance would she have to survive?

Stuart was chewing the end of his pen, his teeth making a dull clacking noise on the metal. Now, what the hell should he write inside Rose's Christmas card this year? It was always a minefield. Too lovey-dovey and she cooled off; too casual and she teased him about treating her like a patient. That was what kept him on his toes, kept him interested. Her capriciousness.

Mind you, it was frustrating as well. Still, Stuart thought, everyone knew that nice girls didn't sleep around. And Rose was a nice girl. Besides, if he tried anything, he would have her father to contend with . . . Stuart thought of an inscription for the card and then threw down his pen, irritated. Bugger the bloody card! He would marry Rose if she agreed to it. Why not? She was good-looking, funny and outspoken – and according to the old man she came with a dowry from the Widow Miller.

Stuart smiled mischievously to himself. It was rather amusing to have two ageing matchmakers leaping about on hot coals, waiting for the announcement. And it did no good for his father to nag him.

As if he had read his son's thought, Cedric walked into the surgery at that moment, looking round at the empty waiting room.

'Not many patients today.'

'Pray for a fight.'

Cedric looked at his son in total bafflement, his eyes moving towards the surgery chair and fixing on the steel drill above it.

'I've been thinking. You and your lady friend should settle down, Stuart. I'm not a man to hurry things and I think a long courtship is sound to find out if the woman is the right one for you. But I do feel that . . .' his gaze moved to the water basin and remained there, '. . . the time has come. After all, what can be holding things up?'

'Rose hasn't said yes,' Stuart replied, almost happily. 'That usually stops a wedding – if the bride-to-be isn't playing ball.'

'I don't understand a half of what you say,' Cedric intoned. 'Are you telling me that Rose Bradshaw has *refused* you?'

'Seven times.'

This was unthinkable. Cedric's gaze bored into the water basin. He would have to talk to Henrietta. The girl was impossible. Refusing his son! Some upstart from Gull Road! And seven times!

'Maybe she didn't understand you?'

'I said – will you marry me? And she said – no,' Stuart

replied. It was worth getting rejected just for the amusement value. 'I think she understood me, Dad –'

'Call me Father.'

'*Father*,' Stuart replied accommodatingly.

'Is there someone else?'

Now this was a sticky one, Stuart thought. He wasn't sure about Rose, although he knew that she *had* loved someone in the past. But as for himself – he did have a girlfriend in Blackpool. A girl who liked to fool around, just as he did. Well, some types you had a laugh with, others you married. And all men had sexual needs – unless they were Cedric.

'Stuart, *did you hear me*?'

'What?'

'Is there someone else?'

'No, Father, no one else. Neither Rose nor I has anyone else.'

Towing his gaze from the wash hand basin, Cedric looked at his son studiously. 'Perhaps you should . . . romance her.'

This was too good an opportunity to miss, Stuart thought delightedly.

'*Romance her*?' he repeated innocently. 'You might be right there, Father. Maybe I'm doing it all wrong. Have you got any tips?'

Unbelievably, Cedric fell for it.

'I find that a good restaurant and a nice glass of wine – only one – sets the evening off. Then a walk along the sea front. Not Blackpool. Lytham, of course –'

'Of course.'

'Then possibly you could read her something.'

'*Read her something*?' Stuart repeated, fascinated. 'Like what?'

'A good book. A novel, but not one of these dreadful commercial works. Nothing like *Gone With the Wind*, something improving – poetry even. Lord Tennyson has a masterly way with words.'

Stuart could imagine Rose's face.

'What about kissing?' he asked, his father's gaze moving away from him immediately and fixing on the ceiling rose.

'*Kissing?*'

'You know, kissing.'

'I know what kissing is, Stuart!' he replied curtly. 'But I feel that might be a little presumptuous.'

'After four and half years? You feel we might be rushing it?' Stuart asked, his tone ingenuous.

'Maybe a kiss on the cheek.'

'On the cheek,' Stuart replied, reaching for his pad. 'Now I see where I've been going wrong. Would you hang on a minute, Dad? I want to make some notes.'

Even Cedric knew he was being mocked. Dragging his gaze from the ceiling, he walked, stiff-necked, to the door. Then he paused, his nasal voice condemning.

'Perhaps if you took life a little more seriously, Stuart, you might get on better. As you know, no one likes a laugh more than myself, but the Fallow men are known for their dignity.'

'And their kissing,' Stuart called after him, laughing. 'And for their kissing.'

That did it! Hettie thought, enough was enough. And she had had more than enough of Rose's hesitation. Never one to like being out of control, Hettie resented the fact that she was now at Rose's mercy. How had that happened, she wondered fitfully. Hadn't she planned out the whole scenario? Who would marry whom? Who would live where?

And Rose – peevish, selfish Rose – hadn't fallen into line. After all she had done for her! Hettie raged. After all the kindness, the money, showered on her. To turn on her benefactor like this! To throw her kindness in her face! To look such a gift horse in the mouth . . . Hettie stopped, having run out of clichés.

That was the trouble with the working class: everything had to be spelled out for them. They had no subtlety, no sense of loyalty either . . .

The doorbell ringing broke into Hettie's thoughts, her eyes marble as Rose walked in. She was wearing a red coat with a black velvet collar, her hair hidden under a black fur hood. Her good looks were unexpected, even to Hettie.

'You look well, my dear,' she began, motioning for Rose to sit down. 'Anything nice happened?'

'Nothing out of the ordinary,' Rose replied, taking off her hood and shaking her hair loose.

The thing about being young was that you believed it would last for ever, Hettie thought. Plotting, she eyed Rose up and down. *She* might have time on her side, but Hettie hadn't. And neither had Cedric, who, with any luck, would never make old bones. Besides, there was a war on, people got killed. Futures were ruined, no matter how carefully planned.

'I'm having a Christmas party,' Hettie said, out of the blue.

Rose raised her eyebrows. 'With a war on?'

'I wasn't thinking of inviting Hitler, dear, just some old friends.'

Poison was in the air – Rose could feel it.

'Here?'

'Of course. Where better? Unless you think that we should hold it at the Fallow house?'

To Hettie's chagrin, Rose laughed. 'That would be presuming a bit much, wouldn't it?'

'Cedric and I are very close. Almost engaged,' Hettie said, her tone freezing. 'In fact, we want to settle down together –'

'That's wonderful,' Rose said, genuinely pleased. 'Is that what the party's for? Your engagement?'

'Are you being stupid, or deliberately provoking me?' Hettie said, her face set.

'What?'

'You know exactly what I mean! For long enough, Cedric and I have been waiting for you and Stuart to make an announcement. But nothing's happened. And both his father and I want to know why.'

This was the first full-on challenge Hettie had ever made about the matter. Over the last few years she had hinted, intimated, but never come out with it directly.

Equally direct, Rose answered her. 'Stuart and I aren't ever going to be getting married –'

'You bloody fool!' Hettie said violently. 'What do you think you're playing at? You think you can just take and take from people and not pay them back?'

'I'm very grateful –'

'I don't want your gratitude!' Hettie raged. 'I want you to do your duty.'

At that, Rose's eyes blazed. 'My duty! My duty is first to myself, not to you.'

'Selfish, that's what you are,' Hettie snapped back, fiddling with the cuffs of her expensive suit. Her colour was high on her cheeks, one foot tapping impatiently on the floor. 'There is more at stake than you realise.'

'Your marriage to Cedric, you mean?' Rose replied, curtly. 'Does it rely on my marrying his son?'

'How dare you talk to me like that?' Hettie shouted. 'Is this all the thanks I get? Dear God, I'm willing to leave my inheritance to you –'

'I never asked you to!' Rose answered. 'I'm not on the make. I never was. You've done more than enough for me –'

'Well, you haven't done enough for me.'

'So that's bloody it, is it?' Rose snapped. 'Payback time?'

'Stop being so dramatic,' Hettie replied, her tongue running over her dry lips. The gloves were off. If the ungrateful bitch wanted a fight, she could have one. 'Nothing's for nothing in this life. You would do well to remember that.'

Stung, Rose got to her feet, Hettie looking up at her.

'If you walk out, you walk out on your job and the good wage it pays you. Which you – and your father – sorely need. You can leave the clothes and everything I ever bought you behind too.' Hettie paused, sure of triumph. 'Go back to Gull Road, my dear. Go back to being ordinary. Like your old friend, Trudie. Perhaps you could work in Myers, or I hear they're looking for women to do war work in the factories. I don't think you'd like your old life so much any more, but I could be wrong. Perhaps Gull Road has a potential I can't see. Go and find it, dear. And whilst you're at it, go and find yourself a man there –' Hettie stopped short. She had seen the slightest flicker in Rose's eyes and was suddenly alert. *There was a man! Of course, how stupid she had been* . . . Breathing in, she modulated her voice. 'I think perhaps we should have a proper talk, woman to woman.'

Rose kept staring down at her, her expression hostile.

'Oh, come on, we've often fought over the years, you and I. Sit down, Rose. You know how I get angry at times. You frustrate me, being so stubborn. You should think nothing of it.' She gestured to the seat next to hers. 'I care about you, my dear, and I want to understand.'

It was like being mesmerised by a snake, Rose thought. Her instinct told her leave and yet if she did, she would lose everything. She knew full well she could live without the clothes, but the job? The wage? Rose winced. Who was she kidding? She *liked* the life in Lytham, liked going out to dinner with Stuart, liked working in a nice place, surrounded by money. There was no way she could go back to working in Blackpool. Back to where she had been a runty, squint-eyed kid. Back to the streets that reminded her of Lester.

'Rose, *please* sit down.'

Deflated, she did so. 'I don't want your money.'

'Forget the money for a moment,' Hettie said, leaning

towards her. 'I think I know why you don't accept Stuart. There's another man, isn't there?'

This was the last thing Rose wanted to discuss with the Widow Miller.

'No.'

'Don't lie to me, dear. I've been married twice, remember?'

'There was someone. Once.'

'But no more?'

'No,' Rose replied, acutely uncomfortable. Why didn't she just tell Hettie to get lost?

'What happened?'

'He died.'

'I don't think so,' Hettie replied, exquisitely astute. 'You would have moved on to someone else if he'd died . . . Ah, is he married?'

'I don't want to talk about it!'

'He's married,' Hettie said, sighing and leaning back in her seat. 'What a waste, Rose, to pine over a man you can't ever have.'

'Let it drop!'

'But I'm worried about you,' Hettie persisted, then some hunch made her take a shot in the dark. 'It's not that young man you were so hung up on before, is it? Lionel, or some name beginning with an L?'

Her face white, Rose turned to Hettie. 'His name is Lester. And he's married – and besides, he's signed up.'

Now that *was* a problem, Hettie thought to herself. Stuart wasn't ever going to be a hero and yet here was Rose's true love on the front line. Her own private Sir Galahad. The stuff that dreams are made of – in romantic novels. And the very fact that Lester was unattainable would only make a woman like Rose want him more.

'I hate to pry, my dear, but why didn't he marry you?'

Rose looked down. 'He married someone else.'

'Well, I can see that. But why?'

'He had to marry her.'

Hettie acted naïve. 'Why, dear?'

'Because she was bloody pregnant!' Rose hurled back, turning to look Hettie in the face. 'Go on, tell me what you're thinking. I imagine I know already.'

'That you're a fool to carry a torch so long?'

Rose winced. 'That hurt.'

'Good. What hurts makes an impression – or so I've found. Pussyfooting around leads to all kinds of misunderstandings. Take me, for example: I know what I want and I go out and get it.'

'You haven't run Cedric to ground yet.'

Stung, Hettie smiled bitterly. 'Such a sharp tongue you have at times. Remember, you can catch more flies with honey than you can with vinegar.'

'Flies are ten a penny.'

'Stuart Fallows, however, are not.'

Hettie let the words sink in. Outside snow had begun to fall, the light dimming in the room, the fire making shadows on the far wall. From somewhere else in the house came the sound of a radio, the voices low and sonorous.

'Clinging on to the past is pointless, Rose. If you do, you can never move forward. Life becomes a drudge, always longing for what – and who – you can't have. You lose sight of a future. Of the potential of others. Of other men.' Hettie paused, careful with her words. 'I know what *I* want. But I also know what would be good for you. There's a way out for you, Rose. An exit that doesn't come to everyone. I found mine; now is the time to recognise yours.'

Rose's voice was very low when she answered. 'I don't love Stuart Fallow.'

'But you care about him. You like him?'

'I've always liked him –'

'Many marriages flourish on that alone,' Hettie replied pragmatically. 'I was in love once. Crazy, absorbed by a man. He died. Did I pine for him? No, I got on with my life. Am I cold-blooded? Probably, but I didn't marry again for love. I might not have had the passion any more, but I had power and position instead.'

'If I'd married Lester we would have had love *and* power.'

Impatiently, Hettie waved aside the words. 'Lester Williams – oh, don't look so surprised, Rose, I do *know* who we're talking about – has done well for himself. As far as it goes. But he's not from good stock, or old money. He couldn't give you the life you want. Oh, for God's sake, Rose, why are we even talking about it? Lester isn't yours and never will be. Stuart, however, *could* be yours. So could a fine house, money in the bank and status.' She sighed. 'All I ask is that you make the decision, Rose.'

'What decision?'

'Are you going to move on and move up? Or fail?'

FORTY

Winking over the patient's head, Stuart caught Rose's attention and then crossed his eyes, his tongue lolling out of the corner of his mouth. Smiling, she looked away, determined not to laugh.

When the man left she turned on Stuart immediately. 'Stop doing that! I nearly burst out laughing – and *you* wouldn't have been if you'd lost a patient.'

Stuart's eyes fixed on the ceiling rose, his voice suddenly nasal. 'We Fallow men know how and when to be serious. A tooth cavity – although in itself not amusing – can, however, provide levity for the select few.'

Rose gathered together the patient's notes, her tone mock-severe. 'Your father will catch you mimicking him one day. And then you'll have had it.'

'He wouldn't realise it was him,' Stuart replied, leaning over the desk towards Rose. 'You look adorable today. Edible, in fact.'

'You look pretty good yourself.'

He preened. 'Marry me?'

'No chance.'

'Lunch on the sea front?'

'You're on.'

Stuart's high spirits continued all morning and continued as they chatted all the way to the Promenade. In the distance a clock chimed one o'clock, and on the horizon

Stuart pointed to a boat, riding the high waves. The winter chill was vicious, the sea dark as pitch.

'That out there, Miss Bradshaw, is a *boat*.'

'You don't say.'

'Spelled B-O-A-T,' Stuart went on, still imitating his father. 'We Fallows dream of having our own boat.'

'You Fallows do?'

'Indeed.' Stuart nodded. 'A boat large enough to hold parties on –'

'That reminds me,' Rose said suddenly, 'Hettie's throwing a Christmas party.'

'Let's hope it doesn't hit someone.'

Rose jammed him in the ribs. 'You're invited, with your father.'

'As a couple?' Stuart teased her. 'I must tell Dad, he'll be *thrilled*.'

Laughing, Rose began to eat the sandwiches she had made earlier. Rumours were rife that soon food would become short, rationing biting into everyone's larder. But would it affect the Fallows? Padded comfortably by money, would they go short? Surreptitiously Rose stole a glance at Stuart. He was so funny, she thought, such easy company. And attractive. She could learn to love him, couldn't she? *Shouldn't she?*

'Too dark and cold for even the serpents.'

Rose frowned. 'What did you say?'

'The sea,' Stuart replied, unusually serious. 'It looks so godforsaken.' His mood had shifted, catching her unawares. His gaze fixed on the horizon where a storm cloud waited for its moment. 'To be honest I feel embarrassed, Rose. About the war. About all the other men being called up, or volunteering.'

She thought first of Lester, and then, guilty, hurried to console Stuart. 'But you can't fight. You're medically exempt.'

'Yes, and I suppose everyone will believe that.'

Rose winced, remembering how she had doubted it at first.

'I imagine some men will envy me. Think I'm a lucky sod. Lucky in so many ways. And now even managing to get out of the war. But they won't understand how it feels – to know that people might envy you, but despise you at the same time.'

'Stuart, listen to me,' Rose said, startled by his uncharacteristic depression. 'No one will think any the worse of you.'

'What about you?' he said, turning to her. 'Will you think badly of me?'

'No –'

He hurried on. 'I can't ever be a hero for you, Rose. Can't come home with a medal, in a flash uniform. Can't impress the girls with stories of my bravery. Will it matter?' he pressed her. 'I'd like to know. Here and now. The truth. I *really* would like to know.'

And in that moment, whilst Stuart was at his most exposed and vulnerable, Rose felt the first shudder of love for him. When the joking had been put on pause, then the real man had shown himself and his shortcomings. And in doing so, Stuart Fallow had managed to achieve what humour and persistence had failed to do: he had finally won his lady over.

As everyone had hoped, Lester and Joe were granted a forty-eight-hour leave at Christmas from their barracks at Catterick. Ruby was ecstatic: both her sons home. It was more than she could have wished for. As the only guest still at Sea View, Miss Vernon found herself unceremonially shunted to one side. Ruby *did* remember to make her dinner, but for once it wasn't on time. And when Miss Vernon had the nerve to ask why her towels hadn't been changed, Ruby's response was acid.

'Have you got children?'

Miss Vernon prickled. 'You know I'm a single lady.'

'Well, I've got two boys fighting for this country, and they're coming home today. So you'll forgive me if I'm a little preoccupied, Miss Vernon, but your flaming towels will have to wait.'

So much for the towels, Gilbert thought, hurrying off to the theatre before Miss Vernon could nobble him. Walking as fast as his limp would allow, Gilbert mused about the evening to come. To see both of his nephews again – now that *was* something to look forward to. And both alive and well. Which was more than could be said for sons of several families in the neighbourhood.

At the same moment that Gilbert was walking into the backstage entrance of the Pavilion Theatre, Joe was slipping into the kitchen of number 99 Gull Road. It was warm inside, a fire lit, a kettle singing on the grate. Above him, he could hear voices and crept silently upstairs, looking in at the bedroom door. Maisie had just bathed Lesley, the toddler wrapped in a towel. As she bent over her daughter, Maisie's hair was coming undone, her glasses sliding down her nose. But she was laughing, and Joe thought that he had never heard so beguiling a sound.

For a long moment he watched his family and then suddenly Maisie turned.

'Joe!' she said, jumping to her feet and hurrying over to him. 'Oh, my love, I'm so glad to see you.'

Drawing her to him, Joe wrapped his arms around his wife and pressed his child against his chest as he kissed the top of Lesley's head.

'She's grown so much.'

'And she looks like you,' Maisie said, her voice wavering. 'Oh God, Joe, I'm so glad to see you. I've waited and waited, and longed for you. It's been so hard. Well, not hard like it is for you . . .' she paused, smiling wistfully. 'I've missed you so much.'

Laughing, he led them over to the bed and sat down, rolling the three of them over, so that Lesley was lying on her back between them. Taking off his soldier's cap, Joe put one arm across his child and then stretched his other arm over Lesley's head to stroke Maisie's hair. His eyes met his wife's eyes and held her gaze.

He told her about fighting, about being afraid and longing for home. He told her about dreaming of her and their child, of the sight and sound of gunfire coming in blasts through the dark reaches of the witching hours. He told her about wanting to run, and knowing he never would because he had a family he would never disgrace. He told her about men who had died – some next to him – and others who had been recalled, some mutilated, some mad. He told her that without her he could never have borne any of it.

And he told her everything with his eyes. Without saying a word.

Standing by his back gate, Lester paused and lit a cigarette. He had no stomach for coming home, had even toyed with the idea of going to Sea View to stay for his leave rather than run the gauntlet of Gate Street. But then again, there were other memories at Sea View . . .

It was bloody grim, he knew that much. Cold, the streets snow-bound, slush in the gutters, the windows criss-crossed with tape. And no lights burning. A cold night. A cold welcome . . .

Inhaling, Lester thought about his brother. At least Joe had been looking forward to coming home. They had been lucky, being given the same leave. God grant we are always so lucky, Lester thought dully. He had seen the change in Joe and regretted it. Gone was the mischievous, slightly dopey kid; now his brother seemed quiet, at times almost melancholic. If he had been on his own, Lester feared that Joe wouldn't have fared well either physically or mentally. And yet he always held his own. Never complained on the dawn raids into Northern France, never seemed nervous on the long cold journeys to their hit-and-run missions. Ran quick, responded fast, kept silent. But what did he *think*, Lester wondered. After so many dangerous, potentially fatal missions, how did he manage to hold his nerve? To prove he was brave? Or to please his brother?

Lester knew the war was easier for him. People responded to Lester. A born leader, someone had said. But Lester had no interest in promotion. He loved the danger, the excitement of being one of the chosen. One of the élite Royal Marines. It was obvious, even to him, why he liked the risks – because he could be careless with his life. Only the thought of his empire held him back from total rashness. The empire he had been building up so well. The empire that was now on hold. *For his son.*

Not his wife. Beth never played any role in Lester's future plans. He knew she would be there, as certain as his own shadow. But – like his own shadow – he had grown used to her and ceased to see her. She might always be present, but she was ephemeral, without substance in his heart.

Stop daydreaming, he thought suddenly. It was time to go home. Lester flicked the butt of his cigarette into the gutter. Only forty-eight hours to go.

'I thought you said she was throwing a Christmas party.'

'She changed her mind,' Rose replied, looking over her shoulder to Stuart. 'Women do that a lot.'

'So now it's a New Year party?'

'You catch on fast.'

Pulling a face, he clinched her round the waist and then leaned his head on her shoulder. '1940 – I wonder what it'll bring?'

'Undoubtedly 1941,' Rose teased him, cupping his face in her hands. 'It'll bring all kinds of wonderful things. Fabulous things –'

'Like what?'

'What do you want it to bring?'

'Our marriage.'

She smiled, kissed him lightly on the lips. 'We've only just got engaged.'

'I like being engaged,' he said, hugging her to him. 'I wonder if marriage will be as good?'

He kissed her slowly, longingly, Rose leaning against him. They had become lovers over Christmas, actually making love in the surgery when Cedric was away visiting Hettie. It had been dark, Rose banging her head on the drill as they kissed on the surgery chair, Stuart laughing and pulling her over to the couch.

Everyone would be outraged if they knew, Rose realised. Her father, Hettie, *Cedric* . . . it made it all the more enjoyable, in a way. And her feelings for Stuart had grown steadily with their intimacy. She liked the way he touched her, made love to her, made her feel beautiful. With Stuart, her emotions finally caught up with her appearance. And as she lay in his arms, she smiled to herself. Oh yes, he would do well for a husband. Mr Stuart Fallow would definitely do.

'I mean – what if you got fat?' Stuart went on, letting his fingers run over her stomach.

'What if *you* got fat?'

'It's all right for men. A bit of weight makes you look prosperous.'

'Then you must be worth a bloody fortune,' Rose replied, laughing as Stuart chased her around the reception desk.

They hadn't noticed Cedric standing in the doorway, his expression pained. Finally, he coughed, Rose stopping at once and smoothing her hair. Unabashed, Stuart smiled at his father.

'What on earth is going on in here, Stuart?'

He never missed a beat. 'We were practising.'

Cedric's nasal tone rose. 'Practising! Practising what?'

'The new dance,' Stuart said smoothly, Rose watching him in open admiration. 'It's called the Waterlily.'

'The Waterlily?' Cedric repeated. 'I've never heard of it.'

'It's very new,' Stuart replied. 'You run round and round in the shape of a waterlily.'

'And?' his father intoned.

'And what?'

'And what happens then?'

'You start again – in the other direction,' Rose answered, her tone composed.

Impressed, Stuart gave her a sidelong look.

Cedric might doubt his son, but Miss Bradshaw was not a flippant girl. If she said that there was a dance called the Waterlily, then there was.

'Anyway,' Cedric continued, 'I came to say that we can all go over to Henrietta's party together.'

'Great,' Stuart muttered.

Cedric turned to Rose. 'I'll pick you up tomorrow evening at seven. Then we'll all go on to Heathcote Place. I will, of course, run you home later.'

Rose nodded. 'Thank you.'

'I could take her home myself, Father,' Stuart interjected swiftly. 'You might want an early night. I mean, we won't want to keep you up.'

Cedric fixed his son with rheumy eyes. 'Petrol is on ration, Stuart. We are lucky to have one car, never mind two. And as such we must set an example. We will use my car. And my car only.' He looked his son up and down. 'Anyway, why would I want an early night? No one goes home early at New Year. That's the point of having a New Year, to welcome it at midnight. Twelve o'clock.'

They both expected him to point to the clock and were almost disappointed when he didn't.

'So you'll be ready at seven, Rose?' he concluded. 'Then we can all have a lovely evening.'

It should have been a lovely evening, but despite everyone being determined to enjoy themselves, there was a melancholia about the night. Too many of the guests had sons, nephews, husbands, away fighting, and although everyone was talking about an early end to the war, no one really believed it.

As a skilful hostess, Hettie was irritated by the flatness of the proceedings.

'Whatever's the matter with everyone?' she asked Stuart. 'Really, people can be so dull.'

'Especially when they're wondering if this New Year's Eve will be their last.'

Hettie gave Stuart a bleak look. He could be so tiresome at times.

'I imagine things will liven up when midnight comes.' She looked round, her guests hanging about in the drawing room, the music lifting no one's spirits. 'What about some more food?'

Rose materialised beside her at that moment. 'You've fed everyone plenty, Hettie. They're just a bit quiet, that's all.'

'I've never had a quiet party before. I mean, what's the point?'

Irritated, Hettie looked round again, her peach silk dress perfectly tailored, her hair newly done. In fact, Rose thought, Hettie was at her most attractive. For the party? Or something else?

'Are you going to announce your engagement tonight?' Rose whispered excitedly, Stuart straining to hear.

Hettie's eyebrows rose. 'Cedric and I have talked about it –'

'Oh, good on you!' Stuart said approvingly. 'I can't wait to see my father as a nervous bridegroom.'

When she had finally nabbed the father, Hettie thought meanly, she would get her own back on the son.

'We *might* announce our engagement,' she continued cautiously. 'Or not. It depends how the evening goes. Although frankly it would be like announcing it at a wake with this lot . . .' For a moment Rose could see a little of the old Hettie. Her guard was down, her annoyance obvious. 'I've fed them with my best food and my best booze and what difference has it made? None! Not one happy face.' She turned to Stuart, her tone warning. 'And if you say one word about the war, I'll wrap that ham shank round your neck.'

Smiling, Stuart watched her walk off and then turned back to Rose. 'Are you thinking what I'm thinking?'

'Which is?'

'That my father might be holding back?'

'Never!' Rose replied, watching the obviously irritated Hettie try to liven up the vicar. 'Why would he? I mean, you and I are engaged, so the first part of the dastardly plot has gone through. So what's stopping your father marrying Hettie?'

'Cold feet?'

'No,' Rose said flatly, 'Cedric's keen to get the whole thing tied up. And get his hands on Hettie's money.'

'How could you talk about my father like that?' Stuart replied, feigning outrage.

'Because it's true.'

'Oh yeah, I forgot that.' He leaned further towards Rose. 'Do you think Hettie might scare him a little?'

'I doubt that. She's very clever with men – always plays down her natural killer instincts.'

'So perhaps the old man's worried about her reputation? Two husbands dead. And not from laughing.'

'Hettie didn't kill them!'

'No, but you have to ask yourself – what is my father thinking? Is it worth allying himself to a black widow for the money? Or will she mate with him once and then eat him? Like those insects,' Stuart answered her. 'The females mate, then kill the males.'

'You're lucky you're alive then,' Rose said slyly, nudging him, her gaze following Hettie.

It was odd how things turned out, Rose thought. For years she had been resistant to Hettie's plotting and now, suddenly, at the thought that it might go awry, she was anxious for her mentor.

'Oops,' Stuart said suddenly, 'the first people are leaving.'

'It's not midnight yet!'

'They're leaving anyway,' Stuart replied, moving into the hall and watching as Hettie pressed her guests to stay. But they were adamant: It's been a lovely party, thank you, Hettie dear. We'll see you for bridge next week . . .

Behind them, in the drawing room, they could see Cedric turn on the radio. Suddenly the room was filled with the sounds of people celebrating, the chimes of Big Ben counting down the seconds to the New Year. But at Heathcote Place the guests merely stood, smiling politely, as the year limped out.

'Happy New Year!' Hettie cried pathetically as the last chime struck. 'Happy New Year, everyone!'

Thus prompted, there followed a lot of gracious smiles and kisses on the cheek, but no real merriment – however much Hettie tried to force it. As for Cedric, he was sipping a pink gin in an armchair by the fireplace, staring into the flames blankly. Determined, Hettie still tried to make her guests respond, but she had no luck that night. In dribs and drabs they wandered off and by the time quarter-past twelve had come, there was no one left.

'Well!' Hettie said, her temper rising like a geyser. 'That was a waste of time!'

'I enjoyed myself.'

She spun round to face Cedric. 'You enjoyed yourself! You looked like you'd just had a kidney removed! My lovely party, what a disaster –'

'My dear,' Cedric intoned nasally, Stuart nudging Rose to get her attention, 'I feel that you're a little too skittish tonight. A party is a party, after all, and not of great importance.' He paused, looked up at the ceiling and then continued, oblivious to the steaming Hettie standing beside his chair, 'I myself can admit that I have attended livelier functions, but there is a war on, and as such I think the decorum of the evening will stand you in good stead.'

Stuart glided over to Hettie with a brandy and handed it to her. Still listening to Cedric, she downed it in one gulp.

'. . . As people of some stature in this town, we have a position to uphold. An example to set . . .'

Hettie refilled her glass herself, then turned back to Cedric, who was still staring at the ceiling.

'. . . we must be grateful that we are alive and well, and that we have not lost any of our loved ones in this dreadful war. For that reason – and that alone – we should be quietly at peace . . .'

Hettie finished the second brandy, Rose watching her in silent amazement. Then she refilled her glass again. Exchanging a look with Stuart, Rose shrugged.

'. . . What good is it worrying about silly things?' Cedric blathered on. 'A party is just a party, nothing more . . .'

God, Rose thought, he's going to pay for *that* remark.

'. . . the evening was pleasant and without incident . . .'

With that, Hettie moved. She walked over to the grand piano and flung up the lid, sitting down and cracking her knuckles. Amused, Stuart watched her, though Rose was getting more than a bit concerned when Hettie downed most of her third brandy and then crashed her fingers onto the piano keys.

As though electrocuted, Cedric leaped in his seat, turning round awkwardly and frowning.

'I didn't know that you played the piano, my dear.'

'Oh, I play,' Hettie said, her voice a little slurred. 'I can play you a fine song, Cedric,' she laughed. '*A fine song, Cedric*.' Lisping, she laughed again. 'That's hard to say when you've had a couple.'

Cedric's eyes fixed on her with complete disbelief.

'My dear –'

'What d'you want to hear?' Hettie slurred. 'Something cheerful?'

'Henrietta, I think you're a little unwell –'

'Or something a little naughty?' Hettie replied, giggling happily to herself. 'Personally, I think you need a bit of pepper in your sporran, Mr Fallow.'

Laughing outright, Stuart sat down to listen, Rose watching her mentor incredulously. Hettie wasn't lying, she *could* play, a talent she had hidden from everyone. But where in God's name had she learned?

Running her hands up and down the keys skilfully, Hettie played some scales, grinning happily. Then she paused and finished her third brandy.

'Hettie,' Rose said anxiously, walking over to her. 'Perhaps you should lie down –'

'Oh, lie down yourself!' she barked back. 'No one knows how to have fun any more. That's the trouble with people,' she laughed. Not the tinkling laugh she usually employed, but a huge belting Gull Road guffaw. 'They're dull!'

'Hettie, please –'

She shrugged Rose off. 'Leave me alone! I used to have fun once, you know. Before I got rich. Used to have a lot of admirers.' She laughed again. 'Not great long dopey things who can't make their minds up.' She looked over to Cedric accusingly. 'Oh yes, I could tell you some tales, some real tales about real men –'

Catching hold of her arm, Rose tried to get Hettie to rise.

'Come with me –'

'Get off!' Hettie slurred. 'I know how to have a good time. And I'm making the most of it. Not that I've had a good time for years. Money's all right, but look at that lot tonight. All dead from the neck down! But not me. *Not me!* There's lots of life in the old girl yet.'

And then the Widow Miller, a.k.a. Henrietta, began to sing:

'Oh, the white cat peed in the black cat's eye,
And the black cat said, "Cor Blimey!"
And the white cat said, "It's your own damn fault
You shouldn't stand behind me!"'

When she finished, Stuart applauded appreciatively, Rose hurrying the drunken Hettie upstairs. And Cedric – like an elephant hit with a rubber bullet – fell back in his seat, blank with shock.

FORTY-ONE

On the 3 January 1940 Unity Mitford, 'The Storm Troop Maiden', was sent home from Germany. She had fallen in love with Hitler, the rumour went, and had tried to kill herself. But she had survived, and was now back in England. Ruby blew out her cheeks and put down the newspaper.

'Silly cow.'

Alfred looked up, his porkpie hat perched on the back of his head. 'Who's that?'

'Some toff got besotted with Hitler and tried to blow her head off.'

'So he's dead?'

Ruby frowned. 'Who?'

'Hitler.'

'She tried to blow *her* brains out, not his. Although I grant you, that would have been a better idea.'

Ruby regarded her husband thoughtfully. Over the months Alfred had improved and now vacillated between withdrawal and fantasy. Ruby was cautiously optimistic: maybe in time Alfred would get back to his old self. Then she wondered if the same could ever be said for Joe . . . Ruby didn't like what she had seen at Christmas. A few times she had wondered if she should talk to Maisie, but decided against it. If her daughter-in-law had been worried, she would have come to her.

But Ruby herself was worried. She wanted him home.

312

She wanted both her boys home, but knew in her heart that Lester could fend for himself. As for Joe – she had just wanted to keep him on Gull Road, hide him away, disguise him until the war was over. He wasn't the soldiering type. He wasn't up to it. When she spoke to Lester, he told her that Joe was doing well. He didn't have to say that it was only due to the fact that he was with his brother. That was obvious to both of them.

Sighing, Ruby pushed aside the newspaper and began to read Lester's latest letter for the third time.

We're fine, me and Joe, doing OK. It's bloody cold, but what d'you expect? Spring's coming, so they say. I'll believe it when I see it. You know, Ma, life looks so different from where we're sitting.

Joe made us all laugh the other night, telling the lads about how they make rock in Blackpool and showing them Trudie's photo. She's got fans. Too many. Watch out for her, won't you, Ma? And watch out for Daniel for me?

I've still got my dreams. About the dance hall mainly. Sounds strange, but I see it at night and walk the floor, like it's real. I'll finish that dance hall, Ma, and pass it down to Daniel one day. You see if I don't.

Bye for now, from me and Joe, who says he'll write later.

Lester

Hearing the back door open, Ruby looked round to see Trudie walking in. She was wearing a bright wool coat, her hair waved, her lips dark red.

''Lo there. Letter from Lester?'

Ruby nodded. 'He says Joe will write separately.'

'Joe never writes! He says he will, but it's Lester who does all the letters.'

She went over to the kitchen cupboard and looked in. Two tins of corned beef, half a loaf of bread and a tin of pilchards sat unappetisingly on the shelf. Britain was already on short rations. God knows how she was going to feed her guests, Ruby had said only that morning. It didn't bear thinking about.

'You want something to eat?'

'No thanks, Mam, I'm going out.'

'Tonight, Trudie?' Ruby queried. 'You're always going out.'

Suddenly galvanised, Alfred threw in his pennyworth. 'You should stay home and keep your mother company.'

'What the hell are you for?' Trudie replied, her eyebrows raised.

'Don't talk to your father like that!' Ruby snapped, returning at once to her original theme. 'I'd like you to stay home tonight.'

'Mam, I've promised my friends.'

'But there was an air raid Thursday. I worried about you.'

'Three men were killed over in Morecambe,' Alfred cut in. 'Blown to bits. Pieces as far as Southport. They said that one of the men's legs came to rest at the end of the North Pier.'

Both women ignored him.

'I can't stay in all the time because of the war, Mam,' Trudie replied sullenly, then modified her tone. 'I'll be careful, honest I will.'

'Decent girls don't stay out late.'

Trudie put her hands on her hips. 'What's *that* supposed to mean?'

'It means that someone told me you'd been hanging around the Roxy with a soldier the other night,' Ruby replied, shortly. 'You have to watch out, or you'll get a reputation.'

It was almost funny, Trudie thought. Her mother had everyone's number but hers. She couldn't see what was under her very nose. That her own daughter was a tart. Ah well, Trudie thought, who cared? She was having a good time, there were plenty of soldiers about, and someone even said that the Americans might get involved in the war. She liked that idea; liked the thought that she might grab herself a Yank and go to live in the USA – where no one knew her.

For a moment Trudie felt an overwhelming sadness. It was all right for the lads, but when a girl slept around she was rubbish, no longer wife material – for anyone decent. The thought jolted her. She had no one to blame; she had ruined her own future entirely by herself. But the thing about losing a good name was that you couldn't ever restore it. Like losing an arm, there was no way you could sew it back on and pretend that nothing had happened.

'Trudie?'

She snapped out of her reverie at once. 'What, Mam?'

'You OK?'

'Sure, I'm fine.'

'You look different –'

'Oh, leave off,' Trudie whined. 'I'm just a bit tired, that's all. A bit of a laugh and a dance will cheer me up no end.' She walked to the door, wanting for an instant to run back to her mother for comfort. But she resisted the impulse. 'I'll be back a bit later,' she said, her voice brittle. 'Don't worry about me, Ma. I can look after myself.'

The Lazy Eye was doing better than Len had hoped. The war might be on, but people still wanted their racing. Naturally the customers had changed. There *were* a few younger men left, but they were the wide boys: lads who had ducked enlistment and were working the black market – dodgy types, profiteers. Len had seen them in the pubs and by the track, flogging cigarettes and booze and then running off when an official appeared.

Sneezing loudly, Len tipped his trilby further back on his high forehead and then blew his nose.

'Well, hello,' Dave Lincoln said, smiling at him warmly. 'You've got a right cold.'

'You look well enough,' Len replied, patting Dave's stomach and pulling a face. 'Quite a bay window you've got there.'

'That's what age and a good wife does for you. You should marry again.'

'Nah, not me.'

'You'd have someone to warm your bed, Len. That keeps the colds away all right,' Dave replied, passing Bunny his winning slip. 'I did well on the three thirty. Hardy Lad came in for me.'

Len looked surprised. 'I've never seen you on the track before, Dave. I didn't even know you betted.'

'I don't,' he replied, dropping his voice. 'I'm here to keep an eye open. See what's what. I heard there was some black-market trading going on.'

'They come and go.'

'Like Lady Luck, hey?' Dave replied, smiling and looking across the course. 'I'm going back a bit now, but I were glad that nothing happened with Gilbert Beardsley.'

'It was good of you to tip me off,' Len answered gratefully. 'I believe Ruby had a word with Gilbert's boyfriend.'

Dave laughed. 'I imagine that word went a long way – coming from Ruby Williams.'

'Well, Wilkes certainly left town fast,' Len answered, his thoughts running on. 'Did it help you out? You know, with your own spot of bother at the station?'

A beatific smile passed over Dave Lincoln's moustached features.

'Let's put it this way, Len. The bugger that was after Gilbert is no longer in Blackpool. In fact, the last I heard, he were over in Barnsley. And before long there's another promotion coming up . . . Our little arrangement worked like a charm. You helped me out there, Len.'

'My pleasure. Everyone benefited.'

Suddenly glancing at his watch, Dave frowned. 'I've got to be off! Look, if there's anything I can do for you, Len, just let me know. Before long I'll have quite a bit of clout – if things go the way they should. And I could be useful to my friends. You just have to ask.'

'There *is* one thing –'

'No, not yet,' Dave replied, already knowing what Len was about to ask. 'I've heard nothing about Roy Howell. But I keep asking around, Len, and one day I'll find him. And then I'll let you know.'

Dave strode away like a man with confidence; like a man who scented a promotion in the air. Well, why not, Len wondered. Dave Lincoln wasn't the brightest copper around but he was solid and loyal. And the war might actually do him a favour; putting all his younger rivals out of the running.

Sneezing again, Len accepted the whisky Bunny offered him, together with the day's takings.

'We did well today,' Len said approvingly. 'Better than I'd have thought.' He then offered Bunny a note. 'Go on, have that.'

'What for?' Bunny replied, his fur collar pulled high around his neck.

'For being a good clerk,' Len said. 'Honestly, it's a bugger when a man can't make a spontaneous gesture without it being questioned!'

'I never question money,' Bunny replied, pocketing the note. 'Thanks, Len.'

'I have to say that I wondered if we'd still be making a living in wartime. But life goes on. People like to gamble and the bloody toffs have to have their little bets.'

'God bless them,' Bunny answered, giving Len a sideways glance. 'I got my papers this morning.'

'You can't have! You're too old.'

'I look older than I am,' he replied ruefully. 'Unfortunately I'm still young enough to fight.'

This was unexpected news. Len had presumed that Bunny would never be called up. Had relied on it, in fact. But now here was his clerk about to leave. All the familiar faces, going one by one.

'I'll miss you,' Len said sincerely.

Bunny nodded, his milk-white hair ghostly in the light. 'Same goes for me, Len . . . I wanted to ask you something.'

'Go on.'

'I feel a bit soft, talking about it. But I wanted a bit of advice. It's about Trudie Williams.'

Surprised, Len raised his eyebrows. 'What d'you want to know, Bunny? She caused some trouble for Rose a while back. You know all about that. But lately, Trudie's not been around Gull Road a lot. Doesn't mix with the neighbours.'

'I hear she's a bit of . . . you know, a bit fast.'

'And then some.'

Bunny paused, shivered and drew up his collar. 'You think her reputation's deserved?'

Curious, Len studied his clerk. 'Funny thing to ask. What's it to you?'

'I just wondered, that's all,' Bunny replied, looking away. 'Well, to be honest, Len, I went out with Trudie a while back. Only a couple of times. Nothing happened, you know. But I liked her. Thought people had her wrong . . . She played on my mind a bit. I would have asked her out again, but I never bumped into her and time passed. You know how it is. But lately I've been wondering if I shouldn't call and ask her out, proper, like.'

Len sighed. This was a sensitive subject.

'I'll be honest with you, Bunny. Trudie Williams was a great kid when she was growing up – funny, liked a laugh – but now she's gone a bit bloody wild.' Len paused, trying to let his clerk down gently. 'I'm fond of the Williams family, but Trudie's got a reputation – and it's deserved, from what I hear. I suppose she'd be all right if you just wanted to go

318

out for a good time, but she's not a girl to get serious about.'

Nodding, Bunny digested the information.

'Well, now, Len, I don't say you're wrong. But I've a hunch about her. I think she's been judged unfairly. You know, people get a name and it sticks – even if they change.'

Len kept his voice even. 'She's not changed, Bunny.'

'Not yet,' he replied, turning his pale face to Len. 'I liked her. *Really* liked her. She isn't what people think. Oh, I've seen her around, brash and all made up. But when I went out with her Trudie was thoughtful, like a different person.'

'Because *you're* thoughtful, Bunny.'

'No, that wasn't the only reason. She seemed . . . sad.'

Sighing, Len tapped Bunny on the shoulder. 'Listen to a word of advice – Trudie Williams is not a woman to dream over. I understand what you're getting at; I know something of how you feel. You've no family and you want someone to come home to. Especially now you've been called up. It helps to have a woman at home to keep your spirits high.' Len's voice hardened. 'But don't pick Trudie Williams. She'll only let you down, Bunny. And you don't need that.'

'You could be wrong, Len.'

'I could be,' he agreed. 'But then again, *you* could be wrong. And I don't want you to find that out the hard way.'

FORTY-TWO

'I don't want bloody charity!' Len barked, uncharacteristically cruel. 'You can take that back where it came from.'

Stung, Rose put the food back into her basket. 'Stuart said –'

'*Stuart said this, Stuart said that!*' Len hurled back at her. 'Who is Stuart Fallow – the Second bloody Coming?'

'Dad –'

'I've managed to bring you up and fend for us both nicely enough. I'm grateful for what Hettie did, but I'm not going to have it forced down my throat for ever.' He turned on his daughter, his voice raised. 'You've changed, Rose. I don't like to say it, but you bloody have. You kept your head for a long while with Hettie, but since you got engaged to Stuart Fallow you've got above yourself. Bringing bloody food home for me! What the hell's got into you?'

Shaken by her father's anger, Rose flushed. 'I didn't mean –'

'You didn't think!' he roared. 'All you think about is bloody Lytham, Stuart Fallow and your new life. Fine, it's to be expected from a bride-to-be, but don't start looking down on Gull Road –'

'I never have!' Rose shouted back, close to tears. 'I've never looked down on my home!'

'You have now!' Len snapped. 'You've got all high and mighty, the Lady Bloody Bountiful. *Bringing food home to*

320

me!' he paused, unable to believe it. 'Since when couldn't I afford to put food on our table? Since when?'

'Oh, Dad,' Rose said, running over to him and putting her arms around him, 'I'm so sorry, so sorry.'

His anger evaporated in an instant.

Tightly, he hugged her to him, his voice apologetic. 'Sorry, luv, I don't know what I was thinking of. I should have known you'd never look down on me. Sorry, luv, sorry. It's just with Bunny going off, and you getting married –'

'I could postpone it.'

He pulled back to look into her face.

'Not likely! There's no reason to postpone anything. God knows, it's taken you bloody ages to get this far. No, Rose, I'm a jealous old man. And I'm only just realising it. I've had you to myself for so long I can't bear the thought of you not being around.'

'I won't *stay* away,' Rose reassured him. 'I'll come by every day –'

'Oh, your husband will love that!' Len replied wryly. 'You'll come and see me when you can and that'll do me. Besides, I've got plenty of friends in the street. And Clovis.'

They exchanged a knowing look.

'And don't forget Nan Wilmslow,' Rose teased him. 'She's always good for a chat.'

'That's true. You can't shut that bloody woman up when she gets started.'

Laughing, Rose sat down at the kitchen table, pushing away the offending food basket and looking enquiringly at her father.

'I didn't know Bunny was called up.'

'Yesterday,' Len replied. 'I thought he was too old and, worse, I told him so.'

'How will you manage, Dad? Can you get another clerk?'

'I'll find someone.'

At once, the old memories returned, the call of the track. 'I could help, Dad.'

Len gave her a sharp look. 'No, you couldn't! The days of you being a ticktack woman are over. That was in the past, Rose, before you met Hettie and went up in the world.'

'No one would mind me helping you out!'

'You're so naïve,' Len replied quietly. 'Of course they'd mind.'

'Well, they can just get used to the bloody idea!'

He laughed, then shook his head. 'Can't you see that everything's different now? You can never live like you used to. Not any more. Your place is in Lytham, with Stuart. You'll be the wife of a professional, well-off man, with a grand home to look after. How could a woman like that work on the track?'

Impatiently, Rose shook her head. 'I worked the track before! I was going to the bloody races when I was in my pram, and remember how I worked for George to help you out? You know how good I was, Dad. And I loved it.' She had forgotten how much until that moment. 'And more than that, the people liked me. I got on with the bookies and the punters –'

'You can say that again,' Len said drolly. 'Remember how you clipped Freddie Marsh round the head for trying to lay a bet too late?'

Rose shrugged. 'He had it coming . . . Oh, come on, Dad, how *can* you disapprove of me helping you out? It was second nature to me before –'

'Yeah, and you had a squint before, Rosie. You want to be like that again? I don't think so. That was another girl who went to the track with me. A funny, runty misfit who was bolshy and awkward. A girl no one took seriously. She's gone now, that girl. Turned into a beauty, who hooked a great catch. You're not who you were. Never will be again, luv. You have to realise that.'

For the first time Rose saw how far she had travelled. That runty kid *was* gone. But Rose could still feel for her.

And for a moment she could still see her old self; scratching her arms in the sunshine, watching Trudie pedalling down the pier with the boys. The kid who sat on the front steps staring at Sea View; the kid none of the boys wanted; the kid who stole a kiss from Lester Williams. *That* kid. That poor, feisty little sod.

And suddenly she missed her.

'Oh, Dad,' Rose said, laying her head on Len's shoulder. 'I don't know if I *want* to get married and leave you. We were so happy here.'

Len could feel his throat tighten, but his voice stayed calm. He might want to say, leave Stuart Fallow and stay with me, but he had never got in the way of his daughter's progress, and he wasn't about to start now.

'You talk nonsense, luv. Every woman wants her own husband and her own home. Think what a waste it would be for you to end up in Gull Road.'

'There's nothing wrong with Gull Road!'

'It's not thrilling.'

'No, but it's my *home*,' Rose said quietly. 'And as long as my dad's here, it'll be the best bloody place on earth.'

Pushing the letter deep into his pocket, Joe glanced over to Maisie. Should he tell her? Why not? He told her everything else. But then again, Lester had made him promise to keep it a secret. Joe wavered. It was too much! Lester was home on leave too; why hadn't he done his own dirty work? Joe felt immediately guilty. How could he begrudge one favour, after all the favours his brother had done for him?

'Maisie,' he said, and his wife turned to look at him. 'Is it wrong to break a promise?'

She sat down on his lap, kissing his cheek. 'I suppose it depends on the promise.'

Joe considered her words carefully before continuing, 'If Lester asked me to do something and made me promise not to tell anyone – and I did – would that be wrong?'

Maisie stroked her husband's forehead. He was such a child really, she thought. Hardly able to cope with something so small, let alone a war.

'I don't think it would matter if you told *me*.'

Joe nodded. 'OK . . . it's like this. Lester's given me a letter that he wants me to give to someone.'

'Who?'

'Rose Bradshaw.'

Maisie took in a breath. This wasn't good. Rose was due to marry at the end of the month and Lester knew that. What possible reason could he have to write to her now? And *what* was he writing?

'Rose? She's not interested in Lester any more.'

'I know that,' Joe replied. 'Before, she always used to ask me about Lester when we came home on leave. But she hasn't done that since Christmas. Since she got engaged to that Fallow chap.' He pulled the letter out of his pocket and stared at it. 'I promised Lester I'd deliver it – and that I'd tell no one.'

Maisie's eyes fixed on the letter in her husband's hands. Something warned her that it was destructive, the kind of missive which undid lives.

'What do you *want* to do, Joe?'

Confused, he shook his head.

'I'm not sure. If I don't deliver it, I'd have to lie to Lester – and I've never done that before.' His eyes fixed on his wife, his voice quickening. 'Our Lester takes good care of me. You don't know what it's like over there. If I didn't have him with me, I'd find it hard going. I wasn't really made for fighting, it's not –'

'Sssh . . .' she said simply, laying his head against her bosom. 'Sssh now. It's all right, we'll sort this out.'

Gently, Maisie took the letter out of Joe's hand and stared at the envelope. On it was written 'Rose Bradshaw'. Just her name, nothing else. The writing was firm, in black ink.

Holding it up to the light, Maisie tried to see through the envelope, but couldn't.

'Lester's married,' she said finally.

'I know that.'

'And Rose is about to be married.'

'I know that too,' Joe replied, drawing back from his wife to look at her. 'Maybe Lester's just writing to wish Rose well.'

Maisie didn't know that much about life, but she knew trouble when she saw it. And she would bet that the letter was no congratulations note.

Taking off her glasses to polish them, she queried: 'Why don't you ask Lester what's in the letter?'

Shocked, Joe looked at her. 'I couldn't do that!'

'Why not? He's your brother,' Maisie replied, putting her glasses back on.

Then she realised that of course Joe *couldn't* question Lester. He had hero-worshipped him for too long; relied on him too often; admired him too much.

'Joe, luv, why don't you stop worrying about this letter and go and have a rest?' She kissed him gently and slid off his lap. 'I've only got you for another day and I want to make the most of it. I've settled Lesley down for the night. So why don't you go and have a little sleep and I'll join you later?'

Relieved, Joe nodded. He wanted to forget about the letter, about Lester and most of all about the war. A sleep would be welcome, sweet.

'See you soon?'

'See you soon,' Maisie agreed.

Sitting stock-still in the kitchen, she waited until she heard the bedroom door close upstairs. Then she picked up Lester's letter. When the kettle had boiled, she steamed open the envelope.

'God forgive me,' she said, taking in a deep breath. Then she pulled out the letter and began to read.

Rose,

I thought of how to begin this letter – should it be Dear Rose, Dearest Rose, My Darling, or just Sorry? I couldn't decide, so I just wrote your name. Your beautiful name, the name I've tried so hard to forget. But couldn't.

I write this as we are about to be dropped on a mission into France, and Joe is asleep beside me. He looks like a child.

Maisie paused, glancing upwards. But not a sound came from the bedroom overhead.

This war has changed him. And me. Suddenly you realise what's important. And *who* is important. I shouldn't be writing to you. I heard that you were engaged to someone – but this isn't an attempt at a reconciliation. I have nothing to offer you. Except my love. And that was never enough, was it?

I let you down. The failure of my marriage is only what I deserve. Beth isn't to blame, but you can't force love. And I never loved her. *I loved you.* And this letter is self-pitying because it's night, we have to press on tomorrow and I'm bloody scared. I pretend not to be – as much for myself as for Joe – but I do wonder if I'll get out of this alive.

If I don't – and this is the point of the letter – I want you to know something. You were the one and only woman I ever loved. I wanted to marry you, have children with you and take to the floor in my dance hall, with *you*. We could have done so much, gone so far. And I ruined it all. The only thing that remains, and will always remain, is my love.

Don't acknowledge this letter. If I come back from the war in one piece, I'll go back to Gate

Street and never mention it. You'll be married and living in Lytham. Our paths won't cross again . . . But if I *don't* make it home it will be more bearable to know that at least I got the chance to tell you the truth. I loved you and through my stupidity I lost you.

Have a wonderful life, my darling. In this world, or the next, I'll be watching. The stupid angel who will always wish you well.

Yours always,
Lester

Slowly, Maisie replaced the letter in its envelope, resealed it and then put it under a plate to press it flat. Soon no one would know it had been opened. Especially not Joe. Uneasy, Maisie then got to her feet and moved to the front door, opening it and looking down Gull Road. There were no lights on because of the blackout, but after a moment she could just make out number 139.

It would be so easy to walk up and slide the letter under the door. It would be so easy to tear the letter into pieces and burn it. Or replace the letter with another one . . . Maisie shook her head. What was she thinking? How could she forge a letter? And, anyway, it wasn't her business to interfere. But she *had* interfered, hadn't she? And now she had a decision to make.

Damn it! Maisie thought to herself, she wasn't a clever woman. How could she work this out? All she knew was that if she had been Rose and received the letter it would have haunted her. Rose might marry Stuart Fallow and live well for the rest of her days, but Lester's words would echo relentlessly. And if he died . . . Maisie shivered. If Lester died, might Joe? Dear God, it was too much to think of . . . If Lester died, Maisie repeated firmly to herself, then the letter would be his epitaph.

Stuart Fallow wasn't medically fit to fight. Stuart Fallow

could give Rose love, money and status. But he was never going to be a hero. He might make a good husband and a good provider, but women admired heroes. They admired the men who fought, who laid their lives on the line. Like Lester. And they loved them for their courage.

Alive. *And* dead.

FORTY-THREE

Rushed into hospital with an appendicitis, Cedric missed the registry office wedding of Rose and Stuart. After Hettie's drunken performance, he had been shaken for days. But she had won him over, putting her antics down to some bad fish, not the excess of brandy she had consumed. It was a tribute to her skill that she managed to convince him, but then Cedric was getting used to Hettie being in his life. Besides, her fortune remained whether she was drunk or sober. And, he told himself, anyone could have been caught out by some bad halibut, couldn't they?

But despite all Hettie's skill at manipulation, Stuart and Rose had managed to resist her plea for a big wedding. It was wartime, Rose said; a big wedding wouldn't look right. Miffed, Hettie agreed to the civil service, but was infuriated that Cedric couldn't attend.

'Well, honestly,' she complained to the registrar, 'Stuart is his only son; he could have made an effort.'

She was also incensed to find herself alone when faced with the combined force of Len Bradshaw, Ruby and Alfred Williams, Gilbert with his stick, Clovis, Nan Wilmslow, and Maisie carrying Lesley.

'I thought,' she hissed to Stuart before the ceremony, 'that it was supposed to be a quiet affair?'

He smiled, delighted at her discomfort. 'Rose wanted her friends to be here.'

'What about your friends and your father's?' She looked at the procession from Gull Road and shivered. 'Ah well, perhaps it was better to keep it quiet.'

'You are a *terrible* snob,' Stuart teased her, taking in her expensive outfit and what was probably the biggest hat he had ever seen. 'Father would have been proud of you.'

'I dare say,' Hettie replied, secretly flattered, 'if he had got out of his bed and taken the trouble to come. I mean, people have their appendices out every day and don't go around making a song and dance of it.' She eyed the motley congregation and then looked back to Stuart. 'D'you know there are even *soldiers* waiting outside?'

'No! Soldiers getting married!' Stuart replied. 'It should be stopped.'

Hettie gave him a slow look. 'You have *such* a way with words, Stuart.'

'So do you, Hettie. You swept my father off his feet when no one else ever managed it.' He glanced at his watch. Rose was late, but he expected that. 'I suppose you and Father will be getting married before too long?'

She bristled. 'I think your father has an adverse reaction to weddings. It makes me wonder if he would rather have brain surgery than attend ours.'

Laughing, Stuart turned as he heard the door open. Dressed in a pale cream coat and hat, Rose walked in with her father, taking her place next to Stuart and squeezing his hand.

Spotting Hettie, Len moved into the seat next to hers, his voice an amused whisper.

'You know what they say Hettie? If you can't fight, wear a big hat.'

Her eyes narrowed. 'Good to see you too, Leonard.'

The wedding seemed to be over in moments. One minute Stuart and Rose were lovers, the next, a married couple. Mr and Mrs Fallow. Stunned by the speed of the proceedings, Len found himself oddly unmoved, staring at the couple without taking in what had just happened. Meanwhile, Ruby had walked over to Rose and hugged her, Rose momentarily disappearing in the folds of her dark wool coat.

'You're married!' Ruby said, pulling back. 'Sorry Trudie didn't come. Jealousy doesn't do anyone any good . . .'

Smiling, Alfred waddled over to them, his porkpie hat perched on one side of his large head. 'I were married myself three times.'

'. . . and you look wonderful,' Ruby went on, ignoring her husband and shaking Stuart's hand until his eyes watered. 'You've a real good girl here. You look after her, you hear? Or you'll have me to deal with.'

'Yes, I were married in the Sudan to a princess,' Alfred went on, talking to no one in particular. 'She were rich as Midas.'

Materialising by his side, Clovis nudged him with her elbow. 'Haven't you got another hat, Alfred? You must have been wearing that for twenty years.'

'This hat's been everywhere with me,' he replied, launching into yet another story. 'When I were in Panama . . .'

From the back of the room, Maisie's gaze fixed on Rose. She looked wonderful, quite a stunner. Lifting her daughter onto her lap, Maisie nuzzled Lesley's neck tenderly. Joe had gone back to France, with Lester on some raid they couldn't talk about . . . Laughing, Lesley wriggled on her mother's knee, while Gilbert nodded a hello from across the room.

She had never lied to Joe before, Maisie thought. Never. Not even a little white lie. And this hadn't been a small lie. This had been massive. And she had taken the responsibility for it, Maisie thought, amazed. *Her*, simple, bespectacled Maisie.

What would they think of her if they knew, she wondered. Worse, what would *Joe* think? Maisie kissed the back of her child's neck, feeling Lesley's welcome warmth.

She had done the right thing, Maisie reassured herself, look-ing over to Rose again. What point would there have been delivering Lester's letter? It would have stirred up so much. Might even – God forbid – have stopped Rose marrying Stuart Fallow. Because although Maisie might be stupid, she knew how much Rose had loved – and might *still* love – Lester Williams.

Maisie's gaze fixed on Rose. She was her friend and she had helped her in the only way possible. The letter was hidden where no one would find it. Even Joe – who thought that it had been delivered. Maisie couldn't have told him the truth because he wouldn't have been able to lie to his brother. Better to lie for once and let Joe off the hook.

Besides, maybe one day the letter *would* be delivered. When it had no power any more. When Rose was settled, a mother perhaps. When no letter from a lost love could upturn her life.

And if Lester didn't come back, Maisie thought, it would never see the light of day.

Rolling his eyes, Len gestured discreetly over to where the Widow Miller was standing. 'Just look at the silly cow, Rosie. If she took off that hat four more people could get in the room.' He squeezed his daughter's hand. 'You have a good life now, you hear me? I want you to be happy, luv.'

'Oh, Dad, I *am* happy. I'm so happy.'

She kissed him on the cheek and was about to say some-thing else when Stuart dragged her away. Smiling, she waved to her father and the guests, Stuart hurrying her into his car and then pulling away from the kerb. In another moment they were out of sight.

'Is that it?' Hettie asked, her eyebrows raised.

'I've put on a little spread at my house,' Len replied, noting with amusement that Hettie balked.

'I should . . .'

'Yeah, you should,' Len agreed, looking away. 'The newlyweds were in a rush to be off.'

'Young love,' Hettie said wistfully.

'I hear you're going to marry again.'

'Really, Leonard, how people do gossip!' Hettie replied, turning and catching his eye.

'It worked well, Hettie.'

'I don't know what you mean!'

'Your plan,' Len said, beginning to roll a cigarette. 'You plotted for all this to happen and it has. Rosie is set up nicely now, should have a cushy life. And she'll always be grateful to you, her would-be mother. Better than that, she's married a man she loves.' He licked the paper and then rolled the cigarette tightly. 'Appears I have something else to thank you for.'

'I just wanted to help Rose,' Hettie said magnanimously. 'She's very dear to me.'

'So is Cedric Fallow – and Rose marrying Stuart gave you the in there.'

Hettie's eyes turned cold. 'How calculating do you think I am?'

'Come on, we've both been around long enough to know how the world works. Nothing's for nothing,' Len replied, lighting up his smoke. 'I just wanted you to know that I appreciate what you've done, Hettie – but I know why you did it.' He inhaled deeply, choosing his next words with care. 'Oh, and if the man you matched my girl up with ever lets her down, I'll know who's to blame.'

Hettie's tone was glacial. 'Is that some kind of threat, Leonard?'

He thought for a moment and then nodded. 'I suppose it is, Hettie. I suppose it is.'

It was past eleven that night when a dark figure moved into Gull Road and walked up to number 111. Furtively, she looked around, knocked on the door, then walked in because she knew it would be open. Nan was putting some tins into a small cardboard box, her angular face serene as she turned to her visitor.

'Beth.'

Beth moved further into the kitchen. Nan's flat had not been converted yet and was still illuminated by gaslight, the strange, bluish light giving the narrow kitchen an unreal atmosphere.

'I need to talk to you, Nan,' she said, sitting down at the scrubbed table. The kitchen was immaculate, every surface clean, nothing out of place, a tidy fire burning in the iron grate. 'I need some help.'

Without expressing any emotion, the diminutive Nan took the seat next to Beth. Carefully she studied her: the fathomless eyes, the thick black hair, the wildness of spirit. And the sadness.

'Help?'

'You do things. I know you do . . . people talk about you, Nan. About you being in with the black market.' Both of them glanced at the cardboard box, but neither commented. 'But that's not why I'm here,' Beth reassured her. 'I want some other kind of help. Women's help . . .'

Nan nodded, her tiny frame ghostly in the gaslight.

'I'm pregnant. Two months gone.'

Remembering that Lester hadn't been home on leave for over three months, Nan remained silent. So Beth had cheated on her husband, had she? And got pregnant. Things were bad with that marriage.

'It's not Lester's baby,' Beth went on, dropping her voice. 'Don't look at me like that, Nan! We hardly talk, let alone sleep together. He hates me . . .'

Nan watched her, silent.

'. . . Lester mustn't find out. No one must.' Beth leaned towards Nan urgently. 'You have to help me. I can't go on like this, worried out of my mind. I can't sleep, can't think. *I can't live like this!*' Her voice rose, hysteria under the words. 'I should never have married Lester, it was the worst day's work I ever did. For him and me. You don't know what it's like living in Gate Street, waiting for Lester to come home and then wondering why he bothers. I hate my life. I hate it!'

In one quick movement, Nan gripped Beth's wrist. Her grasp was unexpectedly strong.

'You have a son.'

Shaken out of her imminent hysteria, Beth nodded.

'I know. But Lester will leave me if he knows what I've done, if he finds out about this baby.' Her voice rose again. 'And how will I cope then, Nan? How will I bring up Daniel on my own? You *have* to help.' She reached into her coat pocket, drawing out her purse. 'I have money. I've saved what I could. I've got enough, I'm sure I have. If it's not, I could pay what I have now and give you the rest later.'

Rising from her seat, Nan moved to the sink.

Panicking, Beth pleaded with her: 'Listen to me, please. You have to help! There's no one else I can turn to. Not my mother – she wouldn't understand – and who else is there? I never made friends in Gate Street. And even if I had, who'd be on my side anyway? Lester's good-looking, successful, and I was the woman who managed to get him – me, Beth Hodges. But if you don't help me now I'm going to lose him.'

Filling the kettle, Nan calmly set it on to boil and then moved back to the table. Slowly she checked the tins, packing them one by one into the box.

Unnerved by her composure, Beth began to bluster.

'What's the matter? Is it money? What? You need more? Nan! Talk to me. Why won't you tell me what you're thinking?'

Nan was sure that Beth wouldn't want to know her thoughts. She had seen a lot of life, and people, but Beth Hodges unsettled her. It was obvious that her passion was beginning to slide into instability – her frustration driving her to insanity. It should make her feel sorry for the woman, Nan thought, but it didn't. Beth Hodges was pitiful, that was true, but she might also turn out to be dangerous.

Silently, Nan made them both a mug of tea, putting extra sugar in Beth's.

'Drink.'

Obediently, she did so, her gaze never leaving Nan's face.

'Come back tomorrow. Seven thirty.'

Weak with relief, Beth put down her mug and stood up.

'Thank you, Nan. I'll be back tomorrow.' She made to go, then turned back to the tiny woman watching her. 'Is that enough money?'

Nan picked up the purse and passed it back to Beth: 'No fee.'

Beth frowned, wrong-footed. 'I don't understand. You must have a fee. I have to pay you something. Or give you something.'

Nan smiled faintly. 'Silence.'

'What?'

'I want silence. Never tell Lester, or anyone else,' Nan said, turning away. 'And after tomorrow, never come back here again.'

FORTY-FOUR

Wartime food shortages bit hard. German bombing raids inflicted momentous damage, especially in London, and what was being called the Battle of Britain was fought in the skies above southern England. Women were working in the munitions factories and in every street some family had a son, father or brother away fighting.

And yet people were still people and they still wanted amusement. The enticement of Blackpool, of quick sex, sun and sea. The freedom of forgetting the war whilst watching George Formby or Gracie Fields or visiting the Tower Circus was irresistible. Whilst many of the top-line entertainers visited the troops overseas, the middle-of-the-road actors like Gilbert stayed home and performed in variety shows, always with some character dressed like Hitler: a figure of fun that the audiences could mock. And the soldiers home from leave came to the theatre and laughed and then went for walks with their sweethearts on the beach, or made love behind the Rock Emporium.

As for Trudie; she was having the time of her life. Servicemen came to Blackpool looking for a good time, and she was always ready to give it to them. The war was her perfect excuse – why worry what people think of you when you don't know if you'll even be alive tomorrow?

Ruby thought differently. It had taken her a long time to see her daughter for what she was and when she did, the shock nearly floored her. Her only daughter, a scrubber! Her only daughter, a cheap tart, a bint! Jesus, had she worked so hard all her life to see this happen?

'Oi, you!' Ruby called out to Trudie, one afternoon in late summer. 'I want a word with you.'

'Aw, Mam –'

'Don't "Aw, Mam" me!' Ruby hurled back, slamming down her bag on the top of the draining board. 'You've been fooling around, haven't you?'

Bugger! Trudie thought. Her mother had found her out. The day had finally come.

'I just like to have a good time –'

'You're putting it about like a slut!' Ruby roared, grabbing Trudie by the arm and almost lifting her off her feet. 'What example have you been set? Have you ever seen me fool around? I've been with your father all my life, never had another man –'

'I'm not you.'

'More's the pity!' Ruby roared, chucking Trudie on to the battered kitchen sofa. 'I've been a fool, I can see that now. I trusted you. Had too much on my mind to watch out for you. And this is my reward! I overheard some women on the tram talking about you, Trudie. They said you'd soon be taking money for it, the way you were going.' She stopped short, sitting down heavily and shaking her head. She looked older suddenly, her massive frame shaken. 'My girl, *my Trudie* . . .'

'Mam –'

'Why?' Ruby said, looking over to her daughter incredulously. '*Why* would you want to stoop so low?'

Stung, Trudie retaliated. 'Maybe I just like company. I mean, it's hardly thrilling here, is it? Being with you and Dad and the creeps you get as guests.' She looked around her, contempt obvious. 'You think you've done well, do you, Mam? In whose eyes? This is just some down-at-heel bed-and-breakfast dump up the road from the station. Just some place people come when they haven't enough money for the good hotels.'

'Is that what you think?' Ruby asked, her voice disbelieving. 'Have you lived here all these years and looked down on it? Have you been laughing at my place? And us? Me and your dad?' She got to her feet, her booming voice restored. 'You think you can laugh at me, Trudie? Well, just try it! I worked my way up from a bloody tinker's caravan to get here. When I was a kid I was lucky if I had a pot to piss in. If not, I went behind a bloody hedge. And you think *you're* hard done by. I grew up with nothing – but my own self-respect. And my ambition – that ambition you find so funny.'

Scared by her mother's anger, Trudie tried to calm her down. 'I didn't mean it, Ma –'

'Oh, you meant it, you bloody little bitch! You meant it, every word. You wanted to try your teeth out on me because your life hasn't gone the way you wanted. And whose fault is that? You've been choked up with jealousy ever since Rose Bradshaw did so well. Well, she *did* fall on her feet, but, God knows, she had a bloody rocky start. You can't bear to see anyone happy, can you? You had to stir it up with Lester and Rose, ruin their romance. *And* you enjoyed it. I saw another side of you then, Trudie –'

'I shouldn't have done that! I know I shouldn't,' she blustered. 'I was just –'

'Being spiteful. Seems like you've been spiteful for a long time, now I think about it. And I should have put a stop to it. Knocked it out of you. Maybe all this is my fault . . . I thought you'd grow out of it, Trudie, but I was wrong. You've grown *into* it. And now you're being spiteful all over again. *Only this time with yourself*. You've done your best to spoil other people's lives and now you want to spoil your own.'

All of a sudden the sulky, bitter young woman was gone and Trudie Williams was back to being a child. And all her bravado had folded.

'Mam, listen to me,' she pleaded. 'I've gone off the rails a bit, but I'm not hurting anyone –'

'What about *me*?' Ruby shouted. 'I'm your mother, I gave birth to you. My little girl, coming after the lads. My little Trudie, the baby I could spoil. You could do no wrong in my eyes. You made me laugh, told me gossip, kept me company. And I loved you so much that I never saw you for what you were –'

'Mam,' Trudie implored, '*Mam* –'

'Look at yourself!' Ruby snapped. 'Look at that make-up. All that lipstick. I should have said something before – why didn't I do that? I should have stopped you. You've ruined yourself, girl. There's no decent man who'll have you now. No honest guy who'll want to marry you when you've been with God knows how many others. You'll end up with some rough-arsed slob, some hard case who'll get pissed on a Friday night and knock you about for fun. Some fella who'll treat you like dirt, because that's what he thinks you are.' She shook her head, defeated. 'I've been a lot things, Trudie. There's many who'd say I'm coarse, blunt, working class – but I've always been decent.'

Crushed, Trudie stood up, her voice lost, childlike. 'I've got to go out, Mam.'

'Where?' Ruby asked, her eyes fixed on her child. 'Who are you meeting, Trudie? You going for a fumble under the pier? A quick snog behind the Pavilion? That's what the rough girls do, isn't it? Drop their knickers in any convenient alleyway.'

'I *have* to go,' Trudie said helplessly. 'I'm meeting someone.'

'You'll get pregnant, or catch something. You'll throw away your life, and for what? It's not too late,' Ruby said, her voice imploring. 'Don't go, luv. Stay with me now. Take off your coat and stay home tonight. We can sort it out. Make it all right again.'

Close to tears, Trudie shook her head. 'No, we can't, Mam. It's too late.'

And they both knew she was right.

Downstairs Beth could hear her mother moving around. She had fed Daniel and was talking to him in that high-pitched voice some women use to communicate with children. Turning over, Beth pulled the blanket over her head, her hand going to her stomach. It was gone. The baby – that terrible memento of a hurried coupling – had been aborted.

It hurt, but that was bearable, Beth thought. What wouldn't have been bearable was Lester finding out. Not that she need worry about Nan Wilmslow telling him. The woman was strange, but totally reliable. And Beth didn't worry about her mother guessing. She thought her daughter was just suffering a particularly bad period pain, nothing more.

She had been so stupid! Beth thought, putting a pillow over her head to keep out the sounds of her mother and son below. Another child would have been a disaster – and she could never have passed it off as Lester's. But what could he expect, she thought, suddenly petulant. He never touched her any more. Not even on leave, when most men were mad for their wives. Most men, but not Lester. Not Lester Williams.

He thought he could treat her any way he liked – ignore her, reject her – and she was supposed to take it? Beth flung the pillow across the room, her thick black hair framing her alabaster-white face. Most men were fascinated by her. But not Lester. Not the man she married. But then again, he wouldn't have married her if she hadn't trapped him into it. He would have married that Bradshaw bitch . . . Sitting bolt upright, Beth thought of Rose.

No one had seen her watching outside the registry office,

341

but she hadn't been able to stop herself. She had *had* to see her old rival married and out of the way. So Beth had looked on as Rose left with her new husband, apparently happy, judging by the way they were acting. But somehow even seeing the marriage with her own eyes hadn't soothed Beth.

Rose Bradshaw might be married, might have moved to Lytham St Annes, might have put some distance between herself and Gate Street – but whilst she was *alive* she would always be first in Lester's thoughts. Whatever she did, wherever she was, Rose would always be between them.

Beth could hear her son laughing downstairs and turned over again, covering her ears with her hands. There had to be a way out of this hell of a life, she told herself desperately. There *had* to be.

In France, Joe was also lying awake. His eyes were wide open, staring unseeing ahead. Only a little way off he could hear the guns and began to shake, Lester hunkering down beside his brother.

'You all right?'

Joe tried to nod, but could only move his head slightly.

'I got a letter today,' Lester went on, pretending that he hadn't noticed anything. His uniform smelled of damp wool and sweat, and was oddly comforting. 'From home. Ma.'

'What does she say?' Joe asked, still looking ahead, his teeth clenched, his hands tight.

'She says that they're getting some things off the black market,' Lester answered, the gunfire sounded again. 'You'll never guess from who.'

They were going to be caught. Joe thought helplessly. They had been lucky too long. This time they would be caught, taken to some prison camp in Germany. Tortured, maybe shot. This time they wouldn't escape . . .

'Joe, are you listening?'

Slowly he moved his gaze over to his brother. Lester looked so normal, no tremor in his voice or hand. Joe would have died without his brother.

'Joe –'

'Yeah, I'm listening. Go on.'

'It's Nan Wilmslow. She's into the black market.' Lester laughed, leaning back. 'God, she's only the size of a flea and into everything. She might be able to get you some stockings for Maisie.'

Joe nodded, his hands still clenched. He wouldn't panic; it was no good thinking of panicking. It would be OK. He had his brother with him.

'Lester?'

'Yeah?'

'What else does the letter say?'

Lester lifted it closer to the flickering lamplight. 'Ma says that Dad's cheered up. He told her that some clairvoyant had told him he would live to ninety.' Lester laughed and read on, '"Bloody ninety! Can you picture your dad at ninety? Can you picture *me* putting up with him so long? He was driving me crazy the other day and I lost my rag. He said – when you're dead I'll dance on your grave. Fine, I said, I'll be buried at sea . . ."'

Joe laughed softly, thinking of home, of the kitchen at the back of Sea View, and the rickety stairs up to the top bedrooms.

'". . . Maisie's well. Looked ever so pretty the other day. She's written to you again, Joe. And Beth's coping, Lester. The little ones are fine . . ."'

Lester paused. He knew how wary Ruby was about his wife, but also knew that his mother would keep tabs on his family whilst he was away. His family, and Joe's.

'It will all be over soon, lads. And then you'll be home and we'll have a real do. Things will be like

343

they were before. Even better. Look out for each other. Keep your heads down and know that we're all thinking of you at home.

'Your loving mother'

Sighing, Lester folded the letter and tucked it into his back pocket. Joe had fallen asleep. Thank God, Lester thought, ever anxious for his brother. How long could Joe go on like this? His nerves were shot, but he wouldn't complain. And sometimes when the gunfire started he would shake uncontrollably, hardly able to keep himself upright. Other times he would be still, barely moving.

But he would get through it. They both would. Lester had made himself that promise at the beginning of the war. He and his brother would get back home one day. Together. They would never be parted . . .

In the meantime, Joe lived for his leaves, for time with Maisie and Lesley. Whereas Lester missed only Sea View and his son. Never Beth, never Gate Street. In fact, if he could have lifted Daniel out of that house and put him with his parents Lester would have been happy . . . Thoughtful, Lester stared at his boots, then fiddled with the laces. He wasn't in the least tired, just restless.

He and Beth were miserable, but how could he end the relationship? Divorce wasn't an option at present, but maybe a separation was. They could live apart and share Daniel. Lester would see that Beth was well provided for, and in time she might grow used to the idea of divorce. Might even meet someone else and want to wed again.

Or *he* might . . . Lester smiled bitterly to himself. Ruby had written and told him that Rose was married. Not engaged any more, *married*. Unobtainable. Out of reach for ever. Well, Lester thought, who could blame her? He had left her and married someone else; she had no reason to wait for him. No hope for any future. So she had made another future with Stuart Fallow.

Ruby had said that he was a nice enough fella. Although medically unfit to fight, he was, however, attractive, well off, a dentist in Lytham . . . Lester frowned. He couldn't see Rose with a dentist. Wouldn't a dentist be dull? No, Rose would never have ended up with a bore. And Stuart Fallow was rich. That was good, Lester thought magnanimously, Rose was made for the better things in life. The things *he* would have given her.

The things he had never given to Beth . . . But what was the point? If he *did* offer his wife expensive furniture or clothes, she would refuse. Save the money, she would say, put it towards your business. She never understood that part of his business was showing off his family. Instead, Beth was keeping more and more to the shadows, still sometimes wearing that dark green dress he had come to hate so much. The drowning dress.

Rubbing his forehead, Lester tried to dislodge the old memories, but they were too strong: he and Joe on the pier, filling the slot machines, Trudie riding the boy's bike, and the sound of gulls overhead in a clear blue sky. Another remembrance made its appearance: Rose's face after Trudie had told her about Beth . . . Lester shifted his position, unbearably moved. All he had to do was to get home. To survive the war. Then he would sort out his life again. He would get out of his marriage and bring up his son. He would build his business up and . . .

And what? Unexpectedly deflated, Lester closed his eyes. What point was there in living without Rose? Because that was now his life sentence. To live without her. She was another man's wife, as he was another woman's husband. Lester could feel himself drifting off into grateful sleep . . . *She was another man's wife and he was another woman's husband . . . Rose was married . . . he was married . . .* And then – somewhere between sleep and wakefulness – Lester saw Rose reading his letter.

He watched her face change as she read the words. Then

she called out to him, running and waving the letter high in the air.

'Lester!' she was calling. 'Come home and we can sort it out! Lester, we can sort this out . . .'

FORTY-FIVE

Feeling like a total clown, Bunny Lambert arrived outside Sea View with his naval cap in his hand. Smoothing his white-blond hair, he lifted his hand to ring the bell and then thought better of it. He was just trying to summon up courage to have another go when Gilbert arrived.

Leaning on his stick, he studied the stranger. 'Hello, can I help?'

Bunny shrugged, feeling awkward. 'Does Trudie Williams live here?'

Taking one at a time, Gilbert mounted the four steps to the front door.

'She does. She's my niece.' He looked Bunny up and down. 'Don't I know you?'

'Maybe.'

'You look familiar.'

'I'm Bunny Lambert. Len Bradshaw's clerk.'

'I knew it!' Gilbert said, letting them both in. 'I remember you from before the war. I put a bet on a horse that fell at the first fence at Aintree. I was never lucky with the gee-gees.'

Looking round the hallway of Sea View, Bunny waited while Gilbert called out lustily, 'Trudie!'

But instead of Trudie, Ruby appeared, Bunny taking in the apparition with obvious trepidation.

'What the hell are you yelling about, Gilbert? We've got guests.'

He smiled winningly at his sister, jerking his head towards Bunny. 'This is a friend of Trudie's.'

'Really,' Ruby replied, her tone arctic cold.

'He was Len Bradshaw's clerk before the war. Bunny Lambert.'

The thaw was immediate. 'You work for Len? Come in, come in, lad.'

Shown into the family kitchen, Bunny was offered a seat and a cup of tea.

'Nice dog,' Bunny said, looking at Chase, who was snoring loudly by the grate.

'Nice, but useless,' Ruby replied. 'We could be invaded by a dragoon of guards and he'd never move unless they banged the door when they left. Tea?'

Bunny blinked. 'What?'

'Would you like some tea, lad?'

He nodded. 'That would be nice.'

'So you're a friend of our Trudie's?' Ruby asked, studying Bunny and deciding that if he was Len's clerk he was decent enough. Probably *too* decent for Trudie.

'I just called by on the off chance that she might be in.'

'She's at work. At Myers.'

Bunny nodded again, sipping his tea.

'You in the navy then?'

'Nearly a year now.'

'I always get so seasick,' Gilbert chimed in, helping himself to some tea and sitting down at the table to join them. 'All that water – just makes me feel queasy to think about it.'

'Don't you have some lines to learn?' Ruby asked, wanting her brother out of the way.

'Oh no, I'm fluent in Coward,' Gilbert joked, Bunny looking from one to the other and wondering how he could leave without seeming rude.

'So,' Ruby continued, 'you're home on leave?'

'For two days.'

'That's nice. I suppose you've got lots of people to visit?' Gilbert asked, Ruby kicking him violently under the table.

'Not really. I've no family,' Bunny answered. 'I was going to call by and see Len first and then I just wanted to see Trudie.' He looked around. 'What time does she get home?'

Gilbert and Ruby exchanged a glance.

'She sometimes works late,' Gilbert replied deftly, 'but you're welcome to stay for supper. Isn't he, Ruby?'

Picking up the cue, she nodded. 'Oh, yes. Yes, of course. I serve the guests at seven thirty, but we eat before then. You could pop upstairs and freshen up first, if you'd like.'

Whether he liked it or not, Bunny was soon being directed upstairs to the guest bathroom, Ruby returning to the kitchen to nobble her brother.

'I thought you were making a play for him at first!'

Gilbert rolled his eyes.

'Well, you know what I mean,' Ruby said impatiently. *'Hello, sailor.'*

'I was thinking of Trudie,' he explained. 'This Bunny looks like a good catch for her.'

'He says he knows her,' Ruby replied, putting out some knives and forks hurriedly. 'That means he must know *about* her too.'

'Of course he does, he worked with Len.'

Ruby paused to listen. Footsteps were descending from upstairs – just at the precise moment that Trudie walked into the kitchen. Ever since her argument with her mother she had been reserved. But she hadn't stopped going out – only avoided Ruby's eyes when she left. However, she *did* come home earlier than before. And she usually wiped off most of her make-up before entering Sea View – Ruby had noticed that. But Trudie hadn't really changed. It was, as she had said so hopelessly, too late.

Regret was new to Trudie and it hurt. In the days that followed her run-in with Ruby, her mother's words kept coming back relentlessly, and she knew her mother was right. She could have any man she wanted – for a couple of hours. And all the men wanted her – for a quickie. None of them would have looked after her if she had been ill, none would have been proud of her, or ever shown her off to their families. And she had only herself to blame.

So although Trudie was still going out, she had begun to feel differently. The fumblings and snoggings weren't fun any more. The servicemen's hands inside her blouse, or up her skirt weren't exciting any longer. For the first time she saw herself as others saw her. She was a scrubber, Dirty Gertie, and the nickname was suddenly damning. What the hell had she done? Why had she ruined herself, Trudie thought despondently, as though finally coming out of a stupor. Had she hated herself – and life – so much?

'You look nice,' Bunny said awkwardly.

'You do too,' she replied, looking at his uniform with interest. 'I heard you were going into the navy.'

'I'm on the *Ark Royal*.'

'You don't say!' Trudie replied, her cynicism for once deserting her. 'That's the best ship in the navy, isn't it?'

Bunny beamed with pride.

'She is that. Everyone keeps trying to claim that they've sunk her, but no one can sink the *Ark*.'

Butting in, Ruby laid down some food on the table. 'Come on, you two, time to eat.' Then she exchanged a glance with Gilbert over Trudie's head. Well, the look said, what d'you make of this?

'How long are you home on leave?' Trudie asked Bunny, helping herself to some bread and corned beef.

'I go back tomorrow.'

Almost shyly, Trudie studied the visitor. He was strange-looking, always had been – all white, like a glass of milk. But he was kind. Gentle. She liked that; it was different from any other man she had known. And she felt oddly comfortable with him. Why hadn't she gone out with him more? Trudie asked herself. They'd dated a while back, but she had cooled off, gone for the more flashy lads. And some good *that* had done her.

'More bread, lad?' Ruby asked, sitting down beside Bunny.

'Oh, give him some more meat!' her brother chided her. 'This lad's fighting for King and Country. And he's on the *Ark Royal*. You miss the racing, Bunny?'

'I do that. Heard that Billy Stevens – the jockey – got called up the other day. And there was word that Dorona had a bad fall and had to be put down at Catterick.' He shook his head. 'It all seems such a long time ago now. Such a lot has changed since I was working with Len.'

You can say that again, Trudie thought sadly.

'So you've got a whole day to yourself tomorrow?'

Bunny nodded. 'I want to see Len, but after that my time's my own.' He turned to Trudie, embarrassed and dreading rejection. 'You wouldn't like to go somewhere, would you? I mean, seeing as how it's a Saturday –'

'She'd love it!' Gilbert chimed in, answering for his niece. 'Wouldn't you, sweetheart? A day out would do you good. Where were you thinking of taking her, Bunny?'

Fascinated, Ruby watched the exchange.

'Well, we could go to the pictures –'

Gilbert beamed his approval. 'There's a Gracie Fields film on at the Winter Gardens . . .'

'Gilbert!' Trudie admonished him. But it had no effect.

'. . . She has a wonderful voice. Not too pretty, but you can't have everything. I hear she's going out to the Middle East to entertain the troops. I always say –'

It was Ruby's turn to intervene. 'Well, if you've finished your meal, you two, why don't you go out for a walk? It's a nice night.'

Bunny didn't need telling twice. In an instant he was on his feet, ushering Trudie to the door. They were almost halfway down Gull Road when she suddenly stopped walking and turned to him.

'Bunny, you don't have to spend tomorrow with me.'

'I want to,' he replied, with total sincerity.

He had remembered her as attractive and he hadn't been disappointed. And the hardness others talked about he didn't see. In fact, Bunny thought with relief, Trudie looked soft, almost subdued. And her make-up – that dreadful daubing he had sometimes seen her wear – had gone.

'Bunny,' Trudie began again, chewing the side of her fingernail nervously, 'I'm really pleased to see you, I am. But I have to talk to you.' She paused. It was painfully hard to be honest. But he was a good man, and deserved some respect. 'I think you've got an image of me that's not right.'

Bunny raised his white eyebrows. 'It's a big ship, the *Ark Royal* –'

Wrong-footed, Trudie stared at him.

'Didn't you hear what I said? I want you to know the truth about me. I'm not the kind of girl you want, Bunny.' She hated having to admit it, but couldn't lead him on. Bunny Lambert needed a nice girl, not her type. 'I've been around a bit.'

'You know, the Germans put it out that they had sunk the *Ark*, but it was just propaganda –'

'Bunny! Listen to me.'

Taking in a deep breath, he looked at her. 'I know what you're trying to tell me. I know all about you. I know you've been playing the field and that you've a bit of a name.' Trudie winced, looking down. 'I've heard what people say, what they think. But I've made up my own mind. What you seem to others isn't what you ever seemed to me. And looking at you tonight, I'd bet my life on it.'

'Oh, Bunny,' she said helplessly, 'don't . . .'

He fiddled with his cap, then put it back on his head. Awkwardly, he pushed his hands in his pockets and then took them out again. His voice was hurried, nervous.

'For the first time in my life I wished I smoked,' he said, looking down at his feet in an agony of embarrassment. 'I like you, Trudie, I like you a lot.'

'I'm no good.'

He shook his head. 'What's *good* when it's at home?'

'*Respectable!*' she snapped. 'I'm not respectable. Even my mother's told me that, and she loves me more than anyone. And she's right. I don't deny it.'

'Are you proud of it?'

Trudie flushed to her hair roots. 'No!'

'Seems to me that's the important thing,' Bunny replied phlegmatically. 'I mean, I could be wrong – maybe you want to go on the way you are, maybe it's fun.' He studied her. 'But it doesn't seem like you're having much fun to me, Trudie. I look in your eyes and you look sad.'

Her heart shifted. 'Bunny, don't say any more. I couldn't bear it if you liked me and then regretted it and went off with someone else.'

'I'm not like that. I'm not flashy, handsome or particularly good company. And it takes me a while to think things out. But when I do, Trudie, I stick with my decision. I don't go back on it. If I chose to do something – or if I chose to love someone,' he flushed and looked down again, 'I don't waver. My heart's my own, to give to who I please. And whoever gets it, has it for life.'

Moved, Trudie reached out and timidly touched his arm. 'You might think that now, Bunny, but people change. You might get to know me and what I've done, all the mean things, and realise you were wrong about me –'

'You might find out things about me you don't like. Life's not simple, Trudie, but you have to have some trust.'

'And how could you trust me?' she countered. 'Honestly, Bunny, with my reputation, how could you trust me?'

'Aren't you bigger than your reputation?' he asked, obviously surprised. 'What rules you, Trudie? You? Or your bad name?'

His attitude came as a shock to her. She hadn't anticipated his strength of character.

'I regret what I've done –'

'So it's over then?'

Trudie tried to think clearly. Could it be possible? Could you cover up your past that easily?

'Bunny, it's not that simple! The first argument we'd have you'd throw everything back in my face. You'd hold it over me for ever. You think you wouldn't, but you would,' Trudie went on relentlessly, pushing him, willing him to reassure her. 'I don't want that to happen, Bunny. I'd rather we never took this any further than have to live with your disappointment.'

He held her gaze for a long moment before speaking again.

'They keep saying that they can sink the *Ark Royal*, but they haven't. Maybe they will, one day. But no one will sink me, Trudie Williams. No one and nothing can drag me down. I'm my own man, with no one else in this world to answer to. I was free to pick anyone – and it's to you I've given my heart.' He studied her face tenderly. 'So you can stop your warnings. It's too late for me. All I can say to you now is this – do you want me, or not?'

FORTY-SIX

Cedric recovered slowly from his appendicitis, stretching his convalescence into November so that he could postpone his invalid status for as long as possible. As Stuart and Rose now lived with him in Lytham, Cedric had expected them to do the nursing – but Hettie had had other ideas.

From the day of the wedding, Hettie had expected Cedric to name the day for *their* nuptials. But still he hesitated; his convenient appendicitis pushing marriage into the background. But Hettie wasn't prepared to let it stay there. So daily she visited the patient, Rose and Stuart delighted to let her do the nursing.

'Of course it's no trouble, Cedric, my dear,' Hettie said, feeding him some beef tea whilst secretly wanting to tip it over his head. 'Stuart and Rose are busy with the practice. I have nothing to do, but look after you. And anyway, it's a real pleasure. A joy to be helpful.'

His pyjama top buttoned to the neck, Cedric held the sheet high over his scrawny form. He had got used to Hettie when fully clothed, but in pyjamas she always undermined him.

'I feel, my dear,' he intoned, still pompous in striped cotton, 'that you're doing *too* much. I mean, coming over here every day – much as I look forward to seeing you – is very tiresome.'

Not half as tiresome as you are, Hettie thought meanly.

'Now, Cedric, we have to get you on your feet again. You've had a terrible time of it lately. God knows, another man might well have succumbed to the pain.'

She paused, smiled sympathetically, and then shovelled some more beef tea down his throat. How to get her reluctant suitor out of his bed was proving to be a problem. And if Cedric *stayed* laid up, there would be no trip to the altar.

Then suddenly an idea occurred to her – an idea that would get Cedric moving. Pronto.

'You know, a man of your age has to be careful –'

'I'm not an old man!' Cedric replied, stung. 'I'm in good shape for someone of mature years –'

'I don't mind, my dear, if you're getting on. I can look after you.'

Cedric's expression was pure terror. 'Hettie –'

'I always wanted to be a nurse, my dear Cedric. Did I ever tell you that? I think I have a natural caring instinct. To look after you would be a pleasure.' She put down the beef tea and tucked the blankets around him. 'Goodness knows, you've had a busy, long life, and you deserve a rest now –'

'I'm not old!' Cedric blustered, suddenly feeling like a corpse. 'I've still got plenty of life in me.'

Hettie smiled, as though humouring him.

'I thought so too, my dear. But now I see how much this operation has taken out of you, I understand your condition better. You have to pace yourself to enjoy what time you have left.'

This was too much! Infuriated, Cedric threw back the covers and got to his feet.

'My dear Henrietta, I must assure you that I am a fit man with all my senses. And plenty of years left in me. Indeed . . .' he went on, leaping into her trap like a demented salmon, '. . . there are so many things I want to do. Travel, for one. Hobbies. Sport –'

'Oh, Cedric,' she said indulgently. 'You're in no fit state.'

'I am perfectly well!' Cedric hollered, his eyes fixing on a point just over the top of her head, his tone even more pretentious than usual. 'Henrietta, I don't think you realise that I am a very vital man. Age has only improved me and honed my skills. I am not decrepit, just beginning another phase of my life.' He paused, adding for emphasis, 'You're not looking at an old man here, Henrietta. You're looking at a man ready for a challenge. In fact, mentally, I would still call myself young.'

Amazing, Hettie thought, how vanity could lead a person by the nose.

'I think you're putting a very brave face on your condition,' she went on kindly. 'I don't mind nursing you, Cedric. My last husband was an invalid –'

'Look!' Cedric hollered, leaping up and down in his striped pyjamas, incensed beyond reason. 'Look! I can hop and jump about like a two-year-old.' He pranced around the bedroom like a frenzied rocking horse, his breath rasping in his chest when he finally stopped. 'What invalid could do that?' he gasped. 'Well, my dear? What *old man* could do that? You don't have to worry about me. I'm fit for anything. Absolutely *anything*.'

A moment later Cedric found himself agreeing to their wedding date. It took him nearly a week to work out how Hettie had managed it.

Lying in Stuart's arms, Rose closed her eyes and thought drowsily of their lovemaking. She was, she had to admit, perfectly content; utterly happy. Some new brides might not have liked the idea of sharing a house with their father-in-law, but it had turned out surprisingly well. Always busy with his local politics – and the newly formed Home Guard – Cedric was out a great deal. The war had provided him with endless opportunities to order people around and organise their lives. At the rate his father was going, Stuart said wryly, Lytham would soon become *Fallowland*.

Even Cedric's imminent marriage to Hettie had hardly dented his bureaucratic fervour. In fact, he was already laying down the ground for his future married life – being out of his wife's way as much as was humanly possible. What he didn't realise was that Hettie wanted it that way too.

Hettie . . . Rose thought about her mentor, soon to be mother-in-law, and laughed to herself. At last Hettie was within reach of her goal. Having brought Cedric to heel she would soon slide into the Lytham house and take over . . . Rose didn't mind in the least. Cedric had already said that he and his new wife would occupy the ground floor, whilst she and Stuart would have the first. And anyway, Rose thought with relief, it was only temporary. Cedric and Hettie might not realise it, but after the war the newlyweds were going to find a home of their own.

Turning over, Rose ran her index finger along Stuart's bottom lip. He stirred in his sleep, but didn't wake. For a moment she was tempted to let her hand slide under the covers and down his stomach . . . No, Rose thought, let him sleep. It could wait. They had all the time in the world.

Her thoughts moved reluctantly on to the war. Dear God, how could so many women live, day in, day out, waiting to know if their husbands were alive or dead? Much as she knew that Stuart felt guilty for not fighting, Rose was glad that he couldn't be called up. Yes, it was selfish, but love was selfish. They were together, and they were happy. And she wanted them to stay that way.

Only one thing worried Rose. Stuart was funny, loving, kind, generous, everything a woman could want – but he could also be possessive. She had seen it on a couple of occasions, and dismissed it. They were newly married, it was to be expected. Under Stuart's fluid charm there was a layer of his personality she had never suspected: his jealousy.

But then it only meant that he cared, didn't it, Rose told herself. The fact that he had accused a good friend of wanting to seduce her was just silliness, wasn't it?

Stuart's friend had laughed it off, and then Stuart had made a joke out of it. But for a moment – Rose tried to forget the image, but couldn't – Stuart's eyes had been hostile. Unnervingly so.

It was all so silly, Rose thought. Stuart didn't have anything to worry about. She wasn't going to be unfaithful, and she could bet her life that her husband wouldn't cheat on her. She didn't even look at other men, didn't want another man . . . Rose felt every one of her muscles tighten as an image of Lester came into her mind. Irritated, she turned over in bed. That had been a long time ago. Another life really. He had been important to her, that was true, but it was in the past now. Where it was going to stay.

'Darling?' Stuart stirred, rolled over and stroked her back. 'Are you awake?'

She didn't know why, but she didn't answer him. For the first time in her marriage the spectre of Lester Williams had slid between them in the marriage bed.

'Darling?' Stuart repeated. 'We have to get up, we have patients.'

She smiled, the uneasy memory fading as she turned to her husband.

'You're a liar, Mr Fallow.'

'We Fallows never lie,' Stuart intoned, using Cedric's voice. 'We Fallows are men of honour. Not a lying toerag amongst us –'

'It's Saturday,' Rose said, laughing and kissing him. 'We don't have patients on Saturday.'

'You're very pretty,' he said, looking at her intently. 'And one day you'll be very rich – when the ghastly Hettie dies. Unless she's already one of the undead. Which wouldn't surprise me.'

Rose punched him in the chest, mock-angry.

'I suppose you only married me for my expectations. Well, don't get your hopes up, Mr Fallow, the Widow Miller looks set to outlive us all. Anyway, if I do anything to displease her I'll be cut out of the will just like that!' She clicked her fingers, then sighed. 'Poor Hettie, she really does think that she controls me with the promise of her inheritance. And I don't give a damn about her bloody money.'

'Only because *I'm* rich.'

'Why d'you think I married you?' Rose replied, laughing, then becoming serious again. 'I'm worried about Dad. He's not found a good clerk since Bunny left. Oh, he's got help, but no one he's really taken to. Not *family* . . .' She snuggled up to Stuart, choosing her words carefully. 'But I know he's struggling. I could help him out now and again. I mean, we're not as busy in the practice –'

She stopped. Stuart was looking at her oddly. 'You're joking!'

'What?'

'About helping your dad out at the racetrack.'

'No, I wasn't joking,' Rose replied, sitting up in bed, her expression combative. 'Why would I be joking?'

'You're married to me now, Rose. You're living here, not in Gull Road. You can't go back working on the track –'

'What the hell are you talking about?' Rose responded angrily. 'If my father needs help, I'll help him. If you needed help, you'd expect me to be there for you.'

'But I'm not a bookie.'

Her eyes blazed. 'No, but you're a bloody snob!' she hurled back. 'My God, you did well to keep your contempt under wraps until now!'

'Darling,' Stuart said, trying to mollify her, 'it's just that you're not in that world any more –'

'And how it must have pained you that I once was,' Rose responded, insulted for herself and her father. 'Dad brought me up better than most parents ever could. Lowly ticktack man though he was.'

Stung by the tone of her voice, Stuart tried a different approach. 'I didn't mean that I looked down on your father –'

'He'd make ten of you any day!'

'Jesus!' Stuart exploded. 'I can't say anything right.'

'No, you can't! And if I want to help my father out on the racetrack, then I bloody well will. Whatever you say.'

They stared at each other for a long instant, both wondering who would be the first to speak.

Finally, Stuart relented and stroked her cheek. 'Did I tell you I loved you?'

'I don't care! I hate you!'

'Oh, come on,' he teased her. 'Don't be so unkind. I *do* love you, Rose.'

She relaxed, leaning back against him. 'You can be such a pig at times.'

'Oink, oink,' he replied, adding: 'You'll never leave me, will you?'

'Why on earth would I leave you?'

'I dunno, things happen.'

'You chump, Stuart!' Rose replied, laughing. 'You're stuck with me for life – just like I'm stuck with you.'

'Unless a bomb falls on the house and wipes us both out.'

'In that case,' Rose said, kissing him again. 'You're stuck with me for bloody eternity.'

There had been an air raid over Manchester way, someone said on the tram. Doris hurried down Gull Road. The Germans weren't heading for Blackpool, just the industrial centres, but then again, the Tower was too good a target to miss.

Knocking once on the door of number 139, Doris hurried in, Len smiling when he saw her.

''Lo there, luv.'

'My God, Len, I've had a time and a half getting here,' Doris said, by way of greeting. Taking off her scarf she then fluffed up her tinted red hair. 'One bus after another late and then I couldn't get a tram.' Hurriedly she kissed

361

him on the cheek. 'Mind you, it were my own fault I said I'd come tonight.'

'You should have let me meet you halfway,' Len replied, reaching for the teapot.

'I don't want tea!' Doris rebuked him, taking off her coat and sitting down. 'Where's your beer?'

Pouring them both a half, Len sat down next to Doris and turned on the radio. The news was bleak: not only Manchester but Birmingham, Sheffield and Glasgow had received air raids.

Surreptitiously Len snatched a glance at Doris. He was completely comfortable with her, completely at ease. Deep in thought, she listened to the news, her head on one side, her lips pursed. He had seen her age over the years, neither of them beauties, but well-matched. And now she was sitting, listening to the radio, as though she lived with him.

It wasn't a bad idea, Len thought. Since Rose had married the house had been bitterly quiet. No strings of lady's washing across the bathroom, no scents of perfume or nail polish. No feminine touches, flowers, or even a postcard propped up above the fire. When Rose had gone, the female heart of the house had gone with her. Len frowned to himself. The last thing he had expected had now happened to him. He felt lonely.

But why *now*? he asked himself. Surely he should have felt it straight after Rosie left, when the house was suddenly quiet, when there was no one there at breakfast, or playing the radio in the evenings. But funnily enough Len's loneliness had crept up on him gradually, the house getting more silent by the week, the awful sounds of a one person home jarring on him. How bloody loud *could* a clock tick? Or a tap drip? How *could* the stairwell echo so much when only one pair of feet used it? And worst of all, how *could* the post slam on the doormat like a clap of thunder?

No use denying it, Len thought, he was bloody lonely. God, what an awful word, he thought. Old maids were lonely. Widows, widowers, the aged, they were lonely. Not a bookie who still had plenty of years ahead of him.

'How's business?' Doris asked suddenly, turning off the radio and looking at him.

'We had quite a good day at Catterick. Not like the old times, but not bad. I miss Bunny, though.'

'He were home on leave the other week, weren't he?'

Len nodded. 'Came to see me. Good lad, that. He's on the *Ark Royal*.'

'Never,' Doris said, taking another sip of her beer. 'The *Ark Royal* . . . How's your Clovis?'

'Bought an empty bomb shell the other day,' Len replied, rolling his eyes. 'This war's like all her dreams come true at once.'

'And Nan Wilmslow?'

'Who knows with Nan?' Len replied, leaning back in his seat. 'She's into everything. Black market, for sure. You name it, Nan will have it, or be able to get it. I keep my mouth shut, though, because half the stuff she gets she passes on to the folk that need it most.'

Doris nodded. 'What about you, Len? Still not found a good clerk?'

'Nah, the one I've got now is all right, but I keep hoping the war won't last and Bunny'll be back.'

'I wouldn't bank on that,' Doris replied, giving him a warning look. 'Best sort it out now. Be wisest course of action, luv.'

She was right, Len thought. Doris was always good at giving advice. Not cramming it down your throat, but just coming out with it. No introduction. No 'Do you mind . . . ?', 'I hope you'll bear with me . . .', 'I thought maybe . . .' Just came out with it. Her opinion. And if you ignored it, it wouldn't matter to her. Good old Doris, Len thought. It was nice having someone to share the house with again. If only for an evening.

Unless . . .

'I saw Beth Hodges – well, Beth *Williams* I should say – is looking thin.' Doris paused before continuing. 'Lost a lot of weight, that girl. She's an odd one. Always was. Looks it too. All that dark hair and those eyes.'

Lester finished his half-pint and filled up their glasses.

'You want to make me tipsy!' Doris laughed. 'Oh, go on, fill her up, I won't say no.' Her thoughts turned back to Beth. 'I wonder about that marriage. Beth and Lester Williams. I wonder if it'll last.'

'They've got a son.'

'That never stopped a man straying,' Doris replied drily. 'Or a woman – if it comes to that.'

'I'm just glad Rose is settled with Stuart now,' Len admitted. 'I was always a bit uneasy about Lester. I liked him – don't get me wrong – but he was a bit of a wild card. She's better off with someone steady.'

'I heard,' Doris said, leaning towards Len, 'that Trudie Williams was seen out with Bunny.'

'*Trudie Williams?*' Len repeated, shaking his head. 'That doesn't surprise me. He always had a soft spot for her. Told me as much himself.' Len sipped his beer, taking Doris's hand. 'I warned him off – said she wasn't likely to bring him much joy. But he'll make his own mind up. Just like we all do in the end.'

Doris nodded, staring into the fire grate. Together they sat, hand in hand, looking into the flames. For a moment Len thought of saying something. Even suggesting that he and Doris get together. But he didn't and the moment passed. For her part, Doris had been well aware of his intention and had done nothing to encourage it. She didn't want to fill a space left by anyone, even a beloved daughter. Her time for sharing a house and a bed had come and gone. She had made peace with her own loneliness and prized her own independence. If anyone had asked she would have told them that she was as happy as anyone had a right to be. So no, Doris had decided, she didn't want another husband. Even Len.

Gently, she squeezed his hand. They were all right as they were – her and Len. Free to hold hands. And free to let go.

FORTY-SEVEN

A year passed, each movement of the war trumpeted in the papers. The fight had gathered momentum, British troops in France and Holland, whilst Hitler neared the gates of Moscow. 'Grit your teeth! Squeeze the enemy's throat!' was the cry sent out by Stalin. The Russians had held back Napoleon, he told his people, they would defeat Hitler also. Germany was told the opposite: the German army would take over Moscow. It was all part of Hitler's plan, his Reich to last for a Thousand Years.

Having visited her father alone, Rose left Gull Road and decided to walk a little way down the Promenade before catching the tram to Lytham. The night was getting cold, winter just beginning to flex its muscles, the sea a dark, serpent-thick lair only yards away from her.

Shivering, Rose pulled up her collar and pushed her hands deep in her pockets. Perhaps walking hadn't been such a good idea, after all. Turning round, she looked down the seafront for a tram, but there was none in sight. Her head ducked down against the breeze, she began to walk again.

And then she saw him. Sitting on one of the benches, looking out to the inky sea. *Lester.* Rose stopped walking. He hadn't seen her, that much was obvious, and if she retraced her steps now he would never know she had been there. Hesitating, Rose paused – and in that instant he turned.

His expression was unreadable; lost. 'Rose.'

She nodded stupidly, then walked over to the bench. He was smart in his uniform, more handsome than he had ever been in civilian life. But he looked older, much older.

'How are you, Lester?'

'Fine . . .'

'And Joe?'

'He's fine too.' Lester gestured to the bench. 'Can you stay for a while?'

She hesitated, then sat down, keeping as much distance between them as she could. 'I suppose you're home on leave?'

He nodded. And for an instant Rose wondered why a man on leave would spend his time alone, staring out to sea.

'And is Joe home too?'

'Yes . . . gone over to be with Maisie.'

Rose found it difficult to talk to him, this man she had loved so completely, so easily. Now even pleasantries were excruciating.

'How's Daniel?'

At the mention of his son's name, Lester smiled. 'He's doing well. Growing fast.' Then, just as quickly, the smile faded, sadness replacing it. Beyond them the sea ebbed and flowed darkly. 'I've often wondered what it would be like to see you again, Rose . . . I'm sorry for what happened. You know that, don't you?'

She said nothing, just wondered why she was still sitting there. A tram passed by them, moving slowly. At any moment she could have hailed it and left. Made for home, Lester's figure growing smaller and smaller as it faded into the distance. But she didn't move.

'I shouldn't have sent you that letter.'

Baffled, she stared at him. 'What letter?'

'The letter I sent through Joe,' Lester replied, suddenly anxious. 'You *did* get it, didn't you?'

'I never got any letters from you.'

'But Joe said he gave it to you.' Lester paused. Had his brother lied to him? No, never. Not Joe. So had the letter gone astray? Or had Len picked it up? Yes, that was it, *Len* had intercepted it.

Bitterly, Lester smiled. 'I'm glad you never got it. I always regretted sending it. I was full of self-pity at the time.'

'That's not like you.'

He ached to reach out to her, but resisted. 'I thought you lived in Lytham.'

'I do.'

'Are you happy with Fallow?'

'His name's Stuart,' she said coolly, 'and yes, I'm happy. What about you?'

'Need you ask?'

'What was in the letter?' Rose asked, surprising herself. Suddenly she wanted to know every word he had written to her. Every word she had never read.

'I wrote a lot of things.'

'About you and Beth?'

'Some things about us, yes,' he agreed. 'And about you. What I felt about you –'

'On second thoughts, I *don't* want to hear it, Lester!' she said, her tone more brutal than she intended. 'I don't even want to think about the past.'

He nodded. 'I understand.'

'I doubt that,' she responded, looking away from him.

Go on, she willed herself, get up and leave. He's made his bed and now he's lying in it. But he was *Lester*, she thought, and she had loved him so much once. Loved him enough to still feel for him – and wonder why he was sitting in the semi-darkness, alone, looking out to sea.

'What are you doing here?'

'I told you, I'm on leave.'

'Then you should go home to your family.'

He turned to her, then looked away. His expression was unfathomable.

'Go home for your son, at least.'

'I've already seen him. Earlier today.'

Rose frowned at him. 'So why aren't you *still* with him?'

'Daniel's in bed now,' Lester replied, as though the answer was obvious. 'And I leave first thing in the morning.'

'So you're planning to stay here all night?' she asked, her tone incredulous.

'I'm not going back to Gate Street,' he replied, abruptly. 'Go on, Rose, go home. I'm fine.'

Logic told her she should leave Lester to his own devices, but she couldn't. She had no intention of betraying Stuart; she felt no sexual desire for Lester at that moment – just pity. And that was somehow more potent. And more perilous.

'I'm not going home until I know you are.'

'Then you'll be here all night,' Lester replied bitterly. 'I'm sorry, I didn't mean to be sharp with you. But I'm not going back to Gate Street. Don't ask me to. I have my reasons, believe me.' He smiled distantly. 'Hey, I'm not your problem, Rose, I can look after myself. Go on, go home.'

'No,' she said flatly.

'You were always stubborn.'

'And you were always bloody-minded,' she replied shortly. 'Come on, Lester, be sensible. If you can't go back to Gate Street, go to Sea View. Your mother will be pleased to see you.'

'I don't go there any more. That is, I *didn't* go there any more. I didn't want to bump into you. I didn't want to remember what had happened there.'

She put her head on one side. 'Poor street,' she said, with mock sympathy. 'What a burden for bricks and mortar to carry.'

He smiled. 'You're laughing at me!'

'Well, it *is* pretty funny, don't you think?' she asked him. 'I mean, what happened is in the past, Lester. It's over and done with. I'm not angry with you any more. But I'll only catch the next tram when I've know you've gone to Gull Road. Don't act daft, Lester. You've no reason to be alone tonight. I don't know what's going on with you and your wife – I don't care – but you need company. And you've a family who want you. Think of your mum and dad – what they'd feel if they knew you were out here alone.' She paused. 'Your father was telling me about parachuting into Germany. Said he'd volunteered and was waiting for the call.'

They both laughed, Lester finally getting to his feet.

'Thanks.'

'For what?'

'For caring.'

'You're welcome.'

'And for your friendship,' he replied. 'I can't ask for any more. I don't have the right.'

'So we'll be friends,' she agreed, nodding. 'I like that idea.'

A tram came slowly into view, Rose putting out her hand. When it drew up to where they were standing, she climbed on. Then, without thinking, turned back.

'Lester!' she called out urgently as the tram moved off. 'Lester!'

He turned, then began running beside it.

'Lester, write to me!' Rose called out, her words growing fainter as the tram pulled away. 'Write to me.'

On 13 November the *Ark Royal* was hit by Italian U-boat torpedoes. The news, a shattering blow, was all over the English newspapers and Pathé News. One eyewitness described the shock of the sinking graphically, making it real for everyone: '. . . it was as though an athlete at the prime of his powers, with a score of laurels to his credit, had been knifed in the back in a dark alley . . .'

Apparently the boat had been heading for shelter in Gibraltar when she was hit, immediately listing. At one time she managed to right herself, but finally sank whilst under tow. Eighteen sailors were reported missing.

Ruby listened to the news on the radio and then hurriedly turned it off when she heard footsteps overhead. Trudie was coming downstairs, ready to go to work. Obviously she hadn't heard the news. Her calm romance with Bunny had transformed her. No more the good-time girl, she stayed in at night and wrote long letters to him, her head bent down over her writing pad, her attention focused. Work was no longer so bad at Myers because Trudie had found some direction in her life. And love – which was something totally different from sex.

Dear God, Ruby prayed, please let Bunny be all right. She remembered the newscaster's words – 'eighteen sailors have been reported missing'. Missing, not dead. Even if Bunny was amongst the missing, he might well be alive. But now she had to tell her daughter. Ruby felt suddenly, unexpectedly, angry with God. After so much, why this now? Trudie had finally found a good man, who loved her, so why had this got to happen? Wasn't it enough that her two boys were away fighting? Wasn't it enough that she might lose *them*? Ruby railed inwardly. Please God, don't take Bunny. Please God, don't take Bunny away. If you do, Trudie will go off the deep end. If you take her man, her life's over.

'Mam?' Trudie said softly, standing at the doorway of the kitchen. 'What is it?'

'Sit down –'

'What is it!' Trudie asked, alerted.

'Calm down,' Ruby said firmly, taking hold of her daughter's shoulders and looking her square in the face. 'The *Ark Royal*'s been hit –'

'Oh Jesus.'

Ruby shook her daughter gently. 'Hey, come on, some of the sailors survived and there are eighteen missing.'

'So some died!' Trudie asked, her eyes blinded with panic. 'Not Bunny! It can't be Bunny –'

'We don't know yet,' Ruby said, her voice calm. 'We

371

have to find out what's happened to him. Trudie, listen to me, it will be all right –'

'How can it be all right?'

'Because it is,' she insisted. 'I don't feel bad about it. I can't explain, but I don't think Bunny's dead.'

Shaking her head, Trudie slumped into a chair. 'I knew it was too good to be true. I knew it. God, Mam, I couldn't live without him. I just couldn't, I just couldn't –'

'No one gives up whilst there's hope,' Ruby replied pragmatically. 'We'll find out what happened to him, Trudie.'

'What if he's dead?'

'I don't think he is.'

'Missing then,' Trudie said, her eyes wild. 'What if he's one of the missing ones?'

'If he's missing, he'll be found. That's what happens, luv. You lose something and then you find it again.' Ruby hugged her daughter tightly, her voice certain. 'He'll come back, I know he will. Bunny Lambert will walk up this street again. He'll knock on this door again, and then – someday not so far off – I'll dance at your wedding.' Trudie was sobbing against her mother's shoulder. 'Oh, come on, luv. Didn't he tell us that he was born with a caul on his head? Well, a baby born like that never drowns. You ask Nan Wilmslow, she'll tell you. A baby with a caul on its head *can't* drown.'

FORTY-EIGHT

Dear Rose,

I've been thinking about you since I saw you on leave. I was in a stupid mood, feeling sorry for myself. I seem to have been doing a lot of that lately. So it was good of you to take the trouble to knock some sense into me. You never did pull your punches!

We press on fighting – Joe with me, thank God. It was a bugger about Pearl Harbor, but it got the Yanks moving and we needed that. Joe's sure that now they have come into the war it will all be over soon. I hope he's right. We may, or may not, get home for Christmas. I hope so, for Joe's sake. He can't bear the thought of being away from Maisie and Lesley then.

It's so good to have you to write to. Ma sends letters, but yours make me laugh. We've had many casualties lately and we could certainly do with some good luck . . . I'm talking about the war again. Sorry, Rose, but that's all I *can* talk about at the moment.

But I still dream. At night – when I can't sleep – I think of my dance hall and imagine it finished. Keep an eye on it for me, will you? I know it's boarded up for the duration, but before long the lights will be on again, the floor polished, and the

glasses ready at the bar.
Save the first dance for me, Rose.
   Lester

Dear Lester,
   Your dance floor is still standing! Not looking
too cheerful, it has to be said, but promising. You
always liked that word, didn't you? *Promising* – all
your schemes and deals were either no good, or
promising. That always made me laugh.
   I haven't mentioned to anyone the fact that we're
in touch. You know how people get the wrong idea.
Your mother, for one! Of course Maisie knows –
otherwise I wouldn't get your letters – but I can see
she was shocked. For no reason, Lester; we both
know that we're friends, that's all.
   And so, my good friend, goodbye for now. The
rock stand, fortuneteller's booth and your dance
hall are tucked up for the night. Keep dreaming!
   Rose

'I know you'll think it's none of my business,' Maisie said
soberly, 'but I don't think you should be writing to Lester.'
   Surprised, Rose looked up from where she was kneel-
ing, piling some cheap coal onto the fire at number 99.
   'Why ever not?'
   'It's not right.'
   'Maisie, we're not doing anything wrong.'
   'So why doesn't Lester write to you at your home address?'
It was a good point.
   'Because Stuart wouldn't like it,' Rose said, getting to her
feet. 'He can be very jealous. You know how some men are.'
   'Does he have reason?' Maisie asked, keeping her face
averted.
   She wasn't used to confrontation, didn't like it, especially
confronting Rose, who – without realising it – always made

her feel inferior. Lord, Maisie thought, all this business of the letters was so confusing. Hadn't she hidden Lester's letter all that time ago? Intervened then, to prevent them getting involved again. And what good had it done? She had lied to her husband and deceived Lester, and now here he was, in touch with Rose anyway.

'Lester and I are friends,' Rose said, looking at Maisie with curiosity. She seemed flushed, embarrassed almost. 'Do you mind having his letters sent here?'

'Well . . .'

'Maisie, I'm sorry, I shouldn't have just presumed that you'd help me out,' Rose said hurriedly. 'But we've been friends for a while and I thought you wouldn't mind.'

'I know we're friends,' Maisie replied, her voice as quiet as ever. 'But I can still say what I think, can't I?'

'Of course you can.'

'Then I think it's dangerous,' Maisie said, taking off her glasses and polishing them vigorously.

'Dangerous?' Rose laughed. 'I'm just writing to your brother-in-law – how on earth can that be dangerous?'

'Because he's married, and so are you.'

'But we're just *writing* to each other,' Rose replied, her voice cooling. 'Nothing else. I thought you'd understand that, Maisie.'

'I understand that you *think* you're not doing anything wrong,' she said anxiously, pressing on regardless, 'but you and Lester were very close once, and he's not close to his wife –'

'But I'm close to my husband,' Rose interjected. 'I don't want Lester.'

'*But does he still want you?*' Maisie replied, her aim precise. 'He's never loved Beth and now he's away at war, writing to *you*, not her. How do you think that looks? Like he cares about *you*, not his wife. He has a son, Rose; you should think about Daniel, if nothing else.' Maisie paused, flushing. 'It's not right. You should stop writing to Lester.'

'He's just a friend,' Rose insisted. 'Why are you saying all this, Maisie? Has Joe said something?'

'I *can* think for myself,' Maisie said, a little shortly. 'I don't need Joe or anyone else to tell me what to do. There'll be a tragedy if you keep this up. I feel it, I really do. Stuart or Beth will find out – and believe me, however much you insist, they won't think you and Lester are just friends.' She moved over to Rose and touched her arm. 'Ignore his next letter. Pretend you never got it.'

'I never *did* get one of his letters,' Rose replied, remembering what Lester had told her. 'He sent me one a while back, but I never got it.' She could sense Maisie flinch and stared at her, understanding coming quickly. 'You stopped the letter?'

'Rose, I was –'

'You stopped a letter addressed to me!' Rose said angrily, stepping back. 'How dare you?'

'I thought it was for the best –'

'You *interfered*, Maisie. You had no right.'

'And Lester had no right using my husband as a postman – and you have no right using *me*.' Surprised by the outburst, Rose stayed silent, Maisie's voice warning. 'You and Lester are playing with fire. Fine, your choice, but I don't want my husband or my family being drawn into it.' Her face was ruddy, her eyes bright behind the thick glasses. 'I care about you, you know that. But this is wrong. And you know that too.'

Stung, Rose looked away.

'I care about Lester, Maisie. But I *don't* love him any more. I swear I don't.' Her voice softened. 'How can I just stop writing to him? It would hurt him so much.'

'And if you carry on?' Maisie asked. 'Who will that hurt? And do you *really* want to find out?'

The following day Ruby finally discovered that Bunny Lambert was one of the sailors listed as missing. One of the eighteen. It was good news, she told Trudie. Missing meant he could be found.

'Or not.'

She looked at her daughter, irritated. 'OK, let's play it your way! Let's all expect the worse.'

'But if he's missing, where could he be?'

'I don't know,' Ruby said honestly. 'We just wait and hope.'

An unexpected knock on the kitchen door made Ruby turn. Honest to God, no one could have a conversation these days without being interrupted by someone.

'I'm coming!' she shouted, opening the door.

To her surprise, a smiling Miss Vernon greeted her.

'Good morning, Mrs Williams. I want to ask you something.' She paused, waiting for Ruby to speak. When she didn't, Miss Vernon hurried on. 'I wondered if I could stay here?'

'You *are* staying here.'

'No, I mean permanently.'

'What?'

'I have no family, as you know, and I only rent my flat in Liverpool. I'm a retired lady, with few needs. I could pay you the going rate – well, possibly we could come to some understanding – and it would be good for you, off season. I mean, when you have no regular money coming in. What with us being at war and money being tight for everyone. Not that I'm implying anything –'

Butting in, Ruby stemmed the flow. 'You want to live here full time?'

'Yes,' Miss Vernon said, as though it made perfect sense.

'I don't have lodgers, only seasonal guests.'

'But I could be a *permanent* guest.'

Who would bring in a routine payment, Ruby thought, weighing up the offer. But could she stand Miss Vernon around constantly – the ex-tax official sliding around Sea View day in and day out, complaining about the sausages

377

and the thin towels? And in the off season, would she mind serving the pernickety Miss Vernon alone in the dining room? It would be, Ruby thought suddenly, like having another pet.

'Permanently?'

'For as long as I live.'

Ruby looked Miss Vernon up and down and reckoned on at least another ten years of income. Then another thought struck her – *Gilbert*.

'We're not your family, Miss Vernon.'

'I know that,' she sniffed, as though the very thought was abhorrent. 'I don't need a family, just a place to call home. And I've grown to like it here.'

'You didn't say that the other month when you complained about the fire –'

'The coal was wet and made the dining room smoky.'

' – and what about those powdered eggs? I mean, food's on ration, I can't make exceptions for anyone. There are plenty who'd be glad of any eggs. Powdered or not.'

Miss Vernon looked up at her gigantic landlady.

'I've nowhere else to go.'

Touched, Ruby immediately relented. 'All right. But if you start complaining, you're out. As for Gilbert . . .' she paused. Better to make things clear at the start. It was one thing having Miss Vernon for a couple of weeks a year, but poor Gilbert would be exhausted, having to dodge her full time. To explain the situation, however, was going to be difficult. Miss Vernon was a maiden lady.

'My brother is –'

'Very talented.'

'– and very –'

'Amusing?'

'– yes, but also –'

'Gifted?'

Exasperated, Ruby put her hands on her hips. 'Look, Gilbert's not interested in romance. With anyone. Any *lady* at all.'

To her complete amazement, Miss Vernon began to laugh. 'Whatever you say.'

Ruby frowned, Miss Vernon smiling at her knowingly.

'I mean it, Gilbert's not available.'

'Of course not,' Miss Vernon replied, chuckling to herself, then sobering up. 'So I can take it that we have an agreement, Mrs Williams?'

'We do. But if it doesn't work out, I'll give you three months' notice. And you have to agree to do the same.'

Miss Vernon was still twinkling. Shaking hands with her landlady she then walked off, smiling. 'Romance,' Ruby could hear her say merrily to herself. 'Romance. Well, I never . . .'

Hardly enough wardrobe space, Hettie thought, but she would see to that. Critically, she looked around her. Cedric's house was hardly chic, but it would do. Besides, as she was going to sell her own place and put aside the money she might even contribute to the alterations herself. Although where she was going to get good carpenters in wartime she couldn't guess. Still, that was a minor problem. What really mattered was that Hettie had finally seen her plans fulfilled.

Sitting down on the edge of the bed, she took off her shoes. She would have liked a big wedding, but Cedric had been against it. Still, having her picture in the paper had gone part-way to easing the disappointment. As for the wedding night . . . Hettie rolled her eyes. Cedric was a disaster. It was a miracle that Stuart had ever been conceived. And there poor Cedric was, bossing people about, right, left and centre, when he couldn't even get an erection in the bedroom.

Hettie doubted that Stuart would have that problem. She had seen how he looked at Rose, how he doted on her. It was sweet in a way, but also a bit suffocating. Hettie rubbed the sole of her right foot. In her experience, trying to control a person only made them want to rebel. Especially a person like Rose. But maybe she had changed. She certainly seemed to have settled down – even though she had mentioned wanting to help Leonard out at the track.

They would have to put a stop to that, Hettie thought angrily, knowing already that she had an unexpected – but unequivocal – ally in Stuart. A racetrack was hardly the place for Mrs Fallow, the future mother of the next generation of dental luminaries. Oh no, Hettie thought, she and Stuart would have to band together to make sure that Rose stayed on track. And she didn't mean the racetrack.

A warm glow filled Hettie. She was back where she loved to be: in the thick of a family; ready to manipulate and control the lives around her. Ready to make sure that no one moved too far out of her game plan.

It was her life's work, after all.

FORTY-NINE

February 1942 came in violent and ominous. Huddling against the wind, Nan Wilmslow turned into Gull Road, making for her house. When she finally got inside, she locked the door and set down her bag. No one thought that she travelled about so much, but distance didn't faze Nan. In fact, that very morning she had been in Liverpool, visiting someone. So when she saw a man she knew in the city centre Nan had stopped to watch him.

There was no mistake, it *was* Lester Williams. And there was no mistaking who was with him: Rose Fallow, née Bradshaw. Hidden from view, Nan had scrutinised the two of them. They were chatting easily, but not touching, only talking. Innocent. Almost. But Nan hadn't been fooled. If they weren't lovers now, they would be.

And then Nan thought about Beth. That strange dark woman. The highly strung Beth Hodges, whom Lester had never loved. The kind of woman who wouldn't take kindly to being betrayed – even though she had deceived her husband already. As for Stuart Fallow . . . Nan thought of what she had heard about him. A good sort, apparently, but with a jealous streak. Hadn't Len told Clovis that? And of course Clovis had passed the information on. Nan frowned. So put together two betrayed spouses, both jealous by nature, and what have you got? Disaster.

Slowly she emptied her shopping bag, the pickings leaner

every day. Rationing was difficult for everyone, but Nan only really missed the sugar. Not that she couldn't find some if she tried hard enough. Her mind wandered again. Should she tell Len what she had seen? Nan paused, thinking. Her nature was reclusive and secretive. Nothing she heard or saw she passed on. But this was somehow different. This had the whiff of tragedy about it.

Because one thing Nan knew for certain, and it was something people only learned when they got older and understood more: sex and passion were violent emotions – but friendship and empathy were deadly.

He was sick of the remarks about the servicemen. *Our brave boys* – the sailors, the soldiers, the airmen – all so wonderful. Stuart weighed the dental drill in his hand. It wasn't his bloody fault that he wasn't fit to serve. But it felt as though it was – that somehow he hadn't tried hard enough, or was skiving off. And there was Rose at breakfast, banging on about Bunny Lambert being found. Bunny, her father's clerk, who escaped drowning when the *Ark Royal* went down. Another blasted hero. Stuart was glad that the man was OK, but the way Rose had repeated the story got on his nerves. And then she began to talk about Joe Williams . . . Stuart had exchanged a glance with Hettie. His stepmother might be irritating at times, but he had found an unexpected confederate in her. After all, Hettie understood about position, about class.

Annoyed, Stuart let the drill bit fall into the basin noisily. People didn't seem to want their teeth filling as much in wartime. Mind you, there wasn't the same amount of sugar around to keep him in work. He thought of Rose again and then wondered why she was being so difficult about her father. Surely she could see that it wasn't right for her to help him at the track? Stuart had tried to explain why, and so had Hettie, but Rose was being stubborn.

Stuart didn't like the racetrack. He didn't like the whole idea of gambling and he especially didn't like to think of his wife mixing with the rough types there. She might have been used to it once, but that was a long time ago. Now she was a married woman, a respectable woman, who should behave like one.

Stuart's temper uncurled. Who was going to stop any man from making a play for her? Maybe one of those adored servicemen on leave? After all, Rose was very good-looking, and there were seldom other women working at the racetrack. Oh, it was all right Rose talking about just going there to help her father out, but one thing led to another. Besides, what kind of woman worked a racetrack? Only one kind. And they weren't decent.

He would have to have words with her, Stuart thought. It was all right Rose laughing and asking him where his sense of humour had gone, but he was serious this time. He might not be some serviceman, some bloody hero, but he *was* going to be the boss in his own house.

And the master of his own wife.

'Are you sure it's OK with Stuart?' Len asked, rubbing his hands together to warm them.

The race meeting was a small one. Len could have managed alone, but Rose had been adamant. Who did Stuart think he was, telling her what to do? And what a secret snob he had turned out to be, despising the racing, and her past. Well, if he thought he was going to rule her, he had another think coming.

'Stuart doesn't mind, Dad, honest,' she lied, 'although Hettie had to put her tuppence worth in.'

'I don't know how you live with that bitch.'

'I don't know myself,' Rose admitted. 'It was fine at first. Cedric and her lived on the ground floor and Hettie kept banging on about how she wouldn't get in our way. But she soon changed. She's always hanging around us now –

and she keeps siding with Stuart.' Rose thought of the run-in they had had that very morning. 'I can't understand Stuart. He hated Hettie before and now he's listening to her, agreeing with her. Bloody snobs.'

Annoyed, she fell silent. The day was cold, Rose shivering as she stood next to her father's stand. 'Leonard Bradshaw – The Lazy Eye' was emblazoned on the board, the smaller note – 'NO CREDIT' – printed underneath. In the misty morning the smell of the horses and the murmur of men's voices seemed oddly comforting.

She could hardly disguise her excitement. God, how she had missed it! How had she lived without the tension, the thrill of the track? Smiling, she suddenly caught a man's eye, Freddie Walsh walking over to her, grinning knowingly.

'So you're back. Lady Muck, married and rich. You're slumming, aren't you?'

'I'm not proud, Freddie. I'll talk to anybody,' Rose replied deftly, tapping the board. 'What's your bet?'

'That you don't stick it out.'

'Really?' Rose replied, raising her eyebrows. 'You always were a loser.'

Noticing that the horses were being lined up for the off, Rose called out loudly: 'See you after the race, Dad.'

Then she walked across the track to the other side and climbed onto her box. It gave her a good feeling to look out over the punters, several nodding hello as they recognised her. It took a few moments for Rose to get back into the swing, but soon she was ticktacking to her father across the course, giving him the odds. Her hands moved fast in their white gloves, tapping her wrist for 5-4 and then tugging her ear for 11-10. Her confidence came back quickly, as did her homesickness. How in God's name, Rose thought, could someone miss *racing* so much?

But she had. It was all right being genteel, the model wife, but this was exciting – and she had forgotten that.

The mist was lifting, the horses finally lined up ready for the start. Then the pistol fired and off they went, in unison. But not for long. Almost at once a jockey was jostled out of place, another over-using his whip and trying to fight for the lead. And before she knew it, Rose was calling out, urging on the favourite, jumping up and down on her box, her voice raised amongst the rest.

Smiling, Len watched her. *That* was his girl, the one he recognised. Oh, Mrs Stuart Fallow was a fine woman, lovely and respected, but this excitable yelling kid was the Rosie he remembered. And if things had been different she would have stayed with him in Gull Road and come into the business, inheriting it one day . . . Len shook his head as though he was trying to physically shift the thoughts. No, that wasn't the way life was to be for Rosie. She was meant for better things, even Hettie's inheritance – if the manipulating cow wasn't just carrot-dangling. He should be proud of his daughter, Len told himself. He should be so proud.

But at that moment, on that misty February morning he let himself relish – momentarily – another destiny. His and Rosie's, both of them working together on the track. His girl, inheriting his pitch one day. One of the few women bookies around. A one-off in these parts. His daughter, smart as a whip, quick with her sums, her brain flexible, her intelligence obvious.

Not someone fitting quietly into a respectable life, but standing out from the crowd. Literally head and shoulders above the rest . . . Len sighed to himself and began to roll up a cigarette. It was just a dream – the way things might have been. The way they would never be now.

'Good race,' Rose said, having moved back across the track to where Len was standing.

'They didn't want you to come here, did they?' he asked, putting his head on one side quizzically. 'Don't lie to me, Rosie. They didn't, did they?'

She wouldn't meet his gaze. 'Stuart doesn't think racing is respectable,' she replied at last. 'Thinks a dentist's wife shouldn't be on a track.'

'He's right.'

'No, he bloody isn't!' Rose snapped back. 'I was brought up here, and I'm helping you out. He shouldn't mind that.'

'I could have managed today,' Len replied, 'and you know that. You just wanted to defy Stuart.'

'And Hettie,' Rose agreed, smarting. 'I can't live with her under the same roof. I thought I could, but I can't. I said so to Stuart only yesterday and I thought he'd agree with me. After all, we've always talked about moving after the war. But no, he's happy, he says. Well, I'm bloody not!'

Stunned by the outburst, Len was then surprised to find that the race was over. Hurriedly he turned to Rose, but she was already organised, ready to pay out on the winning tickets as soon as he passed them to her.

'He's changed,' she went on, paying out on a ticket and smiling to the punter as she did so. 'Stuart's not at all like he was.' She turned to another punter. 'Your horse came in second, here you are. No, *second*. You know that as well as I do.' Glancing up at her father to check that he was listening, Rose carried on. 'Did Mum change when you got married?'

The clamour around them made Len pause before replying. His daughter was fast, totting up and paying out without seeming to have to concentrate. But he wasn't so quick and only after the winners had been paid and moved away from his pitch, did he finally reply.

'No, your mum didn't change. She was exactly the same girl I met after I'd been married to her for years.' He looked at the takings Rose passed to him. 'Not much.'

'You managing?' she asked him carefully, not wanting to provoke accusations of charity.

'Oh yeah, I don't need a lot.'

'Good thing,' she said drily. 'Why don't you come over to Lytham with me? You could have dinner.'

'I could choke too,' Len teased her. 'Now come on, luv, you know that I wouldn't fit in. Especially now that the Widow Miller's there.'

'She's not the Widow Miller any more.'

'No, but if she has her way she'll soon be the Widow *Fallow*,' Len replied, winking at his daughter. 'I actually feel sorry for that pompous old sod.'

'I do too,' Rose agreed. 'Honestly, Cedric's hardly around any more. Always out and about, doing good and organising fund-raising for the war effort. *And* he set up the Home Guard.'

'Against Hitler? Or Hettie?'

She laughed, linking arms with her father. 'I miss you, Dad. And I miss all this.'

He pulled a face. 'No, you don't. It just reminds you of your childhood. Everything looks good when you look back.'

For a moment she longed to confide in him, aching to share the secret. But what would her father say if he knew that she was friendly with Lester again? Writing to him?

Rose looked down, staring at the track and the horses' muddy hoof-prints. Lester wouldn't have minded about the racing. He liked it, in fact; had often joked about her being a ticktack woman, in the old days. When they had been set to marry. He would have built his empire and his ballroom and she would have inherited The Lazy Eye. No worries about snobbery, no having to visit her father in Gull Road because he felt uncomfortable coming to his daughter's house. If they had married, Lester and Rose would have been well matched. In the right class. In the right place. In their element.

'Rosie?'

She blinked, coming out of her reverie with a bump. 'Sorry, Dad, I was thinking.'

'I could see that,' he said anxiously. 'And I hope you were thinking about Stuart, luv, because you had a look on your face which only a husband should see.'

FIFTY

Plimsoll lines made their first appearance at Sea View at the end of February. It was said that the King had such lines painted on his bath at Buckingham Palace, so that he would set an example and not use more than five inches of water for his bathing.

'Hah!' Ruby said, standing back to observe the line she had drawn inside the family bath tub. 'The water will hardly cover your arse.'

'Wouldn't cover yours and that's a fact,' Alfred said, pushing his porkpie hat to the back of his head. 'In the newspaper it said that people should share water and share baths.'

'If we could ever get into this bath together, Alfred, you can be sure that we'd never get out. We'd be wedged like a cork in a bottle.'

'I can think of better ways to go.'

Rolling her eyes, Ruby pushed past her husband. She had to make sure that everything was ready – her lads were coming home tonight *at last*, although they hadn't got even twenty-four hours at Christmas. It was a disgrace, she had said to anyone who would listen. How could they expect lads to fight if they didn't get home to spend Christmas with their families?

It was obvious how much Joe was longing for home, but although Lester had always seemed indifferent before, this time there was a change in his manner – a lightness of spirit in his letters he hadn't shown for a long time. He would even joke and talk about the future.

'Maybe he and Beth have come to an understanding?' Ruby said hopefully. 'Maybe they've sorted their marriage out. And not before time.'

'Mrs Williams!' Miss Vernon called up from the lower landing. 'Oh, Mrs Williams!'

Ruby looked over the banister rail. 'What is it?'

'There's a moth in my wardrobe.'

'So kill it.'

'I *can't* kill it!' Miss Vernon said, shocked, her voice rising higher as she spotted someone Ruby couldn't see. 'Oh, Mr Beardsley, would you mind? I've a moth in my wardrobe –'

'"I've a hole in my bucket, dear Liza, dear Liza, I've a hole in my bucket, dear Liza, a hole,"' Gilbert sang, his voice rising upwards and reaching Ruby above.

Clapping appreciatively, Miss Vernon carried on simpering. 'Oh, that was very good, very good indeed. But I *do* have a moth in my wardrobe, Mr Beardsley, and your sister suggested that it should be sent to the next world.'

'What?' Gilbert said, baffled.

Bellowing, Ruby leaned over the banister: 'I said – flatten the bugger! I don't want moths in this house.' Ruby's attention then moved back to her guest. 'Miss Vernon?'

Her head appeared timidly, looking up at Ruby. 'Yes?'

'Baths from now on can be only five inches deep.'

'Only five inches? Oh, I see . . .'

'It's to save water. Like the King.'

'We have to save water for the King?'

Give me strength, Ruby thought helplessly. 'No! You just can't have a bath any deeper than five inches.'

'I could manage with four inches if it would help the King.'

'I don't care if you get washed in the sugar bowl!' Ruby

roared down the stairs. 'Just make sure it's not more than five inches deep.'

Smiling wanly, Miss Vernon turned to Gilbert.

'Your sister has such a vigorous nature. An example to us all, is Mrs Williams. Now, if you wouldn't mind coming this way, Mr Beardsley, I'll show you the moth.'

Dutifully Gilbert followed her into her room, Miss Vernon throwing open the wardrobe door and pointing to the offending insect, fast asleep on the shoulder of her outdoor coat.

'Kill it.'

Gilbert hesitated, Miss Vernon handing him a rolled-up newspaper.

'It looks very peaceful,' he said, eyeing up the moth sympathetically. 'I mean, how would you like it if someone killed you in your sleep?'

'You've such a kind nature,' Miss Vernon replied, then pointed to the moth again. 'I'm sure if you act swiftly the moth will be with its Maker before it knows what hit it.'

'But don't you think,' Gilbert began, turning to Miss Vernon, 'that in days like these – when there is so much violence already in the world – we could let a moth live?'

'Not if it's eating my coat,' she said quietly. 'I understand your sentiment, Mr Beardsley, but I do feel that killing a moth is a very small crime in the grand scheme of things.'

Gilbert wasn't sure. In fact, the more he thought about it, the more he didn't want to kill the sleeping moth. For all her outer gentility there was something quite merciless about Miss Vernon, something sinister about the way she was egging him on.

'Just hit it.'

'*You* hit it.'

She balked. 'I'm a woman.'

'I'm a pacifist,' Gilbert replied smartly.

'Oh, really, Mr Beardsley, a big strong man like you can't be frightened of a moth!'

'I never said I was frightened of it,' Gilbert responded, miffed.

'It's a lot smaller than you are.'

'I'm *not* afraid of it!'

'What a baby you are –'

Provoked into action, Gilbert moved. With one swift movement he pulled back his arm then whacked the moth with the rolled-up paper.

'There!' Miss Vernon said triumphantly, looking at the floor, where the powdered ex-moth lay in dust. 'No more nibbling my winter coat, you villain! You see, Mr Beardsley, these insects are vile. They have to be exterminated, even if it seems cruel. No point letting one moth make a dinner out of a lady's winter wardrobe, now is there? What d'you say, Mr Beardsley? *Mr Beardsley?*'

When she turned round Gilbert had already gone.

Standing with her back against the window, Hettie pursed her lips. Rose had gone too far this time – working at the racetrack again! It was ridiculous, and she was obviously doing it to annoy everyone. Hadn't they complained enough last month? And now here she was again, off to help her father. As though Leonard Bradshaw couldn't help himself! Hettie smouldered, Len had always been an irritant. Even now, when she had done so much for Rose, the damn woman was still devoted to her father. That common, squinting bookie of a man, with his nasty little pitch and his poky house on Gull Road. Dear God, Hettie thought impatiently, didn't the girl know when she was well off?

Furtively, she stole a glance at Stuart. He was infuriated too, she could see that clearly enough, and with good cause. Naturally Cedric had been no use whatsoever. When Hettie had tried to talk to him earlier he had been dismissive, hurrying away to be with his wretched Home Guard.

'You should be firm with her,' Hettie advised, focusing

her annoyance on Stuart. 'When Rose comes down, tell her what you think. Forbid her to go again.'

'I *can't* forbid her!' he replied shortly, suspecting that Hettie viewed him with contempt. 'Rose isn't the type to boss around.'

'Nonsense! All women like strong men. That's why they fall for the servicemen. It's the glamour, the aura of power they have.'

Was she talking about servicemen deliberately to provoke him, Stuart thought bitterly. Ever since Hettie had moved in, he had noticed her many references to heroes, almost as though she was baiting him, reminding him of his own uselessness. Or maybe he was just imagining it. Hettie had been a good ally in other ways. And she always took his side against Rose – something he appreciated as his wife seemed determined to go her own way.

Uneasy, Stuart shifted in his seat. 'I'll talk to Rose –'

'*We'll* talk to her,' Hettie corrected him. 'I know her better than you.'

'I don't think so!' Stuart replied, some of his old humour coming to the surface. 'I do believe that Rose is *my* wife.'

'But she was my protégée before that,' Hettie responded evenly. 'Rose was moulded by me, encouraged by me. If I hadn't paid for her eye operation, where do you think your wife would be now? I'll tell you, Stuart, *in Gull Road*! Rose Bradshaw had a squint and no future when I took her under my wing. With my guidance she did very well, and made a good marriage. It's time she was reminded of what she owes me.'

How the conversation had turned round to Hettie, Stuart couldn't work out. But then everything came round to Hettie.

'I'll talk to her,' he said firmly.

'My dear boy,' Hettie replied, tapping him lightly on the shoulder, 'you really do need some guidance. Men and women are very different, Stuart. And the distinction has to be maintained. Men go off to fight and women keep the home. Rose has to be reminded of that.'

'Not every man fights,' Stuart replied brusquely, knowing at once that he should have let the matter pass.

'Oh, I didn't mean to offend you!' Hettie answered, shocked. 'Everyone knows you weren't medically fit to enlist. No one blames you, Stuart. No one at all. I mean, you mustn't think that other men are somehow better than you, or that women admire them more. You won't ever be a hero, it's true,' she said, walking to the door, 'but you have your own qualities. Ones that I'm sure are just as important as fighting on the front line.'

Christ! Stuart thought as he watched her leave, if Hettie had set out deliberately to undermine his remaining confidence she couldn't have done a better job.

'Hi, darling,' Rose said, walking in at that moment and kissing him on the cheek.

His spleen needed an outlet – and found one. 'You're not going to the racetrack again.'

'Don't be absurd!' she teased him. 'I'm helping my father out this afternoon. We've been through this before, Stuart, and I'm not arguing about it again.'

'I think –'

'And you shouldn't let Hettie interfere,' Rose went on, kissing him again.

He pulled away, as though repelled. 'You should do as I say –'

'Stuart!'

'You're not going out!'

Her eyes narrowed. This was Hettie's doing. If Stuart had been alone Rose knew she could have handled him, but with Hettie's influence it wasn't going to be easy. Sighing, she studied her husband. He was changing. Only months earlier they would have laughed this off, but lately he'd become embittered, overanxious about not being able to serve his country. In truth, the fact had all but emasculated him –

and although Rose had reassured him, it was no good. In Stuart's mind he was a failure. Impotent, without worth. A man other men looked down on.

And, of course, Hettie had sniffed out his weakness and was already using it against him.

'Stuart,' Rose said gently, 'let's not fight.'

'Then don't go out.'

'I have to help Dad. I promised.'

'And you promised to love and obey your husband,' Stuart replied, a sudden shadow of his father's pomposity creeping in, 'but you find *that* easy enough to forget.'

'Stuart,' Rose repeated, taking his hand, eager to soothe him, 'come on, cheer up. We'll go out tonight, have a walk and a kiss on the sea front –'

'And then everything will be all right again?' he countered. 'No, Rose, it's not that easy. I want you to behave like a professional man's wife.'

'Well, you're certainly behaving like a professional pain in the bloody backside!' she hurled back. 'Snap out of it, Stuart. This isn't like you.'

'You don't even know me!' he replied, goaded into overreacting. 'I thought you did, but now I see that I was wrong. After all, how could you *really* understand how things run in this house? In my life? You don't know how respectable people behave. You're nothing but a working-class girl who got lucky –'

Enraged, Rose walked out, slamming the door closed behind her. Smarting, she was about to leave the house when Hettie came out of the dining room.

Rose stopped dead in her tracks. 'Now you listen to me, and listen good,' she said, her tone menacing. 'Stay out of my marriage, or you'll regret it. You want to interfere with something? Then boss Cedric around, or join the Women's Voluntary Service – *but keep your nose out of my life*.'

'My dear girl –'

'I'm not your dear girl!' Rose shouted, her patience gone,

'and I'm on to you, Hettie. It took me a while, but I'm finally beginning to see you for what you are.'

'Don't talk to me like that!'

'I'll talk to you how I bloody well like. You might have interfered in my life, but you're not messing up my marriage –'

'Which would never have happened if it hadn't been for me,' Hettie replied lethally. 'Remember, you owe everything to me.'

'I owe everything to my *father*, not you –'

'Hah!'

Rose was incandescent with rage. '*You* changed my appearance, but *he* made me what I am inside.'

'You're right there,' Hettie replied, her tone caustic. 'You're as common as you always were.'

FIFTY-ONE

A freezing March wind was blowing off the sea as Rose hurried onto the front, passing the disused lamplights and the virtually silent streets. The few billboards around heralded the merits of buying War Bonds, or digging for Victory, but there were not many people around to dig for anything. For once the cinema looked quiet, even *Mrs Miniver* not tempting people out. War and the bad weather were keeping people in their homes – but Rose wouldn't have stayed in that house if Hettie had paid her.

Hettie – the bitch! Rose thought, smouldering. The bloody, conniving bitch. She thought of her old mentor and then of Stuart. His remarks had cut her to the bone. Was he *ashamed* of her? Did he really think she was just some scrubber who had married well? Perhaps he watched her when they ate, to check if she was using the right knife and fork. Or listened in on her conversation, checking her grammar.

But why had he changed so suddenly? Rose asked herself, knowing the answer already. *It was all because of Hettie's influence.* Yet who would have believed that her husband could have been so easily led? Stuart, of all people. Stuart who had mocked his father and Hettie for years – and now he was getting like them. A Fallow man through and through. Or was that a *shallow* man . . . ?

Tapping her foot, Rose waited impatiently and then climbed onto the empty tram, which had scuffed to a halt beside her. Sullenly, she stared out of the window as they headed along the coast for Blackpool. She would arrive early at Gull Road, but so what? She couldn't have stayed in that house another moment and she was certain of a welcome from her father.

Rose slumped back in her seat. Hadn't Len warned her about Hettie from the start? And he had been right. She was interfering again, making her indelible mark, Cedric and Rose finding more and more reasons to spend time away from the Lytham house. God, Rose thought, leaning her head against the windowpane, how was she going to sort this out? She was losing her husband, she could feel it. And not to some good-looking rival, but to a manipulative bitch with an expensive wardrobe.

The bitch who had been in her life for too long.

Joe was lying in bed, one arm around Maisie, the other around his little girl. Sleeping deeply, Lesley rested her head against her father's shoulder, Maisie watching Joe's chest rise and fall regularly. He was asleep, thank God. She hadn't mentioned it, but she knew how little her husband rested. How he lay in the dark, eyes open, thinking. And not talking. All her efforts to make him confide had been met with gentle resistance. He was fine, he told her, just fine. He didn't want to talk about the war when he was home.

He might not want to talk about it, but its effect was obvious. Joe had lost over a stone in weight, his open-faced good looks marred by distress. The mischievous expression so typical of the earlier Joe had now gone, replaced by a wariness that belonged to a man way beyond his years.

She would talk to Lester, Maisie thought. He would reassure her. And he would look out for her husband, just as he always had done. But the war was going on a lot longer than people had expected – how long could Lester keep an eye on Joe? Don't worry, Maisie told herself, Lester's tough; he'll carry them both. She would have a word with him, and thank him, and because she relied on him so much she would keep receiving his letters and passing them on to Rose.

Maisie remembered the argument she had had with Rose – but she had soon backed down. Maisie might not approve of her friend's burgeoning relationship with Lester, but she was in no real position to oppose it. What came first with Maisie was her husband. Joe had to be protected, brought home safe – and only his brother could do that.

If Maisie's conscience had to take a back seat – so be it.

'You look furious,' Lester said as he caught his first sight of Rose. 'Gorgeous, but furious.'

'I had a row with Hettie and Stuart,' she replied, turning away.

As they had agreed, Lester had caught the tram as it came into Blackpool. No one would see them – it was a cold afternoon – and besides – as Rose said often enough – they weren't doing any harm. He was just a friend, home on leave – surely she could meet an old friend?

'Maybe you shouldn't have come, Rose.'

'Dad needs me at the track. I wasn't coming just to see you.' She winked, lightening the atmosphere. 'D'you really think I'd make such a long journey to see you? God, I must have been travelling for all of *fifteen minutes*.'

He laughed. 'I'm glad to see you.'

'Me too,' she said genuinely. Then, catching an intensity in his expression, changed the subject. 'You've got two days, haven't you?'

He nodded. 'Two whole days.'

'You'll see your family, of course?'

'Daniel –'

'And Beth.'

'Rose, I want to see my son, but I *have* to see my wife. I don't want to. We don't –'

She shook her head briskly. 'Lester, we're not talking

about your marriage. We're not talking about anything personal. We're friends, that's all. You remember – that was the deal we made in our letters – that we would just be friends. And friends talk about rubbish, gossip, light-hearted stuff. Like the National Loaf the Government's introduced. You must try it now you're home, Lester. It's solid lead – only not so light.'

Smiling, he stared out of the window, turning away from her. All Lester wanted at that moment was to reach out and touch Rose, but he couldn't. *Wouldn't.* If he did he knew he would lose her. And having her in his life as a friend might not be what he wanted, but it was infinitely preferable to losing her entirely.

'I could come to the races,' he said suddenly.

'Dad would like to see you.'

'You reckon?' he asked, turning back to her. 'Or d'you think he might jump to conclusions?'

She thought for a moment. 'Maybe . . .'

'Have you told him we exchange letters?'

'No.'

'Because he wouldn't approve, would he?' Lester asked her. 'Oh, come on, your father's still angry with me about what happened –'

'That was a long time ago!'

'– when I hurt his beloved daughter,' Lester added, teasing her. 'He could swing a good left hook, your father.'

She laughed, linking arms with him as the tram rumbled along the seafront. 'He only did what I wanted to do to you that night.'

'I'm sorry,' Lester said quietly, 'so sorry –'

'No more,' Rose replied. 'We said we wouldn't talk about it again. I have to get off soon and go up to Dad's. What are you going to do?'

'See Daniel later, take him out.' Lester paused. 'Can you get away tomorrow?'

'No chance,' she said kindly. 'But I'll write to you.'

'I can't go back without seeing you!' he said, suddenly urgent. 'Please, Rose, get away. If only for ten minutes, but get away.'

She hadn't expected him to beg her. He never had before. But suddenly her heart shuddered. This was Lester, *Lester Williams*, the man she had loved for years. The man she still loved? No, Rose thought angrily, she was married to Stuart. She loved Stuart. Their marriage was going through a rough patch, it was true, but that was no reason to turn her back on him. Stuart was funny, clever; Stuart was her husband. Stuart was also becoming possessive, spiteful, critical . . .

'I can't,' Rose said finally. 'I'm sorry, but I can't.'

It would be too easy to fall into an affair with Lester. Both of them unhappily married, looking for affection. It would be easy. And wrong.

'Rose –'

'You have to spend time with your family.' She stood up, ready to get off at her stop. 'I'll see you on your next leave –'

'And you'll write?'

She turned, smiling at him. 'Yeah, I'll write. Just try and stop me.'

Three times Beth had combed her hair, tying it one way and then another. Finally she left it loose around her shoulders and turned back to Daniel. He had grown so much in the last three months, she thought, quite a little man now. And so like his father. Beth fiddled with her son's collar and then hoisted him into her arms. He was heavy, going to be tall like Lester.

Standing at the window of her house in Gate Street, Beth looked out. Lester had said he would be home around five. *Home* – he had used the word as though he meant it. Maybe he did, Beth thought, her hopes rising. Maybe he had finally got Rose out of his mind and realised what was important to him – his family, his wife, his son.

Fretful, Daniel began to wriggle in his mother's arms, Beth holding on to him a little too tightly as she stood at the window.

'Stay still,' she urged the child, 'stay still for a little longer, Danny. Look for your daddy coming, look for him.'

She would stand by the window with their son and wait for her husband to come home. Soon Lester would walk round the corner and see them framed by the window – his own Madonna and Child – and be moved. He would realise what he had. And what he *should* miss.

Her arms aching from the strain of holding Daniel, Beth stood at the window on Gate Street. And waited.

The afternoon race meeting passed quickly, Rose and Len returning to Gull Road around five. Exhilarated, Rose tossed the takings onto the kitchen table and glowed.

'Look at that!' she said happily. 'You made a mint today, Dad.'

'With your help,' he answered, putting on the kettle. 'Hey, Rosie, tot the money up for me, will you, luv? And take a bit for yourself.'

She pretended to do so, but didn't. Instead she counted the takings, wrote the sum on a piece of paper and then put the money in Len's savings box and locked it away in his desk drawer.

'You should put it in the bank, Dad – remember what happened to George Ogden.'

'Funny you should mention that. I was thinking about old George this afternoon. And that bugger Howell –'

'The Owl.'

Len nodded. 'Eyes like a bloody frog, he had. And he moved odd too. Slow and creepy.'

'Not that bloody slow. They never found him. I reckon Howell's got away with it.'

Len passed his daughter a mug of tea.

'I dunno. I've a hunch he'll get what's coming to him

one day.' Len started up the fire then sat down, still wearing his trilby and overcoat. 'Bloody cold.'

'It's March. What d'you expect – a heat wave?'

Len tapped the seat next to him. 'Sit with me for a few minutes, before you go back. I'll drive you home.'

'I want to walk tonight, Dad.'

'It's late.'

'It's not! It's only going up for six.'

'And dark.'

She pulled a face. 'But lovely. It's cold and clear and there's a full moon . . . Oh, come on, Dad, there aren't any murderers about any more. They've all been called up.'

He stared at her, then shrugged. 'Just walk part of the way, will you? Then pick up a tram to Lytham.'

'I will, if one comes along. But you know what they've been like since the war started,' Rose answered, sipping her tea.

In truth she didn't want to go home at all, and walking postponed the inevitable. If she had confided in her father Len would have sent for all her clothes and belongings and moved her back into Gull Road before she knew what had hit her. His daughter wasn't supposed to be unhappy – with anyone, in any place. And besides, Len wanted her away from Hettie. When Rose's mentor had been involved from a distance, he had been prepared to go along with it. But now that Hettie was living in the Fallow house Len was just waiting for the fallout.

'Is that the time?' Rose asked suddenly. 'God, I must go.' She rose to her feet, pulling on her gloves. 'See you end of the week for the next meeting, Dad?'

'If you're sure it's OK with Stuart –'

'It's fine,' Rose assured him. 'You need the help, you can't cope without your ticktack woman.'

'And you're the best.'

She nodded. 'It's true, I *am* the best.'

Smiling, she kissed him lightly on the head and then left,

closing the front door behind her and looking down Gull Road.

It was quiet. It took Rose only moments for her eyes to adjust to the blackout and then – with the aid of a full moon – she began to walk down to the Promenade. The sea was calm, the wind having finally dropped, and from the elaborate streetlamps, a few lost Christmas decorations flopped down uselessly, unlit and sad.

She would walk and clear her head, Rose thought, trying to cheer herself. Maybe Hettie would be out; maybe Cedric would have taken her to see friends. But she knew only too well that Hettie would be in the Fallow house – the house that had once seemed like Rose's home, but now seemed strange and unwelcoming. Even the surgery bore traces of Hettie's invasion: *her* writing in the appointments book on the two days Rose had been away, helping her father at the track.

Now suddenly, even her job seemed to have been despoiled. Rose didn't want to see Hettie's writing next to hers; just as she didn't want to see Hettie's shopping list replacing hers on the kitchen wall. Life had been good for her and Stuart for a long time at Lytham. Cedric hadn't interfered and Rose had – almost by default – run the house. But no more. Since Hettie had arrived, the pecking order had slowly – but irrevocably – changed. She was now in charge. And she made certain that everyone knew it.

What a bloody fool I've been, Rose thought as she walked along the Promenade. I knew Hettie well enough – why didn't I realise what would happen? Why didn't I get Stuart to move us out before she moved in? But now it's too late, she admitted bitterly.

And worse than losing control of the house, she was losing her husband. Lovely, loving, funny Stuart was turning into his father. Embittered by circumstances and his own guilt about not fighting, Stuart was becoming another man. And Rose didn't know how to get through to him.

'Rose!'

At the sound of her name, she turned, startled. Staring into the dark night, Rose called out: 'Who's there?'

'Guess.'

She looked about her. 'Come on, who's that?'

'Rose,' the voice whispered, unrecognisable.

'I'm not afraid!' she blustered, scared, but not letting it show in her voice. 'Whoever you are, show yourself.'

'Rosie, Rosie . . .'

Jesus, she thought, looking around again. Who was it? She couldn't recognise the voice because it was a whisper, couldn't even make out if it was a man or a woman. Probably just some stupid kid, Rose told herself, walking on. Just some stupid kid having a laugh . . .

'Rose!'

She stopped again, her heart banging. There were no lights on in the surrounding buildings, and the sea – under the full moon – looked like a black trench.

'Who are you?' she called out in reply. 'Stop buggering about, answer me!'

'Who do you want me to be?'

Peering ahead, Rose tried to see in the semi-darkness. It couldn't be Lester. No, he wouldn't scare her like this. So who *would* want to scare her? Trudie? she thought suddenly. Maybe, yes, maybe it was her. It would be like Trudie . . . Or then again, maybe it was some other woman. A dark woman, with dark eyes and hair. Beth.

'Is that you, Beth?'

There was a long peal of laughter. Uncanny, disembodied.

Frightened, Rose began to walk on, every nerve tensed. Should she continue? Or go back home to Gull Road? Did the person just want to frighten her, or harm her? One thing was for sure – Rose wasn't going to run. So, slowly, she walked on, her footsteps unnaturally loud in the silent evening.

'Rosie! Rosie!'

This time she didn't stop, just continued, her eyes staring ahead, praying for a tram to come along. God, Rose thought to herself, why hadn't she let her father drive her home?

'Rose. Stop!'

The voice's emphasis had changed. No longer eerily playful, it was now sinister. And close.

'What is it! What the hell do you want?'

'Don't you want to talk?' the voice whispered.

Unnerved, Rose turned round and round, trying again to see. 'What should I want to talk about?'

'You choose.'

'WHO ARE YOU?'

'Who do you want me to be?' the voice whispered back, repeating itself.

'I don't care! But I know you're a coward,' Rose replied curtly. 'Only a bloody coward would hide in the dark. Anyone with anything about them would show themselves.' She paused. If she could get the person talking, maybe she could guess who it was. If it was someone she knew. Or a stranger.

'Oh, Rose, you shouldn't swear, it's not ladylike –'

'*STUART*!' she shouted, infuriated. 'Is that you?'

He came out suddenly, facing her. 'Would you rather it had been someone else?'

'You bastard!' she snapped, walking off again. 'You bloody bastard!'

'Oh, Rose, you must be so disappointed. Sorry it's just me –'

She turned to face him: 'What *are* you talking about?'

'I saw you. With him.'

Rose paused, realisation dawning. 'What?'

'I saw you. With Lester Williams,' Stuart repeated, his

tone vicious. 'The brave soldier, come home on leave. To see his wife? No. His son? No. Maybe his girlfriend then?'

'Stuart, stop it!' Rose replied shortly. 'Lester is just a friend –'

'So why didn't you tell me about your little friend?' Stuart replied nastily. 'Instead of just creeping around with him behind my back. But then it doesn't matter *what* you do behind my back, does it? I'm a no one, a nothing. A man with no power – even over my own wife.' He caught hold of Rose's wrist tightly. 'Don't you treat me like dirt! I gave you everything –'

'Get off me!' she shouted, trying to shake off her husband's grip. 'Stuart, let go!'

'You should treat me with respect –'

'How can I, when you act like an idiot?'

'Are you sleeping with him?'

Infuriated, Rose tried to push Stuart away. 'Grow up! Lester's a friend, that's all –'

'A friend – I bet! Like all the other friends you've had –'

'I've never cheated on you!' Rose said, trying to break free. 'You're acting stupidly. I've never done anything to hurt you –'

'That's not what I've heard.'

'Then you've heard lies!' Rose replied heatedly. 'Let go of me!'

But he wouldn't. Instead he pulled her towards the steps that led down to the beach, Rose trying to break his grip and failing. Swearing with the effort, Stuart dragged his wife down the steep flight of stone steps, onto the shingle. Then he pushed her violently, Rose losing her balance and falling hard onto the sea-scuffed pebbles. She could hear the water lapping only feet away, smell the ozone and see the vague outline of the Central Pier in the distance.

'Stuart –'

He was suddenly on top of her, straddling her and tearing off her clothes. Stunned, Rose began to punch him, her

407

arms flailing around – but Stuart was stronger than she was and angry. His right hand holding her wrists, his left undid his flies and then tugged aside her panties. Then with a violent thrust, he entered her.

Screaming, Rose tried to push him off, but Stuart didn't stop. He was beyond himself, desperate to reach a climax. And as she lay there Rose heard the sea water lapping, felt the pebbles press into her bare buttocks, and heard the sound of grunting as Stuart ejaculated. Suddenly there was a wet warmth between her legs as he relaxed on top of her.

Her eyes closed, Rose turned her face against the rough pebbles and the stinking seaweed from the last cold tide.

Having a well-developed instinct for trouble, Hettie could feel it the moment Stuart entered the Lytham house. He looked dishevelled, and smelled of whisky, although he hardly ever drank. Glancing over to Cedric, Hettie closed the door of the drawing room and turned to her stepson.

'What on earth happened to you?'

'I don't have to tell you anything,' he replied curtly, moving towards the stairs.

'Where's Rose?'

'I'm her husband, not her gaoler!' he snapped.

Hettie moved up the stairs behind him. 'Stuart, talk to me –'

'I don't want to talk to you!' he bellowed. 'I don't want to hear anything you have to say. You're always interfering, poking your nose in things that don't concern you. We were happy here before you came. *We were happy* . . . I've been working it out, thinking all the way home about how it went wrong. And now I know the answer – it's your fault. All your fault.'

Hettie's expression was complete disdain. 'You're drunk!'

'Yes, I'm drunk! A bad, drunk pig of a man. But I wasn't before you came here. I wasn't before . . .'

And then he passed out, sliding onto the hall floor: his head thrown back, his body as limp as a corpse.

'Hey, you there. You OK?'

Sitting on one of the Promenade benches, Rose was huddled up, her coat pulled tight around her. She had been there for a while, Stuart having run off long ago. Gone back to Lytham, no doubt. But she hadn't moved, hadn't known where to go. Not to her father's – that was out of the question. Len would kill Stuart. So instead Rose had sat on the bench, staring out to sea blindly. Until that moment.

'Are you OK?' the voice asked again, sliding onto the seat next to her. 'Jesus, *Rose*!'

Rose turned to find Trudie looking at her. 'Are you all right? Has someone hurt you?' She touched Rose's arm. 'Talk to me. You're scaring me.'

'I thought it was you.'

'Huh?'

Rose swallowed, then spoke again. 'I heard a voice calling me. And at first I thought it was you – playing a trick.'

Shame-faced, Trudie stared at her. 'Let me help you up, Rose –'

'Leave me alone.'

'How can I leave you alone!' Trudie replied, shocked. 'Let me help you. Come on, Rose, let me help.'

Time had changed Trudie: time – and Bunny Lambert, the man who had come back from the dead. Even the sinking of the *Ark Royal* hadn't fazed him. And because of Bunny's love, Trudie wasn't the vicious slut she had been. Strangely, she had lately been wondering about getting in touch with Rose to make things right between them. But not like this.

'Rose, what happened?'

'I'm cold . . . so cold . . .'

'But what happened?'

'Nothing . . . I'm just cold . . .'

'Rose, you have to tell me.' She took Rose's hands in hers and began to rub some warmth into them. 'Did someone attack you?'

Rose shook her head. 'No.'

'I think someone did. Come on, talk to me. Who hurt you?' She paused, looking round. 'Shall I get a doctor? Or call the police?'

Rose flinched. 'No! Just leave me –'

'How can I leave you! Don't be crazy. You either tell me what happened or I'll go for the coppers.'

'Stuart raped me.'

Dumbfounded, Trudie stared at her: '*Stuart*? Your husband?'

'Go home,' Rose said, her voice flat. 'Let me sort this out for myself.'

'*He raped you?*' Trudie repeated, stunned. 'Jesus . . .'

'Go home.'

'And leave you here? Not likely. Come on,' Trudie said hurriedly, helping Rose to her feet. 'Come home with me.'

'Not Gull Road!' Rose replied, startled. 'I don't want Dad to know.'

'We'll go to Sea View,' Trudie reassured her. 'When you're ready to see him, we'll get your dad. Oh, come on, Rose, please, come home with me.'

Together they walked up to the hotel, Trudie letting them in at the back door, avoiding the Gull Road entrance. There was no one in the backyard, but when she heard voices Rose pulled back suddenly.

'I have to go!'

'Where?' Trudie asked her, raising her eyebrows. 'Just *where* are you thinking of going, Rose? Back home? To that bastard?' Her tone softened. 'Come in and get warm. Take your time to think things out.'

As Trudie opened the back door, the sound of Ruby's voice swam out into the freezing March air.

'. . . I said, I know butter's on ration, but that piece you gave me wouldn't feed a cockroach! And if you doubt me, I added, try it with one of those you've got running about in the back . . .'

The warmth hit them as they walked in, Ruby turning and smiling as she saw Trudie. Then her smile faded, her eyes fixing on Rose.

'What's the matter?' she said, closing the door and sitting Rose down. 'Are you hurt?'

'Stuart raped her.'

'Stuart? Stuart who?'

'Her husband,' Trudie explained, as Ruby looked from her daughter back to Rose. 'I found her on a bench by the Prom, frozen –'

'Get the brandy!' Ruby snapped, putting on the kettle and banking up the fire. Quickly she jerked a blanket off the dozing Alfred and wrapped it around Rose. 'Bastard! What did he want to go and do something like that for? I can't stand a man who'd do that to his own wife. He wants stringing up. If he'd been out there fighting, he'd not have done something like this.'

When Trudie returned, Ruby poured a tot of brandy into a mug, added some hot water, and gave it to Rose. 'Sip that. Take it slow, it's hot.' She looked over Rose's head towards Trudie. 'Was he there?'

'Nah, no sign of him.'

'You can't go home tonight,' Ruby said, talking to Rose. 'You can stay here.'

'I have to go home.'

'To that man? Nah, Rose, I don't think so. If he'd do it once, he'd do it again. And to leave you out in the cold . . . But whatever made him do it? I mean, *something* must have triggered him off.'

'Things haven't been going well between us for a while,' Rose said, staring into the mug.

Dear God, how could she tell the truth? How could she bring Lester into it?

'But something must have sent him over the edge,' Ruby persisted. 'Was it because you were working on the track again?'

'He didn't like that . . . Neither did Hettie –'

'Hah! Living in the same house as that woman would ruin anyone's marriage. You can't have two women running one house, it never works.'

'I can vouch for that,' Trudie said drily.

'But Hettie can't have caused this,' Ruby went on, persistently. 'Not even working the track could have caused *this*. It must be something else. Or someone else –'

'Me.'

Slowly Ruby glanced over to the door. Lester was standing there, his soldier's cap in his hand. He had obviously not been there long.

Ruby looked from her son to Rose. 'Oh no, not you two?'

'We weren't doing anything wrong,' Lester said hurriedly. 'Rose wouldn't hear of it, although I would have left Beth like a shot if she'd asked me to. We just wrote to each other – and we saw each other this morning.'

Picking up the brandy bottle, Ruby took a hurried swig out of it and then sat down.

'You stupid sods! And you, Lester, you should have had more sense. Any man would be jealous of another man come sniffing around his wife.'

'It was innocent!'

'Well, Stuart Fallow didn't think so!' she hurled back. 'And look what he's done to his wife –'

Staring anxiously at Rose, Lester moved over to her and sank to his knees. He could see that she was in shock and when he took her hand, she was ice cold.

'What happened?' he asked gently. 'Did he beat you? Did he hurt you?'

Rose said nothing. Ruby said nothing. It was Trudie who finally intervened.

'He raped her,' she said simply.

Shaken, Lester got to his feet. His face was set, the pupils of his eyes contracted to pinpricks.

'Leave it,' Ruby warned her son. '*Leave it!*'

But she knew she was wasting her breath.

FIFTY-TWO

Driving as fast as Alfred's old van would allow, Lester arrived outside the Fallow house and parked with two wheels up on the kerb. His anger was burning white-hot, but his composure was frightening. Walking up to the door, he rang the bell.

Hettie answered. 'Who is it?' she asked, recognition coming fast. '*Lester Williams?*' Without effort she managed to put a world of contempt into the name.

Lester moved past her into the hallway.

'What on earth are you doing here?' Hettie demanded, affronted.

'Where's Stuart Fallow?'

'He's out,' Hettie lied. 'Perhaps you'd like to leave a message?'

'Perhaps you'd like to get out of my way?' Lester replied, making for the door opposite.

Flustered, Hettie hurried after him, Cedric looking up as Lester entered the drawing room.

'May I help you?' he asked, taking in Lester's uniform and smiling sympathetically. 'Have you come for a donation? If you bear with me for just a moment, I'll get something for you –'

'Cedric, shut up!' Hettie snapped. 'He's come to see Stuart. And I told him that he's –'

'In the surgery,' Cedric replied, ever polite. 'Is it an emergency? I'm sure my son will look after you . . .'

Trailing off, Cedric watched in amazement as, without another word, the soldier ran out of his house towards the surgery annex.

'You fool!' Hettie hissed at her husband. '*Now* look what you've done!'

It was impossible to see if any lights were burning as Lester walked up to the surgery door, because of the black-out. And though he rang the bell constantly, there was no answer. Hurriedly Lester moved round to the back door – and then heard a noise. So Stuart Fallow *was* there, he thought. The bastard was in there, hiding.

Smashing a glass pane in the door, Lester reached in and unlocked it. Moving into the semi-darkness, he paused for an instant to let his eyes get used to the lack of light. Finally he saw Stuart was standing by the dentist's chair, still wearing his outdoor coat. And he was shaking from a mixture of booze and terror.

'What . . . what d'you want?' Stuart blustered, as Lester moved towards him. 'You have to make an appointment.'

'Not for what I'm about to do,' Lester replied, hitting Stuart square in the mouth and sending him over the dentist's chair. 'You want to play rough? Play rough with me, Fallow! Pick me. Not your wife.'

Scrambling to his feet, Stuart backed away from him, terrified. 'I didn't do anything to her –'

'You raped her!' Lester snapped, hitting Stuart again, and then hauling him back to his feet. 'You raped her and then left her. How could you?' he shouted, punching Stuart in the stomach and watching him crumble. 'How could you hurt her? She's your wife, for God's sake! You should look after her – love her.' He leaned down, violently jerking Stuart's head upwards by the hair, so that he was looking directly into his eyes. 'I would have died for her. And you treat her like an animal.'

'You and her –'

'*There's nothing between us!*' Lester roared back.

415

'Nothing! I love her – but she loves you. Rose wouldn't betray you. But I would have. I wouldn't have thought twice about it. Because I'm not as honourable as she is. I would have taken her away if she'd given me half a chance. But she never did.'

Letting go of Stuart's hair, Lester stood back. Stuart's head had fallen onto his chest, blood pouring from his nose. He was finding it difficult to breathe, his lips swollen, his eyes fixed on the floor. He was already sick with drink; now fury and humiliation tightened his chest. He had taken a beating, had been whipped like a dog by Lester Williams, the hero soldier. Everyone would hear about it. Everyone would know what he had done – and what Lester Williams had done to him. Christ, Stuart thought helplessly, he was finished.

'I saw you with my wife,' he said, his voice thick. 'I thought –'

'*Wrong*. You thought wrong,' Lester said, contempt in his voice. 'And you raped the woman I love. *You raped her.*' He lifted his hand to strike Stuart again and then paused, finally stepping back disgusted. 'If you ever go near her again, I'll do more than give you a beating. As God is my judge, I'll kill you! Don't doubt me, Stuart Fallow. I'd kill you – and happily hang for it.'

PART FIVE

I expect to pass through this world but
once; and any good thing therefore that I
can do, or any kindness that I can show
to any fellow-creature, let me do it now; . . .
for I shall not pass this way again.

Attributed in *Treasure Trove*, 1925
Stephen Grellet 1773–1855

We grow to regret what we've said, only after we've said it.

It's still raining. We must be near the end, surely. And then the rain will stop. And the judge will finally cease talking and the foreman will give his verdict.

When he does it will be all over the evening papers. Paper boys will call out the headlines and people I have never known, and never will know, shall read all about me. And what I did. Or what they think I did. They will talk about me, and use my story as a warning to children. I'll become another anecdote from Blackpool.

A black souvenir. Born within sight of the Tower and the serpent-thickened sea.

FIFTY-THREE

Blackpool people talked about the spring of 1942 for a long time afterwards. Not just because of the war, but because of a local tragedy that spiralled into a series of devastating events. Which for a while almost overshadowed world news. Maisie hadn't really understood how right her prediction would prove to be. Lester and Rose's correspondence wasn't innocent – whatever they thought – *it was lethal*. They had done nothing wrong, betrayed no one – but no one believed that. And after Lester gave Stuart Fallow a beating, everything changed, setting in motion a string of events that would unwind towards disgrace and death.

There was a war on, but in some streets there was a more vicious rout taking place. Histories, memories, loves accepted, lost or denied, suddenly came to the surface like scum on a cold bath. Everyone had an opinion; everyone took sides. It would end badly, everyone said. And everyone was right.

It was beyond even Hettie to repair the damage. What Stuart had done was soon common knowledge. None of the participants involved had gossiped, but someone had seen Rose sitting on the Promenade bench, and when the fight between Stuart and Lester came to light, it wasn't difficult to draw a conclusion. Within a day, it was the talk of Blackpool.

Stunned, Cedric demanded to hear the truth.

And Stuart, reckless and cynical, lied. 'Rose is a slut –'

'I don't believe that,' Cedric answered him, staring at the son he had never understood and was rapidly growing to despise.

Misjudging the extent of her influence, Hettie tried to intervene. 'Dear Cedric, let's not get things out of proportion here –'

'Shut up!' Cedric snapped unexpectedly.

Stepping back, Hettie put one hand over her mouth in shock. Dear God, if she wasn't careful all her planning would be ruined. It wouldn't do for her to lose face now. Surely all this unpleasantness could be smoothed over? What Stuart had done was wrong, but things happened in life . . . That fool of a girl! Hettie thought angrily. If only Rose had kept her mouth shut. And now here was Cedric turning on her.

'You attacked your own wife?' Cedric asked his son, his nasal tones no longer funny, only intimidating.

'She was seeing another man –'

'*You attacked her?*' Cedric repeated. He couldn't bring himself to use the word rape, even though it was being bandied about the town. Not rape, surely? Not that. It was immoral, disgusting. Not rape. Not *his* son.

'Rose is my wife,' Stuart responded sullenly. 'You said yourself that she was letting down the family going to the racecourse –'

'Don't misquote me!' Cedric roared suddenly, Stuart paling. This wasn't like his father, not the pompous, rather silly Cedric Fallow. 'Don't twist my words and throw them back in my face!'

'Dad –'

'I'm not your father any more!' Cedric roared. 'I don't want to have a son like you. You're a lying, cowardly creep of a man. You had everything, Stuart: a profession, a home, a beautiful wife, and you threw them away.'

The old man wasn't serious. Surely he *couldn't* be serious. Shaken, Stuart blustered awkwardly. 'I can make things right –'

'HOW CAN YOU MAKE THINGS RIGHT?'

'Cedric,' Hettie said, trying again, 'please calm down. This isn't good for you.'

'Having a son who rapes his own wife in public isn't good for me!' Cedric countered.

'It wasn't in public –'

'It was on the *beach*, wasn't it, Stuart?' his father said, his disgust palpable. 'Like all the day-trippers. Doing it out in the open, like animals. And then you left her there, for anyone to find. Dear Lord, this could have ended up in the newspapers. It *still* could.'

'The papers?' Stuart said, floundering. 'How?'

'If your wife went to the police –'

'Why would she do that?' Stuart replied, suddenly scared and desperate not to lose his father's protection. 'Look, Father, she goaded me into it. She did! She was taunting me, telling me about her man, what a brave soldier he was. What a bloody hero.' He moved towards Cedric, lying to save his skin. 'Father, you *can't* believe her. You wouldn't take her word against mine?'

'I wouldn't have done – a while ago,' Cedric replied coldly, 'but lately I've seen how you've changed. I saw how you began to treat your wife. Saw you criticise, finding fault, making her feel small. And always accusing her of being unfaithful –'

'She was!'

'No, I don't believe she was!' Cedric snapped back. 'You just want me to believe that so I'll take your side, say she was no good, a poor wife for a Fallow. But I've changed too, Stuart, over these last twenty-four hours – since I heard what you did. I've come to realise that there's nothing in life that matters – except honour.'

'Father –'

Cedric put up his hands to prevent his son interrupting

again. Anxiously, Hettie watched. There had to be some way she could smooth all this over, get life back on its pleasant, even keel.

'Cedric, my dear . . .' she began, too stupid to see that anything she said at that moment would damn her, '. . . I think that maybe I should have a word with Rose. Hopefully she will have calmed down now; had time to think about . . . about the *circumstances*.'

Cedric turned to her, watching her, listening. And then Hettie saw it: the look of complete distaste.

'Don't meddle in my family.'

'I happen to be a *part* of your family, Cedric!' Hettie went on blindly. 'It was me that brought Rose into your family.'

'The way things have turned out, am I supposed to thank you for that?' Cedric replied. 'Or maybe I should thank you for being the person to bring ruin to the Fallows?'

'Oh, the damn Fallows!' Hettie snapped, exasperated. 'Fallow this, Fallow that. You're obsessed with your name – you and your son. And what *is* the Fallow name anyway? You're not royalty, just two jumped-up dentists in a seaside town. Who really cares about your family, Cedric? Who cares about what your son did? It's a ten-minute wonder. You could ride this thing out, if you and Stuart just keep your mouths shut and act like nothing's happened.'

Shaking his head, Cedric stared at her. '*Act as if nothing's happened?* Is that what you think I should do, Henrietta? Well, you're right, I *am* a bit of a pompous wind-bag, and the Fallow name does matter to me too much – but not enough to close my eyes and ears to what he's done. Not enough to ignore my own conscience and condone it by brushing it under the carpet. There *isn't* a carpet big enough to hide what my son did.' Cedric pointed to Stuart, his voice rising shrilly. 'I want you out of this house –'

'Father!'

'– out *now*!' Cedric shouted, then turned back to Hettie. 'And you! You can go too.'

Staggered, for once Hettie couldn't find words, could only watch as Stuart moved towards his father, pleading.

'Look, I'll do whatever you say, whatever, but let me stay here. I've got a practice here. Patients –'

'You *had* a practice. You *had* patients! I want you to go now. Get out, Stuart.'

'You can't do this!'

'I can and I will!' Cedric shouted, then suddenly stopped short, slumping back into his seat.

His high colour faded, his face turning paper white, his mouth hanging open. After a moment, Hettie moved over to him and took his hand, her voice soothing.

'There now, look what you've gone and done, Cedric,' she said, breathing evenly as she studied her husband. The signs were so familiar to her. He was looking just like Hubert had done when he had his stroke. Luck, Hettie thought to herself, was back on her side. 'You must rest, my dear. You rest and we'll get the doctor.' She bent down and loosened his collar, Cedric unable to speak, his eyes helplessly watching her every movement. 'Don't worry about what you said. I forgive you. And I couldn't possibly leave you now, my dear. You need someone to look after you. Get you better again.'

She looked at Stuart, her mind working overtime. What route would serve her best? To side with Cedric? He was powerless enough for a while, no threat to her. Maybe she should throw in her lot with Stuart? Was *that* the wiser course of action? But if Cedric died she would inherit everything – she had already seen to that – so what did she need his son for? What possible help could a washed-up, violent, outcast be to her?

Taking in what had happened, Stuart looked from his stricken father to Hettie, relief in his eyes. He was home free now.

'Hettie?'

She raised her eyebrows quizzically. 'Yes?'

'I can help you look after Father –'

'I don't think so, Stuart. You heard what your father said. Get out of this house.'

'What?'

'Get out!' Hettie said sharply. Without Stuart she would have Cedric to herself. 'This isn't your home any more.'

'But what about Rose?' he replied desperately. 'What about my wife?'

'You think she'll come back here?' Hettie said, laughing mirthlessly. 'She'll never set foot in this house again, Stuart. And neither will you.'

Glancing back to his father Stuart realised it was useless even to try to protest. Cedric was watching him intently, then suddenly he looked away, his expression defeated. Incredulous, Stuart studied the woman bending over his father, almost *absorbing* him. It was true that Cedric had turned against him, but there had been a slim chance that in time Stuart might have won the old man round. But not now.

His father was helpless. And Hettie was in charge.

FIFTY-FOUR

Piling the billboard advertising The Lazy Eye into the back of his old Austin, Len glanced down Gull Road. Clovis was waving, trying to get his attention, seriously out of breath when she reached him.

'How's Rose?' she gasped, her dowager's hump pushing her head down between her shoulders.

Strange to think that once his sister had been a pretty girl of nineteen, Len thought sadly. Strange to think that his daughter had once been happily married . . .

'Rosie's doing fine, Clovis. Thanks for asking.'

'I heard that Stuart Fallow's cleared off. And his father's had a stroke. I'd have a stroke – living with that Hettie woman. As for Lester . . .' she sucked her teeth thoughtfully, '. . . beat up Fallow good and proper – or so I heard.'

'You heard right,' Len replied, looking over to Sea View.

He didn't know whether to hit Lester, or thank him. If Rose and Lester hadn't been seeing each other none of this would have happened. But then again, Stuart was obviously no good. Maybe it was better that Rose had got out of the marriage – however drastic the means.

'Are you listening to me?' Clovis asked, her tone abrupt.

'Sorry, luv, what were you saying?'

'About Rose. Is she going to stay with you?'

'Where else?'

'Good,' Clovis replied, smiling. 'Don't let on to anyone,

but I've a present for her. Nan – you know she's . . .' Clovis dropped her voice conspiratorially, '. . . *into things* – well, she got this lovely drugget for me. And I want Rose to have it.'

Trying not to laugh, Len thanked his sister profusely. What the bloody hell Rosie would do with drugget was beyond him, but it had been an obvious wrench for Clovis to part with it.

'Came from a good home,' she went on, still whispering, so that he had to bend down to hear her. 'Doctor's place, or so Nan says, and as you know she's a woman of few words and none of them lies. I'll pop by with it later. But don't tell Rose – I want it to be a surprise.'

Walking down Gate Street, Beth was well aware of people nudging each other and whispering. If she looked in their direction, they glanced away, but she could still hear them.

Her husband damn near killed Stuart Fallow . . . And all because of Rose Bradshaw, as she used to be . . . He never got over Rose, everyone knows that . . . Married Beth, but she tricked him into it . . . Makes you wonder how long Lester and Rose had been seeing each other . . . I feel sorry for the little one . . .

Beth walked on as quickly as she could with Daniel. For days they had been holed up in the Gate Street house, Beth drawing the curtains to keep out curious eyes. To his credit, Lester had explained what had happened and confessed that he had been writing to Rose. And that he had seen her that leave. However, Beth did *not* confess to her own adultery and let herself look like a martyr instead. When Lester had finished his confession he went back to the front with his brother, promising that he and Beth would talk the next time he was home.

They would talk – Beth knew what that meant. They would part, not talk. So all her hopes had been a joke, she thought bitterly. Her husband's eagerness to get home had

428

been to see his first love, not his wife. All the time Beth had been longing for a reconciliation, Lester had been with her, with Rose. And now everyone knew it. And worse, Rose was free again, separated from her husband, her lover riding to her rescue whilst his wife had stood in the window of their home and waited. *For nothing.*

Hurrying along, Beth could feel a vein pulsing in her neck, her breathing accelerated, her mind swimming with overheard whispers. Finally she entered her mother's house and pushed Daniel into the kitchen, kissing him hurriedly before moving out into the lobby again.

'Mum, it's me,' she called up the stairwell. 'I've brought Daniel over. Will you keep him for a while?'

'All right, luv,' came the answer. 'Can you wait for me a minute? I'll be down soon.'

'I can't wait, Mum. I have to go,' Beth called back. 'I've got something important to do.'

It was growing dark as Beth walked down towards the seafront. The weather had warmed up, a few hardy trippers queuing to see *Mrs Miniver*, a boy wolf-whistling at Beth as he cycled past. Taking off her hat, Beth let the breeze cool her forehead, her eyes fixed ahead.

She had the solution at last. It had taken her a while to work it out, but now she had it.

As she crossed the Promenade, the Tower was hardly visible in the dying light. Ahead of her lay the beach and beyond, the sea. When she had been little her father had brought her here once, both of them running, laughing, in and out of the waves, which had snapped around their ankles, the gulls circling overhead. Later she had walked with boyfriends here, kissed under the pier, and made paper boats with their names written on them. *Where will they go? . . . I don't know, somewhere foreign, mysterious . . .*

And she had come here with Lester. Held hands with him, touched his cheek, kissed him, had laid her head on his chest. And later, made love to him. Made a child with him. He had told her that he loved her wildness, her dark hair and eyes, her quickness of spirit. But then he had grown to hate it and inside her the passion had turned to doubt, the insecurity into madness.

And now Beth finally understood what had happened to her. The previous night she had put Daniel to bed and then pulled out an old box from the bottom of the wardrobe. In it she had kept her treasures: a sprig of lavender from her wedding bouquet, one of Daniel's booties, a lock of Lester's hair. And a pair of gloves that she had worn the first time she had gone out with her husband.

She had looked at them and realised that they no longer belonged to her. That woman had gone. Beth could see her, watch her drawing on the gloves, brushing her black hair – but knew she no longer existed.

I was that person, once, she told herself. I was her. Once.

But no more. That was why Lester didn't love her any longer. It was simple. She had changed. Lost him. Lost herself. Whichever had come first.

Without looking left or right, Beth climbed down the steep iron steps to the dark beach. She could hear the pebbles crunching underfoot as she walked on, the town behind her, the sea ahead. Soon she felt the water around her feet and ankles, then pushing against her knees, then her thighs, the effort of walking becoming difficult. Then all of a sudden Beth couldn't feel the pebbles underfoot any more and with another step the water closed over her.

Just breathe in, she told herself, the dark water pressing against her skin and her open eyes. Just breathe in . . . But instinct made her hold her breath. Then suddenly she couldn't hold it any longer and panicked, breathing in, not air but the cold salt water. The effect was terrifying; at once her lungs filled and she began to sink, falling under the oppressive black sea. Jesus! It was a mistake! Beth thought, struggling hysterically and trying to claw her way back up to the air. It was all a mistake!

And then she remembered. Remembered a dark girl drawing on gloves. And stopped fighting . . . Far, far down she went. Down under the waves, under the dark, under the sea. Away from the lights. And the air. Her dark green dress floating around her eerily.

The drowning dress.

'It's none of my business, luv –'

Rose looked up. 'Of course it's your business, Dad. Ask me anything you want to know.'

'About Lester –'

'We were writing to each other. And I saw him when he came home. But there was nothing wrong about it, Dad, I promise you. We were friends.'

'Oh, luv,' Len said, rolling up a cigarette as they sat at the kitchen table, 'you should have told me.'

'You wouldn't have approved.'

'No.'

'That's why I didn't tell you,' Rose said quietly. 'I've made a mess of things, haven't I?'

'A lot of people are going to get hurt, that's for sure. Has he talked to his wife?' Rose shook her head. 'He should. Beth should know what her husband intends to do now.'

Rose looked down at her hands. 'I don't know *what* Lester intends to do.'

'Then ask him,' Len replied, lighting up his cigarette. 'He has a wife and a child to think about. He should make things clear to them – and to you. Does he love you?'

'He says he does.' Rose's voice fell. 'God, what a mess! I should never have got involved, should I, Dad? I should have stayed out of it. But he was just a friend –'

'– that you still loved.'

'Dad!'

'Oh, come on!' Len said shortly. 'You've always loved Lester Williams. More than you ever loved Stuart. Even if you didn't realise it yourself. When Lester married Beth Hodges you were heartsick.'

Rose winced. 'It was a long time ago. I fell in love with Stuart.'

'You didn't fall far enough,' Len answered her bluntly. 'If you had, you would have told him about Lester. The three of you would have met up. You wouldn't have hidden it, Rosie. I wouldn't have hidden something like that from your mother. Don't kid yourself, luv. You might think it was innocent, but both of you were playing with fire.'

Her head bowed, Rose said simply: 'Stuart's disappeared . . .'

'Good. I hope he's dead.'

'All my things are in the Lytham house.'

'You want me to pick them up?'

'No.' Rose shook her head. 'I don't want anything from there. It's almost like it used to be now, Dad, just you and me. Before Hettie, before the operation, before Lytham.' She laid her head on his arm, her eyes closing. 'I should have stayed here with you, then nothing would have gone wrong. Oh, Dad, why didn't I stay with you on Gull Road?'

Clovis was just passing Nan's house when she felt a sudden grip on her arm. Surprised, she turned, and Nan hurriedly led her into number 111.

'Whatever is it, Nan?'

The front room was, as ever, gaslit, the strange light making Nan Wilmslow appear even more spectral.

'Beth Hodges is dead.'

Clovis blinked, unsure she had heard correctly. 'You what?'

'Beth, Lester's wife, is dead.'

'Dead?' Clovis repeated dumbly. 'How?'

'She drowned herself.'

Sitting down heavily, Clovis fanned herself with her hand. 'Whatever would she go and do a thing like that for? She's a mother, got a little one to look after.' Clovis paused, wincing. 'Oh God, does Rose know?'

Nan shook her head.

'And neither will Lester,' Clovis went on, 'not now he's back fighting. They'll have to write and tell him. Oh God, what a mess. What a terrible mess . . . Where's the little one?'

'With his grandmother.'

Clovis didn't bother to ask how Nan knew; Nan always knew everything first.

'Drowned herself . . . Beth Hodges . . . Lester's wife.' Clovis ran over the facts again, as though they were impossible to take in. 'This is going to be a right scandal. And we all know who's going to get the blame, don't we? Rose and Lester. And mostly Rose – seeing as how he's away and she's here. I always said it was going to go wrong, that marriage with Lester and Beth. It was on the cards from the start. But to *kill* yourself . . .' Clovis shook her head. 'That's a wicked thing to do.'

'She was mad,' Nan said simply.

'*Mad?*' Clovis echoed, shaking her head. 'If she was, she made herself mad.'

At Myers the following morning, Trudie was serving a customer when she overheard two other women talking. One was a fat woman from Holland Road, the other a gossip from Gate Street. They were standing at the far end of the counter, their voices animated, excited.

'. . . well, what did anyone expect? That Rose Bradshaw – that was – having an affair with Lester Williams behind his wife's back? Of course her husband threw her out.'

'But didn't Stuart Fallow and Lester have a fight? I heard Rose was raped –'

'She puts it about easily enough. I wouldn't think anyone would need to rape that one.'

Slamming down a half-wrapped parcel, Trudie moved

433

along the counter until she was facing the two women.

'Oi! That's my brother you're talking about! And my best friend. And they *weren't* having an affair.'

The first woman flushed, but the second held her ground.

'How would you know? You're hardly lily-white yourself, if what I hear is true.'

'And your husband is someone I wasn't lily-white *with*,' Trudie responded, the manager appearing from the back room to see what the disturbance was about.

'My husband and you?' the woman repeated, her voice faltering. '*My husband and you?*'

Trudie smiled grimly. 'That should teach you to keep your mouth shut.'

'Miss Williams!' Mr Philpot said, his voice raised. 'If you please . . .'

But Trudie wasn't about to let the matter drop. Looking round at the dozen or so gawking customers in Myers, she said, loud enough for everyone to hear: 'What Beth did, she did for her own reasons. No one pushed her into it. There was no affair between my brother and Rose.'

'Miss Williams!' Mr Philpot blustered. 'Will you *please* stop –'

'Rose was attacked by her husband, and he buggered off because he's the guilty one.'

'If you don't stop now –'

But Trudie wasn't stopping for anyone. 'Stuart Fallow was a violent coward! Rose left him because he was no good.' She looked round the aghast, listening faces. 'Now, if anyone wants to say anything else, please feel free to say it to my face –'

'You're fired,' Mr Philpot said bluntly.

'Yeah,' Trudie replied, taking off her overall and flinging it onto the counter, 'and ain't that a loss.'

FIFTY-FIVE

The spring shuffled past. Along with the news of the war people gossiped about Gull Road, the Bradshaws and the Williamses. When the body was recovered, Beth's funeral was a quiet affair, Lester coming home briefly, Rose seeing him only for an hour with her father present. Her guilt coloured everything. And nothing anyone said could lessen it.

'You were right,' she told Maisie. 'I should have listened to you. Should have stopped writing to Lester.'

'Beth was always highly strung,' Maisie replied, gently. 'Everyone knew that. She was too excitable for her own good. Come on, Rose, you can't let it ruin your life.'

'But it has,' she countered, staring at Maisie's sleeping child on the rocking chair. 'I can't think about Lester without thinking about Beth, seeing her dead –'

'She did it so you'd do just that. To get her revenge,' Maisie answered, taking some clothes down off the rack and beginning to iron a blouse. 'I know you shouldn't speak ill of the dead, but she was wicked to do what she did – leave her own child, just to spite her husband. And you.'

'We gave her enough reason.'

'You loved each other before she came between you,' Maisie replied firmly, touching the iron with the tip of her forefinger to see if it was hot enough. 'Lester was wrong to act the way he did. But Joe says he had stopped seeing Beth before you and Lester got serious. Seeing as how that's the

435

case, Beth should have stayed out of it – but she didn't. She blackmailed Lester into marrying her instead. Everyone knows that. So she only had herself to blame for what happened.'

'Maisie, that's not like you,' Rose said, surprised by the severity of her friend's judgement.

'I just don't hold with what she did. Beth knew the chaos and the scandal she'd cause. She knew what it would do to Lester, to you, and to her son. But it didn't stop her. Men are dying everyday in this war – men who would do anything to stay alive. And she takes her own life . . . She was crazy.'

'She was confused.'

Maisie shook her head. 'Only up to a point. I still think some part of her planned it, just like she planned to get pregnant to get Lester.'

'People look at me so oddly now,' Rose confided, passing Maisie another blouse. 'Like they're wary of me. The only place I feel comfortable is at the racecourse, when I'm with Dad. Everyone at the track automatically took my side, no questions asked.'

'You were always at home there.'

'Maisie?'

She looked up from her ironing, her head on one side. 'What is it?'

'What am I going to do about Lester? He loves me, I know he does. He always has. He writes to me and tells me that we can sort this out in time, that we'll be together after the war. He even dreams of getting Daniel back from his grandmother. Like he wants to get a real family back. But it's changed between us. If not for him – for me. I still want to love Lester, but I *daren't*. You see, every time I think about him, I see Beth. Every time I hear his voice, I hear hers. Every time I see him, I see her. She didn't come between us in life, but now she's dead she's more his wife than I could ever be.'

* * *

He would get his own back. He would, one day. He would show everyone. And not by topping himself either. Oh no, Stuart thought, he wanted to *see* everyone's face when he got his revenge. He might be cowed now, hidden away in some godforsaken hospital on the other side of Manchester, but his time would come.

Slowly Stuart turned back to the shelves and began to stack them with medical supplies. It was a lousy job, but it would do for the time being. After all, he could hardly say who he really was, could he? Who would hire a qualified dentist for menial work without asking embarrassing questions? And he couldn't set up his own practice either. Not for a while, not until things had settled down.

And it was all because of that bitch Rose. That bitch of a wife of his. She had cheated on him, made him feel like dog dirt, and after all he'd done for her. *Married her*, for God's sake. Some little tart from Gull Road – sneaked in by that vicious cow, Hettie . . . Breathing heavily, Stuart tried to calm himself. He would show everyone – his father, the old fool, Hettie, and that bitch wife of his. *And, most of all, Lester Williams . . .*

Seething, Stuart turned back to the shelves. Let everyone treat him like a minion for the time being. He would recover. He would get back on top – and then he'd make sure that everyone who had hurt him would be repaid threefold.

'Hey, you! You new here?'

Stuart turned to find a thin man with large, protruding eyes, watching him.

'Who are you?'

'Name's Gunner, Ray Gunner,' the man replied, putting out his hand. Instinctively disliking him, Stuart nevertheless responded, shaking the bony, moist hand.

'I'm Frank, Frank Biggs,' said Stuart.

'Pleased to meet you. You come from round here?'

'Blackpool,' Stuart lied.

'Blackpool!' Gunner repeated. 'I could tell you some stories about Blackpool. I used to know a bookie who lived there. You'd have remembered him if you'd met him. Had a squint, and a daughter with a squint too. Only she had hers fixed.'

Stuart flinched. He was talking about Rose! He was talking about *his wife*. Who would have believed it?

'That Bradshaw bugger ruined me, he did,' Gunner went on, self-pity in his voice. 'Spread all kinds of lies about me. That's why I had to leave, lie low for a while. Only came back up North a little while ago. Luckily the coppers lost interest in me when the war started, turned their attention to bigger things.'

'You never got your own back?' Stuart asked, trying to keep his voice emotionless.

'No, but I will, one day.' Gunner's expression was shifty, suspicious suddenly. 'Why did you leave Blackpool?'

'Woman trouble,' Stuart replied, turning away. 'Some bitch floored me. Seems we both have reason to get our own back.'

FIFTY-SIX

Gilbert's leg was aching, but he would have to carry on. He only had one scene left, and it was his big moment. Always brought the house down. On the front row sat Miss Vernon, beaming at him. Quite what she expected, Gilbert didn't know, but as the months had passed her adoration was becoming less and less distressing. Almost pleasant.

'My lords, I have today . . .' Gilbert boomed on, working himself up into a Shakespearean lather. Oh, he was on a roll, he thought. Just let the manager see this performance and he was sure to be booked for another pantomime come Christmas. War or no bloody war. '. . . my liege, MY LIEGE . . .'

The audience – all twenty of them – were ecstatic.

The performance over, Gilbert took two bows and limped back to the dressing room he used to share with the Hungarian jugglers, who, sadly, had been called up. Easing off his boots, Gilbert slid his swollen feet into their Turkish slippers and then leaned back in his seat. It was hard work, entertainment.

'Oh, Mr Beardsley,' Miss Vernon trilled, walking in, her hands clasped as if in some form of artistic supplication. 'You outdid yourself tonight.'

'Was I good?'

'Good! Better than good, fine. Excellent. Exemplary. You made everyone else on the stage disappear. I thought to myself, I have never seen anyone who could handle – is that the correct word? – *handle* a stage so wonderfully. Your voice rose . . .' hers did the same, 'in a crescendo of feeling. When I was a young girl, I was sometimes known to tread the boards myself, but now I watch you I see that I was a fool to think I could act.'

Glowing, Gilbert smiled. He had dropped off into a doze several seconds back, but soon recovered.

'Miss Vernon, you're too kind . . .'

'Kindness has nothing to do with it!' she replied. 'It would be easy to be kind – to lie, to beguile a person with falsehoods – but I do not have to lie. You were superb.'

With that, she sat down, passing Gilbert his cold cream. Thanking her, he applied the cream to his face and began to smear off his make-up.

'Your sister – so firm, so full of life – told me today that your nephews were due home on leave in July. You must be so proud of them – only another month to wait. And they must be so proud of you – having a famous actor for an uncle.'

'Well –'

'I said to my late mother once, if I ever have the chance to be friendly with someone very talented, I would consider myself a lucky woman. And here I am – a friend of yours. I may call myself a friend, may I? I wouldn't want to be presumptuous.'

'You're a *good* friend, Miss Vernon,' Gilbert replied, letting her wipe off his make-up and comb his hair.

It was very pleasant, the way she was looking after him. Very pleasant indeed – all the fuss, without the physicality. And she was a dab hand at teaching him his lines. Something his sister was getting more and more impatient with. Still, no wonder. Poor Ruby had been so worried about Lester, and Beth Hodges killing herself like that . . . Gilbert shivered. Still, his nephews coming home next month would cheer Ruby up.

'. . . and when we were children, Mr Beardsley, my brother used to tell me . . .'

Oh, yes, Gilbert thought, letting Miss Vernon's chatter pour over him like a warm shower, life was getting sweeter for him, finally. No more Louis Wilkes, no more tight, bright little boys under the pier. Lovely as they'd been, they'd only brought him distress.

This was better: being older, with a bad leg and a dotty old bird to look after you.

The gossip died down. For a while. On the war front, the Russians foiled the Nazi offensive, just as Stalin had predicted, and the USA routed Japan in the Battle of Midway. As Royal Marines, Lester and Joe were involved in more hit-and-run tactics around France – dropping in, then making quick escapes, the excitement buoying up Lester, but gradually, insidiously, draining Joe.

Then Lester wrote to say that he had been slightly injured – 'nothing to worry about, only a graze to the leg. The bullet didn't have my name on it . . .'

'This time,' Ruby said, passing the note to Rose. 'God knows where they keep sending those boys. And you daren't ask them. Lester goes hairless if you pry.'

Rose read the letter, then passed it back to Ruby. She didn't like to mention that she had already received her own missive that morning.

'When I were fighting –'

'The only thing you fight,' Ruby said to her husband shortly, 'is a cold!' She looked back to Rose and winked. 'They might give Lester some leave – seeing as how he's been injured.'

'You think so?'

'Fat chance.'

In the weeks since Beth's suicide, Ruby had made it clear to everyone that she was on Rose's side. She had never liked Beth, so it was easy for her. But she missed her grandson

Daniel. Repeated enquiries after his health had been ignored by his grandmother, Mrs Hodges spreading lies about Lester around the town whenever she had the opportunity. And Rose wasn't exempt from her criticism either. To hear Mrs Hodges tell it, Rose had stolen Lester away from Beth. Her daughter's death was all Rose's fault.

Some agreed with her. All the people who had been put out by Rose's rise in fortune; all the ones who had watched her glorious progress under the Widow Miller's wing, now joined forces to carp about her. She thought she was too good for Gull Road, they said, well, look where she's ended up! And with a shadow over her name too . . . Back to being a ticktack woman on the track. What a comedown for a dentist's wife.

To Rose it never once seemed a comedown. She might have walked away from the big Lytham house and the money, but so what? She was back with her father and her old friends, the ones who had stuck with her, like Maisie and Ruby – and, unexpectedly, Trudie. All the envy and hatred behind her, Trudie now defended Rose against all comers – and encouraged her relationship with Lester, something Ruby remained cautious about.

'Are you going to write to Lester?'

Rose nodded. 'I'll drop him a line tonight.'

Ruby eyed Rose up and down. 'What about you two? Going to get married?'

'Lester wants –'

'Ah, but what does *Rose* want?' Ruby asked, interrupting her. 'I know my son, he's very charming when he's got a mind to be, and can talk anyone around to his way of thinking. But we're not talking about buying some booth on the pier are we, Rose? We're talking about marriage. About whether you want to marry my son, and – possibly – take on his child. The son he had with Beth.' She folded her massive arms and leaned back in her seat. 'Well?'

'I love Lester –'

'Is that so?' Ruby said simply. 'That's nice, but it's not an answer, is it?'

Before Rose could reply, the back door was flung open, Trudie walking in and flopping down at the kitchen table. Curious, she picked up Lester's letter.

'When d'you get this?' she asked her mother, then paused, looking from Ruby to Rose. 'Oh God! What's going on here?'

'We were having a private conversation.'

'About Lester?' Trudie replied. 'Using the thumb screws, are you, Mam?' She turned to Rose, her voice interrogating. 'And what were you doing on the night of the sixteenth?'

'Cut it out!' Ruby warned her. 'This is serious.'

'Everything's serious,' Trudie replied, slumping further in her seat. 'Nobody laughs any more. I mean, Bunny could have drowned on the *Ark*, but you don't see me with a long face.'

'I should have drowned *you* at birth,' Ruby replied shortly, looking back to Rose. 'Come on, what's your answer?'

Suddenly Rose felt under pressure. This was no idle question from Ruby.

'I don't know,' she replied honestly. 'I love Lester and I want to be with him. But marriage . . . I really don't know. I'm still married to Stuart, and no one's set eyes on him for months. Isn't it a bit premature to talk about marrying again?'

'Sure it is,' Trudie replied deftly, 'but it would make you respectable.'

'Trudie!'

'Oh, come on, Mam, you know it would. If Lester and Rose got hitched everyone would pipe down about Beth killing herself and Lester beating Fallow up.'

'Do you *want* me to marry your son?' Rose asked, her voice so quiet that it caught both women's attention.

Taking in a deep breath, Ruby stared into Rose's face.

A good-looking face, a strong face – but was it the *right* face? She knew Rose had courage – but was it the *right* courage? She knew Rose loved Lester – but was it the *right* love?

'Do you want the truth, Rose?'

'Nothing else.'

'Then here it is. I don't know if you *are* the right woman for Lester –'

'Mam!'

'Be quiet, Trudie! This has nothing to do with you,' Ruby snapped, before turning back to Rose. 'I love you like my own, but my son's not the easiest man to care for. He's too headstrong for his own good. And he always wants what he can't have. Which is fine in business, but not so good in life. God knows what he'll be like when he comes home after the war.' She looked at Rose carefully. 'He's made some big mistakes – I don't want to see him make another.'

Trudie winced again. 'Mam!'

'It's OK,' Rose replied, 'I wanted the truth and that was what I got.' Slowly she rose to her feet and then looked back to Ruby. 'What *would* make me the right woman?'

Ruby jerked her thumb towards the dozing Alfred. 'See him? I'd give my life for him. Go through fire to get him out. God knows why, but I'd do it. Just like he'd do it for me. And *that's* love.' She glanced over to her daughter. 'Wouldn't you do that for Bunny?'

Surprised, Trudie nodded. 'Yeah. I can't believe I'm saying it – but I would.'

Ruby looked back to Rose: 'To put their life above your own – *that's* what makes a woman right for her man. And a man right for his woman.'

One thing was certain: Hettie wasn't about to die for *her* man. In fact, if she could have avoided it, she wouldn't have spent one more day with Cedric Fallow. Didn't anyone realise what she was going through, she wondered, self-pityingly. And who – in God's name – would have thought that the aftereffects of a stroke could have gone on so long without any improvement?

The doctor was as baffled as she was. And so was the next doctor, and the next. They all agreed that Cedric should have been well on the way to recovery by now. After all, they added, the stroke hadn't appeared to be a major one. But as the weeks passed, Cedric did not recover his health, his movement, nor his power of speech.

Daily, the isolated Hettie waited for the post. When it came she rifled through it hurriedly, then threw it down on the hall table in disgust. Oh, of course everyone knew that there was a war on, but the soirées, the bridge club, the ladies' luncheons hadn't stopped. Except for her. Where Hettie had gravely miscalculated was in thinking that people would forget. In peace, maybe they would have done. With Cedric up and about, they might have relented. But in the middle of a war the news that lucky, unenlisted Stuart Fallow had raped his own wife and then run off with his tail between his legs was too much to swallow. He had had so much, had been so lucky – and he had blown it.

They might have pitied Cedric, but they despised Hettie. Her half-hearted attempts to make light of the incident repelled people and the thought that she might be on the side of Stuart was abhorrent. After what he had done, how could she, they muttered. And anyway, wasn't she always going on about Rose being like a daughter to her? What kind of mother would side against her own child in such circumstances? And why? The answer was unpalatable: the Fallows had money, Rose did not.

But Hettie couldn't understand her fall from grace and was peevish with irritation. 'Oh, do eat something, Cedric,' she said, holding a spoonful of soup to his lips.

He took nothing, then finally drank a little, prolonging her torment.

She had wanted to look after him so much, Cedric thought, well now she could do it for life. He stared at his hated wife, this woman who had no morals, no compassion, and mused on his decision. His son had turned out to be a wastrel – worse, an embarrassment. But Stuart had gone. Only Hettie remained. And Hettie – Cedric had decided – was going to stay with him *for life*. That was to be her punishment. And his revenge.

'Cedric, come on . . .' she whined.

His eyes stayed fixed on the spoon. It wouldn't do for him to look up and let his wife see the intelligence in his gaze. For the plan to work, she would have to think him an invalid. Well, wasn't that what she wanted, an invalid? Someone she could help into the grave? Only Cedric wasn't going into any grave. Not without taking Hettie with him.

It was a well-earned reward for all her plotting and scheming. For thrusting that troublesome girl on to his son, for making him into little more than a common criminal. Stuart Fallow – who should have married and had an heir to carry on the line. Stuart Fallow – now a pantomime joke, who had deserted his wife as surely as he would have deserted a regiment. His son, his only son. What a disappointment he had turned out to be.

And then there was his wife. His darling, caring Hettie. Like an anatomist carved up the dead, so she carved up the living . . . After a long pause, Cedric accepted some more soup, taking his time, knowing how his slowness infuriated her. Henrietta – the Widow Miller. *The Widow Fallow* – if she had her way.

Cedric smiled inwardly to himself. Hettie wasn't going to have her own way any more. She might rail against her fate, but she would stay on. Firstly, because she had nowhere else to go, and any desertion would mean her immediate removal from her husband's will. And secondly, because she was stupidly, infallibly optimistic. Hettie would carry on because every day she woke up she would pray that her husband was dead and she was home free – with his money and his house. She would do all the menial tasks demanded

446

of the devoted wife, whilst she dreamed of her escape. She would plot his funeral, her outfit, plan her words of grief, try on various expressions of woe – and wait.

What she didn't know was that Cedric was also waiting. She had ruined him. But he, finally, would be the one to ruin her. In the midst of his disappointment and pain, he had made himself a promise – Henrietta would go before him to the grave, even if she lived to be ninety.

FIFTY-SEVEN

Holding a piece of cloth to the side of Joe's head, Lester rocked him, his eyes staring ahead, fighting panic. Oh Christ, Jesus, he prayed. Oh Jesus . . . He could feel Joe's blood seeping into his own jacket. He had said not to follow him, but Joe had, coming out from the shelter just as the enemy opened fire. Immediately mortar and gunfire had cut Joe up, ripping through his legs and his upper body, sending him spinning round and round like a bloody top.

Doubling back, Lester had grabbed him and then run with Joe over his shoulder, the gunfire still coming. But missing Lester. Hitting Joe. But missing Lester.

'Joe? Joey?' Lester said softly, staring into his brother's face and then looking under the cloth.

The whole left half of Joe's face was gone, the cheek caved in, the bone of the eye socket visible, blood everywhere. Quickly Lester pressed the cloth back on the wound. They would fix him, he reassured himself, the doctors would fix Joe. They did miracles, everyone said that. They did miracles every day. They would fix him . . .

He stared ahead. At least Joe was asleep and not screaming any more. Not calling out, 'Lester! Lester!' over and over again, because he couldn't see his brother and didn't know he was there.

But of course he was. Lester would never have left Joe. Never *had* done. Never *would* . . . And so Lester clung on to his brother and rocked him on that dark road that would take them back to their base at Catterick. The doctors would sort him out there, send him to the nearest hospital. No-one had wanted to take Joe any farther afield. They'd landed near to the camp; Catterick was only minutes away. So at every bump on the road Lester reassured his unconscious brother.

'It's OK, Joe, we're nearly there. It's OK. Hold on.'

She would just finish the page, Maisie thought, and then go to sleep. It was amazing what the people in Hollywood got up to – all those parties and drinking. She found it hard to believe that people lived so recklessly and wanted so much. All she needed to make her happy was her husband and her daughter.

Beside her, Lesley turned over in her sleep. She was very like Joe, same cheekiness he had . . . No point worrying about Joe, Maisie decided; she would just read a bit more and then sleep. Happily she picked up the book again. Now where had she been? It was all about Joan Crawford and how she did her hair. It was easy to look like a movie star, the piece said. You can create the same hairdo for yourself at home, using just sugar water. Maisie decided that she would do just that, try the style out tomorrow.

With luck she would have it perfect by the time Joe got home.

Just across the road, at Sea View, Lester woke his mother, Ruby jumping out of bed and following him downstairs.

'Are you all right? Where's Joe?' Her eyes widened. 'Where's Joe?'

How could he say it? Say – they've moved Joe to Manchester Infirmary when they saw how bad he was. Say – he's lost an arm and a leg. Jesus . . . how *could* he say it?

'He's alive –'

'Thank God!'

'– but he's bad, Mam. He's bad.'

She took the news squarely, still standing. 'How bad?'

'He's lost an arm and a leg. And he's disfigured.'

Her eyes never left her son's face. 'What else? I know there's something else.'

'He's blind, Ma. Joe's blind.'

Shaken, she reached out to her son and held him, Lester dry-eyed, expressionless with shock.

'I *told* him to stay behind! I told him to let me go first, to see if it was safe –'

'It'll be all right,' Ruby said, not knowing if anything would ever be all right again.

'– but he followed me, Ma. He bloody followed me!'

'I know. I know,' Ruby replied, holding on to Lester tightly. Joe, her Joe, blind. Her lad . . .

'Will he live?'

'They say he will.'

'Thank God –'

'No!' Lester said, pulling away. 'You don't want him to live like that. No one wants to live like that.'

'Joe's got a family –'

'Maisie can't see him!' Lester said firmly. 'He wouldn't want her to see him.'

'*She's his wife!*'

'You haven't seen him!' Lester shouted. 'You haven't bloody seen him!'

'Lester?'

Alerted, the nurse moved over to Joe's bed and touched his forehead. 'Your brother said he would be back as soon as possible.'

'Lester?' Joe asked again helplessly, his mind confused. '*We're hit – Lester!*'

The nurse soothed him, resting him back against the pillows, a doctor walking in and giving Joe sedation.

'You've been in the wars, young man –'

'My brother?'

'Is fine. No injuries.'

They could both see Joe relax, the doctor continuing carefully, 'but you've got some serious injuries –'

'Will I live?'

'Yes.'

Joe nodded, then felt the bandages around his face. 'I can't see. I've got bandages on – why's that?'

'You rest now –'

'Why have I got bandages on?' Joe repeated, his voice rising with fright. 'Lester! LESTER!'

Gently, the doctor touched him on the shoulder. 'Your brother had to go back to his unit. He'll come and see you soon. You have to be very brave –'

For a long moment Joe lay there, without moving or responding. The only real fear he had was that Lester wasn't there. How could he face anything without his brother? And then he realised that Lester had no choice. He would have been recalled, back on duty.

For the first time in his life Joe was completely alone.

'Tell me what happened.'

'You were hit by mortar and gunfire.'

'I don't remember . . .' Joe said distantly. 'Will I be all right?'

'With time you'll be able to adjust –'

'To what?'

'You should rest –'

'Oh, Doctor,' Joe said quietly, 'I'm not tired.'

He could see nothing, just hear his own head noises, which seemed incredibly loud. And the noises of people moving, the rustle of what he took to be the nurse's skirt and the sound of a car scrunching on gravel.

'Joe, please rest. We can talk in the morning.'

'Let's talk now, Doctor,' Joe said, turning his head in the direction of the physician's voice. 'What's happened to me?'

'You've lost an arm . . . and a leg.'

Nodding, Joe turned his head back, as though staring up at the ceiling. 'No more dancing then?'

'Not yet,' the doctor replied, smiling.

'What else?'

'Rest now –'

'Come on, be a man,' Joe said, teasing him.

'You're blind, Joe.'

You're blind, Joe . . . You're blind . . . Never to see Maisie's face again, or Lesley's, or Lester's, or any of his family. Never to see a garden, a tram, or read a paper. Never to see colours, the pier, the sea on a cold March day. Never to know how much money's in your hand. Oh God, Joe thought: to be helped along, to be pitied, a war hero with a medal he couldn't even see . . .

'Christ!'

'Joe, be calm, you'll adjust –'

'I don't want to adjust! I want my limbs back, and my eyes, and I want to walk out of here!' He stopped, mortified to feel tears coming. 'Let me alone, please.'

The doctor hesitated, but when Joe said nothing else he left the room, pausing in the corridor outside, thinking. He had a son around Joe's age, fighting in Burma.

'It's a blessing he's blind, the way he looks, poor thing,' the nurse said sympathetically. 'Will he live?'

'He's lost an arm and a leg, he may lose the other leg. He's disfigured and blind. He'll never be able to get about on his own again. His face is all but destroyed, but as far as we know, no internal organs have been seriously damaged.' The doctor shook his head. 'So in answer to your question, Nurse, yes, God help him, he'll live.'

Wide awake, Ruby lay in bed, Alfred snoring beside her. She could see nothing, with the blackout curtains drawn, and the room was pungently dark, full of spectres. For some reason she remembered her younger days, when she had first bought the van and made a living selling hot food to the truckers. Like Alfred . . . And then she remembered when she was first married and then having twins. Two sons – now that was something to be proud of.

Life had, to all intents and purposes, been good to her. She had had to work hard, but she'd ended up with Sea View and a nice little business – despite the war halving her profits. Even her disappointment in Trudie had diminished, Bunny Lambert making his timely appearance. All in all, life had treated her well. So why was she railing at God for hurting Joe? When she knew how many other women had lost their lads, shouldn't she be thanking God for *saving* him?

'I feel so angry,' she said to Father Anthony when he called by later that morning. 'I know I shouldn't, but I do. Our poor Joe, blinded – and worse, by the sound of it. I'll know tomorrow, when I've seen him at Manchester Infirmary.'

'You're going to visit?' the priest enquired, wondering why he hadn't seen the monumental Mrs Williams in church for over six years. Another lapsed Catholic come back to the fold in wartime. 'Do you think that's wise?'

'He's my son! Of course it's wise!'

'I mean, in his condition. I thought you told me that your other son said you shouldn't see him.'

'That was just Lester being protective,' Ruby responded. 'I have to visit Joe. He's been in this hospital for two days now, and has had no visitors. What the hell – excuse me, Father – will he think has happened?'

'Has his wife seen him?'

Ruby shook her head. 'No, not yet. I'm going first. I reckon that'll be best. Then I'll know what to tell Maisie.'

Father Anthony sucked his teeth. 'You must pray that your son accepts his injuries with a good grace.'

'*A good grace!*' Ruby exploded. 'Having an arm and leg shot off and being blinded he has to accept *with a good grace*! Who said that, when he's at home?'

'God, actually.'

453

Ruby waved aside the words and God with a whisk of her hand. 'I won't hear another word! I couldn't think why I didn't go to church any more, but you've reminded me, Father.' Hoisting the priest to his feet, Ruby showed him the door.

'Mrs Williams, we have to come to terms with what God has decided for us.'

'And what if God has decided that we should argue with him, hey? What then?'

Whilst the priest was thinking of an answer, she shut the door in his face.

It would have made her laugh at any other time, but not now. Instead Ruby changed into her best clothes and called for Alfred, his porkpie hat jammed on the back of his head, his suit newly brushed. It was a nice touch, Ruby thought, and she hadn't even had to ask him to do it. Together they walked down Gull Road to the station, passing Clovis, who sent her best, and Nan who watched, silently, from her window.

For once the noise and bustle of the town seemed worrisome to Ruby. Strangely she wanted to be back home, safe in her own four walls, but that was out of the question. They were going to see Joe. Whatever Lester had said.

'Hello there, Ruby,' a voice called out.

Ruby turned to see Len standing in his doorway.

'Hello there, Len. We're just going to see Joe.'

He blew out his cheeks. 'Hardly any trains running, and it's a long trek to Manchester.'

'We'll manage.'

'You'll do better than that,' Len said shortly. 'I'll take you over.'

'You can't! You'd use up all your petrol coupons,' Ruby replied, 'and lose a day's work.'

'Things are slow at the moment, and the race meeting's been cancelled for later,' Len replied, adding: 'I'd like to take you over to see Joe. Honest I would.'

He was true to his word. After leaving a hurried note for Rose, Len brought his battered Austin round and then helped Alfred into the back seat, wedging him firmly between the door and the arm rest. Holding onto his porkpie hat, Alfred, without complaining, allowed himself to be jammed in, and his legs scrunched up, as his wife got into the front.

'Did I ever tell you about when *I* were a driver?' Alfred asked, only minutes into the trip.

Ruby shook her head. 'You never did, luv. Tell us now.'

'Well, it were in the last war. We were posted to . . .'

Past the window went the views of Blackpool and then the car snaked into the countryside, winding its way over to Manchester. And all through the long journey Alfred talked about his exploits, Ruby half listening, but soothed by his words, as a child is soothed with a lullaby. Now and again Len would interject, picking Alfred up on some point in his story, but nothing stopped him from continuing.

The morning slid on, every mile bringing them closer, every turn of the track making an image bigger and bigger in Ruby's head. Joe blind, mutilated. Joe, her Joe, hurt beyond recognition.

'Don't go and see him, Mam, don't go . . .' – hadn't those been the very words Lester had used? *Don't go . . .*

But she had to. Joe was her child, after all and – how bad could it be? How could her lovely, pretty Joe ever frighten her?

'. . . and they said they would have to shoot me at dawn . . .' Alfred went on, Len laughing to himself as the car moved into unfamiliar landscape.

'Soon be there now,' he said at last.

'I thought it would be further.' Ruby's voice dimmed. She was close now. Close to her Joe, to her boy.

But when Len drew up in the car park outside the hospital she stayed rigid in her seat.

'Ruby? Are you all right?'

A moment passed, then, slowly, she got out of the Austin, helping Alfred from the back seat.

'I'm fine, Len. Just fine.'

Len would tell the story many times over in the years to come. How the three of them walked down the hospital corridor, finally being directed to a separate side ward. He would recall how they had looked through a porthole window to see a body, its top half shielded with a screen. And then Len would describe how Ruby walked in, hand in hand with Alfred. And how she turned at the last moment.

'Come with us.'

'You sure?' Len asked, surprised.

'I'm sure.'

He would stop at that part of the story and roll a cigarette, or cough, to control his feelings. Then he would continue . . . Joe Williams had been lying on his back, the sheet flat where he was missing an arm and a leg. His eyes were covered by bandages, his face mutilated, only an inch of flesh remaining perfect. The handsome young man was now a ghoul.

But Ruby didn't see it. Whilst Alfred hung back and Len looked away, Ruby walked over to her son.

'Hello, luv,' she said, as though everything was normal. 'It's me.' And then she leaned down, found the only unspoiled patch of skin, and kissed it lovingly. 'It's me, Joe, luv. It's your mam.'

FIFTY-EIGHT

'I can't bear to see him like that,' Lester said, his voice breaking, 'Jesus, he can't live like that.'

Gently, Rose took his hand. 'Does Joe know how bad it is?'

'No, and naturally Maisie wants to see him. She can't do that, though. It would kill her. I told Ma not to go, but she would and now she's talking bloody nonsense. All about how she'll take Joe to see that MacIndoe doctor and he'll build his face up again.' Lester hung his head. 'Joe's lost an arm and a leg, and he's blind. Jesus Christ! What difference would it make if they repaired his face?'

'It might make a difference to Joe.'

'I know my brother!' Lester snapped. 'He would rather be dead than be like this!'

Resting her head on Lester's shoulder, Rose kept her voice steady. 'He'll adjust. Joe's got family, Maisie loves him and they've got Lesley. He'll want to live for them.'

'How do you know?' Lester countered. 'I wouldn't want to live for anyone if I looked like that.'

Stung, Rose resisted the temptation to ask the obvious question and instead pressed on.

'But Joe isn't you, Lester. He never was. He never had your ambition. He has different values. And a life that might not seem like much to you, might still mean a lot to him. And to Maisie –'

'She won't think that when she sees him.'

'She already has.'

'*When?*'

'Yesterday. I only knew about it when she came back and told me. She'd gone on her own to see Joe. Said she wanted it that way.'

'How did she take it?'

'Hard to tell,' Rose replied truthfully. 'She was very quiet and she'd obviously been crying, but she was determined to make the best of it. Talked about how the doctors had told her Joe could have false limbs, and how –'

'And false eyes?' Lester said bitterly. 'Did they mention how they could make him see again?'

'They're doing their best!'

'Which is what I should have done!' Lester shouted, standing up and walking over to the window. 'I told Joe to stay behind. I told him to wait – but he followed me. I should have known he would. I should have looked back, checked.'

'It wasn't your fault –'

'It *was* my fault!' Lester snapped. 'He's my brother, my twin. I was supposed to look out for him.'

'Who said?' Rose replied. 'Who said that, Lester? Who laid down the rule that *you* should always look after *him*? Why didn't Joe look after you? Why were you always responsible for him?'

'That was the way it was.'

'That was the way you both *wanted* it to be,' Rose replied gently, moving over to Lester and standing next to him.

Gull Road was empty and dark, no lights showing in any windows. Only yards away was Sea View, only doors away was Maisie and Joe's house.

'I *liked* looking after him,' Lester admitted finally. 'It felt good keeping an eye out for Joe.'

'Lester, don't give up on him.'

'I wouldn't give up on my brother!' he retorted sharply. 'What the hell made you say that?'

'Because you referred to him in the past tense,' Rose said quietly, 'as though he was dead. And he isn't, Lester. He's still your brother and he probably needs you now more than he ever did.'

On 16 August Joe Williams' other leg was amputated. Complications set in with an infection, and then gangrene followed. He was for a week in and out of consciousness, unaware of who he was, or who anyone was around him. At times he would be delirious, babbling nonsense; at other times he would rock his head from side to side on the pillow, the open wound of his cheek gaping under his bandaged eyes.

Their daughter was too young to see her father, Maisie told Rose. She wouldn't understand. To be honest neither did she. But Maisie reassured herself that surgery would repair Joe's face, make him presentable. Then, as the days wore on, Maisie came to accept that Joe was never going to be anything but a freak. The doctors might fit him with false limbs, but he would never be able to see where he was going, would fall and stumble around like a blind drunk. It would be too much to ask of anyone, but especially gentle, courageous Joe.

So when the second infection set in, Maisie stopped praying for Joe to recover. She stopped seeing the vicar and stopped going to church. And she waited for the inevitable. And longed for it. As she had never longed for anything, she longed for her husband to die.

When he had gone, she would learn to live with it. Tell Lesley about all the wonderful things Joe had done, and put up a photograph of him, handsome and young. She would keep him alive without medication, bandages, blood or surgery – because Joe would live in her memory. And in time, please God, she would forget the deformed body with the missing face.

When Joe died. . . . Which they all knew was inevitable.

* * *

'We could bring him home,' Ruby said in the darkness as she lay next to Alfred. 'You know, let him be here when he . . . goes.'

'No point moving him, luv. Joe wouldn't know.'

Sighing, Ruby turned over and buried her face against her husband's chest. 'I keep waiting for them to tell us he's . . . you know.'

'I know, luv.'

'It's been days and he's gone on and on. Why doesn't he let go? The doctors all expected him to be dead by now.'

'Maybe Joe's got a reason to live,' Alfred said, gazing at the ceiling. He couldn't think of any words to comfort his wife or himself, so instead he reverted to what he always did. 'Hey, Ruby, did I ever tell you about when I were a nipper and stole a church candlestick?'

Despite herself, Ruby smiled. 'No, luv, go on.'

'I were ten, or maybe eleven, smart as a whip, and there I was in the church . . . and the priest . . .'

Thank God, Ruby thought as she listened. Keep telling me stories, luv. Make them as silly and crazy as you like, but talk to me. And make me forget, luv. Make me forget . . .

'I've got a rag rug for Maisie,' Clovis said, walking into Nan's house and sitting down. 'Something to cheer her up. God knows, she needs it. Her Joe will die any day now, from what I hear.'

Looking up from her cooking, Nan shrugged. 'Maybe. Maybe not.'

'He can't recover! And who'd want him to, like that, poor luv? I mean, he'd never be able to do anything for himself – not even get about, and that's no good for a man, feeling helpless. No, it's sad, but it'll be better when he's passed on. Better for everyone – Joe included.' Clovis leaned forward and stared eagerly at Nan's pastry. 'That's nice, where did you get that lemon curd?'

Nan gave her a warning look and Clovis leaned back in

her seat hurriedly. 'Yes, it'll be a relief when he goes, poor lad. But no one could live like that.' Sniffing, she leaned forward again. 'You've got *eggs*! Dear Lord, Nan, however did you get eggs with all the rationing?'

Again she was met with a warning look, so Clovis reluctantly continued her one-sided conversation.

'Mutilated, he is. Torn apart. Like nothing you've ever seen,' she went on. 'Poor Maisie, enough to turn her brain. And as for Ruby – well, how could you see your own like that and carry on?' She stopped short, her nostrils twitching. 'I smell meat! You've never got *meat*!'

With a flourish, Nan opened the oven door and pulled out a meat pie. Goggle-eyed, Clovis watched the aromatic steam rising from the air holes in the pastry, her tongue running over her lips, saliva collecting at the corners of her mouth.

'By God, that's a tasty meal for anyone,' she said, looking at the pie hungrily and then glancing over to Nan, her voice accusing. 'Are you going to eat all of it *yourself*?'

'It's for Maisie and Lesley,' Nan replied simply, banging the oven door closed and then placing something on a plate in front of Clovis.

Eagerly she looked down – then her face fell. A lumpen, cold, rock bun stared up at her.

'Are you sure you can spare it?' she asked meanly.

'If you don't want it –'

'No! No!' Clovis assured her, taking a greedy bite. 'God knows, I wouldn't want to offend you by refusing, luv.'

FIFTY-NINE

But Joe didn't die. Somehow he overcame the infection and lived, although his heart had been seriously weakened. Ruby and Maisie visited him constantly. And sometimes Rose joined them. In her letters to Lester she told him all about Joe's progress; about how the doctors were declaring it a miracle. He wasn't out of the woods yet. But his recovery was remarkable.

Rose would never have said it, but she wondered just how remarkable the recovery was for Joe.

'Hey, you were miles away, luv,' Len said, watching his daughter. 'Penny for them.'

'I was thinking about Joe.'

Len pulled a face. 'I'm one of the few who'll say it – he should have died.'

'Lester thinks so too,' Rose replied, looking away from her father to stare into the fire. 'He blames himself. I thought he would come to terms with it, but he hasn't. All he can think about is Joe, how he let his brother down. It's becoming an obsession.'

'Because it's the first thing he's failed at,' Len replied perceptively. 'Lester's been a success in everything he's turned his hand to. But not this. And worse, it's his brother and he can't ever make it right.'

'It's not for him to make it right. It's up to God, or whatever you believe in.'

Len eyed his daughter quizzically. 'Do you believe in God?'

'I'm too much of a coward not to,' she replied, laughing when her father did. 'I dunno, Dad. I look at Joe and wonder what kind of God would do that. And then I look at Maisie and see how much she still loves her husband and think – that's proof of God. But I don't really know.'

'I don't suppose Lester has much time for God.'

'I think God and Lester fell out the day Joe was injured,' Rose replied evenly. 'To be honest, I don't think Lester is in awe of anyone – let alone someone he can't even see.'

Len nodded, reaching for his baccy. 'I reckon it helps to believe that there's someone bigger than you are. Stops you getting arrogant.' He paused to set a light to his cigarette. 'I think you can only tell what a man's really like not when he can *do* something, but when he *can't*. That tells you his real character. When his hands are tied, when he's completely useless – then he shows his true colours.'

Dr Leigh was watching the monumental Ruby Williams. He was thinking that if he was ever helpless he would like someone as big – and as fierce – on his side.

'So when can we bring him home, Doctor?'

'Not for a while, Mrs Williams. Joe has a long way to go before he can even think of going home. In fact, you might consider having Joe placed somewhere more suitable for his needs.' Dr Leigh paused, then tried to explain. 'There are places, quite nearby, where Joe could have a happy life –'

'You mean a home,' Ruby said flatly, turning to Alfred, next to her. 'He means a home! You hear that? The doctor doesn't think we can look after our own son –'

'Mrs Williams, I know you mean well. I understand your feelings, but you have to think this out. Joe is not a child, he's a married man. If he wanted to go home, he would probably want to go to his married home –'

463

'No problem. Maisie lives only a few houses away from us.'

'– and then his wife would have to do everything for him. Joe can't walk, and because he has only one arm he can't dress himself. He's blind, he can't see his way around. He would have to rely on his wife for everything –'

'Maisie's a good girl, and she knows she would have our full support. Doesn't she, Alfred?'

He nodded, his porkpie hat wobbling precariously.

'Mrs Williams, listen to me, please,' the doctor said calmly. 'We're not talking about a child here. We're talking about a man. Joe is not a lightweight. It would be more than his wife could manage, lifting him in and out of bed, washing him –'

'We could help her,' Ruby insisted. 'We could all pull together.'

There was a long pause before Dr Leigh spoke again.

'We're all forgetting the most important thing – what does Joe want?'

'And? What *does* he want?' Ruby barked. 'To come home, I'll be bound!'

'No. He wants to stay here. Or somewhere they can look after him.'

'He never said that!' Ruby exploded. 'And if he did, you don't want to listen. He's just depressed, that's all. I know Joe –'

'He *is* depressed,' the doctor agreed sombrely, 'very depressed. With good reason. But in the end, I have to listen to what my patient wants – not what his family want.' Dr Leigh picked his words with care. 'Joe was a very active young man. He misses that, he misses being able-bodied, being able to see. He doesn't want to be a burden, a cripple for his wife and family to look after. He wants to keep his pride. You can understand that, can't you?'

Ruby stared at the doctor for a long moment before

replying. 'I understand. But let's just give him a bit more time, hey? Before anyone puts him in some home, let's just see if Joe doesn't come round.' She glanced over to her husband. 'If Lester was here, he'd rally.'

'He would that,' Alfred agreed.

'We'll review the situation in a month, in September,' Dr Leigh replied, getting to his feet. 'But then we must decide what to do. And that means what's best for Joe – no one else.'

Dearest Rose,

I'm due some leave at the end of the month – 24 hours, they say. Not much, but better than nothing. Tell Joe, will you? And tell him to hang on.

How are you, my love? Things have been tough for us, haven't they? But it will all be better before long. We'll get over the bad patch, get Joe organised, and then we'll have our whole lives left to live together. And a ballroom to finish, remember?

I love you. I can't say any more. Or any less. I couldn't live if I didn't have you.

Lester

My darling Lester,

I look forward so much to seeing you and holding you again. I miss you so much, every day drags.

Joe is holding on and I told him you were coming home to see him soon.

As for me, I want to see you too. I miss you, Lester, and being apart from you only makes it harder to bear. We can sort everything out, I know, and we will. When the war's over. When the world is back to normal.

I was scared before. I was *afraid* to love you, but not any more. I see Joe and now realise how

precious life is. And as for love – I would give
everything for your love. Everything I have, everything I own, everything I am, I would give for you.

    Your loving, loving

    Rose

Weighed down under a pile of files, Stuart was struggling
to open the door of the hospital storage room, finally pushing it open with his back and almost falling in. Annoyed,
he slammed down the papers and turned back to close the
door. Bloody manager, he thought, exasperated. Who the
hell was he to talk to him like that? All he was was some
old crock that had been drafted in because of the war and
now thought he was running the blasted place. Seething,
Stuart leaned against one of the many filing cabinets. To
talk to him as though he was a no one – when he was
Stuart Fallow! It was getting unbearable.

Sullenly, he looked round the cramped, dusty filing room
and then his gaze came to rest on the pile of patients' notes
ready to be filed away. He would do it in his own time,
and not a moment before – although the sound of footsteps outside made Stuart leap back to work.

Hurrying in, Roy Howell grinned. 'You look guilty. What
were you up to?'

'Nothing,' Stuart replied, leaning back against the filing
cabinet as Howell offered him a smoke. 'You're joking!
We'll get caught –'

'Nah,' Howell assured him. 'The old bugger's gone over
to the main hospital for a while. And if I know him, he'll
be there for at least fifteen minutes. He's a thing about
one of the sisters over there.' Howell's expression grew
animated. 'Here, you'll never guess what I've just found
out.'

'What?'

'You know I told you about the Bradshaws,' he had
Stuart's full attention, 'well, someone from their street's in

here. I didn't put two and two together at first, but then I saw bloody Rose Bradshaw visiting.'

Stuart's heartbeat quickened. 'What?'

'I looked up the notes to see *who* she was visiting. It's Joe Williams.'

Brother of Lester.

'Cut up like you'd not believe. Not half of him left. Jesus, you should see him.'

Emotionless, Stuart asked: 'What happened to him?'

'He was a Royal Marine – one of those bleeding hot-shot heroes – and he got injured on a mission.' Howell dropped his voice, leaning towards Stuart. 'It should have been Len Bradshaw. I'd like to have seen him laid out.'

Stuart was finding it hard to breathe. So Lester's beloved brother had ended up in the very hospital where he worked? Joe Williams, helpless, half dead. And Rose – like a good family friend – had been visiting. And if Rose had called by, so would Lester.

'Where is he?'

Howell frowned: 'Huh?'

'Where's this Joe fellow?'

'In a private ward, at the back, separated off from the rest on the fourth floor. One of the nurses said he was real mutilated, no legs, one arm, face missing. And blind. Not much of a hero now, hey?'

'Not much of anything, it seems.'

'Yeah, right,' Howell agreed, relishing the ghoulish prospect. 'I wouldn't mind sneaking a look. How about it?'

For a moment Stuart felt complete revulsion for the man beside him, but covered it well.

'Nah, I'm squeamish.'

'I hope his wife isn't,' Howell replied, stubbing out his cigarette on the filing cabinet and putting the dimp behind his ear. 'See you later.'

'Wait a minute –'

Howell turned. 'What?'

467

'Do people visit him?'

'I told you, Rose Bradshaw's been in, and his parents. They let people visit when they want,' Howell sneered. 'War heroes – always special cases, hey?'

'Yeah,' Stuart agreed, 'always special cases.'

That night Stuart stayed late at the hospital. He waited until all the other menial staff had left and then made his way upstairs to the fourth floor. It was a dark night, made darker by the blackout. The small side room off the main ward faced him, its door closed, a label reading 'Joe Williams'. He knew the name and something of the man. A nice guy, which was a pity, Stuart thought. It should have been Lester.

He could hear movement inside – a nurse's voice low and soothing – but no sound from the patient. His hand itched to open the door, to look in, to see the ghoul on the bed, but he didn't dare. Instead he waited in the shadows. A minute passed, then another. Finally the nurse left, the door swinging closed behind her.

And then Stuart took his chance. Silently he crept in, and moved over to the bed. Christ, he thought, as he looked at what remained of Joe Williams. It was incredible to see a man so disfigured still breathing.

'Nurse?' Joe said suddenly. 'Is that you?'

Stuart said nothing. Just kept looking at Joe and remembering his brother. His hated brother, Lester.

'Nurse? Is someone there?'

God, Stuart thought, why didn't he shut up? Someone would hear him. Motionless Stuart stared at the monstrosity. What point was there living like that? He would be better dead. Joe Williams, Lester's beloved brother . . . Rage crept up inside Stuart as he stared at the helpless man. He felt no pity, saw only a way to get his revenge on Lester.

And it would be so easy.

'Is there anyone there?' Joe repeated, moving his head from side to side. 'Please, say something.'

Slowly Stuart moved towards the bed, his shadow vast on the wall behind it, the night falling like a blanket to smother them both.

SIXTY

That night Lester was flown over to Germany on a mission, returning at dawn. He was shaky with exhaustion, falling back on his bunk and closing his eyes. But he couldn't sleep, could only see – over and over again – Joe being hit by mortar fire and bullets, his body hurled round and round against the glowing red light that had enveloped him.

'Lester, help me! Lester, please, for God's sake, help me!'

At six, Lester woke with a start, the stuffy morning making his head ache as he sat up in bed. It had been a nightmare, that was all. And then he remembered Joe . . . Getting stiffly to his feet, Lester threw some cold water on his face. He was going to visit his brother that evening, when he got home. When he got back to Gull Road, to Rose's arms and Sea View, to the scent of the ozone and the sound of the trams on the seafront. To the sight of the Tower, the smell of the bladder wrack and the cheap signs on the boarded-up shops. To the pier and the slot machines, the dirty postcards and the graffiti on the Pavilion doors. And the beach. Where – once – Joe had scratched his initials on the rock face, 'JW'.

Still visible and strong, even after a thousand tides, the initials were unchanged, the marks more lasting than the man.

'No, Dad, I'm not going with him this time.' Rose said, pulling on her coat. 'Lester said he wanted to see Joe alone.'

470

'Well, I'll be glad of the help at the track,' Len replied, picking up his board and passing Rose the cash box. 'Let's see if we can fill that today, shall we?' He looked into her face sympathetically. 'Lester will come by later to see you.'

'He sounded so down when he rang. Almost like he was dreading coming home –'

'He's tired, luv, worn out,' Len assured her. 'When you see him, everything will be all right again.'

'I had a dream –'

Len shook his head. 'Don't go reading things into dreams, luv. They're just dreams, that's all. Nothing more, nothing less.'

'Even the bad ones?'

'*Especially* the bad ones.'

'Joe?' Lester said quietly, drawing up his chair by his brother's bedside. 'It's me, Lester.'

There was no movement.

'I've come to see you, Joe. Talk to me.'

Slowly, painfully, he moved his head, his voice faint. 'Lester? Is that you?'

'Who else?'

'I was dreaming about you.'

'Well, I'm here in the flesh now.'

'On your own?'

'On my own.'

'Good.'

'What time is it?'

Lester glanced at his watch. 'Eight o'clock.'

'Is it dark yet?'

'No, dusk.'

Gently, Lester took his brother's hand in his own. 'The doctor said –'

'I don't want to talk about what the doctor said,' Joe replied, interrupting him. 'How's everyone?'

471

'Everyone's fine. Maisie's coming tomorrow, with Mam.'

'But you're alone?'

'Yes, I'm here on my own, Joe.'

'I can see things in my head . . . like the windmill at the bottom of . . . I can't remember.'

'Rigby Road.'

'That's right. And the slot machines on the pier. You remember those, Lester?'

'I remember. When you get home –'

'No.'

'Joe, come on, don't be like that. We all want to get you home.'

'I can't.'

Lester's grip tightened on his brother's hand. 'Joe, it will get better.'

'How? How will it get better? You've never lied to me before, Lester. Don't lie now. I can't live like this. I can't. I can't let Maisie look after me, or any of you. I don't want that.'

'You're just down –'

'Stop it!' Joe said suddenly, his tone uncharacteristically sharp. 'This is you and me, Lester. Just you and me . . . I'm not going to live like this. I've heard them talking. They think I'm asleep, but I listen. My heart's damaged; I could die any time.'

'Or you could live for years.'

'*Like this?*' Joe countered. 'Would you? Would you want to live like this?'

A long moment passed before Lester spoke again.

'No.'

'And neither do I.' Joe paused, then went on steadily, 'I've asked a lot of you over the years, I know I have. But you were always stronger, smarter than me. People expected you to do well, get on in life. I didn't mind, Lester. I want you to know that. I never minded playing second fiddle. I liked it, it took the pressure off me.' He stopped, listening. 'Can you hear that? Dr Leigh's car. I know it from all the others now. I suppose doctors don't have their petrol rationed . . .'

'I suppose not.'

'. . . seeing as how they have to get about so much.' Joe coughed, his chest congested. 'I could die anytime, Lester, with this bad heart of mine. Could just peg out, stop breathing.' Lester could feel his brother tighten his grip on his hand. 'No one would be surprised. They'd say it was a mercy. A blessing . . . What time is it?'

Lester glanced at his watch, his hand shaking. 'Ten past eight.'

'Not dark then?'

'No, not dark.'

'That's good. I don't want to go when it's dark.' Joe sighed. 'We had some laughs, you and me. I keep thinking of the pier, of the way the gulls crapped on you the day you bought your first sports jacket.' Lester laughed, the sound painful in his ears. 'And that ballroom of yours – how's it getting on?'

'It's not. The war's put paid to that.'

'Finish it, Lester, after the war. Have a dance with Maisie there. Pretend you're me.'

'Joe –'

'No, don't tell me what to do, Lester! Not this time. This time *I* take responsibility. I tell *you* what to do. But you know, don't you? You know already?'

Lester was finding it difficult to talk. 'Joe, I can't –'

'You *can*. Only you could. Only you have the guts, Lester. No one else would help me. They'll patch me up and push me around in a pram like a cripple, wipe my arse, and tell me what Lesley's doing – because I won't be able to see my own child growing up. Do you want that for me, Lester? Want to see me as a blind freak in a pram? If I go now, they'll remember me *walking* down Gull Road, calling out of the window for you, or bringing Maisie home to number ninety-nine. They'll remember me like I was –'

'Joe,' Lester said hurriedly, 'listen to me, please.'

'No, Lester, *listen to me*! Listen to your brother. We came into the world together and we've stayed together all our lives, but now I'm going off on my own.' He sighed, took in a hurried breath. 'What time is it?'

'Fourteen minutes past eight,' Lester replied, tears burning behind his eyes.

'No one will suspect anything. My heart would just have given out. They'll be sorry, but relieved . . . Please, Lester, do it.'

'Joe, don't ask me to do this,' he said, his voice hardly more than a whisper. 'Joe, don't ask me.'

'Who else *can* I ask? Who else has the courage? You're my twin, you understand. You, better than anyone.'

'But you're my brother –'

'Yes, and you're mine.' Joe gripped Lester's hand so tightly his knuckles whitened. 'Don't make me beg you.'

Lester tried to pull away, but Joe held on.

'Please, Lester, I know you love me, but you *have* to do this. If our situations were reversed, I'd do it for you . . .' His grip relaxed, now holding Lester's hand tenderly. 'Come on, do it now, before it gets dark. I want to be able to see my way – wherever I'm going.'

Shaking almost uncontrollably, Lester pulled a pillow from under his brother's head and then placed it over Joe's face. At first he felt a slight resistance, Joe's chest rising as he gulped for air, but instead of pulling back, he leaned his full weight on his brother, his arms pushing down on the pillow, his head resting on top of Joe's face.

'God, forgive me . . .' he whispered helplessly. 'Please, God, forgive me.'

A moment passed, then another. Then there was silence. Lifting up the pillow, Lester looked at his brother and then felt for a pulse.

Joe had gone.

SIXTY-ONE

Rearranging the bed, Lester slid the pillow back under Joe's head, smoothed the sheet and then touched his brother's chest. Joe was perfectly still in his death, his mutilated body and face calm. Lester knew he should leave, but couldn't. Perhaps it would look suspicious if he hurried off, but then again, perhaps he didn't care about that. He had killed his own brother; maybe it was right that he should be punished for that.

But that hadn't been what Joe wanted. Their pact had been no Cain and Abel rivalry; Lester had killed with compassion. But would anyone else see it that way? He looked at the still figure on the bed, his stomach tightening into a knot. *Jesus, he had killed his brother.*

Calm down, Lester told himself, calm down. It was what Joe wanted. But would it be what Ruby wanted? Or Maisie?

His hand moving to his forehead, Lester could feel the nauseous thump of a headache in his temples. It was all right. It was all right, he had done what Joe wanted. He had looked after his brother at the end, just like he had always looked after him in life. *But he could tell no one.* He had killed his own flesh and blood – no one could condone that, or forgive him that. It would have to be a secret, between him and Joe.

And Joe wasn't about to tell anyone.

* * *

Incredulous, Stuart flopped into a chair in the rest room, staring ahead. He couldn't believe what he'd just seen. *Lester Williams had killed his own brother.* Stuart shook his head, reaching for a cigarette and lighting it. *Lester Williams had just smothered his own brother.*

It was almost too good to be true. Maybe his luck had finally turned. And about time, Stuart thought bitterly. Wouldn't everyone love to know about the soldier hero being a killer? Wouldn't that sell a few newspapers? Even knock the war off the front page for a day. The glamorous Royal Marine who had killed his mutilated, defenceless brother – how sensational was that? Lester Williams would be charged, arrested, and found guilty – after all, they had an eye witness – and possibly even hanged. And if not, his life would be ruined, the slur on his reputation marking him out for ever. People would shun him, even his own family. Even Rose . . . Stuart inhaled deeply to settle his excitement. If he went to the police he could get his own back on Lester Williams *and* Rose in one fell swoop.

So it was a shame that no one was going to find out, Stuart thought, almost regretful. He had been lucky to have the tip-off about Joe Williams being a patient: even luckier to have happened along the corridor of the fourth floor just as Lester Williams had come out of the lift.

Stuart had ducked out of sight, certain that Lester hadn't seen him. Then after a little while he had grown curious and when the nurse had left the room, moved to the door to listen. What Stuart *hadn't* known until the previous day was that the adjoining room was empty. So, surreptitiously, he had made use of this fortuitous knowledge and eavesdropped at the door of the vacant room. And had heard everything the brothers had said.

It was almost touching – if it had been anyone other than Lester Williams. And, although the idea had crossed *Stuart's* mind, he never suspected that *Lester* would kill Joe

Williams. And Stuart had seen it all; peeking through the keyhole to witness Lester pressing down on his brother's face with the pillow.

God, Stuart thought, shaken. Who would have believed it?

'You look like you've seen a ghost,' Roy Howell said, walking in unexpectedly.

'I'm tired, that's all,' Stuart snapped, irritated to have his solitary thoughts interrupted.

'Want to go out for a drink?'

'With you? Not likely!' Stuart replied, as though mortally offended by the remark.

He wasn't some grubby menial worker, not on a par with the likes of this toerag. And soon everyone would realise that. He had no money, but Lester Williams had money – oh yes, he'd made quite a pile from his wheeling and dealings – and now Stuart was going to help him to spend it.

'You've no need to be bloody rude!' Howell said, stung by Stuart's rejection. 'I only asked you out for a bevy because I felt sorry for you.'

About to leave, Stuart flinched and turned at the door.

'Look in mirror, pal. *That's* the person you should feel sorry for. Not me. Oh no, no one's going to feel sorry for me ever again.'

It was almost eleven o'clock when Rose came down to the Promenade to find Lester sitting on the bench. She had guessed he might be there and slid next to him, laying her head on his shoulder.

'What is it?'

'I was bad company tonight, sorry.'

'You were terrible company,' she teased him, 'but that's OK – if you tell me what's worrying you.'

Lester shrugged. God, could he really carry this secret for life? It had been only hours since he had killed Joe and

477

it already seemed like an eternity. An eternity where he was cut off, detached from everyone he loved.

'I'm just tired,' he lied.

'Did you see Joe?'

'Yes.'

'How was he?'

Lester closed his eyes and stared out to sea. 'Bearing up.'

'I'll go and see him tomorrow.'

You can't, Lester wanted to say. He's dead. I killed him. If you went to the hospital now he would be lying there, cold. Or maybe they'd already found him and telephoned Sea View. Surely at any minute he would hear his mother calling him. God, Lester thought desperately, oh God . . .

'Rose?'

'Yes, love?'

'What if –'

He was interrupted by the sound of feet running towards them. Lester knew without turning round that it was Trudie, her steps coming closer and closer. He had been about to tell Rose what he had done – but now he knew he never would.

'Lester! LESTER!'

They both turned round, Trudie crying as she reached them.

'It's Joe. He's dead.'

Without talking, Nan Wilmslow made tea for Maisie and her mother. Quietly she then laid the cups and saucers in front of them and sat down.

'I'm all right,' Maisie said, for the tenth time, 'honestly. It's better this way. Better for Joe.'

Her mother nodded, then burst into tears again, Maisie catching Nan's gaze and holding it.

'He's fine now.'

Maisie smiled faintly. 'I think so too.'

'But he was so young,' her mother wailed, 'such a lovely

boy. And what will happen to you now, Maisie, with a child to bring up? I can't help you that much, luv. I would if I could, but times are hard, and what with the war and everything . . .'

On and on she rambled, mostly about herself, Maisie staring at Nan, and Nan watching her steadily, as though by averting her eyes, Maisie would collapse – fall in pieces at her feet.

'He was a hero,' Nan said simply.

'In war and in life,' Maisie agreed, picking up the cup and taking a sip of her tea.

She grew up in that moment; stayed very composed. Maybe she had never been that intelligent, or that worldly, but Mrs Joe Williams carried her grief like an empress. She would cry alone, not in front of her mother or anyone else. She would remember her Joe and long for him, but at the same time she would be glad that he wasn't that disfigured carcass on the hospital bed. It would have been too cruel to want to keep her husband alive like that.

She had been a wife. Now it was her time to be a widow.

By contrast, Ruby was distraught, Alfred giving her brandy and Ruby knocking it out of his hand. Up and down the kitchen she paced, backwards and forwards like something distracted. She had lost Joe. How had she lost her son? How could she have lost Joe?

'I should have been there when his heart gave out.' She turned to Lester, white-gilled, by the door. 'You must have left not long before he died. Poor Joe, he would have been alone. If you'd just stayed a bit longer . . .'

She began to pace again, no one able to stop her.

'Mam, sit down,' Trudie pleaded. 'Come on –'

'I should have been there!' she snapped.

Lester looked away. He couldn't touch his mother, couldn't hold her in his arms – because the same arms had held Joe down. The same hands had smothered him.

'I should have been there!' Ruby repeated again, her voice as loud as a gun crack. 'He was my son – and I wasn't there for him!'

'He felt nothing,' Rose said quietly, moving over to Ruby. 'You said that was what the doctor told you . . .'

'Yes!' Ruby nodded eagerly. 'Yes, he *did* say that.'

'. . . so Joe wouldn't have known what was going on. He would just have slipped away.'

Ruby stared at Rose, clinging to the words. 'You think so?'

'Yes, I do. I think he just fell asleep and died. Because he wanted to –'

'He wanted to live!'

'No, he didn't, Ma,' Lester said suddenly. All eyes turned to him, listening. 'Joe was in pain and he wanted it to stop. He wasn't a coward – he'd just had enough.'

'He would *never* have given in!' Ruby retorted heatedly. 'Look how he got over that infection – no one expected that. Not even the doctors –'

'Joe recovered once, but he couldn't have done it again,' Lester replied, his voice thick with emotion. 'He was a *cripple*, Ma, when can you see that? He was blind, mutilated. He had no bloody face –'

'LESTER!'

'He didn't want to live! And neither would I, like that. Neither would you, nor anyone else.' Lester paused, struggling to find words. They were all looking at him curiously and for a moment he wanted to confess. But he knew he never could. It would be unbearable for his parents. Enough to lose one son, not both.

'He's at peace now.'

'Peace!' Ruby snorted. 'What's this peace everyone talks about? I'm not at peace –'

'But Joe is,' Rose interrupted, guiding Ruby to the sofa.

At once, Alfred put his arms around his wife, tears running down his cheeks and wetting his shirt front, his porkpie hat falling from his head and rolling under the table.

The next day seemed like a lifetime to Lester. He longed for seven o'clock when he could catch the train back to his barracks. Longed to be away from his parents, even Rose. When he was away from Gull Road it would be easier to cope, he told himself. When he wasn't having to make the funeral arrangements for his brother; the arrangements which would never have been necessary if he hadn't killed Joe.

Lester had never been a liar, and found the deception tore him apart. His parents had each other to comfort, but when Trudie had turned to him Lester found himself relying on Rose to console his sister. It was impossible for him to reach out to any of them. He was as effectively crippled as Joe had been.

Glancing at his watch for the third time in a minute, Lester willed the time to move on. When he was back at the barracks he would be busy; they'd send him off on a mission soon. Please God, he prayed, pleading with a deity he had never recognised before, let me be busy, let me have no time to think.

'I want a word with you, Williams.'

At the sound of his name, Lester turned, surprised to see Stuart Fallow watching him at the corner of Gull Road.

'I'm surprised to see you in Blackpool. You want another beating?'

'But it's not my turn,' Stuart replied, smiling grimly. 'It's *your* turn to take a beating. Metaphorically speaking, that is.'

Irritated, Lester moved away, but Stuart ran alongside him. 'Aren't you interested in what I might have to say?'

'Nothing you say interests me, Fallow.'

'Fallow rhymes with gallow – I've only just noticed that,' Stuart replied, and Lester's pace slowed slightly. '*Gallow* –

horrible word, conjures up terrible images. Swinging figures, men hanged –'

Lester felt his chest tighten, but kept his voice steady. 'Get to the point, Fallow.'

'What's the hurry, Lester? Why don't we go for a drink, like the old friends we are.'

'We were never friends.'

'Well, I think you should be grateful that I'm being so pleasant. After all, you stole my wife.'

'Your own actions drove Rose away! You only have yourself to blame for what happened to your marriage.'

'You're quite a moralist, aren't you, Lester?' Stuart replied, his eyes dark in the shadow of the street. 'Even though your past isn't exactly snow-white. I mean, you drove your wife to drown herself –'

'Now look here, Fallow!'

'– and then there's the question of your brother's death.'

Lester could feel the colour drain from his face. Did Fallow know? *How could he?*

'What are you talking about?'

'You look rattled,' Stuart replied, glad to see that his words had taken effect. 'Guilty conscience, I suppose.'

'I don't know what you're talking about!'

'Yes, you do,' Stuart replied, his tone sinister. 'I saw you, Williams. I work as some menial dogsbody at that hospital – I couldn't get a decent job after you ruined my life – and I saw you. I watched you kill your own brother.' He looked round to check that no one was about. 'Now, don't you think the police should be informed? I mean, as you're such a decent law-abiding citizen, a man who volunteered to fight for his country? Hey, Williams, what d'you think?'

Lester *couldn't* think clearly. He only realised that he was cornered. Fallow would have his revenge in spectacular style. He closed his eyes for a moment to steady himself. Oddly, Lester didn't mind facing punishment, but he dreaded seeing the look in his mother's eyes; the judgement of his family – and Rose. Dear God, what would Rose think? She would turn her back on him now, for sure. And maybe that was what he deserved.

But he couldn't let it happen.

'You're very quiet,' Stuart said, smiling benignly. 'So you won't mind if I pop off to the police?'

Lester saw a chink of hope and took it. 'Why haven't you gone already?'

'Oh, I think we both know why. You see, I think you should swing for killing your own brother – but on the other hand, that would be too easy. I want to give you a way out, Williams, and help myself in the process.'

'You want to blackmail me,' Lester replied, his voice cool with disgust.

'You can't moralise with me,' Stuart answered. 'You're hardly in a position to get snotty. If you do what I say, I'll keep quiet. Your family will never know, and as for my wife, she'll never find out that she's sleeping with a murderer.'

'It wasn't like that!'

'But it *was*,' Stuart said, almost charming. 'You killed him. Smothered him.'

'I was –'

'What? Tucking him in? Oh, come on, Williams! What you did is murder in anyone's book. I grant you, some might say it was a mercy killing – but do you really want to risk taking that line of mitigation? And if you *do* face the music, your reputation's shot anyway.' He leaned towards Lester. 'I know my wife. She wouldn't approve. And I doubt she would sleep well next to you wondering if she was going to live to see the morning –'

'You bastard!'

'Yes,' Stuart agreed, 'I wasn't before, but I am now. I've been down to the bottom, Williams, and some bad traits rubbed off on me. Of course, I could be saved – which is more than your brother can hope for – if you helped me out a bit.'

Lester swallowed, his throat dry. 'What d'you want?'

'Money.'

'I'm not rich –'

'You have money,' Stuart replied dismissively, 'some put away, I know that much. And property, shops, booths, that wreck of a dance hall you want to impress Blackpool with after the war.'

Lester stared at him blankly. 'You'd force me to sell everything I have?'

'I'd say it was cheap at the price,' Stuart replied, 'compared with gaol and the rope.'

His head thumping, Lester nodded. 'OK, I could get some money. How much d'you want?'

'I want to bleed you dry,' Stuart answered, smiling pleasantly. 'But not yet. I really want to have you on a string for a while, Williams, let you have a taste of how it feels to have your life jerked about by someone else.'

'I won't give you the satisfaction,' Lester said, knowing that, in the end, he would be forced into doing anything Stuart Fallow said to protect his secret. 'Go to hell!'

'You want to watch that temper of yours,' Stuart replied, his tone hardening. 'I'll give you one hour to make up your mind, Williams. I know you're leaving tonight, so don't think about running off. If you do, I'll just let the cat out of the bag and you'll be court-martialled. That is the word, isn't it? Court-martialled? No more being the brave hero soldier for you.'

'You have to give me more time to think!'

'Actually I don't have to give you *anything*,' Stuart replied, glancing at his watch. 'I'll see you back here in one hour. If you're late, I go to the police. And I will, Williams, believe me.'

Rose was just leaving Sea View when she saw Lester at the end of Gull Road. Running up to him, she threw her arms around his neck, a neighbour smiling at them as he passed.

'We've got three hours left before you have to go back,' Rose said eagerly, looking up into Lester's face and then drawing back. 'What's the matter, love? You look awful. It's Joe, isn't it? Oh, Lester, it must be so hard for you, going back on your own when you were always with Joe before. You must miss him so much.'

Taking Lester's arm, Rose led him towards the seafront. A late summer breeze was blowing, making froth on the waves, a boat dancing giddily beside the pier. Sitting on a bench, she patted the place beside her.

'Come on, sit down.'

Expressionless, Lester did so, his gaze fixed on the ground flecked with the shadows of the hungry, circling gulls calling overhead.

'You're not *really* alone,' Rose told him. 'I'll be with you every step of the way. Every minute, every hour, Lester. Please, darling, don't be upset. You're not really alone.'

He could feel a buzz begin inside his head and thought for one sickening moment that he might faint. Rose's voice seemed far away, her words nothing more than a dull murmur.

'Lester, talk to me,' she urged him, 'or d'you want to be on your own for a while? I'd understand if you did, sweetheart.'

He straightened up, his eyes looking out to sea. In amongst the waves he seemed suddenly to see faces: his wife in her drowning dress, and Joe, his arms flailing under the press of water.

'Lester!'

Blinking, Lester sat up, realising he had, for a moment, passed out. 'I'm OK,' he assured her. 'It's just everything . . . everything's that's happened.'

'You can't go back like this!' Rose replied shortly. 'You're not well.'

'I have to go back –'

'You need a doctor. Joe's death has been too much for you.'

He laughed then, the sound mixing eerily with the calling of the gulls, Rose shaken as she looked at him.

'You're scaring me. What's happened?'

'I've just seen Stuart Fallow –'

'*Stuart!*'

Lester could feel his head swimming and wondered if it felt like that to drown; if Beth had felt the same as the waves pulled her under.

'He's blackmailing me.'

'Blackmailing you? How could he?'

Her voice was coming from under a blanket, muffled in his ears. For one heady moment Lester wanted to throw himself into the cool water until he could hear, see, and feel nothing.

'Lester, talk to me! Talk to me!'

The rise in her voice jerked Lester back to the present.

'What was I saying?'

'You said Stuart was blackmailing you,' Rose replied edgily. 'What about?'

'He wants money –'

'Don't give him any!'

'He'll go to the police if I don't.'

She frowned, baffled. 'And tell them *what*?'

'That I killed Joe.'

Rose flinched. Suddenly the sun was boring down on her shoulders, pinning her to the bench. All their warm summer moments dissolved in that instant; all their hopes and dreams slid over the Promenade onto the shingle to be dragged out to sea.

Her voice was low, strange in her own ears. 'You *didn't* kill him, did you?'

'He asked me to –'

'*And you did!*'

Lester buried his head in his hands. 'He begged me! He said he couldn't live like that, that he'd had enough. What could I do? I couldn't leave him like that. He was

486

in that state *because* of me, because he followed me.'
Lester's fingers dug viciously into his scalp. 'It was so
quiet in the hospital, so quiet in that room . . . and Joe
kept talking and talking, so reasonably. Making his case
. . . And suddenly it seemed logical. More than that, it
seemed the *right* thing to do to help him. Like I'd always
done before . . .'

'But he died of a heart attack!' Rose said, bewildered.
'The doctor said his heart gave out –'

'I smothered him.'

'You did what?'

'I held a pillow over his face and smothered my own
brother.'

She stood up. Then sat down again, gazing out to sea
without seeing anything. *Lester had killed Joe.* No, she had
misheard.

'His heart gave out.'

'No, it didn't.'

Shock silenced her again, but her mind ran on frantically. Her first reaction had been horror, but then she
realised that this had not been a decision lightly taken. Her
beloved Lester had killed his brother, but only because Joe
had *wanted* him to. It had been Joe's decision, Rose thought
desperately, and Lester would always do anything to help
his brother. And Joe had been so mutilated, so damaged.
Everyone had said that no one could live like that, could
they?

'Did he ask you to do it?'

Lester nodded. 'You don't think I'd have done it without his permission, do you?'

'No.' Her mind scrambled over the images pouring into
her head. God, if Ruby found out, or Maisie . . . Then she
remembered something else Lester had just told her. 'You
said that Stuart was blackmailing you? Why? Because he
knows about Joe?'

Lester nodded dumbly.

'How could he?'

'He's working at the hospital. He saw me do it.'

Rose shook her head. 'No, he can't have! He's lying. Tell him you won't give him anything! Tell him he can go to bloody hell –'

'He saw me.'

'He can't have seen you!' she repeated madly. '*He can't have!*'

'Do you want to risk it?' Lester asked, turning to her. 'I killed Joe. I did it and nothing can change that, however much I want it to. If I don't pay Stuart Fallow he'll go to the police, and then everyone will know what I did. And they won't understand, Rose. I'll swing for this.'

A long minute passed, both of them silent, staring out to sea, sitting on the bench, but not touching. Lester was drained, beyond emotion. It seemed that having carried so much for so long he could no longer even summon up the energy to move. As for Rose, she was sitting beside the man she had loved for most of her life – and he had just admitted that he was a killer. She should, she thought, be revolted by him. Hadn't she always believed that there was *never* a good enough reason to kill?

But this was Lester. And the life he had taken was Joe's. Because Joe had wanted it. And Lester had never refused his brother anything. And Lester – she stole a look at him – was now in hell.

Tentatively her hand reached out for his and clasped it.

Lester felt the touch and turned to her. 'What do we do?'

It was the first time in his life he had ever asked anyone's advice.

'We take our time.'

'We can't, Rose. Stuart wants his answer in half an hour. Before I go back tonight.'

Her thoughts leap-frogged over one another, then she spoke again. 'Meet him, tell him you'll pay him. Stall him.'

Her voice was certain, quick. 'Tell him you'll raise the money – that I'll give it to him –'

'No! I don't want you to do that.'

'We have no choice!' Rose snapped. 'You're going back on duty in a few hours. I *have* to help you.'

He clung on to her hand, as a child might. 'I didn't want to involve you in any of this.'

'I *am* involved, Lester. For the rest of my life. From here on in, what involves you, involves me.'

'But what about Joe? Can you forgive me that?'

She paused before replying. 'I know you'd have done anything rather than see him suffer. But he *was* suffering, Lester, we all knew that. Ruby might have deluded herself, but we all knew there was no hope. Even Maisie.' She stared into his eyes, her voice commanding. 'They can never know what you did. They wouldn't understand. I do. I never thought I would, but this is you. And if *you* did it, then you did it for the right reasons. But others wouldn't see it that way.' She grasped his hand, her grip strong. 'I won't lose you, Lester. As God is my judge, I won't lose you again.'

SIXTY-TWO

Lester saw Rose an hour later. His face was grey, his eyes shadowed, his movements jerky with exhaustion and anxiety. Luckily Len was out visiting Doris.

Without asking him what had happened, Rose made tea and passed Lester a mug, topped up with the brandy Len had put aside for special occasions.

'Go on, drink that.'

He sipped it gingerly, as though everything was an effort. But gradually the brandy took its effect; his colour returned and his voice became stronger.

'I saw Fallow. He agreed to arrange all this through you. He wants a hundred pounds. This week.'

'A hundred pounds! Is he bloody crazy?' Rose snapped. 'And what will it be *next* week?'

'I don't know, but you can give him everything I've got. Sell up –'

'I don't think so! Stuart's not stealing what you've worked so hard for.'

'I don't care. I just want him off my back,' Lester replied, shivering although the night was clammy. 'Jesus, Rose, what are we going to do?'

'We're going to take it one step at a time – that's what we're going to do.' She moved over to him, stroked his hair, his head resting against her stomach. 'Don't worry, my love, we'll get through this. We can get through anything when we have each other. We're a team, you and me. Lester and Rose – the world could rise up against us and we'd still win out.'

He clung to her, absorbing some of her strength. For a man who had never relied on anyone before it was a humbling experience. Dear God, Lester thought incredulously, why had it all gone so wrong for them? They should have married, had children now, been happy. Instead there were two dead people and Stuart Fallow casting a acid shadow over their future.

'Lester,' Rose said soberly, 'I want you to go back and leave this to me.'

He shook his head. 'No! I've been thinking about it. I don't want you dealing with Fallow.'

'Stuart Fallow is my husband,' she replied steadily. 'I know him. I can handle him.'

'But after what he did before –'

'He won't try it again,' she reassured him. 'He doesn't want *me*, he wants revenge. And money. Stuart wants his power back – and this is the only way he can manage it.'

For a moment Lester was silent. When he spoke again, his voice was hushed. 'I should go to the police –'

'No! No police! You can't lose your nerve now, Lester. You have to go back on duty, darling. Stuart is a problem, but one we can solve.'

'How?'

'I'll know how to handle him when I see him again. But I promise you one thing, Lester, no one will *ever* know about Joe.' She kissed him tenderly. 'Go back on duty, sweetheart, and trust me.'

Lester arrived back at his barracks that night to be told that he had a mission at dawn. He was given his instructions and advised that he was going to be flown over to Northern France where he was to sabotage a bridge. Then he – and two other men – would be picked up later. It was a dangerous hit-and-run exercise, Lester was told, and he knew he'd need all his wits about him.

As he packed his kit, Lester thought of Joe. As he lay down on his bunk, he thought of Joe. As he lay in the darkness, he remembered Joe. They would have gone on the mission together, Joe quiet, Lester talking to cover his own nerves. And later they would have returned, Joe chatty with relief, Lester wrung out, watching his brother as he slept.

But this time there was no Joe. This time there was only a long night to get through and the mission to face, come morning. Every time he fell asleep, he dreamed of Joe or Stuart Fallow, and when he woke, sweaty with unease, he stared into an inky blackness that gave no comfort. And so the night dragged on.

Dawn was, that August morning, taking her truculent time.

Rose woke from a dream-thick sleep to find Len standing at her bedside.

'Hey, you, you took some waking up. It's nine o'clock.' He passed her a cup of tea, sitting down at the bottom of the bed. 'Lester's gone back then?'

She nodded. 'Last night.'

'He'll be fine,' Len assured her, studying his daughter's face carefully. 'You look all done in, luv. Why don't you stay in bed?'

'When you need me?' she answered, trying to sound light-hearted. 'There's a race meeting today, over at Catterick –'

'But I *don't* need you,' Len interrupted her. 'I'm meeting up with a bunch of fellas I haven't seen for a while after the meeting, and I don't want my beautiful daughter around!' He tapped her knee. 'Stay in bed, Rosie, have a rest. You don't look yourself.'

She was tempted by the idea, but resisted, swinging her legs over the side of the bed and sitting up. 'I've got things to do, Dad. I thought I'd drop in and see Maisie. Joe's funeral's on Monday; she might like someone around.'

'I saw Nan Wilmslow and Clovis go in an hour ago. I hope to God Clovis didn't take a carpet with her.'

Rose smiled. 'You can't beat a bit of good carpet.'

'Nothing soothes like a drugget,' Len replied, laughing. 'Bloody hell, that's her cure for everything! World war? Roll of lino sort that out in a minute.'

Rose laughed, but the sound wasn't true in her ears. She was holding something back from her father – from Len, the kindest man on earth. But although he had always been kind with her, would he extend the same grace to Lester? If he knew what Lester had done – if he knew that she was going to be the go-between for him and Stuart – what would he say then? It didn't bear thinking about.

'Go on, Dad, have a good day with your mates. And don't come back drunk!' she teased him.

But when Rose heard the front door close a few moments later the silence landed on her like a shroud.

All day she waited for something to happen. And nothing did. She visited Maisie and was astonished by her friend's composure, finding it hard to control her own when Maisie talked about Joe's death. The doctor told me that he hadn't suffered, she said happily, thank God for that.

'He's at peace now.'

Without speaking, Rose took her hand.

'It must be hard for Lester – he must miss him so much,' Maisie went on. 'He thought Joe being hurt was his fault – but it wasn't. Joe just followed him, like he always did.' She smiled dimly. 'Lester spent his life protecting him.'

It was getting unbearable, Rose thought, watching Lesley playing on the floor in front of them. Joe's daughter was so like him, so much an eerie reminder of the dead man.

'Can I do anything to help?'

Maisie shook her head. 'No, I'm fine. Everyone's been so kind. Nan and Clovis came round earlier, and Ruby's calling by any time.'

Rose flinched. The one person she didn't want to see

was Ruby. Ruby, who had worked as a stooge for a clair-voyant once. Ruby, who saw through people like a pane of glass. Ruby, who would never, *ever*, understand what Lester had done.

'I should be going,' Rose said, getting to her feet. 'I'll call by tomorrow.'

She was just stepping out into the street when Ruby arrived. She was wearing black, which looked hot and dusty in the August heat, and her skin was waxy from strain.

'Hello there, Rose,' she said simply. 'You off now?'

'I should be getting home,' Rose replied, looking away, sure that her guilty conscience was as visible as Alfred's birthmark.

'You don't look too good,' Ruby replied, tipping up Rose's chin and looking at her face.

A couple of instants ticked past, Rose certain that Ruby had read her mind: Ruby aware on some level that Rose was holding back.

'Are you OK?'

'I'm fine, Ruby, honestly.'

An uncomfortable moment held them both immobile – then Ruby moved past her into Maisie's house, calling over her shoulder: 'You look out for yourself, Rose, you hear me? Don't do anything daft.'

Slipping back home, Rose closed the door behind her, taking in a deep breath. She had to be calm, or someone would notice her acting strangely. This wasn't going to blow over, this would go on for some time. Time when she had to appear normal, drawing no attention to herself.

Sighing, Rose looked down, and then noticed a letter at her feet. Although the writing was printed, she knew it was Stuart's.

My dear wife,
    Which you still are, by the way. Even though
your lover would like it to be otherwise. I think

you and I should have a little chat, don't you? And as your father is away – yes, I saw him go out – I could call by and see you this afternoon. Around four be OK for you?

    Your loving husband,
    Stuart

Rose pushed the letter into her pocket, dreading four o'clock and yet wanting it to come at the same time. Somehow she would talk Stuart round. *Somehow* . . . Unsettled, she made a corned beef sandwich, but couldn't eat it and pushed it away. How sarcastic Stuart was, even in a letter. *Your loving husband* – as though he still cared about her. When all he wanted was to blackmail Lester and bleed him white.

Rose glanced at the clock. Three o'clock. She had an hour left. But how did you prepare for this kind of meeting? She busied herself with chores until quarter to four, then changed and splashed cold water on her face, her shaking hands brushing her hair. Surely she was a match for Stuart Fallow. She knew the man, she had married him, slept with him, looked after him when he was sick. *She knew him* – and if she knew him, surely she could reason with him?

On the fourth chime of Len's old clock, there was a knock on the door. Rose let Stuart in without saying a word. He moved on into the kitchen and looked round, smiling warmly as he turned to her.

'Not exactly Lytham, is it?'

'No, thank God.'

He raised his eyebrows in surprise, then sat down at the kitchen table. 'So you're going to be acting for your lover, are you? I have to admit I was surprised. I mean, weren't you the one that used to say that all life is precious? But now here you are, left behind to clean up Williams' mess –'

'Lester's back on duty, fighting. Which is more than you ever managed.'

Stung, Stuart retaliated. 'I wasn't fit to fight!'

'You weren't fit for much,' Rose replied coldly. 'Now, let's talk.'

'I want money to keep quiet –'

'No,' Rose replied, sitting down in the chair opposite Stuart, the kitchen table between them.

He looked shocked. 'No? I'll go to the police if I don't get money. I swear I will.'

'Oh, Stuart, can't we talk properly, without hating each other?'

Carefully she watched him, trying to gauge his reaction. She was gambling and wondering if she could pull it off. Wondering if – as she now suspected – she had been wrong and Stuart *did* still care for her.

'Well,' he said at last, 'I'll admit I would like to have seen you under different circumstances.'

'You left me no choice, Stuart. I had to leave you.'

He nodded, relaxing slightly. 'I was jealous, Rose. You messed up my head.'

It was so hot in the kitchen, flies buzzing around the windowsill, the clock ticking loudly into the stuffy air.

'I didn't cheat on you, Stuart. You drove me away.'

'I thought –'

'You were wrong!' she replied, holding his gaze. It was there, she thought, the look that told her Stuart still loved her. 'We should have stayed friends, if nothing else.'

'How could we,' he said bitterly, 'you running off like that, and my father chucking me out? And that bloody Hettie woman taking over the house.'

'Whatever Hettie wants, Hettie gets.'

He nodded, agreeing with her. 'You're right there. She's poison. And she's got my father in her grip now.'

'Grip, spelled G-R-I-P,' Rose said, reminding Stuart of the old times.

He laughed, the sound thunderous in that clammy kitchen. 'Yeah, right. Poor old sod can't even talk now. Just had enough voice to throw me out –'

Deftly, Rose guided the conversation round to less bitter memories. 'We were happy once.'

'We were,' Stuart agreed, late afternoon sunlight creeping round the house and pouring in through the kitchen window. 'We had some laughs . . . I was sorry for what I did, Rose. I'd been drinking, and things got all mangled in my head. I shouldn't have done it.' He slid his hand across the table, letting it rest only an inch away from Rose's. 'I still care about you.'

'You hurt me, Stuart.'

'I know, I know,' he said, hanging his head, 'but I didn't mean to. People do things they don't mean to all the time. And then have to pay the consequences.' He remembered Lester in that moment and his voice hardened. 'Like your lover, killing his brother.'

'Stuart, you and I both know it was a mercy –'

'Not for Joe.'

'He didn't want to live. How could you endure a life like that? You're strong, young, with your whole life ahead of you. And Joe was smashed up, ruined –'

'But alive.'

'He had a weak heart.'

'If someone put a pillow over my face I'd have a bloody weak heart,' Stuart replied bitingly.

Rose winced. 'You're not really like this,' she said softly. 'This isn't you, Stuart. You were never vicious. Don't do this, please. Don't act like a criminal.'

'Williams is the criminal.'

'You're *blackmailing* him,' Rose replied, trying to soothe Stuart's flickering emotions. 'That's criminal. And you're not that kind of man. I know you: you're clever, intelligent, funny. Not some low life . . .' He was listening, watching her. 'You can start again, get another practice in time. People forget –'

'Forget me raping my own wife and her lover beating me up? Forget my own father throwing me out without a penny? Bloody hell, Rose, you'd need to be an amnesiac to wipe all that out.'

'You *could* make good again, Stuart. Put your mind to that, not blackmail.'

He stared at her for a long moment before speaking again. 'People would forget if you came back to me.'

The words came out of his mouth like gunfire. Wrong-footed, Rose blinked in the hot air, the flies buzzing and battering themselves against the windows.

'It's too late for us.'

'Why?' He leaned forward, taking her hand. 'I've changed, really I have. Had a taste of a life I don't like much. If you came back to me, people would accept me again. I could get that practice you spoke of, even get back with the old man.' He squeezed her hand gently. 'I can give you so much more than Lester Williams. Not now, maybe, but we could build it up again. You and me –'

'Stuart –'

He cut her off immediately. 'Listen to me, Rose. You want to talk, to bargain, well, let's bargain. If you come back to me as my wife, I'll forget all about Joe Williams' murder. There now – you wanted a way out for your lover and I've given you one. Give up Williams, come back to me, and I'll keep my mouth shut.'

Rose could feel his hand pressing hers and her mouth dried. She had never expected this.

'I can't do that –'

'Why not?'

'You wouldn't keep your word,' she said, thinking quickly. 'What's to stop you exposing Lester the first time we argued?'

'You'd have to trust me, Rose. That's all I can say.'

And then she saw it: the enormity of the trap. She would give up Lester in return for Stuart's silence. She would live with her husband wondering daily if – or *when* – he would tug on the leash. He would have her under his thumb completely. Shackled by the love she had for Lester, she would be stuck in a marriage with a man she hated, and who she could never leave.

Anger made her reckless as she snatched her hand away from Stuart's. 'You can't control me, you bastard!'

'Language, Rose, language –'

'You think I could trust you?' she said, Stuart's expression hardening as she laid into him. 'You! Of all people! You got what was coming to you, Stuart. You deserved it –'

'Now look here!' he snapped, standing up and grabbing her arm. 'You don't want to be my wife, fine. But you and your lover can pay me –'

'You lying, cheating sod!' she shouted, trying to pull away from him.

'Rose –'

'You bastard! You bloody, stinking, conniving pig. You're no good, Stuart. You had every chance in the world and you botched your life up. You lost your wife, your home and your inheritance.' She laughed, beside herself. 'And now you're showing what you really are. A criminal. And a bloody coward!'

The word punched through the thick air, Stuart losing his temper and slapping Rose hard across the face. She fell backwards, towards the work top, putting up her hands to protect her face.

'And you're a whore!' he snapped, now punching her, Rose trying to move out of his way and losing her footing, her hand grabbing the side of the kitchen table to steady herself. 'A bloody cow! A tart! A cheap, Gull Road bint!'

Beyond control, Stuart put his hands around Rose's neck and squeezed, Rose choking, her hands scrabbling on the table top to find something to protect herself with. She was getting dizzy, about to lose consciousness, when her hand closed over the handle of the bread knife. In one last desperate movement she reached behind her and then jabbed the knife into Stuart's body.

He let go at once – Rose turning as he fell heavily to the floor. He was silent, but there was blood gushing from him, the knife sticking out of his chest, the flies buzzing hysterically against the hot glass of the windowpanes.

SIXTY-THREE

'Did you hear that?' Mrs Lyman said to her son.

'What?'

'That thump – sounded like someone falling.' She moved over to listen at the partition wall that separated the Lymans from the Bradshaws. Disappointed, she then shrugged. 'Nah, it's nothing. Len was probably just moving the furniture around again.' She glanced over to her sixteen-year-old son. 'How many of those sweets have you had?'

'Not many, Ma –'

'Too many,' she said, snatching up the brown bag. 'There's rationing on, you know.'

Honestly, Mrs Lyman thought, you had to keep an eye on everyone these days.

Laughing, Len was standing amongst his old friends in the racecourse bar, Dave Lincoln – newly promoted – fanning himself with a copy of the *Racing News*. It had been a slow day, but no one really cared. The weather had been good and after a few beers and more reminiscences, no one was too bothered about their takings.

'So how does it feel to be a big shot, Dave?' Len asked, mocking him gently. 'I'll have to watch my p's and q's.'

'Too right, Bradshaw,' he teased him back, his voice dropping. 'I've got a bit of news for you – I've found Roy Howell.'

'You never!'

'I told you, everyone gets found in time. He'd been down South and changed his name, but then he came back, chancing his arm.' Dave winked, his moustache as luxuriant as ever. 'We've got him in custody now. He'll get what's coming to him. Everyone does in the end.'

'And about time,' Len replied, ordering another round. 'Thanks, Dave. Thanks for remembering. I was fond of that old bugger Ogden, and Howell as good as killed him.'

Dave nodded solemnly. 'Well, I'm not the brightest copper that ever lived, but I'm thorough. And I never give up.'

A while later Len toyed with the idea of going over to visit Doris, but then dismissed it. He was in high spirits, but not drunk, at peace with his own world. The business was chugging along, and his Rosie was back at home – what else could he want? Of course it would be good when the war was over, when the likes of Lester and Bunny came back, but at this moment in time, Len thought with relief, he was a happy man.

Over at Sea View, Trudie was painting her toenails red, Ruby watching her.

'How can you? What with Joe being dead, and all.'

'He wouldn't mind me painting my nails,' Trudie replied, 'honestly, Mam.'

They both looked up as Gilbert walked in, hand in hand with Miss Vernon. Incredulous, Ruby glanced from one to the other, Miss Vernon blushing.

'We've something to tell you, Ruby,' Gilbert began. 'We know it's a bad time – what with Joe dying – but we wanted to tell you *we're married*.'

On cue, Alfred woke up.

Ruby stared at the happy couple with her mouth open. 'Don't be bloody stupid,' she said at last, 'you *can't* be married.'

Trudie was so engrossed that she had let her nail varnish drip all over her foot without noticing. 'Married? But you're –'

Ruby cut her off. 'Miss Vernon, I think you and I should have a word.'

'I'm not a silly woman,' Miss Vernon replied, clinging to Gilbert as keenly as a coat of paint. 'I know what you're going to say – that you didn't expect it. But you see, my mother always used to tell me that life was full of things you didn't expect and that, if you were wise, you could recognise happiness where other people might not see it.'

Taking a deep breath, Ruby glanced at her brother. 'Will you tell her, or shall I?'

'I could tell her.'

'Shut up!' Ruby snapped at her daughter, Trudie looking away, disappointed.

'Gilbert is –'

'A fine man, who needs a woman's love,' Miss Vernon went on blithely, 'and I can give him that love. I wasn't always the silly old lady you see today. I was quite a looker in my day, I can tell you. There were many young men after me –'

'But I was the only one who caught you,' Gilbert simpered, glancing over to Ruby. 'Lydia –'

'*Who?*'

'Lydia, Miss Vernon's first name is Lydia,' he explained, then carried on. 'Lydia knows everything about me. I have no secrets from her.'

'But you can't have . . . have . . .' Ruby blundered on, '*carnal knowledge.*'

Now it was Alfred's turn to interrupt. 'I was always good at that.'

They all looked at him.

'At *what*?'

'General knowledge.'

'Oh, for God's sake!' Ruby replied, Trudie laughing helplessly as her mother faced the couple again. 'Well, if you

503 .

really think you know what you're getting into, I'm happy for you.' She studied Gilbert, who was beaming with contentment. 'I really am happy for you, luv. And you, Miss . . . Lydia.'

She twittered a thank you and then snuggled up to Gilbert, happiness making her almost young again.

And so life goes on, Ruby thought, birth and sickness, loss and triumph, love and marriage, round and round in a giddy circle, which you managed to cling on to – if you were lucky. Some people kept their grip, but others weren't so lucky and were spun off, all the casualties of the world losing their hold on life. Like Joe. Her Joe.

Ruby sighed to herself sadly. In the end it was the most unexpected people who triumphed.

SIXTY-FOUR

Carefully Len locked up the old Austin and then searched for his key. Trying not to make a sound, he opened the front door, the clock chiming eleven as he entered. The house was in darkness as he fumbled for the lobby light switch. Rosie would be upstairs asleep, he thought, moving into the kitchen.

His attention was caught by an unfamiliar shape in the semi-dark, Len flicking on the light and seeing his daughter. 'You still up, luv?' he asked, surprised. 'And sitting in the dark?'

He moved towards her and then stopped, realising that there was something terribly wrong. And there was a smell in the air; unfamiliar, sickly. His daughter was sitting rigidly on a kitchen chair, blood on her skirt, and on the floor at her feet was Stuart.

'Christ!' Len said, kneeling down and feeling for a pulse. 'He's dead . . .' Turning round, he looked at his daughter urgently. 'Are you all right? Did he hurt you?'

She shook her head.

'What happened, Rosie? Rosie, tell me what happened.'

'I didn't mean it, Dad. Honestly, I didn't mean it . . .'

Automatically, Len put his arms around her. She was cold to the touch, although the temperature in the kitchen was stifling, a solitary fly still buzzing madly against the window.

505

'What happened, luv? You've got to tell me what happened.'

'He came to see me . . .' she paused.

Where had her carefully worked out plan gone? Hadn't she rehearsed it over and over again, ready for her father's return? She couldn't tell Len the whole truth. Instead, she would have to tell her father *some* of the truth. No one – not even Len – could find out about Joe.

'Stuart wanted us to get together again, but I said no. I said no, Dad! And then he lost his temper. He grabbed me around the neck.' She touched her throat, Len's gaze resting on the livid bruising there. 'He would have killed me! I was fighting for my life . . . I just grabbed the knife without thinking and jabbed it into him. But only so he would let go – not so I would kill him.' Her eyes were unblinking, the pupils dilated with shock. 'I didn't mean to kill him!'

'It was self-defence, luv,' Len said, his mind whirling. 'Everyone will realise that.'

No one could blame Rose for trying to save her own life, he thought, no one could. And yet didn't everyone know about the bad feeling between Rose and Stuart Fallow? About the ugly break-up of their marriage? And Lester's fight with Stuart? Len tried to see it from an outsider's point of view. A jury might not believe her story, might find her guilty of a capital offence . . . Len was suddenly terrified. No one was going to hang his child – not Rosie. Not his baby. He had to get rid of the body. Yes, that was what he would do. Hide the body and then no one would know.

'We'll have to move him, luv.'

'I can't, Dad.'

'We have to! We'll hide him somewhere, somewhere no one will find him.'

'They will find him! They will!' she said, her voice rising. 'People will look for him. Someone might have seen him come here.' She clung to her father desperately. 'Daddy, help me. Please, *do something*.'

But Fate was against them. By mistake Len had left the front door ajar, Mrs Lyman's son passing and looking in. Through the kitchen door he had seen Len and Rose with the body of Stuart Fallow – and had run, screaming, into his mother's house.

SIXTY-FIVE

Of the three men who went off on that dawn mission to Northern France, only two returned, one man reported missing. The Marines told their commanding officer that as they descended by parachute they had been seen. The enemy had opened fire. A splattering of bullets had missed two of them, but had hit their companion. Their last sight of him had been his body hanging limply in its harness as the parachute floated to earth. No one, they said, could have survived.

That day Lester Williams was posted missing, presumed dead.

SIXTY-SIX

The police came for Rose that night and she was taken to the local station to be questioned. After the police had talked to Mrs Lyman's son, and to Mrs Lyman herself, they then talked to other witnesses. All of whom repeated the old gossip – Stuart Fallow had raped his wife, and her lover, Lester Williams, had then beaten Fallow half senseless. When pressed they admitted that Rose had always been in love with Lester Williams and that his forced marriage to Beth Hodges had all but destroyed her. Then, when Lester and Rose got cosy again, Beth Hodges committed suicide.

Everything the witnesses seemed to say made the case more damning – although Len gave a spirited defence of his daughter.

'She killed him in self-defence! I know Rosie, I brought her up single-handed. She's a kind person, who'd never hurt anyone –'

The police officer looked up. 'But she had a public fight with a local woman.'

Len frowned. 'Who?' He shook his head. 'Oh, you mean that scrap with Trudie Williams. That was years ago –'

'The fight was about Lester Williams.'

'Well, in a way –' Len stopped short, looking at the officer. 'I'm not saying anything else, and neither is Rosie, until I get some advice.'

The following morning it was all over the local papers:

'BLACKPOOL WOMAN KILLS HUSBAND', and by the following morning it was on the front of the national press. The scandal even managed to knock the war into second place, the press photograph of Rose staring out of a police car window riveting people's attention. Those who knew her – and many who had never known Rose – talked incessantly about the case.

Her friends from the racetrack – apart from Freddie Marsh – all decided that she'd acted in self-defence. Fallow was a bastard, there was nothing else to say. Let our girl come home, they insisted, comforting Len. You'll see, she'll be all right.

But on the Blackpool streets other voices came to other conclusions. She had always acted like a man, doing a man's job, swearing like a man – and she was always mad about Lester Williams. Would have done anything for him . . .

'You can't tell me,' a woman said to her companion on Derby Street, 'that Lester Williams and her weren't having a fling. Stuart Fallow was in the way, wasn't he? Some surprise he ended up dead.'

'But he'd raped her –'

'Oh aye, she *said* that. But were it true?' the woman went on, banking up the moral outrage. 'Remember that poor Beth woman? Drowned herself – and all because of them two. A disgrace, I call it.'

Despite enlisting help from local solicitor Ernest Jenkins, Rose was – two days later – charged with murder. Because it was wartime there were legal staff shortages up North, and so the case was transferred to London, Rose taken to Holloway Prison. Almost overnight her story grew from a crime in a seaside town to a national scandal.

Rose Fallow was on trial for murder – a crime that called for the death penalty.

Holding the change of prison clothes they had given her, Rose was ushered into a cell in Holloway, the door locked behind her. Panicking, she looked up at the barred window but could see only a patch of dull September sky. Shock had all but paralysed her, the events of the previous few days blurring in front of her eyes: the police, the station, the questions, the charging. And the whispering about her and around her, the glimpses of newspaper headlines, the camera bulbs flashing in her face every time she was glimpsed.

One minute she had been in Gull Road, the next she had been propelled into a nightmare. Her clothes had been taken from her, the clothes with Stuart's blood on them, Len bringing a summer dress to the police station for her to change into. But now that was going to be taken away too. Her hands rested on the prison clothes. How had she got here? How?

She had hardly uttered a word to the police – only to say that she had killed Stuart Fallow in self-defence. Len had been with her as much as he could, but this time there was very little even he could do. Sitting on the edge of the bunk, Rose watched a fly walk across the floor. Her mind went back to the flies in that hot kitchen the day she had killed Stuart. It will be all right, she told herself. When she explained, people would understand. About her and Lester.

'You've a visitor,' an officer said suddenly, hurrying Rose out and up, across the landing, crossing the rows of cells and the sounds of women calling out or crying.

Finally Rose was shown into an ante-room. Len looked up as she entered and she ran to him, holding on grimly. 'Dad, Dad . . .'

'Oh, luv,' he said simply, 'my little girl.'

'It'll be all right,' she said, drawing back, trying to comfort him and console herself. 'Honestly, Dad, when I tell them; when I explain about me and Lester. People will understand. He'll be in touch any day now. He would have been in touch sooner, but you know how it is with the war.

He'll have been on a mission and not heard about all of this. But when he does, he'll be here. He'll explain –' She stopped. Her father was looking at her strangely. 'What?'

'Rose, luv –'

'What!' she almost shouted.

'Lester's been posted missing. Presumed dead.'

'No!' she snapped, pushing her father away. 'NO!'

'Rose –'

'Get away from me!' she screamed. 'Get away from me!'

Blindly, she backed away from him, as far away as she could in that ante-room. He was lying to her! He had to be. Lester wasn't dead. He couldn't be. If Lester was dead who would speak up for her? Jesus, Rose thought desperately, was it true? Was it true? And then she realised that it *was* and that in her heart she had already known. If Lester had been alive he would have been there for her. He would never have deserted her, never allowed her to protect him by endangering herself.

Unless he didn't know. Unless he had no choice. Unless he was dead . . . Slumping in a seat, Rose stared ahead, her breathing shallow. Suddenly there was no feeling left in her. No screams, no tears, no raging. Nothing. She didn't even care about fighting for her own life. Without Lester, there was *no* life. She had loved him and lost him, and now lost him again. Only this time there was no way he could get back to her.

And only one way she could get back to him.

Sitting in the snug of the Almoner's Tavern, Dave Lincoln saw Len and waved him over.

'I got the drinks in,' Dave said, gesturing for Len to take a seat. 'Now, what about Rose? What can I do to help?'

Len's face was pinched from lack of sleep, his voice edgy. 'Funny thing, you know, Dave. Last time I spoke to you it were about Roy Howell and how you'd found him. Seems so unimportant now.'

'Strange, though. The fact that he was working in the same hospital as where Joe was.'

Len looked up. 'I didn't know that! Stuart Fallow and Roy Howell together? Life makes for some strange bedfellows.'

'Stuart might have found out about Joe being in there, and seen Rose visiting.'

'He might,' Len said, his expression helpless. 'I can't believe Rose has been taken to Holloway. They said it was because hers was a sensational case – like the papers keep telling us. She's even been on the Pathé News.' Len took a sip of his whisky to steady himself. 'Christ, it'll go to court and then what? She can't be found guilty, she can't! They'd hang her –'

'Hold it there,' Dave told him. 'Just keep calm.'

'She's my daughter!' Len snapped. 'How the hell can I keep calm? They've been talking to the Lymans and the Williamses. I don't worry about Ruby. But Trudie? She's desperate to help Rosie now, but she can blurt things out so stupidly at times.'

Dave watched him. He knew what the police gossip was and knew that it was looking bad for Rose Fallow. No one seemed to believe her story of self-defence. After all, hadn't she been raped by her husband? Then left him for another man? Hardly any love lost between them. And why, they asked, would Stuart Fallow suddenly want to get back with his wife? Her defence was that when she had refused, he had tried to kill her. But no one believed it. No, they said, she had killed him. Got rid of Stuart Fallow once and for all to leave the way clear for her lover.

'That bloody solicitor Jenkins is no help,' Len said, interrupting Dave's thoughts. 'You can see what he's thinking, and it's not encouraging. Besides, he's not up to it. Not here, and definitely not in London.'

'You need a good barrister.'

'I know! But I don't know where to start looking. I mean,

I don't have much money, but I could sell the house and the car.' He gripped Dave's hand. 'Find me the best barrister in London, will you? I don't care if I have to give him the skin off my back, I'll pay him somehow.'

Dave paused, trying to remember a name – and then he suddenly slapped the table with his hand. 'Randles!'

'What?'

'Gerald Randles,' Dave repeated triumphantly. 'I remember him well. We had a case a while back and he took it and won. He's been climbing the ladder steadily since then. If he believes his client's innocent no one can shake him. He's like a big slow dog – then, when he needs to, he clamps in his teeth and doesn't let go.'

Gerald Randles was shaving for the second time that day. It infuriated him, but by afternoon he always had a five o'clock shadow. Why did they call it five o'clock? he wondered, when the bristles always started appearing at four? Slowly, he shaved. Like he did most things. *Slowly*. At fifteen stone in weight he wasn't fat, being six feet in height, but when he'd passed forty the pounds had slid around his waist and jowls and taken up early retirement there. Scrutinising his reflection in the mirror, he checked his fleshy chin for any rogue bristles and then rinsed his face, patting it dry with a soft hand towel.

The heat in court had been intense, and Gerald didn't like it. Not personally, or professionally. When people got hot, they got tired. And then they didn't listen – which was always dangerous. A jury member who knew only some of the story was a loose cannon.

A loose cannon. Gerald considered the phrase as he refastened his waistcoat and put on his jacket. He had something of a loose cannon coming to see him. A Mr Leonard Bradshaw, father of the suddenly notorious Rose Fallow. Gerald had read about the case, and had wondered from the start why it bothered him. It should, by rights, have been clear cut, but it wasn't. There was a dud note in it. And Gerald – as a barrister and a skilled pianist – prided himself on spotting dud notes. They rattled him, like someone playing G flat when it should have been G sharp. He knew that something so small could easily be overlooked in an orchestra playing Beethoven's Eighth Symphony, but it was still there. Still wrong. Still needing correction to make the piece run smoothly. Just like life.

Precisely one minute and thirty seconds later, on the dot of four fifteen, Len was shown into Gerald Randles' rooms at Lincoln's Inn, the barrister shaking his hand and offering him a seat. Then the two men regarded each other for a long moment. Len saw a heavy-set, tall man with a round face, a benign expression, glasses pushed up on his forehead. And eyes as alert as a lizard's. By contrast, Gerald saw a wiry man with a high forehead and a squint, in a loud jacket, who was obviously desperate.

'She didn't do it.'

Gerald nodded. He rather liked Len's direct approach; it saved such a lot of time. 'Is that what your daughter says?'

'She admits to killing her husband – but only in self-defence.'

Gerald jerked his head, his glasses dropping down onto his nose in one accurate movement. Then he started to take notes. 'From what I've heard and read, your daughter admits to killing Stuart Fallow because he wanted a reunion.'

Len nodded.

'I would have thought that a reunion with his wife would have been difficult if he had killed her.'

Len leaned forward in his seat. 'Stuart Fallow was a violent man! He had raped Rose before. That's why she left him and came back to live with me.'

'No other reason? Like her old boyfriend?'

Len bridled. 'Now, look here! Lester Williams wasn't Rose's boyfriend until her marriage broke up.'

'Are you sure?'

'She never lies to me!'

'If she was a *good* liar, how would you know?'

'I know my child!'

'Mr Bradshaw, the courts are full of parents who insist that they know their own children, even when it is patently obvious that they couldn't see a monster under their own noses.'

'Don't bloody patronise me!' Len snapped, leaning towards Gerald. 'I came here to ask you to help my girl, not to listen to you spouting off at the mouth.' He stopped, angry at himself for losing control.

'Does your daughter have a temper too, Mr Bradshaw?'

The men exchanged a look.

'Rosie's lively, but she doesn't have a bad temper. She speaks her mind, a bit too much sometimes.'

'I can't think where she got that from,' Gerald replied, smiling wryly and pushing his glasses on top of his head again. 'And what about Lester Williams? I hear that he's missing in action, presumed dead.'

Len nodded. 'That's why Rosie doesn't care any more. Since she heard, she's lost the will to live. Doesn't seem to realise the trouble she's in.'

Randles nodded. 'Tell me about her. What kind of girl she is.'

Smiling, Len stared ahead. 'Feisty, full of guts, more like a son than a daughter in some ways. I used to take her to the track with me –'

'The track?'

'The racetrack. I'm a bookie – The Lazy Eye – and Rosie used to come with me when she was a kid. Her mother died when she was still little, you see. Rosie even helped me out with the ticktacking when she grew up. Before everything changed, before Lytham . . .'

Gerald was getting more and more anxious by the moment. He knew the moral climate was harsh on women criminals, and this girl seemed doomed from the start. She was independent, free-spirited and her father was a bookie. There had been no mother around to guide her. She had worked the racetracks as a ticktack man . . . Dear God, Gerald thought, he would have his work cut out if he took this one on.

'It all changed when Hettie came into our lives,' Len explained, Gerald listening avidly. The sensation of hearing a wrong note intensified, until it became an unpleasant buzz in his head.

'Mr Bradshaw,' he said at last, 'do you believe your daughter?'

'Of course I do.'

'But she lied to you before. When she didn't tell you about writing to Lester Williams.'

'She didn't lie to me,' Len countered. 'She just didn't tell me.'

'Then perhaps she *just hasn't told you* something else. Like why her estranged husband wanted a reunion.'

'Stuart Fallow loved her.'

'But if I heard you correctly, he had been thrown out of his family and home because he had raped his wife. Stuart Fallow's father turned his back on him, he was given a beating and disgraced publicly. His livelihood was curtailed and he ended up in some menial job. Would he *still* love a woman he thought had cheated on him and been the instrument of his downfall? Doubtful, I think. And I believe others would feel the same way. So why *does* Stuart Fallow suddenly want a reunion with his estranged wife? Why?' Gerald asked. 'She had been living without him for a while. She was now seeing Lester Williams, and they were recognised as a couple. So why did Stuart Fallow come back when he did? What did he – or she – say that day that provoked such a violent argument? *What* made her drive a knife six inches into her husband's chest?'

Len winced, then admitted finally. 'I don't know.'

517

'And neither do I,' Gerald replied, glancing down at his notes. 'But your daughter *does* know. And now all I have to do is to get her to tell me.'

SIXTY-SEVEN

By the time the end of November came around, Monty had scored his triumph at El Alamein and the Germans had been routed near Stalingrad. The Russians had advanced so fast that many of the Germans had been shot in the back trying to retreat. But there was no news of Lester, and after being denied bail and spending months in Holloway Prison, Rose's case was finally given a trial date of 14 December. By this time it was generally – if reluctantly – accepted by everyone that Lester Williams had perished. Killed in action. A hero's death.

Which was not what Rose Fallow's death would be . . . Gerald Randles sighed and pushed his glasses onto the top of his head. He was putting the final touches to Rose's case, but there was still that dud note, clanging in the back of his mind. And Rose had done nothing to dispel it. He thought back to the first time he had seen Rose Fallow. He realised then that if he had passed her on the street he would have thought her an attractive young woman, and noted the way she walked, with that totally unaffected sensual gait. When he spoke to her he would have been intrigued; she could be funny, quick, and unlike so many women of her generation, swore openly. He would – Gerald realised – have liked her.

But time had gone on and Rose Fallow had changed. She had lost weight, her colour fading, her hair growing longer and now tied limply at the back of her neck. Her eyes remained clear, but her expression was unnerving, a mixture of world weariness and complete indifference. How many times Gerald had tried to provoke her, he had lost count. Whatever he said, she stuck to her story: Stuart had wanted a reunion, when she refused, he attacked her. She killed him in self-defence.

It didn't ring true to him. Or to anyone else. It hadn't when he first met her, and it didn't now.

'The trial's been set for December the fourteenth,' Gerald said, waiting for a response.

'I see,' Rose replied evenly, her hands on the table in front of her, the nails short and unvarnished.

'We have to make sure that we're fully prepared,' Gerald went on, jerking his head and letting his glasses slide down onto his nose so that he could read his notes. 'The prosecution have a new witness.'

'Who?'

'Henrietta Fallow.'

Rose paled, her hands clasping together. 'She's going to be a *prosecution* witness?'

Gerald nodded. She was finally rattled. Good.

'Mrs Fallow is very hostile to you. Says that you were a bad influence on Stuart, that you cheated on him –'

'No,' Rose replied simply, pushing back her chair and standing up. Slowly, she walked to the window and looked out. 'I've told you all about Hettie. She just wants to get back at me for the way her own life turned out.'

'But she was your mentor – why would she turn against you?'

'Because she wanted me to stay married to Stuart, so that the four of us – her and Cedric included – could all live together as one big happy family. And she wanted us to give her grandchildren, more lives she could manipulate. She's like that, wants everyone to dance to her tune. Or else.'

Gerald nodded. 'She could be dangerous.'

'Hettie could always be dangerous,' Rose replied calmly, sitting down again.

Her temper had evaporated. Of course Hettie would turn against her, Rose thought; hadn't she let her down? Disappointed her? Wasn't she stuck in that mouldering house in Lytham with the invalid Cedric, watching her life ebb by, drip by steady drip? And worse, she would be pointed out everywhere, because of her relationship to Rose. No more bridge parties, no more luncheons, no more invitations falling on the mat. Hettie had wanted to create the perfect wife and mother, and she had created a murderess instead.

'What are you thinking?'

Rose looked up. 'Nothing important.'

'What *is* important to you?' Gerald asked, losing patience. 'Soon you're going to be on trial for your life, Rose. You have to fight.'

'Is Dad all right?'

Gerald nodded wearily. 'Fine.'

'He can't afford your fees. I told him that.'

'We came to an arrangement,' Gerald replied. Dear God, when would the woman realise what was at stake? 'Rose, I'll ask you again – what happened that night?'

'It doesn't matter.'

'"*It doesn't matter*"?'

'No!' she snapped, unexpectedly losing control. 'I don't care what happens to me. Lester's dead. That's all that matters.'

'You can't be sure he's dead –'

'Oh, I'm sure,' she said. 'If he was alive, he would have got in touch. He wouldn't have deserted me.'

Gerald decided to go for the nerve. 'From what I hear, Lester Williams didn't behave well with women.'

'That's a lie!'

'He deserted you once.'

'He had to!' Rose hurled back. 'He had to marry Beth Hodges because she was pregnant.'

'He made her pregnant.'

'Before we got together!' Rose countered, her face flushed. 'He did the right thing. The only thing he could do. He *had* to marry her.'

'He didn't have to cheat on her.'

'How many times do I have to tell you that we weren't lovers,' Rose replied, her tone icy. 'I wrote to Lester when he was away fighting, and I saw him a couple of times when he was on leave. But we weren't lovers.'

'People won't believe that.'

'I can't help what people think,' she replied bitterly.

Gerald pushed his glasses back on top of his head and stared at her.

'No, but maybe you *should* know what people think of you. They see you as some hard-bitten piece who worked on the racecourse with all the men. No shrinking violet. They'll find out that you were outspoken, that you swore – and that you were seeing an old lover behind your husband's back. They'll see an adulteress. And they'll try you for that – and that alone. They might even hang you for it.'

Rose looked down at her hands, lying flat on the table again. 'I can't help my past.'

'No, but you can show them that you're not what they think you are. You can show them a thoughtful woman, who was seriously affected by her husband raping her. An injured woman who ran back to her old lover *as a friend*. A woman who refused a reunion with a violent man – the jealous ex-husband who would have killed her. We have to show the jury a helpless woman – not some hard-nosed bitch playing around.'

'Why?'

Gerald blinked. 'Why what?'

'Why bother?' Rose replied flatly. 'I know you're trying

to help me, but it doesn't matter any more. Nothing does. Lester's dead –'

'And you will be too, at the end of a rope.'

She paled visibly. Hadn't she overheard things at night? Or when some of the women paused by her door and talked maliciously about hanging? Knowing she would hear them? . . . *they put you in rubber pants because you wet and shit yourself as you die . . . they bury you in quicklime . . .*

Abruptly pushing back her chair, Rose stood up.

'I don't want to die – but I don't want to go on without him. Lester was my life. What is there for me out there?' She jerked her head to the barred window. 'You think the jury finding me guilty is the worst thing that can happen? What if they find me not guilty? Where will I go then?' She held his gaze. 'I can't ruin my father's life. Go home, where everyone will be whispering behind my back for the rest of my days. So where else? Some strange place where no one knows me? To do what? Marry again? What man would marry me now? And what man would I *want* to marry after losing Lester?' She smiled briefly. 'You're a good man, but I'm not prepared to live as a freak, a travelling peepshow working the racetrack, my past hanging like a bloody sign round my neck.'

Gerald sighed. 'Did Lester Williams *really* mean that much to you?'

'Yes!' she said simply. 'And don't tell me again that he might not be dead. Months have passed. Mr Randles, I tell you this – and you *must* believe me – Lester would have got in touch by now if he was still alive.'

For a moment Gerald found himself without words. He had agreed to take the case because it was sensational, even waiving his fee because he knew that a win would give him better publicity than he could ever hope to buy. But as time had gone on his ambition had taken second place to his compassion. Something in Rose Fallow's story was missing. And without it, he realised helplessly, she was damned.

But why wouldn't she fight, he thought despairingly. Because she was protecting someone? *Who?* Lester Williams? But if she believed he was dead, he no longer needed her protection. Try as he might, Gerald could not correct the one dud note.

And it was enough to send Rose Fallow to the gallows.

SIXTY-EIGHT

Ruby was looking through the window, then ran out, waving her arms around violently. 'Go on! Get away from here, you flaming ghouls!' she snapped at the curious who had come to stare at Lester Williams' old house – and opposite, Rose Fallow's. 'Go on, get off with you!'

Her size and the volume of her voice deterred all but the most hardy, Ruby thundering back up the steps and slamming closed the front door of Sea View. In the kitchen Alfred sat, gazing into the fire, Trudie rereading a treasured letter from Bunny.

'Pigs!' Ruby snarled as she began to wash the dishes. 'Fancy coming to gawk! And there'll be plenty more, I can tell you.'

'It reminds me –'

'Not now!' Ruby shouted, Alfred falling back into his daze. 'You'll wear that letter out, Trudie, if you keep reading it over and over.'

'You do the same with . . .' she trailed off. Damn it! she thought, what had she been about to say? There *were* no more letters from Lester or Joe. Sheepishly, Trudie avoided her mother's stare and went upstairs.

It wasn't fair to take it out on her daughter, Ruby thought, banking up the fire and then drawing the curtains. It wasn't Trudie's fault that Bunny was alive and Joe was dead. And as for Lester . . . Ruby began to fold some clothes hurriedly, keeping herself busy to stop the deep scream in her belly. She knew her son: if Lester had been alive, he would have been in touch. With her. And with Rose.

Faster and faster Ruby folded the clothes, so quickly that finally they fell from her hands, the sheets all collapsing on the floor, just as Ruby did, flopping onto the lino heavily.

'Ruby!' Alfred said anxiously, leaning down to her. 'Ruby, luv, are you all right?'

She was sitting on her backside, her face as crumpled as the sheets around her.

'I miss them,' she said simply. 'I miss my boys.' She held up the sheets and shook them at her husband. 'I can't wash their sheets any more! Why? Because they don't sleep here. They don't come home any more. I keep washing *our* sheets and Trudie's – but not *theirs*.' She stopped, crying soundlessly, Alfred struggling to get down on the floor beside her.

'I don't know what to say, luv –'

'And now the trial,' Ruby went on. 'Rose so far away, and people talking about her everywhere you go. Newspapers are all full of it, her name on the radio every time you turn it on. That's Rose Fallow, Rose Bradshaw that was, Alfred. The little runty kid who used to live opposite. Not some murderess, not her. They make her sound like a right whore. Every time I go out I can hear people whispering behind my back. Talking about Rose and Lester, *our son*. They make him sound like he was no good. A womaniser, an adulterer, a man who drove his wife to her death.'

'I know, luv, I know –'

'But it wasn't like that! It wasn't anything smutty with Rose and Lester.' She paused, reaching for Alfred's hand. 'Dear Christ, what happened to us?'

'Hey?'

'Once we were all living here, Rose opposite. We were happy, weren't we? Lester always making deals, Joe trailing behind like he always did, Trudie buggering about . . . We

526

were so happy once. Did I know it?' she asked him eagerly. 'Did I know how good life was?'

'It will be again –'

'Without the boys?' she countered sadly. 'Without the noise and the squabbles? Without Lester telling us about his plans for that flaming ballroom? And I always thought he'd pull it off,' Ruby said, gripping Alfred's hand tightly. 'I always thought he'd finish it one day. Then it would be like his monument. Our lad, made good.'

She stopped, resting her head against her husband's shoulder, Alfred putting a burly arm around her. Somewhere, down the street, a paper boy shouted the headlines.

'SENSATIONAL MURDER TRIAL BEGINS TOMORROW! READ ALL ABOUT IT!'

Neither of them spoke, Alfred for once empty of stories, Ruby empty of hope.

Exhausted, Len waited in the ante-room for Rose to appear. He had brought the clothes she had asked for, knowing they would now be too big. Respectable clothes, just as Gerald had asked. Nothing flashy. Rosie was never flashy, Len had retorted, she was elegant, everyone used to say so. But everyone said other things now.

He stood up as his daughter entered, flanked by a prison officer. 'Hello there, luv.'

She kissed him: lips cool. 'Hello, Dad.'

Both of them sat down, the officer standing by the door. 'Dad, I'm so sorry –'

'Hush,' Len said at once, 'there's nothing to be sorry about. You'll see, luv, when the jury's heard all the evidence they'll understand. Mr Randles said that he had some good witnesses, people who would stand up for you. Describe how things were. You know, with you and Stuart.' He squeezed her hand, finding it difficult to talk. 'You have to have hope.'

She nodded listlessly. The trial was due to begin. And

no Lester. Because Lester was dead. There could be no other reason. Only once had Rose wondered if he'd deserted her – but the thought lasted only a moment. If he had been able, Lester would have come to her. He was obviously dead. And she was as good as dead. The trial was just a formality.

But she would never break her promise. Never tell anyone why she and Stuart had *really* argued. No one needed to know about Joe's death. It was her only way out – but she wouldn't take it. Why destroy a dead man's reputation? Why add more heartache to the Williamses' grief? They had had enough.

And so had she.

'You have to convince the jury,' Len said, urging her on. 'Let them know what Stuart was like.'

'Hettie's giving evidence against me.'

Len looked down. 'I know.'

'You were right about her all the time,' Rose said. 'I should have kept away. I'm really paying for having that squint corrected.'

He smiled bitterly. 'Rose, luv –'

'Oh, Dad, don't worry. It'll be all right.'

He held her hand tightly. 'Rose, have you told me everything?'

No, she wanted to say. *This* is the whole truth, make it right, Daddy, make it right . . . But she didn't. She wasn't scared of what would happen, only her death – the prospect looming over her and making inroads into her sleep.

'You've been the best father any child could ever have had,' she said softly, so that the prison officer wouldn't overhear. 'You've loved me and taken care of me and I always knew you would be there for me – whatever happened.'

Len was finding it difficult to talk. 'I wish it were me,' he said finally. 'They could do what they liked with me.'

'But it's not you, Dad, it's me.' She kissed his hand

hurriedly, then stood up. 'I'll see you tomorrow? When the trial starts?'

He nodded firmly. 'I'll be there.'

'I know. You always are.'

SIXTY-NINE

In Blackpool many occupants of Gull Road listened to the news on the radio and followed the trial in the papers. For once Clovis stopped her hoarding and stayed most of the time with Nan Wilmslow, chewing over every piece of news, Hettie pilloried for her evidence. And it had been damning. As the only person who had actually lived in the Lytham house she gave an eyewitness account of their lives. How Rose had been a neglectful wife, an adulteress, making a false accusation of rape against the respectable Stuart Fallow.

Rose had jumped to her feet at that point.

'You're lying!' she had hissed. 'You know you are. How could you say such things?'

But Hettie had stuck to her guns. It was her revenge on Rose for ruining her life. A payback for the ghastly old age she was facing, for Cedric's nursing, and her fall from social grace. In an expensive suit she stood – under oath – and damned her protégée as easily as she would have bought a new sofa. And the jury believed her. That dud note Gerald knew was sounding, they also sensed. They might *want* to take Rose's side, but she was remote, inviting no allies.

Sensing failure, Gerald refused to let Rose take the stand. He knew that she would only alienate the jury further, her story coming out rehearsed, wooden, her emotions held firmly in check. Surely such a cool woman was capable of planning and carrying out a murder? Surely an innocent woman would plead for her life? Would beg to be believed? To live?

Evidence followed evidence. Rose was feisty, they said, and opinionated. She liked male company, liked to work on the track, liked to swear. For the jury – particularly the women – she seemed to come from another world. One of the new sort of women who led their own lives, like men, and lived like men. And loved like men. They saw in Rose Fallow what they feared most – moral laxity. And they judged her for it.

By the second week of the trial Gerald was getting nervous. Rose had remained aloof and distant, whatever was said. There had been only the one outburst when Hettie gave evidence, otherwise she had stayed silent. The fight between Rose and Trudie was picked over in detail. As was Beth's suicide.

And Lester came out of it looking like a bastard, a man who had deserted his lover to marry the woman who was carrying his child. The woman he never loved and who would later commit suicide as a result of his rejection. No one believed that Rose and Lester hadn't been lovers. No one believed that they were innocent. It was a sign of the times, some argued. This was the way the younger generation behaved.

And Gerald knew that unless a miracle happened Rose was going to be found guilty. As an adulteress as much as a murderess. Her downfall would act as an example to others. A reminder of what happened to people who overstepped the social and sexual boundaries.

And *still* Rose stayed silent.

'I brought you one of my dresses,' Trudie said, handing a parcel to the prison officer and then turning to Rose. 'Yours are too big for you now.' She held Rose's gaze for a moment, then looked away. 'I'm so sorry –'

'About what?'

'Our fight. They made so much of it in court.'

Rose shrugged. 'It doesn't matter.'

'Why don't you *talk* to them, Rose? Take the stand, talk to the jury. You could sway them onto your side, I know you could.'

'It's too late.'

'Why is it too bloody late?' Trudie snapped. 'You've got to fight, Rose, not give in. It's not like you.' She paused, staring at her oldest friend. 'It's because of Lester, isn't it? Because he's dead.'

Rose nodded. 'At first I thought he might turn up . . . They said missing, after all. Not definitely dead. But he must be dead – he'd have been in touch otherwise.'

It was unbearable for Rose to talk about Lester, so she changed the subject, going back in time, away from the brick walls, barred windows and the dark skies, back to the salty coast and the hot summer air.

'You remember when you were working at the rock factory?'

Trudie grinned. 'Do I ever! And you came to watch. God, Rose, d'you remember when I got my arm broken on the big wheel?' She paused, thinking back. 'You saved my life. If it hadn't been for you, I'd have died. And I was such a bitch to you later.' She stopped, tears close.

'Everyone fights –'

'No, they don't!' Trudie replied fitfully. 'And don't be kind, just to make me feel better. I should be geeing you up. I don't know how you're so calm. I can't bear it! I can't stand seeing you in the dock like that, all on your own. Everyone knew what a bastard Stuart Fallow was. I'd have killed him myself if I'd have got half a chance.'

'Time's up,' the warden said behind them.

Incredulous, Trudie jumped in surprise. 'But I only just got here!'

'Time's up,' the woman repeated, Trudie turning back to Rose hurriedly.

532

'You hold on, you hear me? You hold on, Rose. There's a new Judy Garland film just out and I want us to go and see it.' She was ushered to the door, fighting tears. 'We're going to see it together. You hear me? *Together*.'

Two further days followed, then the prosecution did their summing up, followed by Gerald Randles' defence. Because it was such a serious case, the judge advised the jury at length. He would only take a unanimous decision, as the sentence for a guilty verdict would be death.

Taken back to her cell, Rose washed her face and changed her clothes, setting out a different outfit for the following day – the day when the jury would give their verdict. Slowly she held the dress up to her body, her gaze resting for a moment on her face.

Time slid back. Suddenly Rose could see herself as a kid, runty, truculent, with a squint and a chip on her shoulder. Scratching her arms in the heat as she sat on the pier, watching Trudie. Then she could see Len whistling for her and waving across a winter racecourse, her hands signalling the odds back to him: and the sound of the horses' hoofs on the hard winter ground. Time passed on. Now she was with Stuart in Lytham, laughing in the surgery. I loved you once, Rose thought with disbelief. And then she remembered Lester. *Her Lester*, dry with remorse, telling her about Joe. His face had been tormented, his voice incredulous. He had killed his brother, his beloved Joe. *No one will ever know,* Rose had promised him. *Trust me.*

She imagined him touching her, holding her and telling her about his plans for the ballroom. Which was now boarded up, falling into disrepair, graffiti on the outer walls. Someone would rebuild it, she thought dully, someone would put lights on and play music. Someone would take their sweetheart onto the floor and dance . . . But it wouldn't be Lester. And that sweetheart wouldn't be her. It wasn't their time. It might have been, once. If Beth hadn't got in the way; if Stuart hadn't married Rose. If Lester and Rose's paths had conjoined at the right moment. *Then* it would have been their time. But not *this* time. Not this life.

Slowly, Rose put down the dress and turned to the window. She had kept her word, but suddenly she realised the enormity of her situation and panicked. If they found her guilty she would be sentenced to death. And she would die horribly. They would take her out in the cold early morning, in a place far from home, buckle her arms to her sides and tie her ankles together. Then they would put a hood over her head and stand her on the trapdoor. When the lever was thrown she would drop into nothing, her body jerking, slowly suffocated as she hanged, her body swinging from the end of a rope, the breath choked out of her . . .

'Oh, Christ, help me,' Rose whimpered desperately, 'I don't want to die.'

So here we are and it's still raining. I can see a single bird pass the window, but only one. It could be going anywhere, or maybe just landing on a nearby windowledge. And I'm cold. The dress Trudie has given me is woollen, but the sleeves are too short and my wrists and hands are numb.

I am no longer looking over to the jury. I don't want to see anyone's face, pick out anyone who has decided what's going to happen to me. Life *happened* to me. Lester *happened* to me. Hettie, *with all her great residue of spite,* happened to me. But I wonder how she'll live with what she's done. How she'll nurse Cedric, and decay in that house, with him. I hope her life is going to be long. Very long. And I hope she remembers me every day of it.

And there's my father, watching me. Smiling, putting on a brave face, Ruby beside him. I loved your son. I loved your son . . .

'Now we're all ready,' the judge says impatiently, 'I'll ask you again. Ladies and Gentlemen of the jury, have you reached a decision on which you are all agreed?'

'We have, your Honour.'

'Do you find the defendant guilty or not guilty?'

And then the foreman of the jury opens his mouth to answer . . .

SEVENTY

But before he could there was a outburst at the back of the courtroom, the door opening and someone hurrying in. In the midst of all the noise and scramble, the judge banged down his gavel repeatedly.

'Silence! Silence in court!'

He was hardly heard over the noise, a figure running up to the judge's bench. 'You have to stop this –'

'Silence!' the judge barked again. 'Silence.' He looked at the intruder. 'What's the meaning of this? There's a trial going on here.'

'I know, that's why I'm here.' The man paused, staring up at the judge. 'She's innocent. You have to let her go. Rose Bradshaw killed Stuart Fallow to protect me.'

Around them the courtroom was growing quiet, people listening with open astonishment, Rose staring at the intruder with disbelief.

The judge leaned forward across the bench. 'And who are you?'

'Lester Williams.' He turned to the people in the courtroom, appealing to them. 'Rose was protecting *me*. She killed Stuart Fallow because of me. Because –'

'No!' Rose shouted, getting to her feet.

'Silence!' The judge roared, as the courtroom exploded with noise. 'I will have silence in my court!'

'Don't say it, Lester, don't,' she pleaded, Lester holding

her gaze for an instant before turning back to the judge.

'*Because I killed my brother . . .*'

Rose could see Ruby cover her face, Len leaning forward in his seat to hear more clearly.

'I killed my brother, and Stuart Fallow saw me do it. He came to see me, to blackmail me.' Lester paused, looking at the judge imploringly. 'Rose offered to act as a go-between because I had to return to active duty that night. She saw Stuart in order to help me, no other reason. And he attacked her because of that.'

'How d'you know?' the judge asked sternly. 'You weren't there.'

'Stuart wasn't really interested in a reunion,' Lester replied with certainty. 'He wanted revenge. On me and on Rose. She killed him because he attacked her. And he attacked her because she was trying to protect me – because I'd killed my brother.' His voice was imploring. 'Please, listen to me. Believe me. Stuart Fallow was a jealous man. How do you think he would have taken to his wife begging for mercy for *me*? Of course he attacked her. He hated her with all his heart at that moment. And he would have killed her for sure. I know that. As God is my judge, he would have killed her.'

And that, Gerald Randles thought with satisfaction, was the missing note. Good for Rose – but not so good for Lester Williams. Slowly, Gerald collected together his papers as Lester was arrested, journalists all vying to get to the phones outside, flashbulbs going off like a hundred comets and illuminating Rose's disbelieving face. She would have a retrial, Gerald knew, but the next time she would get off pleading self-defence. But as for Lester Williams . . . Gerald sighed. A man murdering his own brother? That was dynamite.

Waiting until the courtroom had finally cleared, Gerald moved to the door. Jerking his head in his familiar manner, he let his glasses fall down onto his nose and picked up the morning paper. It read: 'SCANDALOUS MURDER CASE. VERDICT DUE TODAY.' Frowning, he screwed it up and tossed the paper into a nearby bin.

Rose might have escaped the rope, but Lester had just taken over the noose.

SEVENTY-ONE

Charged with the wilful murder of his brother, Lester was taken into custody and interviewed that very afternoon.

'I was shot down in Northern France and captured by the Germans. But I escaped on the way to Germany,' Lester explained. 'I had to lie low for a while because I was injured. After a week or so, I made my way down to Marseilles. There was a Resistance organisation there who helped me out, getting me across the Pyrenees and into Spain. I actually came back to England via Gibraltar. That's why it took so long. At first I could only travel by night, so that no one would see me. I had to watch out for the enemy, and dogs too. If they hear you, they bark, tipping people off.' He paused to light the cigarette that was offered him. 'I had no news from home. There were no radios, no English papers and no one to ask. I was lucky if I heard how the war was going. I didn't hear about the trial until I got to England yesterday.' He shook his head in disbelief. 'I can't believe that Rose stayed quiet. I can't believe she would let herself be hanged rather than expose me –'

The police officer interrupted him. 'You admit to killing your brother?'

'Yes.'

'You realise that you'll be charged with murder?'

'I do,' Lester said calmly. 'I killed Joe – and I'd do it again.'

The police officer looked at him curiously. 'That's no defence. You know, Williams, you could have got away with this. Everyone thought you were dead – you could have *stayed* dead.'

'And let Rose hang?' he replied incredulously.

'But *you* might hang now.'

Lester winced. 'I might. But I've saved her.'

The newspapers couldn't believe their luck. Lester Williams back from the dead to save his lover – by damning himself. It was seen as a tragic romance to some. To others, Lester's actions were damnable. How could any man – let alone some so-called war hero – kill his own brother? Nothing warranted that. No matter how injured Joe Williams had been.

'WAR HERO MURDERS TWIN' – the words blasted from the newsstands, and on radios and in town halls people debated the crime. Wasn't it a mercy killing? some said. Who wouldn't have done the same for their own? Others saw it as Lester Williams playing God. He had no right to kill, they said. No one had. Either way everyone agreed that he was a doomed man. If he got off, his reputation would follow him everywhere. If he hanged, the lover he had saved would live out her days alone.

The night Lester was charged with murder his mother paid him a visit. Lester was nervous, afraid of Ruby's judgement. Should he beg forgiveness? Or plead his case?

She came in wearing a dark coat and a felt hat. Obviously shaken, she was still formidable, her voice challenging.

'I want to know one thing, and one thing only – did Joe want to die?'

'Yes,' Lester said honestly, 'he did.'

She nodded. 'Did he suffer?'

'No,' Lester replied, his voice faltering.

'You should have told me.'

'How could I?'

Her voice rose. 'I *should* have known.'

'I couldn't tell you, Ma –'

'No, I don't mean that! I mean that as your mother I should have known without being told.'

'No one knew. Only Rose.'

'And she can keep a secret,' Ruby said admiringly. Then she reached out for son. 'Christ, Lester! We thought you were dead. And now you're back, in this bloody place. If only you'd stayed away.'

'If I had, Rose would have died.'

'I know, I know . . .' Ruby held her son at arm's length. 'They crucified her and now they'll crucify you.'

'I know that,' Lester said, resigned. 'But I don't regret killing Joe – or coming back. I only care about one thing now: Rose has to get off. They *have* to believe that it was self-defence, that she killed Stuart because of me. That she would have died for me.'

'Yer bastard!' a man screamed at Lester, as they led him from the prison van into the back of the courthouse. 'Yer murdering pig!'

Others had come to cheer him on. Lester Williams, the man who had had the courage to end his brother's suffering. He had become – like Rose before him – a metaphorical board on which everyone could pin their point of view. Many of those opinions then found outlet in the papers, alongside the news of Rose being acquitted. Gerald Randles had done his job well:

'Maybe,' he agreed, 'but this time I had help. My client was on my side.'

But Rose took little time to savour her freedom. Dogged by journalists and photographers, she and her father were followed when they visited Lester in prison and hounded in the days to come. She was constantly pressed for her opinion, for her account of Stuart's murder, for what she knew about Joe Williams' death. And in reply Rose did what now came naturally to her – she stayed silent.

And she prayed.

'Read this, Dad,' she said, pushing a paper over to Len. 'Some women's group has written to say that Lester should hang, that it's justice to have a life for a life.'

Len threw the paper into the bin, and picked up another.

'This says it was a mercy killing –'

'That's not the general opinion,' Rose replied, brushing her hair back from her face. 'The public loves a hero, if they can stick a medal on him. But no one's going to decorate Lester, are they? Whatever happens, his reputation's ruined.'

Len frowned, concerned. 'Come on, luv, sit down. You look all in.'

'Lester looks haggard too,' Rose replied softly. 'I could still lose him, Dad –'

'He's got a good lawyer. And good advice.'

The words had no power to soothe, Rose staring ahead blindly. Lester was pleading diminished responsibility – that he had acted out of a moment of madness, a temporary loss of judgement. He had only wanted to help his brother, believing that he was doing the right thing . . . It was a good defence, but one thing was missing – evidence of his remorse. How had he acted after the murder? Had he shown sorrow? Regret?

They had interviewed his army comrades, his family, but their answers weren't conclusive. Yes, Lester had seemed depressed, withdrawn. But that could have been due to the war, to the stress of his undercover missions. If it was due to his brother's death, who *really* knew that for sure?

Someone did.

'I have to give evidence.'

Len looked at his daughter angrily. 'No! Enough is enough. You've suffered too much already. I won't let you.'

'I'm going to, Dad,' she said firmly. 'Who else knew

what Lester was feeling after Joe died? Who else knew what had happened? There *is* no one else who can tell them, except me.'

SEVENTY-TWO

A bird passed by the window, dipped under the eaves of the courthouse roof and was silent. As was the court, and everyone in it. All seemed spellbound, enthralled by the evidence they had just heard.

She had stood in the witness box wearing pale blue, her suit light against the heavy panelling. People remarked that she looked handsome, but older, yet when she spoke Rose's voice never faltered. Instead she drew a picture of the brothers, the neighbours, she had known all her life – and the night she had found Lester sitting on the Promenade bench.

'Can you tell us,' the defence lawyer said, 'in your own words, how Mr Williams appeared to you?'

'He was blank, white-faced. I'd never seen anyone so pale. He told me he'd killed Joe, his brother, the lad I'd known all my life, the boy from across the street. And I didn't believe him at first – because this was Lester and *Lester loved Joe*.' Rose paused, thinking back. 'Everywhere Lester went, Joe followed. Everyone knew that he wasn't as bright, as smart as his brother, but they knew that Joe would be all right if Lester was looking out for him. Even when they went off to fight, they were together.' She looked at the jury. 'You have to understand, they were twins. Joe was a part of Lester, and Lester a part of Joe. The *stronger* part.' She took in a breath to compose herself. 'That night Lester told me that Joe had asked him to kill him, begged him, and Lester had no choice. *There was no choice.* He had to make it right for his brother, just like he always had. So he killed him out of kindness . . .' she held the jury's gaze. '. . . out of love. But when it was all over for Joe, that was when the hell began for Lester. Did he suffer remorse? You can't imagine how much. He'd killed his brother – and, with that, the best part of himself. It wasn't just Joe Williams who died that night.'

SEVENTY-THREE

And it was a love story that endured. Lester was found not guilty of murder, having pleaded diminished responsibility due to a temporary loss of judgement. Many agreed that Rose's evidence had been vital, swaying the jury on to Lester's side at the last moment.

When he was released, he and Rose dodged the photographers and made their way home by the first train they could catch. It was a night train with few passengers, just some servicemen returning home from leave.

It had been a long time since Lester and Rose had been alone together and it felt strange to them. Slowly the train moved along in the dark night, Rose looking out of the window. If Lester was honest, he could see that the strain had changed Rose: her bloom had gone, maturity in its place. As for Rose, she looked at Lester and realised that however long they lived they would never be like a normal couple. They had shared and suffered too much. It was on both their faces and etched in both their hearts.

Together they sat in silence, holding hands. Finally it was Lester who spoke: 'Next stop Blackpool.'

'Home,' Rose said simply.

'People will point at us, if we stay there. They'll talk and gossip.'

'People always gossip.'

'Gull Road will be buzzing.'

'It's always buzzing.'

'What about Hettie?'

'Leave her alone,' Rose replied bitterly. 'She's in her own misery. And she's got hell to look forward to.'

'We could stay on the train. Go past Blackpool. Miss our stop.'

Rose looked at him questioningly. 'D'you want to?'

'If I did, would you go with me?'

'*Would I go with you?*' she repeated. 'Only to the end of the earth – and back again.'

I did stay with him and life was never easy. It was full of quarrels and makings-up and times when Lester overreached himself, his ambitions making me dizzy. We had two children, a girl and a boy. And the boy we called Leonard, of course. As for the girl, she grew up very like me.

She would ask us over and over again to tell her about the past. The drama of those days seemed to transfix her, and when Lester and I became middle-aged I could see her struggle to imagine the passionate lovers we had once been. Our son grew up steady. Very like Joe.

As for my father, he married Doris, and lived and died in Gull Road, in the same house where he had raised me. Clovis reached ninety, but Nan Wilmslow passed on just at the end of the war, preceding Alfred by a year. As for Trudie, she married Bunny, of course, but they had no children and in time Bunny inherited Dad's pitch. If you look for it you can still find The Lazy Eye travelling the same routes it did with George Ogden, and later, my father.

As for Roy Howell, he was imprisoned and then went abroad, no one knew where. Dave Lincoln was promoted again and retired early to fish in Wales. Miss Vernon – for she was never anything but Miss Vernon to me – died in the early sixties. Gilbert was traumatised by her loss but carried on playing the dame in the pantomimes at

Christmas. Of all the adults who populated my childhood only Ruby and Gilbert remain – and I doubt that anything could kill Ruby.

She still runs Sea View, and after Lester and I married she came to see me: huge in a print dress, her hands on her hips.

'I was wrong,' she said simply.

'About what?' I asked.

'About you. I said once that people who really loved each other would die for each other – and you damn-near died for Lester.'

I didn't need to remind her that he could just as easily have died for me.

So there you have it, and now it's time to stop. It's a warm evening here in Blackpool. Through the window I can hear the sound of the day-trippers, the gulls, the screams of excitement from the fairground. And if you listen carefully, very carefully, you can just make out the murmur of music coming from a dance hall. And if you look carefully, very carefully, you can see its outline reflected magically in the dark and serpent-emptied sea.

Ellie Pride

Annie Groves

A stirring, heartrending story of love, passion, duty and family, set in the North-West in the turbulent years leading up to the First World War.

After the tragic death of her mother, beautiful, headstrong Ellie Pride must forge her own way in the world. Having made a deathbed promise to her mother to forsake passion for stability and social status, Ellie rejects the advances of local craftsman Gideon Walker, despite her deep attraction to him. With her grieving father struggling to cope, Ellie is exiled to live with her aunt and uncle. Her mother hoped Ellie would be able to escape her humble roots forever. But despite the so-called luxury, Ellie is left frightened and alone.

Her uncle quickly reveals a terrifying cruelty that forces her into a loveless marriage in order to escape him. Struggling to support her weak husband against his penny-pinching father, Ellie never forgets her love for Gideon. Their paths are destined to cross again and again.

But when events take a tragic turn, Ellie needs all her pride and strength to overcome hardship, and to triumph.

'An engrossing story.'

My Weekly

'A stirring and heartrending family saga … The choices and dreams of a generation of women combine to create this passionate story.'

Liverpool Daily Post

0 00 714955 7

Sea Music

Sara MacDonald

A wonderful, haunting story of family ties and wartime secrets.

The house opposite the church, overlooking the Cornish coast, is home to three generations of Tremains.

Fred Tremain, the country doctor, came to this beautiful corner of England with his wife, Martha. Difficult and determined Anna, their eldest child, is now a successful barrister and their easy-going son Barnaby is vicar to the parish. Also making her home there is Lucy, their beloved granddaughter.

And it is Lucy whose discovery of family papers, hidden in the old attics, brings to light the first of the long-hidden wartime secrets. As each layer is unwrapped, the family start to question the price paid for the upheavals caused by violence, wars and prejudice today and yesterday; and unlock the way to new relationships and new loves.

0 00 715073 3

The Girl Now Leaving

Betty Burton

Lu Wilmott grows up in the Portsmouth slums of the 1920s. Stricken by diphtheria, she is sent to the Hampshire countryside to recover, and in this idyll she discovers a robust fighting spirit, new and challenging friends, and the first stirrings of sexual attraction.

But, faced with little choice, she follows her mother and aunts into the city's infamous staymaking trade, where young girls and old women endure conditions so appalling that Lu comes to realize that things must change. And she can be the instrument of that change.

Her journey to maturity, from proud but shy child to energetic woman, encompasses love, deep friendship, and a growing political awareness as the Spanish Civil War casts its influence over Europe. Above all, Lu is a survivor – and one to be reckoned with.

'Betty Burton constructs the world from the female point of view . . . carefully considered, subtle, and observant'
Sunday Times

ISBN 0 00 649631 8